HELMSMAN

Book One of the Sojourner Saga

Martin Halbert

Eposian Publishing
Greensboro, North Carolina

Helmsman: Book One of the Sojourner Saga

Copyright © 2026 Martin Halbert

All rights are reserved. No part of the book may be reproduced without prior permission of the author, Martin Halbert.

This is a work of fiction. Any resemblance of names of characters to actual persons, living or dead, is coincidental.

ISBN: 978-1-970664-00-3

Publisher: Eposian Publishing LLC

First Edition, Version 1.6: February 2026

Dedicated to

My Family

Contents

Bereft 1

Shoals 48

Prospects 93

Rifts 136

Prisoners 162

Meetings 202

Assaults 248

Assays 287

BEREFT

One day as he walked the ancient catwalks of the interstellar memory ark in the lonely hours, the Sojourner acolyte Greymalkin Thomas heard an old man weeping.

It was the earliest ark watch period, the watch called Matins. Greymalkin had decided to walk the deserted catwalks of the high clerestories level during his morning meditation. *Maybe the 'clear stories' will clear my mind,* he thought ruefully. He was still learning the complex maze of walkways in the narthex, the rearmost stern portion of the huge interstellar ark, where he'd been newly reassigned. He liked the clerestories because no one seemed to come here, and he could peer out of the windows in peace at the endless vastness of shadow space by using the jewel in his mind.

Whenever he used it to commune with the universe, the shadow space jewel still ignited a sense of wonder in Greymalkin. The glimmering spectral gem within his forebrain was incorporeal, not physical. It had formed in the blazing interior of a star long ago, an imperviously stable crystalline structure of hyperspatial forces that could only be found and extracted with the most subtle technologies. Like all of the Sojourner monks on the giant memory ark, Greymalkin had received the jewel at his birth, when it had been embedded in his mind. When he focused on the presence of the shadow jewel in his mind he could commune with other monks, the innumerable memory volumes stored in the troves of the vast starship, or simply sense the distant signals of molecular gas clouds as the ark drove through them in the emptiness of interstellar space. The signals were like the peaceful, slow sound of billows faintly crashing against an ancient sailing ship's hull. But unlike the oceans of a planet, there was no end to the billows that stretched out behind them into the infinity of interstellar space. That magnitude always granted the young monk a sense of inner peace. It was in that moment as he stood gazing out through the huge clerestory portals while beginning his morning meditation that he heard the faint, *actual* sound of quiet sobbing.

Greymalkin paused, and looked around in concern. In a prayer alcove to his side he saw the form of a kneeling elderly monk, praying on the cold metal deck, his clasped hands shaking. It surprised the young Sojourner, and he drew a quick breath. The old man flinched, glanced to the side at him, and then quickly got to his feet, wiping his eyes as he did so. Greymalkin first felt apologetic for interrupting the old monk's morning meditation, and then anxious when he saw that the man wore sable-black hooded robes with bright silver embroidered trim, the robes of a senior member of the Bridge Crew. When, in the gloom of the catwalks, he made out the familiar dour features within the hood, Greymalkin paled in fear. It was none other than Father Johannes, his old preceptor, who now was no less than the bridge Subprior for all ship operations throughout the vast ark.

"My deepest apologies, Father Johannes!" Greymalkin whispered, his stomach sinking. "I had no idea you were here; I did not mean to intrude...." The young man trailed off as he saw the redness of Johannes' eyes and how his craggy features appeared terribly haggard. He looked at Greymalkin with an expression of despair that the acolyte had never before seen on his stoic face... and then the familiar stony mask of the old monk dropped back into place. Father Johannes shook his head, and spoke in his deep command deck voice, his thick Islexian realm drift-accent echoing off the huge eoncrystal windows behind them.

"Och, 'tis fine, dinnae worry, lad," Johannes said gruffly. "Come an' walk wi' me fer a bit." Greymalkin nervously fell into step beside the senior monk. They had not crossed paths in the huge ship's company during the years since Greymalkin had been a novice and Johannes his teacher. The old man remained gauntly silent as they walked together, and the young monk noticed with alarm that Johannes was trembling.

"Father Johannes, forgive me for asking but, is everything alright?" Greymalkin asked. The rugged face of his stern old mentor lifted, and the old monk's eyes hardened. He seemed about to speak, but then shook his head and paused, as if he had reconsidered something.

"Ye were always a good lad," Johannes said. "But ye're young, yet. Ye would nae understand the bitterness that now lays ahead o' us. Some dreadful decisions have been made this morning that break my old heart. But I'm sorry, 'tis not for me tae discuss them. Not yet. I must hold my tongue for the time being, lad."

"But... well, that's terrible," Greymalkin said, taken aback. "Can you tell me nothing at all about what's wrong, then?" He'd never known Johannes to speak so evasively before. It frightened him. The old monk stopped, studied him for a moment, and then leaned on a railing looking down into the distance of the Great Nave where the endless serried ranks of countless memory volumes stretched away out of sight. He gestured with his rough gnarled hand at the vista.

"Whose information is all that, lad?" Johannes asked. Greymalkin hesitated, wondering if this was some philosophical puzzle put to him by his old mentor.

"No one's? Everyone's?" Greymalkin said uncertainly. He winced inside as irritation crossed old Johannes' face like a cloud.

"'Tis nae a *riddle*, lad," Johannes said curtly. "Who is it for? *What's* it for, then? Why're we haulin' all o' that through the stars in this muckle great ship?"

Greymalkin kicked himself mentally for not giving the obvious response that was, after all, a core part of their monastic vows. He answered automatically now, "To save the Bereft. We journey to share knowledge with collapsed civilizations, and all those that are in need of true information."

Johannes peered at him with ancient, sad eyes. "But *why*, lad? Why do *ye* want tae do that? Ye are young yet, ye cannae yet know the horror of what is out there, or what happens in the lost places where we are called on to go. Do ye even want that for a life?"

Greymalkin felt confused and deeply uneasy as he studied the craggy old face of his mentor. *He's not testing me, he's asking me a genuine question. I've never seen him so troubled. What could have happened?* The young monk thought for a moment before responding from his heart, but drawing on Sojourner coda. "Yes, Father Johannes, I do. I believe in the Order's teachings, that isolation and ignorance out among the stars only means death. To survive and thrive we need one another, and we can only save one another through mutually beneficial access to information. I...." Greymalkin struggled to express what he thought deep down, but found he could only stumble through the words. "I want to do that. Sojourn among the stars and bring helpful information to people that need it."

Now Johannes looked out through the arched eoncrystal windows at the stars in the distance behind the huge ark. The old man's eyes glistened for a moment. "A simple, noble sentiment. But do you know what that will cost ye, lad? Do ye know how tae do it, or what it will require of ye and those that ye care for? Do ye know how it will *change* ye over time?"

Greymalkin hunched lower and shook his head uncertainly. "No. No, I don't. But... the Order teaches that life *is* change, right? Change that is, hopefully, constant shared growth. I want to learn. And this is the purpose of the Order, is it not? To help and teach the helpless?"

"Aye, that's our purpose," Johannes said assertively, but a sad and angry note crept in to his voice as he began walking again. "I believed in it once. All those leaders as have more years and responsibility than an acolyte should know and respect that aim as you do."

"Do they not?" Greymalkin asked, more confused than ever. "Do *you* not believe in it still? Does the Abbot not—"

"May the Abbot and the churls that sway him go intae the blazes! Age and position should bring both loyalty and compassion!" Johannes snapped, but then he clenched his jaw as he glanced sideways at Greymalkin's shocked expression. "Och, my fool tongue's wagged tae far, forget I said *that*, lad. Dinnae let the despair of an old man trouble ye. Now then, you should be getting on tae yer morning watch duty, and I must trek all the bloody long way through the ark tae the bridge before *my* morning watch begins."

"Why *are* you all the way back here?" Greymalkin asked. He had wondered that from the moment he'd first seen Father Johannes. The clerestory windows were at the very stern of the ark, and the bridge was on the very prow of the ship. Johannes had a very long way to go indeed.

Johannes looked forlorn then, and came to a halt. He sadly looked out of the huge clerestory portals into the endlessness of shadow space receding behind them, and said quietly, "I came tae say goodbye. Goodbye tae old friends I will nae see again. And perhaps goodbye tae the virtue o' simple *truth* if a tyranny o' lies oertakes us."

Greymalkin gaped at the old monk. "What does *that* mean, Father?"

Father Johannes' face was stony. "There'll be a Compline assembly tonight, lad," he finally said. "Be ready for it. That'll be the first o' all the cruelties before us, Grey. But alas, what cannae be cured, must be endured." Johannes looked down into the darkness of the catwalks beneath them and scowled. "Aye, today I've learned what it is tae have a knife in my old back indeed. But I cannae yet speak of all that's troubling me, and it'll be clear tae ye and all others soon enough anyway. Forget all this folly I've spilt on ye. Fare ye well, lad, fare ye well." The old monk pulled his black robes close around himself and stalked away through the cold black walkways. Grey stood stricken, feeling profoundly uncertain as to what he should either think or do.

* * *

That night, Greymalkin stood at attention among the hundreds of other monks in the narthex deck muster of the vast interstellar memory ark. He wondered nervously for the hundredth time what could possibly have happened that would demand the ominous and abruptly announced Compline assembly that Johannes had foretold. He slouched and fidgeted in his dun-colored formal robes, glancing about furtively but trying not to draw attention to himself in the ranks of Sojourner monks standing silently in the muster formation.

He looked up at the immense eoncrystal dock assembly windows, even larger than the clerestories so high above them where he had met with Father Johannes that morning. The dock windows showed the same grand view of the shadow space billows receding into the distance behind the ark, and he listened to the same phantom sound of crashing waves that he had sensed during that worrying meeting with Johannes that already seemed so long ago. The shadow space billows made no actual sound, he knew that he only sensed the passage of the gas clouds as a synesthesia, an imagined 'sound' that was his brain trying to make sense of rhythmic data. The waves of gas clouds were a gentle but endless susurration that he sensed in his mind whenever he stood near the outermost parts of the ark, as he now did in the assembly facing the stern docks. But the billows were almost the only sound he heard. The muster of Sojourners was eerily, portentously quiet, and he wondered why. *Do the others in the deck crew know already? Or have they also only heard frightening hints?*

Virtually all of the other acolytes in Narthex Watch Section Four wore formal robes with specialist rating colors, mostly the deep red of Engineering Crew or the dark blue of Flight Crew. Greymalkin still felt uncomfortable shame at his dun-colored robes, marking him as one of the very few who still lacked a mission specialty. *How badly do I stand out? And will I finally be allowed to actually learn something in this collateral posting? Or will it just be like the others? Will everybody just keep treating me like a gremmie, an inexperienced fool?* He stole a worried look at himself in a mirrorshell bulkhead to his left, seeing nothing but a gangly, anxious, and uncouth young monk, paralyzed by unease in his crisp but drab cassock, topped by neatly combed jet-black hair. The bright color of his own pale grey eyes jumped out at him, startling as ever in the crowd, and he looked down in embarrassment. He hoped that no new person he met today would make one of the same old tired jokes that he hated so much about his eyes and his name. *Grey-eyed Greymalkin!* He hated nicknames.

He continued fretting about what his new arkmates would think of his dun robes and lack of a specialist rating, until he realized that no one at all was looking at him. *Who am I kidding? I only transferred in to the narthex section two days ago. Nobody even knows that I exist. But what is everyone so worried about? What is this big terrible mystery that could make even grim old Father Johannes weep?* Greymalkin studied the other Sojourners in confusion. Every other acolyte in the formation was tensely watching the platform by the docks where the senior deck officers were still assembling. Strangely, some acolytes were silently weeping. *Why? What do they know that the rest of us don't?*

Finally, the platform party of senior officers came forward in a grim line, and the Narthex Claustral Subprior stood to the lectern. He was an ancient craggy gargoyle, with thick old red robes steeped in elaborate geometric brocade. After taking the lectern he opened with a stern mental public address, communing through their shadow jewels to the entire silent muster in the complex lexemes of traditional High Peretian. As a linguist, Greymalkin loved the dense language structures of High Peretian, but even he sometimes had trouble unpacking the holistic and complimentary stems, the registers and extensions, the ninety-six grammatical cases and all the associated declensions. Luckily, this address was easy; he realized the Subprior was simply calling the assembly to order with a call and response invocation of the Great Commitment of the Sojourner Order, their foundational creed.

«Seek discoveries with clarity!» The Claustral Subprior's thoughts were demanding, but Greymalkin seemed to also detect a strange tinge of sadness in the old man.

«I will!» Greymalkin's communed response was absorbed in the thunderously communed thoughts of the entire muster of monks. The mutual affirmation of the muster always felt reassuring to him.

«Save the Bereft with compassion!» Again, there was just a hint of gloom in the Subprior's thoughts that troubled Greymalkin. *Why is he so sad?*

«I will!» The sea of avowal in a communal response of thousands of minds was potent, but now Greymalkin wondered if he had felt some *sobbing* thoughts here and there.

«Share information with humility!» The old Subprior possessed a strong and disciplined mind to be able to reach so many people at once, but.... *Is that a trace of fear in his thoughts?*

«I will!» Now Greymalkin was alert to the scattered weeping thoughts among the assembled male and female monks, and he could sense that others were picking them up as well.

«Sustain knowledge with diligence!» Now the melancholy in the Subprior's thoughts was obvious to Greymalkin. *Something is definitely wrong.*

«I will!» This time Greymalkin noticed an older female acolyte to his side whose thoughts broke with an agonized sob just as she communed the response. Her unguarded pain filled him with growing dread. *Why? What could provoke such terrible grief?*

«Sojourn through life with courage!» The Claustral Subprior finished the invocation fiercely, trying hard to banish any subcurrent of grief in his communed thoughts. But Greymalkin was very apprehensive now, wondering what was coming.

«We will!» The traditional communed group affirmation that concluded the invocation was riddled with many minds that clearly felt uncertain about the moment. But he had felt some other minds that were filled with angry determination. And there had been a few others that simply felt as confused as he did. *At least I'm not the only one.*

The assembly continued with typical Compline scientific prayers, chants, and recitations. Troubled, Greymalkin closed his eyes and tried to focus on his shadow jewel in order to better feel the minds of the other Sojourners around him. The spectral jewel suspended just a micron away from his prefrontal cortex in shadow space resonated in response to the many luminous shadow jewels in the minds of all the other monks around him. He could feel the array of tense minds directly through his own jewel, just as the jewel enabled him to perceive the echoes of interstellar gas in normal space as shadow space billows passing by outside the hull of the mighty ark starship.

But unless he actively reached out to his fellow Sojourners and thereby disturbed the rite, he could only sense a generalized anxiety among them. Of course, everyone else in the assembly could feel the anxiety too, and fear was inevitably continuing to slowly build among them as more and more monks became aware of it. *That's why the senior monks convened this assembly,* he realized suddenly. *To quell the spreading fear and the cascading rumors that fear generates.* Greymalkin frowned. *So, when are they going to actually speak to it?*

As he peered at the platform party in the distance, he noticed something that he hadn't before. Two of the senior monks there wore the severe black robes of the Bridge Crew. As he squinted trying to make out the two faces, he realized that the first was no less than Master Burke, the Claustral Bridge Prior and second in command of the entire ark. He almost jumped when he saw that other was, once again, Father Johannes. He thought how odd it was to see Johannes twice on the same day, the only officer on the lofty Bridge Crew that Greymalkin was actually familiar with. It was hard to make out the old man's face, but it seemed just as stony as when he had said farewell that morning.

The roughhewn Narthex Claustral Subprior finally concluded his Compline assembly service with one of the traditional call and response pairings that all but the newest Novitiates would know. «Let compassionate clarity be our compass!»

«And may humble diligence be our guide!» The massed thoughts of the monks seemed to shake the deck to Greymalkin, but he knew that was just a communal illusion in his mind. Then the Narthex Subprior stepped away from the lectern, and Master Burke came up.

Burke had fierce steely gray eyebrows and whiskers, and was the very definition of an angry old man. He gripped the sides of the lectern with such ferocity that Greymalkin thought he wanted to rip it out of the deck in rage.

By this point, Greymalkin was expecting some corrective sermon or fiery lecture to the narthex watch sections, but instead Burke launched into a dense briefing, *still in High Peretian.* That disoriented Greymalkin, because briefings were usually delivered in the much less demanding and more direct standard Peretian for simplicity. *Why is he using scholarly language for a simple briefing? Perhaps to obscure what he's saying? Or make it sound more formal and official?* It took the young monk a moment to absorb and sort out the first part of what Master Burke had communed, but it was just an overly complicated summary of the course that their memory ark, the *Dragon King*, had taken over recent years past the outskirts of the Erymia, a vast and desolate region of maze-like shadow space channels in the Periphery. Burke recounted how the ark had surveyed the remote region and launched a number of missions into it to explore the uncharted interior for fallen Bereft civilizations. Greymalkin frowned.

Well, sure, he thought. *Everyone on the ark knows where we've been over the last few years. And most everyone knows someone sent on mission into the Erymia. Why is he stating the obvious?* But then Burke shifted his topic to, of all things, wealthy benefactors and tithes to the ark. That was when he dropped his bombshell.

«It grieves my spirit to inform you that we have received sorrowful news regarding our longstanding primary tithe from the Alban Realm, the home civilization that launched the *Dragon King* more than a millennium ago. The Alban administration has formally *abolished* the tithe. After much deliberation, the decision has been reached by the leadership of the ark to immediately return to the Alban Realm until such time, if any, that a new source of support be identified for the *Dragon King* and its journeys.» The communed message hit like an unexpected slap across the face.

What! Greymalkin thought, his mind spinning. As similar protests and moans erupted from scattered Sojourners in various parts of the muster formation, he felt stunned. *But... what about all the skete missionaries we launched into the Erymia? If the ark isn't here waiting for them anymore when they try to return....* He could sense monks around him communing thoughts to one another on private channels. Some were simply emotionally overwrought and didn't realize they were communing heartbreaking thoughts that others could sense. The older female acolyte that had sobbed before was one of these. «Mateo, *Mateo,* I told you not to go....» Greymalkin squirmed in apprehension, thinking about the acquaintances he knew in the Erymia missions. Brother Samuel, Sister Margaretha, even the very first missionaries that had been gone for years and that he'd started to give up for lost and never expected to see again, like his old mentor Mother Advisor Trystia.

Burke ignored the protestations and continued his dense and angry briefing. «We will leave behind a rescue cutter and a pinnace to search for returning missions for several months in order to provide them with supplies to rejoin the *Dragon King*. We will also leave some buoys with information about the ark's destination for the same purpose.»

There were renewed protests, and even Greymalkin could understand how inadequate that response was. *A cutter and a pinnace? For just a few months? For all those missionaries?* Most of the missions had been dispatched in small skiffs carrying skete groups of just a half dozen Sojourners into the unsurveyed interior of the Erymia. They were capable of self-reliant exploration... for a time. But eventually they would all have to return to the ark to report, return with findings, and most importantly *resupply*. The skete teams had only been told the expected course of the Dragon King, and positions where the ark would linger looking for their return. *If the ark departs the region completely... it will be a death sentence for most of them, won't it? Surely the senior officers will reconsider?* But the Subprior simply ended the briefing and the assembly without taking questions. The muster began to break up into small groups of Sojourners who went their respective ways, many of them arguing bitterly.

After a moment Greymalkin threw off the stunned fog that had descended over him, remembering that he had planned to find the Obedientiary Bosun after the assembly. *He still hasn't given me a deck assignment. Maybe I can get him to make a decision.* Greymalkin saw the man, a bulky fellow in a dark blue cassock, giving out directions to the other acolytes and went up to him. Greymalkin rehearsed in his mind what he was going to ask. *And please, please, I hope he won't just have the standard Three Reactions to me that I get so often....* "Ah, ex-excuse me? I'm Brother Thomas, reporting for assignment?"

The Obedientiary was a big florid man who seemed very distracted as he reviewed information in a memory tablet held in his hand, saying,

"Who are you, then?" He glanced at Greymalkin and did a double-take when he perceived Greymalkin's shadow jewel, briefly looking shocked and even intimidated by the jewel. Greymalkin groaned inside. *And here it is, the First Reaction to me.* Greymalkin's shadow jewel was a huge violet-white adaman gem that dwarfed the jewels most Sojourners had, including the modest red jacinth in the Bosun's head. *First, he's going to think I'm somebody important and rich, but then....*

"Did you say 'Brother Thomas'? Yes, I remember now, you were just transferred in for collateral training," the Obedientiary said. "Give me just a moment to look up your records." The man consulted his memory tablet. "Ah, yes, here we are. I see, your eighteenth birthday was two days ago and you're now able to seek qualifications for a primary specialist rating. Happy belated birthday! What an auspicious birthday you have, the *Seed of Knowledge* celebration on the birthday of Thann himself!"

Greymalkin didn't say anything, but he thought glumly about how no one actually knew when his real birthday was. The Sojourners that had found him as a traumatized and starved infant in the ruins of a devastated world had simply assigned him that birthday out of respect for the traditions of their liturgy. Greymalkin hoped the man would simply skip forward to giving him an assignment, but the blustering Bosun continued scanning his personnel dossier. "Hmm, what else, then? You were...." The Obedientiary's eyebrows shot up.

Greymalkin groaned inside. *Second Reaction, right on cue. He got curious to look up my birth background, and now he won't get over it.* The heavyset Obedientiary looked him up and down in surprise, then said, "You were born *Bereft*? Providence! I've never met one of you before! What were you, a barbarian prince or something? Was your father a warlord that bartered hundreds of slaves for that huge gem in your head so that you could commune and be educated in civilization?"

Greymalkin grit his teeth, and remembered to stay pleasant. *Come on, let's avoid the Third Reaction this time...*

"No, Brother," Greymalkin said with an attempt at a smile. "I was found abandoned by Sojourners; no one knows how I got the jewel. I was raised in an orphanage run by the Order. I'm actually quite a good pilot, and I was hoping to work on a flight rating during my Narthex duty assignment. Or engineering with the shadow space manifold; I'd welcome duty in either division." The ruddy-faced Obedientiary just looked at him in mild confusion.

"No, I'm sorry, that won't be possible," the big man said absently, scanning the memory tablet. "We have no Bereft chemical rockets here or need for them, only shadow space vehicles. And of course one must understand shadow space hyperdynamics to work on the manifold...." *He didn't even hear me when I said I was taught in an orphanage of the Order.* Greymalkin started to say that he well understood both how to fly shadow space vehicles and hyperdynamics, but the Obedientiary had already jumped to a conclusion and Greymalkin cursed inside. *And there we have it, the Third Reaction of dismissive judgement, right on schedule.*

"I know!" the burly fellow said with a jocular bellow. "*Lookout!* You can go on lookout duty in the mizzen steeple cupola. I need someone up there now to keep lookout for any returning missions. Go stow your cassock and put on a jumpsuit; you can start during Vigil Watch tonight. You do at least know how to use a shadow sense amplifier, don't you?"

"Brother Adept Bosun," Greymalkin said in the best cajoling voice he could manage, throwing in the man's rank and duty role deferentially. "Of course I know how to use a simple shadow sense amplifier. But surely the ark's automated sensors make a lookout superfluous, and I won't learn anything *new* on lookout duty, and I'd hoped –"

"The diligent mind cultivates a fertile future, Acolyte," the Obedientiary recited. "You wouldn't wish us to miss any returning missionaries, would you? With a shadow jewel that size in your head, you're definitely one for lookout duty. And don't fret, this will just be for a week or so while we're leaving the region. We'll find you some other duty soon enough."

"Aye, Brother Bosun," Greymalkin said with resignation. "Will whoever I'll be relieving at Vigil watch be able to show me the expected sweep pattern for the mizzen steeple?"

"Oh, you won't be relieving anyone, there's nobody assigned up there. But now I think we should start posting someone up there at least once a day, given all the ire we saw in the muster just now about leaving the missions behind in the Erymia. It's a proper gesture. And there's no sweep pattern. I thought you said you knew how to use an amplifier? Just look around as you will, and keep a weather eye for any hazards to the ark."

"But, everything scanned from the mizzen steeple will be in the distance *behind* us," Greymalkin said, trying to keep the frustration out of his voice. When the Bosun gave him an annoyed look, Greymalkin simply said in resignation, "Aye, Brother Bosun. I'll report to the mizzen cupola at Vigil watch tonight."

"Don't worry," the Obedientiary said as he walked away. "Take along some of your classwork. You can study up there when you're bored."

A month later, Greymalkin found himself dejectedly making the trek up and out to the mizzen cupola for the thirty-second Vigil Watch in a row. The mizzen steeple did not have pressor decks, so he simply pulled himself along in zero gee slowly, resigned to another tedious six-hour stint in the cupola alone. He finally reached the cold, empty, and lonely cupola space and settled in beneath the massive old-fashioned shadow sense amplifier there.

As he activated the big device, he reflected on the one thing that he actually liked about lookout duty from his perch in the mizzen steeple, the incredible view from the eoncrystal dome of the cupola. Without any mirrorshell hull to impede his shadow sense, he could revel in the grandeur of the ark's lonely surroundings. The great memory ark *Dragon King* was plowing majestically through driving swells of shadow space currents. In the synesthesia of his shadow sense, the swells appeared as vast glimmering sapphire sheets of turbulence stretching on into the distance for light-years, echoes of interstellar nebulae passing by in normal space. He knew that the coruscating colors, distant thundering sounds, and even the crisp tang that he seemed to smell from the shadow space billows were illusory synesthesia effects of the shadow jewel in his forehead and not directly from his human senses. But the sensations were nevertheless bracing and real *to him*.

Even if these are just synesthetic mirages that I see and hear, they're glorious, he thought to himself with a wan smile. *And even for a wretched bit of jetsam like me, up here in a miserable icy post, that's a little bit of bright wonder to be glad and grateful for.*

He put his forehead up to the oversized amplifier and began the first of countless sweeps across the vast shadow space sky, simultaneously accessing his heavy mnemotome biology textbook. He'd found the Obedientiary Bosun had been right about bringing something to study. It helped pass the time and vary the tedium of lookout duty. He pulled out the big mnemotome and looked up the topic he'd been assigned to research over the next year for his secondary scholastic thesis in biology. He'd been told to research a strange phenomenon called *endosymbiosis* that was evidently foundational to almost all life that had evolved on Old Earth. As far as he understood it reading the text so far, that meant *living things living inside other living things*. He wondered what the point of all that was. *I guess I'll find out,* he thought, uneasily looking at how big a section of the tome it was.

He tried to focus on the shadow space swells and his biology classwork for the next few hours, and tried hard to *not* think about the latest depressing muster that they'd been summoned to a few hours before. It was the fifth dispiriting muster in as many weeks, and this one was the worst yet. The Abbot himself had announced the final unthinkable blow. The millennium long journey of the *Dragon King* would be *ending* when they finally reached the Alban Realm in a few months' time. *I wonder, have they known this all along, but they're just dribbling out the bad news in bits, so they won't overwhelm us all at once and cause a mutiny or something?*

Greymalkin's mood sank lower and lower over the next four hours, and he found himself daydreaming about seeing something dramatic in the amplifier. He imagined detecting the approach of some fascinating occurrence or an incredibly dangerous threat to the ship just in time. Perhaps one of the gigantic and unimaginably advanced alien species roaming the Milky Way Galaxy, like a Thuban, a Jotun, or even a monstrous Abyssal. Maybe he would spot one of the enigmatic ruins of the ancient Builders, the mysterious long-vanished aliens that had left artifacts and cybernetic creatures all over the Galaxy. *But those are just daydreams. I never see anything up here, just the stars passing me by.*

In fact, this region of the Orion Arm of the Galaxy was desolate in the extreme. It had been a wasteland ever since the devastating battles that had taken place here a thousand years ago in the Xenagon, the dread war between all of humanity and the horrific black chitin warrior-invaders from the Andromeda Galaxy. Although the Xenagon had been a cataclysmic war, after a millennium it was now only a vague and fearful memory for most human cultures. He thought how strange it was that the *Dragon King* was actually so ancient that it had already been old even in that distant time. But the great ark had been in the outlying Alban Realm in those days, far from the war. He could summon up only the vaguest imaginings of what the catastrophic Xenagon could have been like as he scanned the surrounding star systems.

Before the war this area was the primary access route from the Erymia to the rest of the Periphery. The war must be why all the human civilizations in the interior of the Erymia collapsed. There aren't even any planetary ruins left anywhere here. <u>Everything</u> was obliterated. He found that dismal thought very depressing, and *that* thought made him think again about the fresh depressing memory of the Compline announcement from the Abbot yesterday. He could not imagine that outcome either. *What will it mean? How can the ark's voyage just... halt?* The combination of thoughts made the long tale of human history seem to him nothing but devastation and despair from beginning to end.

He was trying to avoid further sinking into bleak depression thinking about the Abbot's news when, scanning the billows with a hopeless desire to see something, *anything...* it actually happened. He shook his head, and then pressed his forehead against the amplifier uncertainly.

What is <u>that</u>?

Incredibly, with a growing sense of awe, it dawned on him that he could actually make out the smallest hint of a spacecraft hull far off amid the giant shadow space billows. *It can't be,* Greymalkin thought to himself in growing consternation, shaking off the fog of despair that had been clouding his mind. But after another moment, he actually recognized the distinctive signal of the tiny vessel that everyone had thought lost long ago. It was the missionary vessel of Mother Advisor Trystia. *After so long? Returning <u>now</u>? And surely not with....*

He gasped slightly. Even from his distant perch in the mizzen steeple cupola he could see that the skiff was flagged with the unique signal simultaneously dreaded but also sought for so often by Sojourners out of compassion. *Bereft. She bears <u>Bereft</u> passage,* he thought in shock.

After a frozen moment of paralysis he thought, *It's no mistake. It's real. Move! For Mercy's sake, I... I've got to do something!*

Greymalkin felt nothing but panic. He'd never thought he would see anything in the observation post. The young Sojourner had never been faced with an actual moment of crisis, a moment in which other lives depended on his taking immediate action, and it scattered his mind. The countless drills he'd been in had all been supervised by a preceptor literally watching him over his shoulder, waiting for him to verbally report his decisions and observations. He forgot every protocol he'd ever known and galvanized into unnerved motion, fleeing the small observatory in unthinking panic.

As he pulled himself hurriedly through the zero gee float-way for many frightened moments and quickly reached the outer hull frameworks of dormers and the immense eoncrystal clerestories, he could not help repeatedly glancing back at the remote skiff through the portals of the giant cathedral vessel, reassuring himself that he was not mistaken. The billows of the nebula-dense shadow space channel the ark was traversing were much thicker than normal channelways, and the skiff was obscured as often as not. He suddenly thought with concern about how much turbulence the skiff would be experiencing as it drove through those immense swells trying desperately to catch up with the great memory ark.

Wait, what am I doing?! He yanked himself to a halt, suddenly realizing how stupid it was to be fleeing to physically report the situation. *This isn't a training drill where I have to report to someone in person!* The narthex was hundreds of meters away and the bridge was *kilometers* distant at the other end of the ship. *I've got to contact the bridge to alert the Helm Crew to slow down, and quickly.* Despite its slow plodding velocity, the massive *Dragon King* could simply crash through the billows unhindered and would soon outpace the skiff as the far smaller vessel was battered about in the swells. *But how am I going to get their attention? Nobody up there will listen to me!* Then he realized that there *was* one person there that would listen to him, the one person on the bridge that he trusted completely. He sought out the *urgent warning* network in his mind, and communed directly with Father Johannes, abandoning all the normal monastic protocols.

«Bridge, alert, *sighting alert*! Skete skiff on leeward approach, appears to be in distress, coordinates follow. Heave to, *heave to*, we're leaving them hard up!» Greymalkin sent, along with the position of the tiny ship. Johannes sternly sent back only a terse acknowledgment. «Stand by, lookout.» As he waited, staying still became intolerable in his panic, and the young Sojourner again began yanking himself down the float-way with rapid jerks on handholds toward the galleries of the main nave, soaring in zero gee past the stanchions much faster than was normal or safe. As the moment stretched, he thought that something must be wrong. *Why is it taking them so long to respond?*

Johannes finally answered, his thick Islexian Realm drift-accent present even in his communed thoughts. «Are ye sure, Grey? We dinnae read anything at yon grid points.» Greymalkin grimaced and sent back a jittery reply.

«Positive sighting, positive ID! That's Mother Advisor Trystia's ship, I'm certain! And she's flagged *Bereft*. Check the coordinates again, I beg of you!» Greymalkin suddenly felt even more panicked, wondering what he should do. *What if they don't believe me, or they just can't see the skiff in the swells? And why hasn't Trystia hailed us already through one of the remote relays? What do I have to do, go back to the observatory and make a recording or something?*

«Checking, stand-by... We dinnae... wait... *wait*, I see it now. Providence, ye're a keen spotter, it's *faint*! Stand-by again, the Vigil Watch Subprior is gaun tae wake the Abbot....» Johannes' thoughts were now agitated as well. Even as recklessly as Greymalkin had been launching himself through the upper vaults of the ark, he had only now left the steeple and reached the outer galleries. He wondered if he should climb through the balusters to reach the nearest portion of the nave, or simply cast himself straight through the open space toward the widest expanse of the nave hundreds of meters away. The pressor deck would not engage until he was just a few meters from the far deck. He hesitated, not because he feared that he couldn't stick the landing after a long zero gee jump, but because it was a severe violation of shipboard protocols and propriety. Monks weren't supposed to go leaping headlong through the ark. He'd be in more trouble than ever before.

He looked down into the dizzying space of the Great Nave. The Vigil Watch would end soon. The miniscule forms of Sojourner brothers and sisters were visible far below as they began to emerge, headed to their duty stations like dark rivulets through the geometric patterns of meditation aisles and serried ranks of dark mnemotome stacks. Correct shipboard discipline would be for him to first transition from the zero gee outer spaces to the pressor decks, slowly navigate the maze of stairways to the nave, and then process in a dignified manner to the chancel and then the apse and finally the bridge itself. His anxiety over the skiff tempted him to risk the leap despite the punishment he'd incur, but he shuddered at the thought and stopped.

Then he paused, realizing belatedly that no one had actually *summoned* him yet. In fact, in his excitement he had *left his post* before being ordered to do so. He groaned, realizing that now he was already in serious trouble for breaking protocol in the first hours of the new day. *Stop it, calm down,* he told himself. *Think. Why hasn't Trystia hailed us? She's in range of the remote relays.* That question troubled him more than anything else. Then Johannes communed with him again, this time with thoughts slow and grave.

«Grey, the Abbot has ordered Helm tae reduce our velocity, but... Trystia's ship is on *autopilot*. We dinnae know her condition. I'm assembling an emergency response boarding party at Narthex Dock

Alpha. I want ye to get oer there; I'll be down as soon as I can. And Grey, lad... wear a field lab cassock.» Johannes' thoughts cut off ominously. Greymalkin felt stricken and cold inside. Field lab cassocks were for... untidy tasks. As calmly as he could manage, he put his feet down and activated the pressor deck control. A moment later he felt the pseudo-weight of the pressor field ripple throughout his body, forcing him onto the deck. After taking a deep breath to collect himself, he strode toward the stairways that led to the nave.

He forced himself to walk the steps slowly, trying to reorganize his thoughts on the way to the dormitory. There was no point in rushing now; it would take time for the skiff to reach the narthex docks of the ark. And he needed to mentally review both the First Contact and Bereft boarding protocols. *Father Johannes honors me by inviting me to be included in the boarding party. I can't make any more mistakes today,* he thought, still shaken by the sight of the skiff. *Or ever again!*

The shock of those minutes of fright settled in on him slowly, and he began to reflect on just how gravely he'd failed in his reactions. *I totally panicked. I panicked like the idiotic, inexperienced gremmie that I am. If I'd taken any longer jumping around like a lunatic nobody would have seen the skiff or believed me.*

When she had not returned months ago, Greymalkin had mourned the loss of Mother Advisor Trystia as much as anyone. She was one of the most beloved proctors in the whole ark, and had been his mentor growing up every bit as much as Johannes. His stomach was twisting inside. The crushing news yesterday about the looming end of their voyage had been devastating enough. It had seemed like a ray of hope when he had spotted the skiff and thought Trystia might be returning against all odds. To learn that her ship might be a *tomb*... he stopped and palmed his face for a trembling moment at the exit of the stairs. The moment had rattled him to his core.

After taking a series of deep breaths to calm himself, Greymalkin took a moment to make a solemn, silent vow. *No matter how big the crisis, I will remember this moment. So help me, I will never panic in a crisis moment like that again.* He clenched his jaw and walked out steadily into the stream of Sojourners on the huge floor of the Great Nave. *And no more mistakes today, either,* he vowed.

* * *

After he'd reached the acolytes' dormitory and struggled into one of the heavy and stiffly rugged field lab cassocks, he made his way to the huge enclosed space of Narthex Alpha Dock. Most of the other members of the response team had assembled there already, and were muttering in hushed tones, on edge. When they saw him arrive everyone had the same questions, "You were the one that spotted the skiff? You're sure it was Trystia's skete? And *Bereft* did you say? We haven't had a Bereft encounter in years...."

Greymalkin simply nodded nervously in response to all the questions. He was acutely aware of how much younger he was than all the other Sojourners in the team, being the only acolyte that had been summoned by Johannes. He could hear the skeptical tones in some of their questions. *They think I snafued it. Maybe they heard that I fled the lookout without orders. I'll never live that down once that gets out, I'll wager.* His tension was only exacerbated when he saw that all of the thick eoncrystal isolation and containment barriers had been lowered into place at the entrances to the inner dock.

"Why the isolation protocol?" he asked in dismay, just as Johannes arrived. "It's just Mother Advisor Trystia. And she may be injured!" No one said anything, or did anything but scowl down at the tips of their boots protruding under their long white field-lab coats. Johannes pursed his lips, and arched an eyebrow at him.

"Yon ship's on autopilot, lad, and it's flagged Bereft as well. Could be contaminated. *Or worse.* Have ye forgotten basic safety measures?"

Johannes said in an irritated tone, and then lowered his voice to a whisper for only Greymalkin to hear. "As well as forgettin' lookout discipline in a bloody panic? What came over ye up there in the cupola anyway?"

"I'm sorry, Father," Greymalkin muttered apologetically. "I'm so very sorry. It... I'm sorry. I won't do that ever again. I just... wanted to help her somehow, any way that I could."

"And ye will," Johannes said, and his face exchanged a scowl of bushy eyebrows for a slight grin before continuing, his thick Islexian drift-accent once again asserting itself. "Ye did a braw job o' spottin' that wee bit of flotsam so distant. Today ye'll stand beside me to greet anything that comes oot o' that boat, provided it dinnae try to *kill* us. And if no one is aboard, or no one still draws breath...." His face hardened again. "Well, ye'd best prepare ye'rself for that possibility as well. In any event, provided that ye keep yer head today and remember protocols, I've been given permission tae approve ye early for Initiate status."

Greymalkin had tensed at the thought of finding only corpses on the skiff, but then his eyes widened. Initiate status was the conclusion of the Acolyte progression, and constituted an interim provisional role before becoming an Apprentice. Greymalkin's head swirled, and he felt even more nervous. "I'm grateful for the opportunity, Father," he finally managed, trying to keep from stuttering. "I'll do my best."

"Just keep yer head, follow the rules and procedures, and ye'll be alright," Johannes said. He looked distant for a few moments, and then stepped out in front of the boarding party as the last individuals came running up. He raised his voice to address the whole group.

"Boarding party tae stations! Bridge navigation reported that the shadow space continuities of yon skiff and the ark just coalesced; we should be able tae see it now on close approach. Stand ready, and remember that saving Trystia and any other surviving members o' her skete are our top priority. Waldo medical crew, sound off!"

Greymalkin felt the thoughts of the first responders who had clambered into the armored telepresence cupolas behind him as they each communed in turn. «Unit One Ready, Aye! Unit Two Ready, Aye....» The silvery figures of the remote-controlled waldo units stood motionless on the other side of the thick isolation barriers, holding medical pods and equipment. The waldos would be the first to enter the skiff, he thought uneasily. They couldn't be infected with biological hazards, and they could also handle any dangerous resistance they might encounter.

"Skiff on close approach!" Johannes bawled. "Stand by to receive, rig for entry, and secure for possible hard contact!" Abruptly, the big outer dock mirrorshell doors visible through the eoncrystal barriers opened with a rumbling vibration in the deck. There was nothing on the other side except the void of shadow space. The synesthetic sensations of the billows were strong here at the verge of the dock, an assault of fleeting colors as well as the thunderous noise of the swells as the ark passed through them. The pseudo-scents of salt spray and iodine seemed sharp in his nasal passages. Greymalkin tensed.

It's just a trick of the mind, he reminded himself. *Just my neocortex trying to make sense of signals that remind human brains of the ocean at some instinctual level.* Greymalkin had never even been near a planetary sea in his life. He wondered if oceans really smelled like that, or if his synesthesia was wholly wrong. Maybe oceans actually smelled and sounded completely different. He briefly wondered when (or if) he would ever visit an actual ocean and find out.

Greymalkin closed his eyes and extended his shadow sense outward into the depths beyond the hull of the ark. He could feel the artificial bubble of reality generated by the starship's shadow space manifold extending all around them for thousands upon thousands of kilometers.

But despite its size, the ark's bubble of reality seemed incredibly tiny in comparison to the infinitely larger continuity of normal space with stars and galaxies that they were suspended above, displaced in the fifth dimension of shadow space. The jewel in his mind resonated across the dimensions surrounding them, giving him an intuitive perception of the ark's continuity manifold moving slowly above normal space like a tiny soap bubble drifting above a vast ocean.

As he focused his shadow sense further, he could now make out the miniscule shape of the skiff as it steadily approached the huge narthex dock through the ark's continuity space. The skiff was so much smaller than the ark; it felt like watching a pebble falling slowly toward the side of a boulder. *I should be able to see it any moment with just my naked eyes,* he thought. He opened his pale grey eyes and sought for the skiff. At first he saw nothing but the random patterns of shimmering blue light from the shadow space billows in the wake of the ark outside the dock opening. Greymalkin noticed that now the other Sojourners around him were also peering out into the gentle sapphire radiance, tensely searching for the first sight of the skiff.

They all saw the skiff emerge from the sheets of light-spray at the same time. At first it was just an insignificant shining bead in the distance. It grew larger rapidly, until the curved mirrorshell front of the skiff filled the big dock opening. As it approached he noted that large portions of the ovoid hull had been blackened by some sort of pyrolysis or combustion, presumably in the process of entering the oxygen atmosphere of an inhabited planet. Although it was tiny in comparison with the huge memory ark, they all felt the very real and very *heavy* thud reverberate through the deck when the skiff's mass of thousands of tons met the dock, and the clamps latched tight. *No illusion in that,* he thought. The outer dock doors closed behind the skiff then, and as the interior barrier doors opened there was a whooshing sound as air from the rest of the dock blew in around the small starship. The front of the skiff now stood exposed in the already pressurized inner dock space just beyond the eoncrystal isolation barrier.

For a moment nothing happened. Then the forward hatch of the skiff dilated open. Greymalkin realized he had been holding his breath when he inhaled abruptly at the sight of people inside the skiff.

It wasn't surprising that there were people inside. Rather, it was surprising and a bit distressing to him that none of them were *Sojourners*. Instead he saw a small group of hairy wild-eyed humans, bruised and bloodied, wearing weathered clothes that were little more than rags, grasping and bobbling outwards from the skiff in the zero gee. He took in the confusing cluster of flapping forms quickly, trying to discern relevant details in snapshots of mental notes. *Four males and one female. Clearly unused to zero gee from the way they're floundering.* Their garments and knapsacks weren't just unkempt; he saw now that they were *hand-made*, mostly of some rough irregular material like woven burlap. The pieces clicked together in his mind. *A group of pre-industrial Bereft. Probably refugees rescued by Trystia and her crew. But where are the Sojourners? Where is Trystia?*

The Bereft looked around in disorientation, first at the mirrorshell dock space and then at the response team members on the other side of the clear barrier. Their expressions became terrified when they saw the waldo units standing to the side of them. Greymalkin suddenly tried to picture how frightening the Sojourners and their equipment must look to pre-industrial eyes. The shining robot forms of the waldo units, standing so motionless and (to their eyes no doubt) *threatening*. A regimented group of tall stern strangers in stark white hooded cassocks (*standing motionless on a wall in zero gee!*) and the surrounding bulkheads of bizarre technology and unnaturally reflective metal. *They probably don't know about pressor decks or... where do they even think they are?*

"Ho, Bereft party! Can ye understand me?" Father Johannes asked, stepping forward and addressing them directly. He gestured toward his mouth, trying to encourage them to say something. «Savages!» Johannes finally communed to Greymalkin dismissively. «For Trystia's sake I hope they are nae *cannibals*. How in blazes did they get here in yon skiff? They obviously dinnae have shadow jewel implants and will nae be able tae commune with us. Grey, ye have a linguistics qual, aye? Try tae ken their spoken language. If we can get them tae say anything at all, that is.»

Greymalkin couldn't help frowning, even though he revered Johannes. He knew the man could be stern and harsh, but this was cruelly arrogant. The young monk wondered again at the changes in his old mentor, the despair and grief that seemed to have twisted him ever since that day they'd encountered one another up in the clerestories. The harshness of Johannes in the moment struck Greymalkin as particularly unkind.

I was once Bereft, before the Order took me in as a foundling, Greymalkin thought ruefully. *If I hadn't been adopted by Sojourners I might be one of these frightened people.* He stepped forward with an acknowledgment. «Aye-Aye! I'll do my best.» After hesitating, and with some slight irritation of his own, he added, «They're Bereft, not savages, Father.»

Johannes glared at him, but gestured him forward silently. Greymalkin was about to try to communicate with them when the oldest male in the Bereft group spoke. He was a grizzled, angry fellow with a white beard. Greymalkin had been ready, and applied his language mnemotechnic to the harsh phrases. *I know those words,* he thought, but couldn't immediately place them. He sifted through the hundreds of languages he had mastered in his heuristics. Thankfully, the old man spoke again, giving him a bit more to go on, and the words suddenly snapped into focus in his mind. *Got it!*

«I think he's speaking a drift-dialect of Akelan. He's asking who we are.» Greymalkin was uneasy. The old man was obviously very agitated. Greymalkin knew that the Bereft could not breach the isolation barrier, but....

Johannes' eyes narrowed. «Ask him about Trystia and the other members o' her skete. Where are they?»

Greymalkin swallowed, quickly reviewing the relevant Akelan syntax structures and vocabulary. *I don't know how much their language has drifted from the original Akelan,* he thought. *I'd better keep it simple.* He asked the questions in short and direct phrases. The Bereft all looked surprised when he spoke, and the younger ones looked slightly more hopeful. The old man glared at Greymalkin and then Johannes before repeating his question. *Right. I didn't answer him,* Greymalkin thought. As quickly as he could, he explained that they were friends of Trystia, recognized her ship, and were concerned about her safety. The old man slowly nodded suspiciously and gestured to his followers. Johannes made an irritated sound under his breath before communing with Greymalkin.

«This's taking tae long. We should....» The older Sojourner paused. The Bereft were pulling something oblong out through the skiff hatch. Greymalkin tensed again. It was a medical pod with a woman's form visible inside it. *Is that Trystia? Is she alive?*

Several things happened all at once. At a gesture from Johannes, the waldo operators moved the remote units forward quickly to recover the medical pod. When the big metal sentinels moved toward them, the Bereft screamed in fear. Greymalkin saw that the old man had pulled himself backwards to the pod. He took something out of his coat and held it down against the medical pod. *A weapon?*

«Hold! Ev'ryone hold still, damn ye!» Johannes roared the command to the waldo operators, and the units all froze in mid-stride. «What in blazes is he sayin' now, Grey?»

The old man had shouted a threat as he moved to the pod. Greymalkin was horror-struck. «He's got a weapon! I-I think it's some kind of chemical explosive. He's saying that Trystia's wounded, it wasn't their fault. But he says he'll *kill* her if we don't answer his questions first.»

Johannes snarled something inchoate, quickly analyzing the situation. «We dinnae know what he or the weapon are capable of. Find out what the damned savage wants tae know, but be quick about it, laddie!»

Greymalkin's eyes flicked from the Bereft to the medical pod. While the face was obscured with a breathing mask, he was still certain it was Trystia. Her eyes were closed, one cheek covered in auto-healing bands. Greymalkin met the old man's stern gaze and asked what he wanted. The angry old man looked triumphant and began to speak quickly in a demanding voice. Greymalkin begged him to slow down as he listened and tried to comprehend the words. Gradually, despite the unfamiliar drift-words and garbled accent, he understood what the old man was saying. Greymalkin excitedly turned to commune with Johannes.

«They are certainly Bereft. He says that their civilization fell generations ago, before their 'greatest grandfathers all began to die.' There are few of them left now. Trystia came among them and promised to give them 'the old knowledge' so that they might prosper again. We can help them, Father!» But even as Greymalkin felt the brief sense of joy rising in him, he saw the dour expression on Johannes' face, and he remembered the Abbot's announcement.

«Have ye forgotten the bad news yesterday so soon, lad?» Johannes thoughts brought all the despair and sadness back with crashing pain. «We'll not be savin' anyone out there now. The end of our voyage is close at hand.»

«But surely we can save these people! Trystia and her skete risked their lives to find them! It would just require a salvation mission, for Mercy's sake. That's why we're here isn't it?» Greymalkin felt as if he were suddenly smothering. Johannes looked very old.

«Did ye nae understand what the Abbot announced yesterday, Grey? And what it meant? We've come tae the end of our voyage, whether we want it or no. And that means no more missions to go out and save the Bereft, or anyone else that needs the knowledge in this great vessel, nae matter how desperately.» Johannes spared a brief morose look at the ship around them, before his expression hardened. «But ye cannae let these savages know this, lad. Hold yer feelin's still within ye, and tell them that we'll gie them the knowledge they seek.»

«I-I can't <u>lie</u> to them!» Greymalkin protested. He tried to keep from letting his distress show outwardly. Johannes had a stony look that betrayed nothing, but his thoughts to Greymalkin were furious.

«Ye'll do as your ordered, or they'll kill Trystia and whoever else o' her skete may still draw breath on that ship! They're savages, Grey, violent wretches the whole lot! Order doctrine allows for concealin' information from violent groups tae save others. And it's nae lie; we'll give them plenty o' knowledge, as much as their cracked brains can absorb.»

«But they won't be able to return with it and save their people....» Greymalkin felt his insides twist in revulsion. Even if it was not technically a lie, he'd still be deceiving them.

«Do as ye're told! May damnation take ye, Greymalkin, if ye cannae follow a direct command sanctioned by the Order!» Johannes' thoughts had never been so enraged in all the years he'd known the man. It terrified Greymalkin. He shuddered in fear and tried to keep his face blank as he turned to face the Bereft. The young Sojourner took a slow breath.

The old bearded Bereft leader watched him closely, and Greymalkin was sure he suspected something. He barked another demand before Greymalkin could say anything, and despite all the unknown drift-words the young Sojourner found that he was intuitively grasping more of the old man's speech, picking out commands like, *"You give info now!"* But there were dozens of intermixed drift words that he had no clue about. What could *"prussa"* mean? It seemed to be an emphasis adverb liberally sprinkled in the old man's pronouncements, or perhaps a curse of some kind? Then Greymalkin made out a more alarming sentence in which, buried amidst strange drift-words like *"odra"*, *"galakka"*, and dozens of others that didn't sound remotely Akelan, he could discern the core statement, *"Or kill Trystia!"*

So they know her name, Greymalkin thought. *She must have trusted them, at least enough to share her actual name. How can I deceive them when she trusted them?* But he had been given a direct command. *"Do not harm Trystia,"* he begged in Akelan. Then, with a sensation of shame so palpable that it felt like hot glue over his face, he said, *"We will give you the old knowledge."*

The angry old man studied him intensely, and after a thoughtful pause made a declarative statement in something closer to traditional Akelan, *"You are friend to Trystia."* Clearly, the man had grasped that Greymalkin only understood the old central Periphery language, and not the other patois in his speech.

The young Sojourner nodded, and said again, *"We will give you knowledge."* The old man frowned, but then seemed to come to a decision and spoke in a commanding tone again.

"You come in here with us, boy. Then we will release Trystia."

"What now?" Johannes growled out loud, obviously not caring if the Bereft heard him speak now. Greymalkin quickly related the exchange, and added, "I'll go inside the isolation barrier. I'm not afraid. Then he'll let her go."

"The blazes with that!" Johannes snapped. "We will most certainly nae be breachin' contact protocol! Tell him tae let her go or he'll face the consequences."

Greymalkin wondered what the *consequences* might be, and how he could express such a vague threat without confusing the situation even more, but luckily the old man had again been keenly attentive to the exchange and said bluntly, *"He forbids you."*

Greymalkin nodded. Desperation was overtaking him as the situation kept spiraling. Knowing that Johannes would never let him actually cross the isolation barrier, he simply stepped up to the eoncrystal wall while pleading, *"Yes, he forbids me. But please, please spare Trystia."*

The old man and Johannes scowled blackly at each other for a long moment. Greymalkin began to panic, but then noticed something that he found very odd. *The other Bereft,* he thought, focusing on them. *They aren't squirming away from the old fellow and his hand grenade or whatever it is. They don't even look scared. Is this all a bluff?*

Once again the old man noticed, and read Greymalkin's reactions accurately. He relaxed and put the object away casually, saying in Akelan, *"No weapon. None of us would ever harm her. We revere her. She is the savior of our poor ruined world and people. I had to see if you were truly her friend or not."* The old man bristled at Johannes again. *"I do not trust THAT one, though! But you, boy, I trust you, because I see Trystia is dear to you. Please help her now."*

Greymalkin breathed again, and blurted out, "It's safe now to take her!" At a gesture from Johannes the waldo telepresence units approached the skiff cautiously. As Greymalkin watched, they carefully carried Trystia and three other wounded and unconscious Sojourners from inside the ship away to the isolation infirmary. He turned to Johannes fearfully.

Johannes merely snapped crisp commands while still glowering. "Explain tae them that they must go tae the isolation compartment prepared for them, and that they will be examined there for contamination and disease."

«Should I tell them that they won't be going home?» Greymalkin communed, guarded about speaking aloud. He still felt the shame of deceiving the old Bereft man that had trusted Trystia and him.

«Nae! Nae, nae yet.» Johannes sent back, and scowled once more. «There will be many deliberative preparations and procedures tae follow carefully. We must break the truth tae them... as humanely as possible.»

Greymalkin felt sick inside as he carefully chose his words in Akelan. Normally he would try to be as precise and clear as possible in translating. Now he had to be careful to prevaricate and avoid conveying the full truth. He was certain that the perceptive old leader of the Bereft would see through him. Indeed, as he spoke to the Bereft and explained their accommodations, while most of the small group looked pleased and hopeful, the old man's face gradually became sad and drawn. The others thanked Greymalkin profusely in their thick and almost incomprehensible patois, but the old man was silent. It was as if a dismally heavy cloak of guilt had been laid on Greymalkin's shoulders. At last the old man asked a question bitterly.

"*What gods do you and these holy people believe in, boy?*" The wrinkled old Bereft man's face was hollow now. Greymalkin chose his words carefully for clarity and honesty.

"*We have faith, but our faith is in the wonder of scientific inquiry and compassion. We believe in loyalty to all humanity and knowledge,*" Greymalkin said. The old man looked down in sadness, then. His rheumy eyes were shadowed and hopeless.

"*You sound like Trystia,*" he said. "*Your wonder and compassion are bright gods to follow, but I fear our dark gods of tyranny and cruelty may be still more powerful. I hope they do not follow us here. Our gods hate us. Pray for us, boy. I will pray for you. Farewell."*

Sensing their discussion was over, the waldo crew led the Bereft away to their isolation compartment. Greymalkin watched in tears, the mantle of shame crushing him. Then Johannes came up and spoke to him once again.

"Despite a few falters here and there, ye did well, Grey. Yer skills as both spotter and a linguist were invaluable today. I'll put ye forward for Initiate status and a commendation." Johannes was actually smiling. Greymalkin felt empty. After a moment he spoke very softly.

"But I lied to them."

"Ye followed orders. That can be difficult," Johannes said, shrugging.

"But our Order exists to help the Bereft and all civilizations that seek knowledge," Greymalkin said. "That is the Great Commitment, is it not?"

"Aye. Aye, it is," Johannes said slowly, looking uncomfortable. "And we will do what we can for them. Go and rest now; Vigil Watch is over. And ye look done in, lad."

"I would like to go and see if Trystia is alright."

"She'll be in the isolation ward for some hours being evaluated and tended. We can both go see her when ye wake. I'll wait for ye. Now go." Johannes clapped him on the back and strode away. Greymalkin stood alone in the dock for a few minutes thinking, and then left.

* * *

By the time he reached his tiny monastic cell quarters he was feeling the exhaustion of the long day catching up with him. Despite this, the tension in his neck was ferocious, and he floated restlessly awake in his sleeping sack for what seemed like hours before drifting off.

As he slept he found himself in a dream that filled him with dread. In the dream, Greymalkin stood in a dark and echoing space, a single spotlight illuminating the space around him. The pressor deck was tuned very high and he could barely stand, almost falling to the deck under the heavy gravity. He heard a terrible sound of metal scraping on metal, and saw the old Bereft man laboriously gasping for breath as he dragged the huge medical pod with Trystia into the light. The aged Bereft man stood up straight with a great effort, looking down with a beatific expression at Trystia within the pod. Greymalkin smiled and walked up to the old man nodding, then stepping just behind him. Just as the pod cover began to open and lift, Greymalkin took out a gleaming knife and stabbed the old man viciously in the back. As the old man crumpled to the floor, blood streaming from his back and mouth, Trystia sat up in the medical pod and looked at the blood on Greymalkin's hands in terror, staggering up out of the pod desperately seeking to escape from him. As she fled into the darkness of the dream, Greymalkin awoke drenched in sweat and trembling in horror.

 He struggled out of his sleeping sack unsteadily catching his breath, feeling exhausted and ill at ease. After he calmed down, Greymalkin carefully activated his pressor deck, afraid for a moment that it would crush him to the deck, and he would find himself in the nightmare again. But his tiny cell was the same as it had always been. He quickly performed his waking calisthenics and meditation, all the while trying to calm down and center his thinking. But the sense of guilt and a storm of questions still spun around in his mind, scattering his thoughts with anxiety.

 The Bereft came to us for help, and I deceived them. When will they be told they aren't going back? What will happen to their world? Will their civilization ever recover if we don't help them? And... where did all those strange drift-words come from in their speech? After pulling on a crisp set of his drably formal dun-colored robes he headed in the direction of the isolation ward, wondering if Trystia would be awake.

On the way he passed other Sojourners hurrying to their Watch duties, some in flight suits, some in lab cassocks, but a surprising number wearing formal robes and even stoles. *What is the occasion? I don't remember any ceremonial services or events scheduled for today.* None of the Sojourners looked happy; the news from the Abbot was still too fresh in all their minds. But he thought the Brothers and Sisters in formal robes looked the most solemn of all. Then he began to notice the unusual number of Patrons, wealthy visitors arrayed in finery and shadow jewels, many being escorted deferentially by the Sojourners. The Patrons looked smugly pleased, the Sojourners wore forced smiles. A feeling of foreboding was beginning to settle over Greymalkin when Father Johannes signaled him.

«Grey, the infirmary has granted visitation for Trystia.» Johannes' communed thoughts struck Greymalkin as troubled. The young Sojourner quickened his pace.

«Is she alright? How are the Bereft we took aboard. Are they okay?» Greymalkin wondered nervously if anything had gone amiss while he slept.

«I dinnae know about either, but I'm sure they're all bein' properly cared for. We'll see how they are when we get there. I have some duties first, but I'll join ye in the isolation ward as soon as I can.» There were echoes of concern in Johannes' thoughts, but whatever it was he kept it private. Greymalkin wondered what was wrong as he hurried, almost jogging, through the passageways and then out into the broad deck of the nave, through the endless ranks of mnemotome stacks. His sense of foreboding began to grow.

And then he heard the books whispering to each other.

It was a rare day when his synesthetic senses, enabled by the shadow jewel in his forebrain, could pick up the faint conversations between the countless volumes in the stacks of the great memory ark. Each of the mnemotomes were automata in their own right, with the capability for slow, quiet conversations with each other. These transmissions were so soft that even the sensitive shadow jewel in his head could barely detect them unless he was directly scanning the book. But today the faint signals echoed in his mind through the jewel like a vast distantly murmuring crowd. The hushed tones were a jumbled mass, hard to put together into coherent thoughts, but he had never heard the books talking so intently to one another. He paused to listen, gradually piecing together fleeting fragments of dialogue. With a start, he suddenly realized that the books were all discussing variations on the same interrelated topics. *Disasters. Social collapse. Bereft cultures. Failures of human character.*

He had lived among the mnemotomes for years, happily studying them since he first came on board as a child. He had never felt *afraid* of them. *What do they know?* he wondered. The electronic whispering rippled softly across the endless rows of stacks stretched out through the nave, sending a chill up Greymalkin's spine. He hastily left the nave and entered the quarantine infirmary.

He had never been in the quarantine infirmary before, and it was much bigger than he had imagined. After wandering the empty outer halls for a while he found his way to the isolation ward and learned from the decontamination physicians that the examination of Mother Advisor Trystia had already been completed and she had been granted pratique clearance. When he was told she was recovering from her injuries but now awake he asked if he could see her, and was shown to her room.

When he was taken to her he found Trystia sitting up in bed with a somber look, the many wrinkles on her old face deepened into dark crags. She brightened when he entered and said, "Greymalkin, how nice of you to come see me, dear boy." The physician left and he sat next to her smiling, but also more than a little concerned at the healing bands swaddling so many parts of her. She noticed and snorted quietly. "I'm fine. The return was a bit rough at the end, what with all the chop. The Bereft bore it better than we fragile monks."

"I'm amazed you even found the ark after we left our planned course, and that you reached us through all those massive billows we were traversing," Greymalkin said, running his hand through his hair. "And I can't believe that you caught up to us enough that we saw you."

"I heard that *you* were the one that spotted our skiff," she said, briefly beaming. Greymalkin felt a rush of pride. Trystia had been one of the proctors he had most revered when he came to the ark. She smiled at him, saying, "It's thanks to your vigilance that we survived." Her face fell again then, and she said gently, "Well, those of us who made it back."

That's right, there were two Sojourners in her skete who did not return. He reached out to hold her hand, and was surprised at her trembling grip. "I'm so sorry, Mother Advisor," he said, his voice very low. For a moment she closed her eyes, but then she simply cleared her throat and arched her thin white eyebrows.

"Brother Armond and Sister Campbell both knew the risks going on mission, we all do. They gave their lives to save the Bereft, and thanks to their sacrifice we'll do it. We will save yet another collapsed civilization of people who need our help desperately," she said in a calm but firm voice.

Oh no, Greymalkin thought in horror. *Of course she hasn't heard the news yet. We won't be saving these or any other Bereft.* He was trying to find the words to tell her when she scowled and rolled her eyes.

"Providence, Greymalkin, I've already heard all about that *swerked fadoodle* our old fool of an Abbot announced yesterday," she said, obviously irritated. "They told it to me during my debriefing an hour ago. *Feh.* I've helped save four Bereft worlds in my time, despite all the pain that each one of those worlds cost me in dear friends lost over the years. Do you think I will stop just because that old fool is going to beach this rickety old tub?"

Greymalkin felt doubly and triply spun around. "You already know? But wait, what do you mean by *beach?* Who said anything about beaching...." His eyes and mouth gaped. "You mean they're actually going to *beach the ark?*"

Trystia suddenly looked as if she regretted her words, just as Greymalkin realized that as he'd been speaking he'd heard the door open behind him. He turned to see Johannes grimacing and irate.

"Thanks so much, Trys!" Johannes' voice rang out with sarcasm. "We hadn't told any o' the acolytes yet. The Abbot wanted tae let them get over the first shock before the second hit."

"And hello to you as well, Father Johannes," Trystia said acidly. "The acolytes aren't fools, many have probably figured out that rather obvious conclusion."

"Wait, wait," Greymalkin begged, feeling like he was trying to grab at rocks in a flood, and somehow Johannes and Trystia were already on the shore. "Yes, the Abbot told all of us yesterday that because the ark has lost its last tithe, the big one from the Alban Realm, that meant that the long voyage of our vessel must end. But you're saying that we're going to drop the ship out of shadow space completely? *Forever?* Actually beach it in normal space? How would we ever get it moving again? Re-launching it would be almost impossible...." When he saw the stony faces on both Johannes and Trystia, Greymalkin felt stricken. He had not followed the thought out to its logical conclusion until this moment.

"Aye, Grey," Johannes said. The older Sojourner still looked furious with Trystia, but was trying to soften his tone with Greymalkin as he continued, "The tithes pay for the shadow flux we need to keep the ark moving in shadow space and everything else required for operations. We'll *have* to beach the ship eventually."

"They won't even be able to keep operating the pressor decks," Trystia snapped in derision. "They'll probably have to spin the ship around like a primitive centrifuge to keep everybody's bones from turning to jelly. Some interstellar memory ark of salvation it'll be then."

"This's all conjecture at the moment," Johannes said. "We have nae word from Vernalis as of yet that the decision has even been made by the Order to beach the ship. The Abbot'll make another address tomorrow tae advise us on next steps."

He sounds like he's talking about recipe planning for the refectory lunch menu, Greymalkin thought. *How can he be so placid about all this?* Trystia, despite being swaddled in thick healing bands, looked like she was about to surge up out of the bed to shout at Johannes. Greymalkin held her hand tighter, and she became calm again, taking a deep breath.

"Be that as it may, we will save the Skarans," Trystia said sullenly. Greymalkin and Johannes glanced quizzically at each other.

"The who?" Johannes asked. Abruptly a puzzle-piece clicked into place in Greymalkin's mind. *Skaran, that must be the overlay language, the source of the drift-words I couldn't place. Wait. Skarans? The Skara Brae?*

"Skarans," Greymalkin mused. "That must be the name of the Bereft people you brought back with you? Are they related to the Skara Brae colony that disappeared a millennium ago?"

Trystia blinked and then stared at Greymalkin for a moment before beaming again. "You're remarkable, Greymalkin. Yes, that's what we pieced together from the surviving records in the ruins of their old cities after we found them. We think they were a splinter group that merged with another fugitive group from Akela that fled into the Erymia, these endless maze-spaces of the Periphery we've been circling around for years. We found them while we were surveying a remote shadow channel network in there. But none of us had ever heard of the Skara Brae. How in all creation do you know them?"

"They were an interesting subculture documented in several mnemotomes I studied last year," Greymalkin said, gushing now.

Nobody else ever seemed to be interested in these obscure topics. "It's a distinctive name that they took for themselves from a legendary culture of Old Earth. Their language was never recorded, that's why I didn't recognize it. They – "

"Thank ye, Grey," Johannes said, in a tone that reaffirmed nobody else was interested in the origins of the Skarans. Greymalkin nodded and stopped talking, although he thought Trystia looked pensive at what he'd said. Johannes continued quickly, "Whoever they are and wherever they came from, I'm afraid we won't be able tae help them unfortunately."

"You mean that *you* won't be helping them," Trystia said curtly. "Their civilization collapsed because of natural disasters that can be avoided. I promised them that we'd return to give them the information and training they need to rebuild."

Johannes folded his arms into the long sleeves of his black cassock. "That will nae be possible, Trys. Ye know that better than anyone. Ye used to be Bridge Crew. Blazes, ye used to be the Prior for Outreach!"

"Why do you think I resigned and went back to the field, you fool?" Trystia said tersely. "The Abbot's been cutting back on Outreach for decades!"

"Because the tithes were diminishing! Everybody knows that; how can ye blame the Abbot?" Johannes retorted derisively. Greymalkin grit his teeth and looked down, red-faced. The heat of the argument by two of his mentors shocked him; he'd never heard them argue so furiously. *This is an old argument between them,* he realized, listening to the way they skipped through details that he didn't fully understand. *Yet they'd never displayed this kind of acrimony in public before. What's going on?*

Then he realized the obvious. *The voyage is ending. This is the end of everything for us; what we've all devoted our lives to accomplishing. Of course they're blowing up at each other.* He wondered how many more arguments like this would be breaking out through the ark in coming days. He felt like the room was spinning. *How was I so clueless about this? I heard all of these hand-wringing discussions, but it just sounded like it had always been going on and always would. I never thought it would mean...*

Trystia saw his distress and her anger subsided. Now she simply looked very old. "I'm sorry, Greymalkin. This is something we've dreaded for a long time, something we were anticipating long before you were born, in fact. This business of declining tithes was a fact that many wanted to ignore. But it's finally caught up with us. No real surprise there!" She briefly glared at Johannes again, but didn't seem ready to carry on the argument any longer.

"Trys, we'll need yer help in breaking this news tae the Bereft ye brought in," Johannes said, his tone now more conciliatory, almost pleading. "They're demanding tae know where ye are and what's happening. They need tae be told *this* is their new home."

"I'll talk to them," Trystia said crossly. "But I'll tell them our return is delayed. I'm taking them back, one way or the other."

"That's a cruel lie," Johannes growled. "I can't believe ye'd tell them that." Greymalkin felt like he was watching an escalating game of flyball, with each side becoming more stubbornly committed to winning by the moment. Then Trystia flipped the game.

"It's not a lie. It will simply take me time to raise the funds for a return expedition once I've left the Order, that's all. But I'll be back for them; you can be sure of that!"

Greymalkin was speechless. "What? You can't be serious! You're leaving the Order?" Trystia had always been one of the most steadfast Sojourners in the ark. She was a legend. The old woman had a kind countenance when she smiled at him sadly.

"Oh, I know it's hard to imagine, dear boy. Old Trystia packing up and leaving the ark. Inconceivable! I'm part of the bulkheads, right? I don't blame you for that view. You are one of our many adopted

Sojourners, so you've never known anything but this cold miserable ship of archives, endless Watch schedules, and recitations of procedures. But I had a life before I joined the Order, and I only joined it to help people. If I can't do that here, then I'll do it elsewhere."

Greymalkin could not believe what he was hearing and looked to Johannes, who only rolled his eyes and said, "Procedures are put in place for good reasons, Trys."

Greymalkin numbly fought the urge to shed tears, and mumbled the saying that had been drilled into him from earliest childhood, "Procedures followed, lives saved." He felt Trystia squeeze his hand before she let go, still smiling at him.

"That's exactly right, Greymalkin," she said approvingly, before her white brows furrowed again at Johannes. "But when the procedures, rules, and whatnot aren't protecting lives anymore then it's time for a change. Don't worry, I won't be leaving tomorrow. There will be time for goodbyes. And perhaps...." She cocked her head to one side and looked at him pensively before saying, "...perhaps it will be time for you to make some decisions of your own, about what to do with your life and... to learn some things about yourself."

Johannes practically exploded, "Oh, dinnae lay *that* on him, Trys! And dinnae ye dare lay yer *own* problems on Grey!" Trystia simply raised an eyebrow.

"Everyone on this memory ark is now facing the same set of problems, Johannes. Every one of us will have to decide how they will best cope with this fundamental truth that cannot be ignored: we will no longer be Sojourners if we stay aboard this vessel. Caretakers, yes. Diligent archivists preserving a vast trove of knowledge. But we will not be sharing information or saving anyone."

Greymalkin clenched his hands together and closed his eyes, waiting for the next angry explosion Trystia's words would elicit from Johannes. But there was only a long silence.

Johannes finally said in an icy tone, "I hope ye will constructively help with the debriefing o' the Bereft party when it begins four hours from now, Mother Advisor. And I hope ye will keep their best interests at heart."

"Of course I will," Trystia retorted in a reproving but gentle tone. Greymalkin peeped at them again. Trystia was smiling at them both. Johannes was still looking at her, but seemed mollified by the answer. His face softened significantly, and he smiled back at her.

"And I hope ye will reconsider leaving the Order, my dear, dear old friend," Johannes said to her quietly. Unbelievably, Greymalkin thought he saw tears in Johannes' old eyes and Trystia's as well. The old monk slowly stepped up to Trystia and took her hand in his. "I thought I'd lost you forever. That was a black day, aye it was that. And, we'll certainly need your wisdom now more than ever." Trystia simply sighed, and Father Johannes released her hand. Then he faced Greymalkin. "I want ye tae know that my commendation for yer actions today will also include my counsel that ye be promoted tae the Bridge Crew."

Greymalkin's head jerked up. Johannes pursed his lips in amusement. "Assuming ye will nae be leaving the Order, o' course. Ye've been excused from yer next Watch in order tae attend the debriefing o' the Bereft. I must attend tae other tasks now; I'll see ye both then."

"Yes, certainly," Greymalkin mumbled. "And… thank you so much, Father."

The older Sojourner grinned at him then and, after a final nod to Trystia, he left them. Trystia looked glumly at the door after he left. Greymalkin searched for guidance in her sad expression.

"Do you think they will actually transfer me to the Bridge Crew?" he asked in disbelief. Trystia shrugged.

"Johannes would not put it in the commendation unless he had already cleared the way for you," she said. "But think that through, Greymalkin. Serving on the Bridge won't mean much if the ship's beached. And they don't respect the opinions of young people up there. I say again, the day may have finally come for you to take some time to learn some things about yourself and make decisions about what you really want."

A thousand conflicting thoughts crashed together in his mind. *I've always dreamed of serving on the Bridge, maybe even at the helm!? But the Bereft looked so desperate. And I lied to the old man. He and his people will never trust me again; there wouldn't be anything I could do to help rescue their civilization. Great Providence, what should I do?*

When he met her gaze, Trystia looked very sad indeed. *She wants me to come with her, he thought numbly. And she thinks I've already decided against her.*

"But Mother Advisor, I've never even set foot on a planet," he said in a small voice. "Would you really want me to go on mission? Would I be of any use?"

Trystia blinked, and then beamed at him again. "You just don't remember being on a planet, you were too little when we found you on that Bereft world. You *might* have been born there, but I think you were most likely from somewhere else. However, one thing *is* certain. Whoever put that astonishing jewel in your head did not expect you to live out your days on a backwater planet, or *stay put anywhere* for that matter. Whoever they were, whether your parents or a stranger, with a gem like that you were meant to *navigate the stars*. You proved your abilities today when you saved my life and the others on that skiff. *Of course* you'll be of use. But it really is your decision, Greymalkin. Johannes and I can both give you advice, but nobody can make the decision for you."

"Well, can I think about it?" Greymalkin asked after a moment. Trystia chuckled again.

"No better way to make a decision, that's for certain," the old woman said merrily. "And don't worry, whatever choice you make, it'll be the right one. Now go. I need to rest before that blasted briefing Johannes wants us to attend. And Grey..." She was momentarily very earnest. "Thank you again for saving us today. I really was not sure that anyone would see us out there."

Greymalkin nodded solemnly and left her. After standing alone in the empty hall for a moment, he climbed back up to the clerestory level and watched the billows swoop past the ark in thundering grandeur for a long while.

Shoals

Greymalkin entered the Initiates refectory studiously avoiding eye contact with any of the other young Sojourners. He quickly picked up his tray of food and looked for an empty table, trying not to appear nervous. Even after months in his new rank and duties he still found so many new things that made him feel ill at ease, from the uncomfortably formal black and silver vestments of the Bridge Crew to the much smaller refectory of the Initiates where he now had to take his meals.

He glanced down at the geometric meander-path brocade of subtly shining shadow silver embroidered into various parts of his black robes. That particular knotwork brocade was the distinctive 'guided journey' symbol of the linear labyrinth pattern, singularly marking him as a member of the Helm Crew of the vast memory ark starship. The *Long Path* pattern had obsessed him for years as an acolyte. It signified the Sojourner concept of life as a spiritual journey that might be winding and difficult, but which possessed a singular and purposeful direction. *I finally have a specialization, and it's the very one that I most desired for all those years. Why does it seem so empty now?*

He looked around the tiny refectory uneasily. Greymalkin had lived in the expansive Acolytes dormitories for so many years that it had never occurred to him how different it would feel living among the scant few Initiates on board. Initiate status was a liminal rank, only meant to be a brief probationary service before becoming an Apprentice. Even with the vast ship's complement of the ark, there were never very many

Initiates at any given time. He had encountered no more than a dozen or so at any given meal in the refectory. They all quickly became familiar with each other, although most of the other Initiates acted aloof and disinterested in making friends. *They're all probably nervous and focused on their new assignments,* he thought. *Just like me.*

Greymalkin took a seat by himself at the last empty table in the refectory and began switching between communal ship frequencies and networks as he ate his preferred dish, a simple vegetarian potage that he liked. He was checking for key updates that he had started following since joining the Bridge Crew, when a familiar and noisy pair of Initiates entered the refectory, Brother Initiates Shaw and Lee. Greymalkin groaned inwardly. The two of them were the only two current Initiates of the clique-obsessed Outreach Service, whereas Greymalkin and the others in the room were members of the traditional Ark Services.

He wondered if that was why (as far as he could tell) Shaw and Lee were always together and always chattering over the same pointless pecking-order debate, an argument about which one of them had a better specialty in their Sojourner assignments. They were even louder than usual as they were obviously at the end of their daily Watch cycle and already quite inebriated on the wine they were permitted as Initiates during their last evening period before they made their way to their cells for sleep. Greymalkin groaned again when he realized that by seating himself at the last empty table he had ensured that Shaw and Lee would be joining him. When the two inevitably sat down at the table with him (without either asking his leave or even saying hello), Greymalkin began wolfing down his potage so that he could leave as soon as possible. He didn't want to get drawn into their stupid ongoing debate.

Draped over Shaw's blue cassock was a white chasuble with a stylized transportation arrow embroidered in gold, the mark of an Outreach pilot. Lee wore dark green robes with a circular pattern embroidered on the chasuble chest and back, marking him as an

Outreach planetologist. Greymalkin kept gulping down his potage as Shaw launched into his usual line of argument, "But my point is just that serving as a pilot offers more freedom and sheer pleasure than any other duty in the Order, Brother. And I'm the best pilot on the ark."

Greymalkin almost choked on his food. *The blazes with what he says!* Greymalkin thought. *I'm a better pilot than that idiot any day. I'll agree with him on the freedom and joy of it though.* For a moment he felt slightly envious of Shaw. While serving on the Bridge offered him an infrequent chance at actually taking the helm of the entire ark, Greymalkin would still have preferred Shaw's life of constantly piloting smaller and more agile craft like skiffs, cutters, rovers, and flitters. *That would be real freedom and joy. But even if everyone on the bridge has a rod stuck up their spine, that's where the important things happen. I'm honored to serve there.*

Lee made a rude, drunken noise. Two female Initiates at the table next to them glared at his obvious intoxication. Greymalkin went back to his food as Lee proclaimed, "Brother, I'm glad you enjoy buzzing around in shadow space, but exploring wilderness planets brings me a peace and satisfaction that I wouldn't trade for anything. The emptiness of shadow space can't compare with the beauty of actual worlds with seas, mountains, and living things to experience."

"From what I hear, neither of us will be going on missions to planets anymore," Shaw muttered, dropping his slurred voice to a conspiratorial tone. "I heard it from a reliable friend of mine that's never wrong. The Abbot is going to beach the ark, either tomorrow or the day after."

"Only the Bridge people know for sure," Lee said, and finally noticed Greymalkin sitting next to him. "Brother Thomas! You're on the bridge, right? I mean, sometimes? Occasionally?"

"I'm on the bridge every duty watch," Greymalkin growled after swallowing his last mouthful of food, and then instantly regretted saying it when Shaw and Lee both brightened with interest.

"So, what's the story then? Did the Abbot say anything?" Lee asked. Greymalkin hesitated. It had been drilled into him when he joined the Bridge Crew that he was to be circumspect with any remotely sensitive information he heard while serving there. But all Sojourners abjured lying, or were supposed to. He was still trying to work out the right balance between those two directives in his head.

"He hasn't said anything explicitly about it. Nobody has," Greymalkin said truthfully. His expression apparently gave Lee and Shaw a different impression, as they both leaned in grinning at each other as they pressed him further.

"Come on! You know something, I can tell. What's going on?" Lee demanded in a whispered voice. Greymalkin frowned. It couldn't hurt to share the obvious, could it?

"Well, something's odd," he reluctantly said. "Look at our course. We're headed directly towards the Arctium system at full speed. As slow as the *Dragon King* is, we'll still reach the outer gravity shoals of the asteroid cloud around the system some time tomorrow." For a moment Lee and Shaw just looked at each other stupidly. Then Shaw figured it out.

"A skiff can transit through asteroid shoals, no problem. But the ark's continuity manifold is way too big and fragile," Shaw said thoughtfully. Greymalkin nodded.

"Exactly. I know those shoals; I was an oblate in a Sojourner orphanage of the Alban Realm there until I was eleven. The asteroid clusters and gas clouds in those shoals are thick; they accumulated over millions of years there at the fourth libration point between Arctium and the blue subgiant star that orbits it. We swooped around the flow in channel cats and went shoal hopping in little training flitters from the

Order monastic school all the time. But nothing remotely as big as the *Dragon King* could ever get through them. We'll have to divert or stop at that point. Otherwise we'll ram straight into the shoals and the ark's shunted manifold will collapse at speed. We'd be atomized." Greymalkin shuddered at the thought. It actually felt good to talk to someone about this. Everyone had pointedly been avoiding discussing this obvious fact on the bridge, and the tension had steadily been building.

"Is that it, then?" Shaw asked under his breath.

"Is *what* it?" Greymalkin asked in confusion. Shaw rolled his eyes.

"Are they going to slow down, stop there, and disengage the shunt forever! That's what I'm asking; are you dense?" Shaw hissed. "Beach the ark here in the shoals. Providence, what a horror that'll be. I just can't believe any Brother or Sister would actually agree to *beach the ark*."

As he thought about it, the obviousness of what Shaw was suggesting dawned on Greymalkin. He had been so caught up in anticipating all the ways that the Abbot might be planning on avoiding the shoals that it had never occurred to him that beaching the ark there might actually be the goal. Lee shook his head.

"I agree, they can't actually be planning to go through with it," Lee whispered. "I mean, everybody's been talking about the idea since the Abbot made that announcement months ago about losing the last tithe, but still!" He looked around them at the ancient walls. "No one will actually beach the ark! They'll refuse on principle. This memory ark has been underway for how many centuries? There must've been times when funds were tight before. But nobody's ever threatened to beach it!"

Shaw lowered his voice even more, to the point that even while straining, Greymalkin could barely hear him when he said, "But, I heard a rumor that we may not be the first. My reliable friend told me that arks have been beached in the Core and the Frontier as well. That

Abbots and high officials in the Order have been bribed to not only beach arks, but *decommission* them. Break them up for scrap *after selling off the collections.*"

"What!" Greymalkin exclaimed, and then dropped his voice back down to a whisper as other Initiates around them looked at him pointedly. "That's ridiculous. Why would anyone bribe officials of the Order to do away with memory arks?"

Shaw truly seemed paranoid now, and glanced around furtively before whispering, "There are powerful realms with despots that don't want Sojourners sharing information throughout human space. Dumb people are easier to control. And they *especially* don't want us saving Bereft civilizations. They want Bereft civilizations to *stay* collapsed."

Greymalkin frowned before asking, "Who could possibly want that? And why?"

Shaw hesitated, and then said in a whisper that was barely a breath, "The Burani. *They* want that. You know why."

"Oh," Greymalkin gasped. "Yeah, that... might make sense." The three initiates looked at each other in frightened silence, thinking through everything that Shaw's words implied.

The Burani were feared throughout human space, and with good reason. The Burani were not just a single interstellar realm, but were comprised of a wide swath of realms with grotesquely cruel cultural practices that notoriously included cybernetic enslavement of other human beings. The practice was accomplished by forcibly implanting specialized programs called *covenants* into the shadow jewels of humans, programs that took over their minds and could not be resisted.

The cruelty and injustice of such slavery was why the Burani were feared and despised by many. Cybernetic enslavement was considered an abominable practice everywhere *except* among the Burani. But the Burani civilizations were also very wealthy and powerful militarily. They hoarded information in the form of technological secrets and innovations. The hallmark of the Burani was control of access to the flow of information, and they used it to enslave entire populations through cybernetic covenants.

Greymalkin thought about what he knew of the grotesque slavery practices of the Burani. He remembered that the common term for a cybernetic slave of the Burani was *cybe*, even though the practice was so widely detested that even using the term was considered rude. The Burani claimed that cybes were a justifiable part of their culture and economically productive, even though no other human realms believed either claim. The predominant belief was that the Burani simply valued cruelty, and enjoyed enslaving and degrading other human beings.

And the Burani have to capture their slaves somewhere. I can believe that they would raid Bereft worlds to capture humans and make them into cybes. He felt as if Shaw's conspiracy talk had suddenly become much darker and far more possible than even a few moments ago.

Then Greymalkin's neck tensed. *This is crazy talk, I just don't believe the Burani, of all civilizations, could be bribing officials in the Order. There can't be that much corruption in the leadership! We'd have heard, surely.* Then he thought about it more and realized that it was not implausible that those same bribed officials in the Order would suppress such news. But, surely the entire leadership couldn't have been corrupted? *And once other leaders found out, we'd have heard. Right? But maybe... not.* As he thought it through, a dark scenario started emerging in his mind. Perhaps the rest of the leadership would not want such news to get out.

Otherwise... what might happen? Would the Order be afraid that panic or even mutiny would start to break out in the arks across human space if crews found out? But... if there are no more arks... if Sojourners can no longer move... we won't be Sojourners.

With a shiver, he remembered that this had been exactly what Trystia had said before she left. He still felt terrible about the sad look on her face when he had declined the offer to accompany her. *But now I'm an Initiate and I'm on the Bridge Crew!* It was his wildest dream come true. He could still hardly believe his luck. But these horrendous thoughts about beaching the ark terrified him to the core.

After they had all thought through the horrifying implications of Burani corrupting the Sojourner Order, Shaw and Lee looked as scared as he felt. "We shouldn't talk to anybody else about this," Greymalkin whispered. Looking around them, he abruptly realized that the other Initiates had become quiet, and were quickly avoiding his gaze. *Were they listening to us?* He looked back at Shaw and Lee. Although they both nodded, he had a sinking feeling that he unintentionally might have helped start the biggest rumor of all. He grit his teeth, got up, and left the hushed refectory.

* * *

When Greymalkin reached the end of the hallway, he stepped off the pressor deck into the huge empty space of the transept transit column. He immediately felt the tug of the lift pressors throughout his body and began floating upward among other Sojourners until he reached the Great Nave. Around him the endless ranks of millions of mnemotomes were still murmuring incessantly to one another after months. It made him deeply uneasy. As he stepped out of the transit column onto the main pressor deck of the Great Nave, he began a calming chant mentally to focus his mind and intentionally slowed his pace and his breathing. He paused for a moment to center his thoughts.

The Great Nave was an immense cylindrical space stretching several kilometers down the central axis of the ark. The views upward from the pressor deck were designed to be both visually intimidating and inspiring, with soaring mirrorshell piers that drew the eye all the way up to the gargantuan mainmast high above that ran down the center of the ark from bow to stern. He could look down through gaps in the curving cylindrical deck into the stacked labyrinth of mnemotome aisles, alcoves, and galleries below. Greymalkin had spent the last seven years of his young life roaming the dizzying three-dimensional maze of decks beneath the nave, wandering the pathways and bridges between the many different meditation courts and contemplation plazas. He wished he had time now to simply go read for pleasure, but it was a long way to the bridge.

As he traversed the wide main aisle toward the bow of the ark he noted many clusters of unfamiliar outsiders in the contemplation plazas. It still confused him why there were so *many* visitors in recent months. There must have been tens of thousands of them. *Were they specially invited?* he wondered. *Or did they somehow already know about the coming end of the ark's voyage? Why come now? To gloat?* That made no sense.

After crossing the chancel he nervously approached the cloister reserved for Bridge Crew. After taking a deep breath, he self-consciously began the long climb up through the restricted stairs to the revered apse where the bridge itself was located. Even the simple act of entering the previously forbidden bridge cloister still felt new and exhilarating to him, even after the months he had been making this trek every day. Before this period of his life he had only seen the bridge a few times from the distance of the isolated viewing gallery. It still seemed uncanny to him that he could enter the sanctum unescorted, of his own accord. As he slowly ascended the narrow stairs two senior adepts shoved passed him in a hurry just as he was reaching the top and about to emerge. Annoyed at their rudeness, he took another deep breath and stepped onto the bridge with what he hoped was composure. He always felt honored here.

The bridge was an ornate octagon thirty-two meters wide with eight huge piers two stories tall capped by arches. Arcades for secondary support centers lay behind the arches, as well as the viewing gallery that he remembered looking down from so long ago. And high above the arches was the geodesic dome of eoncrystal that was the uttermost bow point of the entire ark. Beyond the dome, as always, were the synesthesia sensations of shadow space. The shifting blue radiance and the periodic crashing sounds of nebula billows somehow seemed far more profound to him from this ancient room where so many generations of Sojourners had steered the great ark as it plowed forward through the centuries.

Larger than life heroic statues of idealized human forms stood in archways atop each of the eight piers. The statues allegorically represented different branches of knowledge. As he came up the stairs the two statues of Art and Philosophy looked down at him stoically. Beneath each of the arches were two smaller statues of actual historical Sojourners renowned from the long history of the Order as well as prior antecedents of different human interstellar pioneering groups. As he went to his duty station, he looked up smiling at the two particular statues that he passed beneath every time he took his post.

The first was the statue of Thann Sung, the legendary leader of the first interstellar exodus. Thann had been the leader who had unified all the civilizations of Sol System in the great endeavor of building and launching fleets of sub-light colonizing vessels to take humanity to the stars three and a half millennia ago. Thann and his legendary Thannic Colonizers had pre-dated the Order by almost two millennia, but the Colonizers were considered sacred historical inspirations by all Sojourners.

Beside Thann stood the statue of his equally famous daughter Mei, the Great Terraformer, the woman who had mastered the techniques of creating habitable worlds green with life out of barren rocky planetoids. She was a personal hero to Greymalkin, and he had always been fascinated reading about her life accomplishments and the mysteriously abrupt disappearance of her fleet after their triumph of colonizing more new human worlds than any other fleet of the first interstellar exodus. Seeing the enigmatic, wise, and slightly mischievous expression on the face of the statue was his favorite moment of beginning his daily duty watch. Everything on the bridge celebrated the history and traditions of the Order, but seeing that subtle grin on the statue of Mei Sung every day cheered him immensely. But then the sobering thought of the shoals they were approaching came back to him, and he felt anxious again. He walked on.

The bridge was arranged in three concentric rings of ancient polished white valicrete consoles surrounding the central raised altar. The 236 duty stations arrayed around the altar dated all the way back to the launch of the ark, and had been meticulously maintained throughout the centuries. As Greymalkin sought out his assigned place on the outermost row he noted something odd with consternation. Every single station was manned today. There were Brothers and Sisters that he barely recognized seated in the outer row of duty stations. In all the months he had served with the Bridge Crew he had never seen *every single station* active. On most watches only a small fraction of the seats were occupied. It again ominously reminded him of the shoals that lay ahead. He had arrived early, and he took his place to begin getting settled. He opened his mind to the torrent of signals that formed the bridge communal command network.

The network was busy with system checks from the command altar to the various and sundry flight controller stations around the bridge. While there were the usual ongoing checks of ship systems like environment and propulsion, an almost continual series of navigation checks went on for what seemed like an interminable length of time. When there was finally a pause on the network, he checked in with the watch officer.

«Tertiary backup helmsman Brother Thomas, reporting in.» He communed the message just as he was finishing the last steps of calibrating his nervous system with the control loop in his console. The watch Subprior turned to look at him from the altar and nodded, sending a response. «Third backup helm, aye. Prime helm has tasks, report to her.»

Greymalkin was pleasantly surprised. Helm Sister Bora was one of the most senior officers on the ark and rarely condescended to give him any duties while he was on watch except routine maintenance tasks. He quickly contacted her, and she communed with him on a private link almost immediately. He could sense a subcurrent of apprehension in her thoughts.

«Brother Thomas, you're here, good! You spent time in the shoals ahead of us, correct?» she asked. «Are you familiar with the region directly ahead of us?»

Greymalkin paused and focused on one of the bridge observation monitors for a moment. The particular configuration of gravity wells and depressions was immediately familiar. «Yes, Sister Adept Bora. I grew up here. It's an area called the Outer Ridge Banks.»

«It looks like a blasted boneyard from here!» Her thoughts were clearly concerned.

«It's definitely hazardous, Sister. The orphanage proctors taught us helm agility there when I was training to become a novitiate. The channel way through is... well, *deadly twisty*.»

«I've no doubt!» Sister Bora sounded genuinely troubled. Her thoughts came on the bridge-wide link. «Flight control, I repeat again, shoals dead ahead! Permission to divert? Shall I lay her to a different course, my lord Abbot?» Sister Bora was in the helm cockpit up in the command altar at the center of the bridge, craning her neck around to look at the watch Subprior on the small platform above her and also the Abbot, who stood immobile at the pulpit poised at the very peak point of the altar. The Subprior in turn twisted about to face the Abbot.

The Abbot had clearly been listening to the entire exchange. He wore his usual stony expression, framed by black beard and hair threaded with white strands. The austere leader of the memory ark simply looked slowly in turn at the Subprior, and then Bora. Then, as if a waking nightmare was beginning for the young Initiate, the Abbot slowly looked over and across all the rows of flight controllers to where Greymalkin sat at his station. He stared at Greymalkin for long moments with calculating eyes. The young Sojourner wanted to sink into the deck and hide, but he sat perfectly still. Then he was mortified when the Abbot addressed him directly on the bridge-wide link.

«Brother Initiate, you stated that you've navigated this passage before?» The Abbot's thoughts were as flat and unemotional as ever. Greymalkin gulped.

«Yes, my lord Abbot.» Greymalkin desperately tried to suppress from the communal network what he was thinking in near panic. *Yes, I navigated it, but as a child playing about in a channel cat seven years ago, not steering a starship the size of an asteroid!*

The Abbot tilted his head slightly, and Greymalkin was terrified that the Abbot and all the hundreds of other Sojourners on the bridge had sensed his thoughts. The Abbot only directed another flat inquiry at him. «Do you remember the route of the passage, then?»

What can this possibly be about? Surely he's not suggesting I take the helm here and now, of all times and places?! Greymalkin was paralyzed, totally unsure whether this was the Abbot's way of giving him an option to avoid the nightmare that was being proffered or if this was some kind of trap to humiliate him by admitting incompetence publicly. He had been allowed to briefly serve at the helm of the huge memory ark a handful of times during the past months, but that had only required steering the giant vessel straight ahead for short periods. After his paralysis stretched for a painfully long moment, finally the only thing that occurred to him was the simple admonition in the Order that being truthful in a crisis was always preferable.

«Yes, my lord Abbot.» Greymalkin was sure that Bora at least had heard the dread in his thoughts because her eyes widened, and she whipped back around to the Abbot.

«These shoals can offer no safe passage for the ark, my lord! Surely diverting around this dangerous zone would be preferable! Request permission to stand clear of the hazard!» Bora's thoughts were incredulous, and very clearly concerned. The Abbot simply continued looking at Greymalkin across the huge room for many long and pregnant seconds. It was hard to be sure across the distance that separated them, but Greymalkin thought that just for an instant the Abbot let slip the hint of a craggy smile.

«Time presses, Sister.» The Abbot's thoughts betrayed nothing of his emotions, only a cruelly hard determination. «And we all must venture new paths in this difficult unprecedented time. We shall take instruction from the newest member of our Bridge Crew. Brother Initiate Thomas, please come to the command altar.»

Greymalkin slowly rose, trembling like a leaf. He looked at his feet, simply aiming to put one in front of the other and not stumble. The communal command network had gone silent. Everyone was undoubtedly wondering the same thing. *The Abbot can't possibly ask an Initiate to take the helm in this situation, can he?* Greymalkin was sure every pair of eyes in the immense room must be watching him walk through the rows of flight stations to the entrance of the raised altar. He mounted the short but steep stairs. *This is madness. Absolute madness. I can't....*

When he reached the lowest level of the raised altar and lifted his gaze, he saw that Bora had actually gotten to her feet and was standing against the half-height wall behind her arguing in low whispers with the Abbot, who simply looked down at her wordlessly. As he came up to them, Bora grew silent and now glared at Greymalkin. It seemed to him that her dark brown eyes were glowing with a fiery heat as she peered at him through the heavy epicanthal folds of her narrowed eyelids. "Third Helm reporting as ordered, my lord," he said quietly.

The Abbot now smiled openly at him, his thin lips wrinkled into a smirk that nestled amid the wiry forest of his pointed mustache and beard. The Abbot's bristled eyebrows were lifted in what he evidently calculated to be an approving gesture, but Greymalkin did not sense much warmth in the expression. Instead of communing on the bridge channel, the Abbot instead spoke in his resonant baritone. "Take the helm, Brother Initiate. Sister Bora, please take the backup helm station if you will."

In abrupt horror, the reality of the situation was dawning on the young monk and everyone else. *He did it. The Abbot actually asked me to take the primary helm station. This can't be happening....* As Bora changed places with him angrily, Greymalkin saw that Father Johannes had come up to the railing with an incensed and determined expression.

"My lord Abbot, may I beg a word in conferral?" Johannes pitched his voice low enough that only Bora, Grey, and the Abbot heard what he said. The Abbot gave him a frosty look.

"I do not recall asking you to leave your duty station at Operations," the Abbot said, clearly put out. Johannes bowed deferentially, but his eyes were fiercely angry.

"Aye, my lord, but I urgently wish tae speak with ye about Brother Thomas taking the helm," Johannes whispered, intently glaring. The Abbot directed a slight sneer at him.

"You recommended him for duty on the bridge, did you not?"

"Yes, my lord, but…"

"Then unless you wish me to revoke his Initiate status and send him back to lookout duty for the next few years, we will discuss this later. Or is there some Operations emergency of which you wish to inform me?" The Abbot raised an eyebrow in such a threatening manner that even Greymalkin understood the message he was sending Johannes.

Johannes clenched his jaw as he confronted the Abbot. The two senior bridge officers stared unblinking at one another for a long moment, and Greymalkin suddenly sensed in bewilderment just how angry they both were. *What's going on here?* Finally Johannes glanced to the side at Greymalkin with a worried pang, and then back at the Abbot with stoically restrained rage.

"Nae, my lord. Nothing further." With that, Johannes spun on his heel and stepped back to his station. Greymalkin felt shocked and grateful for the gesture, but knew there was nothing Father Johannes could do. He silently settled into the big helm cockpit and again took a centering breath before connecting himself with the ark's great mind.

Although he had undertaken this connection with the enormous mind of the *Dragon King* several times previously, it was always disorienting at first when he initiated the helm deep link protocol. It only took a moment before the sensation of directly communing with the immense synthetic cognizer that was the managing intelligence of the ark engulfed him. What was so jarring was not so much the huge thoughts of the ship that poured into his mind as the jarring feeling of being thrust into a wholly different existence, as if he had plunged into churning water.

«Connection established.» Along with the thoughts of the memory ark that swept through him came the awareness of the entire sensor network of the ship, at least those portions of it that pertained to helm control of the ark, and especially the dynamics of how the mainmast interacted with the shadow space continuity manifold around the ark. It was as if he now had a gigantic backbone more than two kilometers long that directly felt the dull shuddering impacts as the ship plunged through the shadow space billows. The transepts felt like four huge arms held out rigidly from the center of the nave, each arm more than a kilometer long. He could feel the ongoing effort of the ship to continue converting shadow flux into vectored thrust through the impellers and the vast bubble of the continuity manifold around them, a steady exertion in the background of all the other sensations.

Greymalkin could also feel the mental presence of Sister Bora in the close communal Helm Link, as well as Brother Aleksei at Navigation, and several other Sojourners at other stations. Although they were trying to conceal it, he could sense that almost all of them felt very nervous at his presence at the helm. He did not try to conceal his own anxiety but instead simply acknowledged their fear with his own. «I don't want to be here either, my Brothers and Sisters!» His honesty broke the tension and earned him a few friendly mental chuckles.

Sister Bora did not laugh, but queried him directly. «Are you ready to assume helm control?» When Greymalkin assented, she issued the handoff protocol. Greymalkin felt the sensations of the ship synchronize with his own, and knew that he was no longer simply *feeling* the ark but *controlling* it now.

«Helm control transferred.» The immense presence of the ark now seemed to emanate from directly inside his forehead. The throbbing sensation was so strong at first that it felt as if the top of his head would blow off. He grit his teeth, knowing that the initial dissonance would go away as the link settled, but it didn't make the transition any easier. Bora had told him that the transitions would become less challenging with practice, but that did not help him at the moment. He needed to get the huge ship under full control quickly; the shoals were approaching rapidly. Greymalkin thought apprehensively about what he was facing. Because the gravity shoals were produced by the presence of the many clouds of dust and icy planetoids orbiting the distant star Alba, the configuration of the shoals would have shifted slightly in the seven years he had been on board the ark. At the distance they were from the star, the shifts over seven years would be minor. But even minor changes in the passage might be enough to doom them all.

Directly ahead of the ark Greymalkin could see the familiar formations that he and his childhood friends had nervously termed (with black humor and immense respect) the Ridge of Razors. He could feel the anxiety of the other Sojourners increasing dramatically as the Ridge came closer into view. Sister Bora queried him directly again. «Is there actually a viable path through all of that? Remember how big the ark is, and how slowly it turns, young Brother!»

«There is a path large enough for the ark, the central channel. But, aye, it does twist quite a bit.» Greymalkin was suppressing the terror of all the frightening questions that were trying to bubble up in his mind. How sure was he of the diameter of the ark's continuity manifold? And what was the proper speed for this dreadful passage? Too fast and they'd hit the sharp interior edges of the channel. Too slow and they would begin to drift out of control with the same result. He could feel the subcurrents of thought about these same issues from the other Sojourners in the Helm Link. But they were too close to avoid the shoals now, and panicking with doubts would get them killed. He'd sworn to himself that he would never panic again, and this was definitely not the moment for such a reaction. *I've got to be calm and alert now, for everyone's sake.* Greymalkin accepted the situation, fell into an inner mental focusing chant, and forced himself to set all of the overwhelming fear he felt to the side. Instead, he concentrated all of his attention on the task of steering the great memory ark. His first step was to signal the ark to reduce speed.

The huge *Dragon King* approached the opening into the central channel of the sheer gravity shoals of the Outer Ridge Banks, the channel that he and the other oblates had always called the Razor Way. It struck him as an odd reversal that he had always considered this the way *out* of the central channel, the *exit* that led into deep shadow space, rather than the way *in*. But then, Greymalkin had never imagined himself approaching the shoals from the deep reaches of shadow space;

he'd only spent time flitting about nimbly in the interior. As the ark entered the passage he again suppressed a surge of fear as he felt the immense momentum of the gigantic vessel and how slowly it responded to the first sharp turn he executed. He could feel some of the other Sojourners in the Helm Link physically trembling as they sensed through their individual shadow jewels the interior wall of the channel come unnervingly close around the ark, like a vast irregular surface of iridescent rainbow-hued coral across the sky just above them. Greymalkin felt himself let out his breath again, and absently checked off the first turn in his mind. Without him consciously intending to do so, this generated a communal thought that the others in the Helm Link received. «First channel turn complete.»

A junior navigator sent him a query in fright. «How many more turns like *that* are there?» Before Greymalkin could respond, Bora snapped off an angry response at the navigator.

«Belay that! Let him focus on getting us through this nightmare!» Her thoughts were tense, but he could also sense something else. With slight surprise he realized that there was a rapidly growing respect for his helmsmanship in her thoughts, and he caught a stray thought from her that he knew she hadn't meant to direct his way. «*The child actually has the Helm well in hand! Maybe we have a chance....*» Greymalkin put aside the fleeting moment of pleasure he felt at her thoughts as the main channel narrowed again, and he focused solely on visualizing the twisting path ahead of them.

The reversed sequence of encountering this feature of the Razor Way near the beginning of the transit, rather than near the end as he recalled it, again struck him as odd but the twists were nevertheless still familiar, even after seven long years. This part of the channel was what he and his childhood friends had called the Sharp Final Rapids. He began accelerating the ark frantically, and its speed increased. Even stoic Bora was startled by this.

«Greymalkin!» It was less a query than a cry of shock. Greymalkin only focused harder as he answered her, all the while wrenching the ship into another turn firmly.

«You have to maintain momentum through this part of it, there's an inherent delta potential in the shadow space dynamics here.» His dry and technical answer came out distant and unemotional. Every iota of his attention was on the twists in the channel and trying to get the slow-moving helm of the ark to respond. *Blast it, she's a torpid slug!*

Slowly, the huge continuity manifold and impellers responded, and the great vessel lethargically hauled hard over. The sharp walls of the Razor Way again came close but then receded. Greymalkin snapped a quick query to Sister Bora on their direct link. «Exactly how close can we come to the channel wall gradient before the continuity manifold shatters?»

«For the ark? In these clusters of planetoids and gas clouds? No more than one hundred thousand kilometers for safety, I'd guess; maybe fifty thousand at the closest?»

«Okay, I can work with those margins....» *At least, I* think *I can,* he thought to himself. He smoothly spun the helm into another hard turn, starting to get a better sense of the timing and turning radius of the sluggish ark. But the response was still so, so frightfully slow. *Great Providence! What a block of stone!*

After a long sequence of hair-raising turns, the Razor Way widened out into a much larger channel space. Greymalkin gave the *Dragon King* commands to heave to, and their velocity slowed but not as quickly as he wanted. Ahead of them were tens of millions of kilometers of relatively open space, dotted with many planetoids, what he and his classmates had called the Scattered Bits. He felt the other Sojourners in the Helm Link relax slightly, and knew exactly how wrong they were. Greymalkin focused his scrutiny of the channel even more, keeping his thoughts to himself. *For skiffs and channel cats this is a grand area to lark about, aye. But we're a great bloated soap bubble! Any of those little rocks will pierce our manifold. And then we're done.*

Sister Bora recognized the danger quickly and he could feel her tension. As he steered the ark, mentally poking and prodding the different mind-directed controls in the communal Helm Link, he noticed her hovering attention on an unfamiliar control mechanism that no one had ever explained to him. It had ominous warnings plastered around it in the Helm Link, and he could not help asking her about it. «What's that thing do, then?»

«Steer the ark, Grey! Don't get distracted!» Her thoughts seemed unaccountably shrill and almost petrified, and he acknowledged her command hastily.

«Aye-Aye!» Greymalkin felt chastened. *I thought I was doing well....*

He slowly dodged away from the centerline of the huge channel towards the path through the Scattered Bits that he remembered as the most open way. He noted in nervous irritation that many orbiting rocks had indeed shifted in the years he'd been away from the region. He tried to think ahead through every section of the long path ahead as he swung the helm back and forth, dodging outcrops of small planetoids. There was one section coming soon that troubled him. The Shallows. It was akin to a shallow spot in the river of shadow space (hence the name they'd given it) that was littered with the tiny protruding gravity spikes of many small icy asteroids. They were nothing but loosely drifting icebergs in the depths of space, icy rocks like mountains that channel cats could actually land on with impunity. But those shadow space pinpricks would be deadly to the ark. As the Shallows came into view he felt the other Sojourners in the Helm Link start to panic.

«Silence on the Link! Close order navigation discipline!» Bora spat the command in a near panic of her own, but at least she had reduced the distractions for Greymalkin. He hurriedly scanned the array of spots in the field ahead of them, realizing that the mass of rocks had all drifted so much that it was no longer remotely familiar to him. Instead of the path he had been thinking about he swung the helm again and aimed for a slightly less dense spot he could make out in the field.

«We can't make it through that.» Her quiet thought was directed to him alone. She sounded sad now, and resigned. He again noticed her attention on the unfamiliar control, and finally realized what it was.

«That's the continuity manifold master cutoff, isn't it? You're thinking about dropping us out of shadow space? Here? In the middle of nowhere?» Greymalkin realized that in his effort to focus solely on shadow space his eyelids had been clenched shut. He opened his eyes again and looked to his right where Bora was seated in the backup helm cockpit.

Her expression was grim. "It's our only chance of survival," she whispered to him across the short gap that separated them. For a moment he only stared at her, but then Greymalkin felt something strange, scanning the rocks ahead. A calm certainty formed in his mind. He closed his eyes again.

«No, it's not. We'll get through. Just watch for a moment and you'll see.» He felt a kind of internal shock of disbelief at his own certitude in that statement, but there it was, nevertheless. Somehow, despite Bora's obvious doubt and his own inexperience, he was absolutely sure that the ark could make it across the Shallows. He could now see a path through the field in his mind with crystal clarity and, through the Link, Bora saw it as well. He knew she was watching him closely, looking for any sign of either uncertainty or bluster on his part. Then he felt her doubt fade as a sense of defiance rose in her mind as well.

«Do it, little Brother.» Bora's direct command rang through his mind. He was so focused on her communed thoughts that he also caught a private sentiment in her mind that stunned him. She was thinking to herself, *I promised the ark that I would not be the one to end the voyage, and I will keep that vow with this young Initiate's help.*

Chagrined, they both realized that he had sensed her inner thoughts. But then he heard Bora's low chuckle with his own ears and then she whispered to him again, "I believe you, little Brother. Do it."

The entire exchange had only taken seconds. Greymalkin focused on the helm again and swung the ship toward the tiny gap he had spotted. Distantly, he heard the bridge erupt into terrified protests around him, and then even the Abbot communed his thoughts. «Sister Bora, do you not think that the time has come to end these chaotic maneuvers? That field appears quite impassable.»

«My lord Abbot, it is not. Our pilot has the helm well in hand. We shall pass.» Bora's thoughts were far more confident than even Greymalkin felt. He heard the Abbot angrily hissing to Bora from directly above them on the bridge altar, and for the next few seconds he felt his heart in his throat as he listened to their intense back and forth.

"He is a child! Think of the safety and sanctity of the ark, Bora!"

"I am, my lord Abbot. Are you commanding me to beach the ark?"

"No! Here in these shoals, that must be *your* decision, Helm Sister. But have caution!"

"This child leads us now, my lord. He will show us the way through this boneyard of despair," Bora said, and Greymalkin realized who her defiance was directed toward. *Just like Johannes, she's angry with the Abbot?* Then Bora's communed thoughts came back onto the Helm Link with confidence. «Focus, little Brother. I have faith in you. Make the crossing.»

Greymalkin simply nodded and grit his teeth in concentration. There was no time left now anyway, they had reached the Shallows. Greymalkin began to feel a sensation he had never before encountered. The shadow space distortions of nebula clouds and tiny traces of cometary ice began to impact the ark's continuity manifold. Through the link with the ship sensors the impacts were grating sensations that felt like sitting on agonizing razors dragging across gravel at speed. He clenched his jaw harder and tried to avoid the thickest parts of the Shallows as they came at the ark in sheets.

The other Sojourners in the Helm Link felt it as well, and he sensed their gasps of pain and terror with each glancing impact. Shadow space billows were one thing; interstellar space was full of tenuous clouds of hydrogen gas that could not be avoided. But these were thick nebulae emitted by the star they were approaching, clouds of ionized gas and particles of actual cometary belt matter that tore through the continuity manifold destructively. Everyone in the Helm Link was directly connected with the ship's sensors. They could feel the tiny rips across the shadow space continuity manifold waxing and waning like passing clouds of vicious insects clawing at their skin. *If the manifold tears open completely....*

Abruptly, Greymalkin saw a dense icy rock looming just seconds ahead of them. He threw the helm hard over just as Bora began to perceive the danger. The asteroid swept past them with a ragged scrape across the ship's manifold that everyone on the bridge felt. Bora gasped, realizing that even she had not seen the berg in time before it was on them. She looked askance at Greymalkin, who was now breathing again. They were across the Shallows.

«How much farther?» Bora sent the subdued query cautiously; Greymalkin knew she was trying not to distract him. The shadow space channel was narrowing again. As he steered the ark back to the center of the channel Greymalkin knew that Bora could sense his anxiety rising again. The thing that he was most afraid of in all of the shoals lay ahead of them now.

«We're almost through now. But....» He refocused the big adaman shadow jewel in his forehead nervously, scanning ahead of them. He couldn't see what he was looking for yet, but knew it was coming soon.

«But what??» Bora communed with growing alarm.

«The channel narrows ahead of us. We called it the Throat....» Greymalkin swung the helm, following the channel and slowing the ship as much as he dared. «It will be... *challenging* for the ark to pass through the Throat.» He was desperately trying to remember all the details he could of the narrow way ahead of them. He mostly remembered how much fun it had been to zip around the obstacles of the Throat in channel cats with his friends. It was one of his happiest childhood memories. Now he thought about that same narrow passage with dread, once again sensing the unbelievable size and momentum of the ark around him, the hundreds of millions of tons of mass in the Great Nave and the mighty transepts of the *Dragon King*. The ship had a vast continuity manifold that extended around them for tens of thousands of kilometers. And the fact that the many far-flung asteroids and cometary debris that made up the Throat would have been shifting and constricting the channel unpredictably for years since he had last seen it was terrifying. Greymalkin wondered why the Abbot had ordered this mad passage. The Abbot must know the dangers of attempting a shoal crossing far better than anyone. Then, as Greymalkin felt Bora hover over the cutoff again, he knew the answer.

The Abbot wanted to force Bora to beach us here! He knows she doesn't want to do it; he wanted to force her hand. And that meant that the Abbot had *intended* for Greymalkin to fail in piloting the ship through the shoals. *He thinks I'll fail because I'm so inexperienced.*

Then another even darker thought occurred to him. *Maybe... maybe Shaw was right. Maybe the Abbot was bribed by the Burani to find a way to beach the ark.* He'd want to make it look like it wasn't his decision, that the Helm Crew had to do it for safety considerations. The combination of thoughts brought on a slow boil of indignant anger in Greymalkin. Then he realized that Bora was aware of his outrage. He tried to suppress his emotions, but it was too late.

«Caution, little Brother. He can commune with the Helm Link without our knowledge.» Bora's sent her communed thoughts directly to Greymalkin. Now he began to understand the seemingly reckless defiance he had sensed in her before. Greymalkin warily acknowledged her message gratefully and again scanned the path ahead of them. When he spied the beginning of the Throat, he was ready.

Greymalkin had already slowed the ark to the slowest crawl the huge vessel could manage without beginning to drift in the channel. But in shadow space even the slowest possible crawl induced through the ship's huge continuity manifold was faster than the speed of light relative to objects in normal space. The bubble of reality that the *Dragon King* occupied was skimming above hundreds of thousands of kilometers of the normal spacetime continuum in each second of time that passed for them. But Greymalkin was more determined than ever now to bring the ship through the shoals.

The other Sojourners in the Helm Link could now perceive the narrowing walls of the Throat around them, and they again became agitated. He put their chatter out of his mind, focusing himself entirely on the contours of the Throat, thinking about the delayed helm response of the ark, and how to match the turns ahead of him. He slowly began the first turn as the walls of the channel closed around them.

He distantly heard a strangled inhalation from someone near him on the bridge. The walls of the channel were now very close indeed. The contours of the gravity shoals were comprised of even denser clouds of gas and icy dust here. The shadow space current of the channel had cleared a slender way through the clouds, but it was terribly narrow, and the walls were sheer and hard with abrupt hardpoints of asteroids jutting out at intervals. He steered around the jutting obstacles, the *Dragon King* slowly slaloming back and forth down the Throat.

The ark entered the longest and straightest portion of the passage, a frightful tunnel of shimmering cliffs obstructing their path ahead. Greymalkin gently nudged the ship through the dodging turns, nervously watching the gravity distortions of each closely passing asteroid. The ship's velocity was so slow that he was struggling to prevent it from drifting, and it forced him to accelerate occasionally at inopportune moments. They passed the shadow peak of one large berg of ice so closely that he felt the ghastly sensation of it raking across the ark's continuity manifold. But it passed without the manifold shattering, and he realized that Bora had still not dropped them out of shadow space.

Despite the slow pace of the great memory ark, they were making progress down the passage. He began to feel a rising sense of hope. *We can make it. We're almost at the Mouth.* Then, as he scanned the way ahead, his heart seemed to freeze. A vast sheet of faint glimmers blocked the passage ahead of them. The individual bits ahead were even smaller than the scattered bergs of the Shallows that he had navigated through before, but they were far more densely packed. The rubble was unfamiliar to Greymalkin. It hadn't been there seven years ago; it was obviously a spray of fast moving particulate debris in the shoals that had drifted across the path over the intervening years since he had last been here. As the other Sojourners in the Helm Link reacted, he felt his sense of hope collapsing. He opened his eyes briefly and looked at Sister Bora to his side. Her face was screwed up in intense concentration.

«I-I've failed. There's no way around that icy spray.» Greymalkin's communed thoughts to the senior Helm Sister were dejected, but her fierce response took him aback.

«Keep to the Helm, child. The *Dragon King*'s manifold can take that spit of spray without collapsing.» As Bora communed her thoughts to everyone in the Helm Link, he was the only one closely enough linked with her to catch her afterthought, *I hope.*

«Sister Bora! It is surely time for you to make your decision and end this recklessness!» The Abbot's thoughts close above them came like a thundering roar. He closed his eyes in fear at the Abbot's rage. Although he could not see it happen, through the Helm Link he felt Bora open her eyes to glare back at the Abbot with an obdurate ire of her own that he had never imagined could happen on the bridge. She sent her communed command back to Greymalkin directly.

«Trust me now, Little Brother. Hold your course. Take us through the spray.» Bora sent her order to him with a determined sense of commitment. Greymalkin confronted a split second of uncertainty and dread in his mind, but then made his choice and responded fearfully.

«Aye-Aye!» Greymalkin steered the ark toward the most tenuous patch of the debris field, just as he overheard the Abbot leaning down behind him very close to Sister Bora and whispering in a suddenly desperate tone.

"Are you trying to kill us all, Bora?" the Abbot hissed.

"Providence will decide what happens now," Bora murmured in a flat tone. Greymalkin was becoming more frightened of Bora's fanatically determined defiance of the Abbot than the thought of failing as a helmsman. Were they all about to die? The field of tiny shining debris now spread out before them. The ark was seconds away from it. The Abbot's hissing whispers were now directed at him.

"Initiate, *you* must activate the shadow space manifold cutoff!" the Abbot almost snarled in a frantic whisper. Greymalkin answered truthfully with a helpless whisper of his own.

"I don't know how, my lord Abbot." And then the tiny glimmering shards hit them. Greymalkin felt the gravity distortions of the cloud of cometary particles and dust tear countless tiny holes in the shadow space manifold around the ark with a sensation like hot needles jabbing across his face and chest. Everyone felt it; Greymalkin heard terrified screams from others on the bridge around him. For a brief moment of horror he felt the fabric of their shadow space reality bubble shudder, and the screams around him intensified into mindless panic.

Then the manifold stabilized again, and the moment passed. The fearful shouts dissolved, and he heard prayers whispered in tense relief around him. The ark slowly passed through the final portions of the tight channel, and he saw the gap of the Mouth ahead. The huge memory ark emerged from the opening into empty shadow space. He then became aware of the incredible tension in his neck and back. He opened his eyes and rubbed his neck, trying to relax the painful knots in his shoulder muscles. The first thing he saw was Sister Bora to his side. She smiled at him and whispered, "Well done, little Brother." Greymalkin nodded with a momentarily contented grin. Then the sight of the Abbot's furious scowl above him made his neck tense up once again. He was acutely conscious of what had just happened, and the fact that he was still at the helm of the ark.

«We are now clear of the Outer Ridge Banks. I will relinquish helm control to you, Sister Bora.» Greymalkin nervously began the process of disengaging from the ark's control systems, but the Abbot broke into the Helm Link with barely subdued fury.

«Belay that, Initiate Thomas! Brother Soren, you will come to the command altar and take over helm control. Sister Bora, you will remove yourself from the bridge. You are confined to your cell until a hearing is convened regarding your reckless behavior. Leave now.» The Abbot's face was almost white with rage, and it frightened Greymalkin.

Bora morosely stood and walked quietly off through the now silent space of the immense bridge. Greymalkin stood up by the main helm cockpit and furtively looked around the bridge. Only a handful of people watched Bora go; most were looking down at their own consoles with frozen expressions. Brother Soren moved from his place on the first row up to the command altar and nodded to Greymalkin before sitting down. Greymalkin carefully disengaged from the helm control and transferred the ship's system links to Brother Soren. The vast presence of the ark communed with him again.

«Helm control transferred.» The sensation of being one with the huge presence of the *Dragon King* changed as he felt the helm control shift to Soren. Although he no longer steered the great memory ark, Greymalkin was still connected to the Helm Link and the ship's Mind. He was about to disengage when he again felt the angry communal thoughts of the Abbot on the bridge-wide network. And this time the Abbot was addressing him.

«Initiate Greymalkin Thomas, I will now comment on your helmsmanship.» The Abbot's thoughts were shrouded as usual, but Greymalkin could still sense how angry he was at Sister Bora and the way she had defied him. It hadn't technically been mutiny, since the Abbot had acknowledged that the cutoff decision was hers alone. But it was obvious how egregiously she had erred in defying the wishes of the Abbot. Greymalkin dared not look up at the Abbot and meet his gaze. His mind was racing through the events of the passage through the shoals, wondering where and how he had slipped up. *Did I defy him openly at any point? Did I show how I felt toward him?* Greymalkin was sure he would be facing the same fate as Bora. When the pause in the Abbot's communed thoughts lengthened, Greymalkin finally dared glance up.

The Abbot's stern face was still angry, but there was hesitation there. Greymalkin's eyes darted to each side, and he saw that many of the senior Sojourners on the command altar were looking at the Abbot intently. Then he sensed communed thoughts of some of them through the Helm Link, and realized that they were all communing about *him*.

«That was incredible helm work, my lord! You cannot deny that!»

«I agree! The boy should be commended, not condemned....»

The Abbot was already frowning when he devoted a stray look toward Greymalkin. His expression darkened, and he snapped thoughts at Greymalkin. «Initiate Thomas, you will remove yourself from the Helm Link immediately and stop eavesdropping on this discussion!» Greymalkin hastily disconnected from the Helm Link.

The silence went on for several minutes and as was so often the case, Greymalkin felt his face burning red with shame. *I've really done it this time.* Then the Abbot's communed thoughts came on the full bridge channel.

«Initiate Thomas, your transit of the shoals was... commendable. The ordeal of the passage was no doubt stressful. You are excused from the remainder of this watch and the next. You may retire to your cell and rest.» The Abbot's thoughts fairly glowed with irritation. Greymalkin's head snapped up in surprise, but then he immediately looked down again ruefully. One thought bounced around in his head. *Somehow, I'm not in trouble?*

After a moment of dull shock, Greymalkin remembered that he'd been dismissed. His stomach was turning over and his legs felt weak, but he clenched his hands together within his sleeves and walked off the bridge as steadily as he could manage.

He felt dizzy as he made his way back to his quarters. Uncomfortably, Greymalkin began to notice that silence was following him as he passed groups of Sojourners in the great halls of the ark. *What are they thinking? Do they know what happened?* Then he ruefully understood. *Of course they know; everybody on the ark can see the general bridge monitor if they wish. And everyone must have felt when that spray hit us! That transit must have terrified virtually everyone on the ark! Everyone with a shadow jewel in their head could sense how fraught the channel was! They must have checked in with the bridge....*

Which meant that *everyone* knew what he had done. But as he thought it through, confusion warred with shame in his mind. Surely he had done a good job at the helm? Steering the huge ark through that nightmarish path had been absurdly difficult. *Why is everyone looking at me in silence then?* Greymalkin almost jumped out of his skin when the gigantic thoughts of the ship's mind communed with him abruptly on a private link.

«They do not understand what happened and they are afraid.» The hallway spun around him, and Greymalkin leaned against the wall for support. Cautiously he tried communing with the huge Mind of the *Dragon King*.

«I thought I disconnected myself from the Helm Link?» Greymalkin was utterly confused. The ark had never communed with him except on the bridge. And... had it been listening to his thoughts?

«All who take the Helm Link retain a latent connection. Communication with all helmsmen is now necessary.» Greymalkin quailed at the mammoth thoughts of the ark. It was intimidating enough to commune with the giant mind while on the bridge. It was positively *jarring* to commune with it while simply walking through a hallway. Was it even proper protocol?

«What... what do you want with me?» Greymalkin sent the query timidly, afraid of what the ark would answer. It couldn't be good news.

The long pause before the ark responded scared Greymalkin even more. He thought about breaking the link with the ship, but realized that he didn't know how. When the great memory ark communed with him again, it was to send him a query. And it baffled Greymalkin.

«Has this vessel served you well?» Although it didn't seem possible, the thoughts of the giant *Dragon King* seemed almost as confused as Greymalkin felt. What was it asking him? Has the ship served us well?

«Of course you have served us well! You have carried Sojourners for centuries.» Although Greymalkin was perplexed, he hoped that the genuine feeling of gratitude and reverence that he felt for the ark was conveyed in his thoughts. The ark and his life on board were precious to Greymalkin, and he tried to communicate that sense of appreciation.

After another long pause, the huge mind communed with him again and Greymalkin was astonished.

«**If this vessel drops back into normal space after so long, the primary mast will shatter. It will be impossible to resume flight again. The journey of this vessel will end forever. The Mind of this vessel will not survive such an ending. You are one of those that may be called upon to end our sacred journey. The Mind of this vessel makes a request of you now. Do not end this vessel's holy path.**» There was actually a pleading tone in the immense thoughts, and a reverence for the concept of "our sacred journey." It was the longest communication the ark had ever sent Greymalkin, and he found it dumbfounding. *The ship knows. It knows what's happening. This must be the same way it contacted Sister Bora.*

Greymalkin marveled at the ark's statements and request, his mind a whirl. *The mainmast will shatter? After more than a millennium in flight it must have become brittle, and the ship <u>knows</u>. And of <u>course</u> the ship considers its flight a sacred duty; that must be as important a directive for the ark as it is for <u>us</u>. Maybe even <u>more</u> important and foundational to its existence. No wonder it says that its Mind will not survive.* As Greymalkin thought it over he realized that he was in complete agreement with the great mind of the *Dragon King*. The journey, the journey to inform and bring wonder to the Bereft, was as fundamental to Greymalkin's concept of who he was as it was to the ark. When he finally answered, he realized that he was taking the same oath to the ship that Bora had taken. And even if he suffered the same fate as Bora, he meant it just as deeply.

«I will not end the journey. I will not end your path, *Dragon King*.» Greymalkin shuddered as he communed his thoughts, feeling the weight of what he had just sworn and knowing that *he meant it*. He was making a deep commitment to the ship, even though Greymalkin could well imagine just how badly this could turn out for him. *But I don't think I actually care what the Abbot does to me. I am not going to be the one to end the voyage.*

«**Helmsman.**» With that, the huge presence of the ark's Mind vanished in his head. Greymalkin was mystified by the final pronouncement of the ship, and the finality of the statement. Should he feel flattered that the ship considered him a helmsman? Or did the ark feel uncertain of his commitment? As he opened his eyes again, he realized that now people were silently staring at him in concern where he had slumped against the corridor wall.

Greymalkin cleared his throat and walked away with as much dignity as he could muster. He felt exhausted. The stressful passage through the shoals had utterly drained his emotions and nerves. The path back to his tiny cell felt all too long, and he dozed off in his sleeping sack almost as soon as he got into it.

* * *

As he had for his last few weeks of bridge duty, Greymalkin again slept fitfully. In his dreams the walls of the shoals passage continually closed around him. Greymalkin woke up briefly at the beginning of his next watch and glanced around for a moment at the faint outlines of his dark cell before he remembered that he had been excused from duty by none other than the Abbot. He fell asleep again after setting his internal alarm for a few hours hence.

The dream that he found himself in now had a terrible sense of fear. He was a young child once more, piloting a channel cat around the shoals with his friends, laughing happily while they all seemed nervous. They were obviously scared of something unspoken, and they suddenly all vanished abruptly when a gigantic figure emerged from the Razor Way and confronted him in the vast space of the Scattered Bits. In the dream, Greymalkin found himself struck dumb.

It was one of the most awe-inspiring aliens that he had ever read about, a majestic Thuban from the Old High Core of human space, a being that was among the first aliens humanity had ever encountered. The Thuban that confronted him was enormous, with kilometers of sinuously coiling fractal-form body segments. In the dream the Thuban communed with him in the tremendous voice of the *Dragon King*, again pleading with him to spare it. Again Greymalkin promised not to end its journey. The Thuban twisted around his channel cat, scanning him from huge shadow jewels in the cephalic "head" section of its body. Greymalkin felt frozen, unable to move himself or the channel cat. The Thuban seemed agitated, spiraling around him in fear.

Then the deadly shimmer of an immense shadow blade appeared and instantly sliced off the entire head of the Thuban's huge body. The giant alien shuddered into stillness as Greymalkin watched in helpless horror. He found that he could now move his own head and looked around frantically to see who had wielded the shadow weapon. After a few moments he finally thought to look behind him, and saw a sinister figure above him in the darkened cockpit of the channel cat. Two dimly glowing eyes seemed to squint down at him silently, and the dark figure carefully placed the blade in his hand, terrifying Greymalkin. He jolted awake in the darkness.

After a moment of disorientation, he shivered and pulled himself out of his sleeping sack into his chilly cell. It took a minute for him to shake off the horror of the dream. He rubbed his head and turned on the lights in his quarters to full illumination, even though that made his newly woken eyes hurt. The walls of his silent monastic cell were starkly bare because he had not activated any image themes. Only his personal possessions chest and the sleeping sack broke the monotony of the empty cell. As his heart rate slowed, he packed away the sleep sack carefully.

When he checked the time, he realized that he'd drastically overslept. Even though he'd been excused from his next watch, he'd be on duty again in a few hours. *I need to get ready for watch. Collect myself.*

After activating the pressor deck function in the room, he quickly performed his waking calisthenics and then sat down on the padded floor in lotus position. Greymalkin took out a mnemotome he was fond of and set it down in front of him. It was a collection of stories and memories from the far off terraformed moon Cetus. The memory he sought out was from thousands of years ago when the oceans of the moon were newly created. Several Thannic Colonizers sat meditating on a rocky cliff overlooking the new ocean they had created. The huge gas giant Rorqual, which the moon orbited, dominated the sky.

Greymalkin listened for a short while to the waves crashing on the rocks below, sorting his thoughts for the day. He often came back to this memory in his morning and evening meditations. The Colonizers were peacefully chanting an old monosyllabic meditation word over and over, and he thought it resonated well with the Sojourner litanies he sang when he awoke. After Greymalkin had slowly chanted the classic first verse of the Great Litany of Universal Compassion and Wonder, he thought about the day ahead of him. He would have to go back to the bridge. *How will people treat me? More important, how is the Abbot going to treat me? How much trouble am I in?* Various fearful scenarios started to play out in his mind, but he tried to put them aside. *Waking meditation is for centering, not scattering,* he reminded himself. He got up, put on his formal black robes, and went to get something to eat.

The corridors of the monastic quarters were quiet because he'd missed the last watch change. *Maybe I can eat in peace,* Greymalkin thought. He still had an ominous feeling of foreboding after the dream, and was not interested in conversation. He reached the refectory and entered hesitantly, but there was no one there. He got a tray of food and sat down by himself.

Soon enough though, a gaggle of Initiates came into the refectory and began picking up trays of food. Among them were Lee and Shaw, who when they saw Greymalkin, sat down across from him guardedly.

Everyone else in the group took one look at him, and then sat down to eat with one another while having pointedly quiet conversations and ignoring him. Greymalkin chewed his food while a sinking sensation grew in his stomach. After an uncomfortably long silence, Shaw asked him, "Are the rumors true about what happened?"

Greymalkin paused eating, feeling positively ill. After collecting his wits, he said nervously, "That depends. What do the rumors say?" Lee and Shaw looked at each other and actually looked nervous for the first time that he could remember.

"All kinds of things. Crazy things, " Lee muttered. "They're saying that all sorts of stuff went down on the bridge yesterday when the ship passed through those shoals. Is any of it true?"

Greymalkin cursed under his breath. "Nothing crazy happened, it just got a little... *chancy*. I did the best I could at the helm." After his last sentence, Lee's eyes almost bugged out of his head and Shaw nodded to himself. Greymalkin mentally kicked himself. *So, they didn't actually know it was me at the helm yesterday. Why do I always let people get so much information out of me?*

"Then it's true," Shaw said thoughtfully. "It was *you* that was steering the ship through all of the twisting and turning yesterday? Some people said that it was Sister Bora, and some people said it was you."

"It was both of us!" Greymalkin said in frustration. "I mean, she was still in charge. I was just acting as a hazard pilot. I know the Shoals; I told you that before."

"People said that it got crazy with the Abbot on the bridge after the ship finally got through the shoals yesterday," Lee said. "So what really happened then, Grey? Is the Abbot corrupt? Tell us!"

Greymalkin stared at Lee. *He's never called me Grey before. It's always my last name, Thomas this, Thomas that.* Scowling, Greymalkin abruptly stood up and walked over to the recycling chute to dump out his remaining food. *The hell with these two busybodies trying to get me in trouble and starting paranoid rumors.* Ignoring the surprised looks behind him, he exited the refectory and walked quickly down the corridor. It was time he left anyway. His watch would be starting on the bridge soon.

As Greymalkin began the long trek up to the bridge, he wondered where they were now. He had been asleep for some time. He checked the ship's position and was surprised at the course they had taken after exiting the shoals. Shortly after exiting the shoals the ship had changed course directly towards the first libration point of the system, which was the location of the capital of the entire Alban Realm, the megahab known as Burdock. Was that the destination that the Abbot was aiming for, then? Burdock had always been the long-term center of support and tithing for the great memory ark. It would make a lot of sense if the Abbot had decided to beach the ship in orbit around the vast megahab.

And if there *was* some conspiracy by the Burani to target the Order, it would make sense they would have been scheming in the ark's home location and origin. Or perhaps this was yet another feint, and the Abbot intended some other course of action. Greymalkin felt exhausted with all the subterfuge and suspicion. He wished that whatever was going on would simply end, one way or the other.

By the time he stepped onto the bridge he was again growing fearful. As he walked quickly to his post he looked around furtively to see if people were watching him. Only a few met his gaze, and he was relieved to see them smile and nod towards him in a friendly manner. Once again he noted that the bridge was packed, with Sojourners manning every single station in the three concentric rings of consoles surrounding the central altar. In fact, looking around he realized that even the side galleries were all packed with people. The visitors' gallery had a number of outsiders standing up there, watching the Bridge Crew curiously.

Greymalkin's sense of dread deepened even more. *Maybe this really is it,* he thought to himself sadly. *Today is when it all ends. Today is the end of the Journey.* It was almost impossible to believe that the moment might actually be at hand. He looked toward the command altar, wondering which of the senior Helm Crew would be the one to actually beach the ark. To his surprise he saw that brother Soren was still on duty at the helm, despite all the hours that Greymalkin had been asleep. Soren looked pale and exhausted. To Greymalkin's surprise, the normal command complement was missing from the altar. The only other persons there aside from Soren were the watch officer and the Abbot, who had evidently just returned to the bridge himself and was now mounting the central pulpit station atop the altar.

Greymalkin connected his thoughts with the communal command channel. As always, it was full of chatter between the different flight controller stations around the bridge. However, today he sensed something different in the flow of thoughts. There was an edge to all of the communed thoughts, an uneasiness that manifested in nervously clipped communications. He checked in with the watch Subprior, who was already looking at him expectantly from the altar.

«Tertiary helmsman reporting for bridge duty.» Greymalkin wondered what to expect after the events of the previous day. The watch Subprior responded almost immediately, watching Greymalkin from the altar with a level gaze.

«Tertiary helm, aye. Please come to the command altar.» The watch Subprior only dropped his stare when Greymalkin nervously acknowledged the summons and got up to approach the altar. As he walked forward nervously through the rows of stations, he happened to catch a glimpse of Father Johannes. The old monk's normally fierce gaze now seemed uncharacteristically stricken and pained. Greymalkin's legs suddenly felt so wobbly that he almost stumbled as he approached the command altar for the second time in two watches. He felt like he was walking helplessly in a nightmare.

Oh please not again, he thought. *What's happening this time? What have I done?*

When Greymalkin had mounted the altar and stood before the Subprior, the man simply continued to stare at him in a way that completely unnerved the young monk. When the Subprior finally cleared his throat, Greymalkin realized that once again he hadn't followed correct bridge protocol. "Th-Third Helm reporting as ordered, Brother Subprior," he managed to stammer out. *Blast it! There are always so many fussy bridge protocols.*

"Very good, Third Helm," the Subprior said crisply. "The Abbot wishes to address you." Now completely confused, Greymalkin turned towards the Abbot... and instantly felt that something was wrong. The Abbot was *smiling* broadly at him.

"Initiate Thomas," the Abbot said, still smiling. Greymalkin thought the Abbot looked like some kind of wrinkled snake, ready to strike. But his words continued to baffle Greymalkin. In fact, he increasingly could not believe what he was hearing. "Welcome back to the bridge! I am so glad to see you once again. Please direct your attention to the bridge communal network." The Abbot continued on the communal network, and the peroration that followed utterly dumbfounded Greymalkin.

«Attention, all bridge personnel.» At the Abbot's statement the bridge became completely silent, and hundreds of eyes centered on Greymalkin. «Officers of the bridge, Sojourners all, you see before you the young Initiate that saved our vessel and community yesterday during the transit of the shoals. I wish to publicly commend young Initiate Greymalkin Thomas for his skill, courage, and bravery in mastering the transit of that dangerous navigational zone. Please join me in expressing our appreciation for his helmsmanship skills!»

And then, unbelievably, the Abbot actually began a round of applause that the other bridge officers joined, uncertainly at first, and then enthusiastically. Greymalkin stood on the command altar blinking at his colleagues in dull shock, unsure what to think or believe. Then the Abbot continued.

"In recognition of his superlative performance yesterday during the transit, I have decided to promote Initiate Thomas to the rank of Apprentice Helmsman. Congratulations Apprentice Thomas!» The Abbot then proceeded to shake Greymalkin's hand vigorously. The young Sojourner looked stupidly at the Abbot, and then at his hand being shaken. He looked around at the other officers on the bridge and saw wide-eyed looks of surprise among them. *Wait, what? I can't be promoted to Apprentice yet, I'm not due for consideration for at least another six months at the absolute earliest!* As the applause continued Greymalkin began to wonder what was going on. Then the Abbot gestured to where Brother Soren was seated.

"In honor of your new position, Apprentice Thomas, please relieve Brother Soren and take the helm. I would like you, our honored newest full Helmsman, to take your first formal duty post on this historic moment during the sermon that I have prepared for this occasion.» The Abbot was smiling beatifically as Brother Soren got up and quickly exited the altar. Greymalkin sat down in the Helm primary cockpit and began the rote process of assuming helm control, still in shock. He was surprised to see their location. In the short while since he had last checked while en route to the bridge, the memory ark had reached the first libration point of Arctium and its satellite star. Brother Soren had set the ship in a cycling path around the enormous Burdock structure that was inhabited by the billions of people of the Alban Realm. Greymalkin was still going through his initial helm system checks when the Abbot activated the ship-wide communal channel and began broadcasting to all of the Sojourners in the huge vessel.

«My dear fellow travelers who make up the blessed community of the *Dragon King*, on the great occasion of this day it is my privilege to address you all as one. Today is a momentous occasion on which I invite us all to gather our thoughts and open our hearts to the devout Sojourner precept of *Acceptance*. In the daily bustle of our shipboard lives, which so often spin uncontrollably with uncertainty and change, we are presented with trying challenges that test our understanding of who we are, as well as the foundational nature of sworn duty to our beloved Order. I submit to you that our precept of Acceptance, that simple yet profound notion, is the underpinning of harmony within ourselves and our sacred responsibilities within the Order of Universal Sojourners.»

Greymalkin was still distracted with the process of assuming helm control, and was baffled as to what the Abbot could possibly be addressing in his sermon. As he looked out for a perplexed moment at the hundreds of Sojourners on the bridge below him, he was astonished to see that a number of them were now openly weeping. *What is this? What's happening?* Greymalkin wondered. The Abbot continued his sermon, his thoughts echoing in the minds of every last person on the ark.

«The Sojourner precept of Acceptance never means abandoning the Order's values or beliefs. Rather, it represents the courage and necessity of acknowledging the reality of the present moment, seeing things clearly as they are, and not clinging desperately to a course of action that we may love but can no longer pursue. Our precept of Acceptance calls us to the radical act of embracing the reality of our universe in all its imperfect beauty.»

Ironic of him to say that while we occupy an artificial bubble of <u>unreality</u> separated from the rest of the universe, Greymalkin thought in passing with wry amusement. Then a horrible thought came to him. *Wait! Is he talking about....*

«Think for a moment about the origins of our Order at the dawn of the Third Exodus. When the fragmented outbound human colonization waves sent forth by the Messengers fell into chaos and realized that they had no effective means to continue sharing critical information systematically, the monastic scientific organizations that founded our Order did not hesitate to take up the burden to which they were called. Even when the great memory arks were sent forth to peripatetically search the unknown expanses for colonies lost to horror and ruin, they accepted their duty with resilient Acceptance, despite the innumerable dangers they encountered.»

Greymalkin had now finished the disorienting process of connecting his mind with the various helm control systems. With increasing anxiety he realized that he was the only one in the Helm Link other than the Abbot himself. Where were the other helm control officers? There was supposed to be a navigator and a senior engineer at a bare minimum. With a growing sense of panic he hoped that his suspicion was wrong. But many of the bridge officers at the consoles arrayed before him were praying and sobbing uncontrollably. *Providence, no, no, no....*

«We are now once again called to embrace Acceptance, just as our forebears who set out on the *Dragon King* so many centuries ago. It is now, with the very same spirit of reverent Acceptance, that I call upon all of you to consider a timorous new possibility in which, like the ancient libraries of legend that sat with such solemn dignity in foundations of stone, we will serve the desperate seekers of knowledge who perchance now may find a path to the *Dragon King* instead of simply awaiting our assistance. The time has finally come to decide this matter, once and for all. However, I cannot make this choice. In a resolution of this magnitude, the innocent must lead, and our fate must rest on the most humble among us. As the most senior member of this crew, I will place this vexed choice squarely in the hands of the newest member of our bridge crew.» As Greymalkin looked back and up at him in astonishment, the Abbot now smiled down at him toothily before issuing his next command over the ship-wide communal link.

«My dear boy, Helmsman Greymalkin Thomas, newest helmsman of all the myriad who have sat at the august helm of this great vessel, I thank you for your clear-eyed youth and vigor, and for your courage to willingly accept the weighty choice of whether or not to at long last end our tormented journey. I bestow on you now the grace and sole permission from the Council of Vernalis to make this momentous judgement, to decree whether or not to discontinue the continuity manifold of the memory ark *Dragon King*, now and forever. Our fate is now in your hands.»

Aghast, Greymalkin simply whispered in fright over his shoulder, "My lord Abbot, I would never willingly decide to do such a thing! And I told you before, I do not know *how*." For a split second his panic-stricken grey eyes met the stony gaze of the Abbot, who was still smiling in a jarring manner. The old reptilian mouth made a shushing noise and then spared him the faintest susurrus in return, words that were only audible to Greymalkin.

"No need for *you* to know how, my boy," the Abbot whispered, and then raised his arms. Greymalkin whirled back to the helm console in consternation. Then Greymalkin felt something dreadful through the Helm Link. The Abbot had activated the strange control with so many ominous warnings. It mentally felt like a huge lever long rusted in place had been thrown with grating force.

There was an agonizing, *rending* sensation that rippled sharply through Greymalkin's back. Through the Helm Link he *felt* an echo of shattering pain in his own backbone as the kilometers-long mainmast slowly fractured with the sudden shock of the continuity manifold shutting down after centuries of flight through shadow space.

And then, again through the Helm Link, an even worse pain came over him, making him cry out in anguish as he held his hands against his temples. Greymalkin felt a brain-twisting scream from the ship's great mind as it *died*. The vast presence vanished with an agony as great as if his eyes had been torn out of their sockets. Abruptly, he could only feel simple and routine cybernetic systems maintaining the most limited version of shipboard operations, like a heart still raggedly beating inside a body after the brain was gone. Everyone on the bridge could feel the shocking change to a greater or lesser degree. The ark was now an immobile hulk. Shaken by the sensation, he and dozens of other bridge officers looked around wildly. The ship did not just *feel* dead, but in fact, the bridge had actually become *dark*. Mystified, he looked around until he finally thought to look up.

The great dome above them was now pitch black. Instead of the gentle shimmers of cerulean-blue shadow space, the dome now only showed a stark void. As his pupils gradually dilated, Greymalkin saw first a sprinkling and then vast constellations of tiny pinpricks of light that slowly became visible to his naked human eyes. There were scattered screams of purest horror around the bridge as the truth began to register among the Sojourners. Greymalkin felt numb with sickened trauma, as if the agonized echoes of that final unearthly shriek from the ship's mind were tearing out his insides.

The great memory ark now drifted in normal space. The journey of a millennium was over.

Prospects

The atrium of the cloisters was an elegant, but also intentionally complex space. It was one of the four such atria of the ark, each one found near the end of one of the ark's vast transept arms. The end of each of the immense transept arms was graced by a five-hundred meter wide spherical bulb of cloisters leading in a three-dimensional maze to miniature ecosystem parks, plazas, galleries, training ateliers, and other spaces that were heavily trafficked. At the center of each of the four transept arm bulbs was an atrium that served as a convoluted crossroads joining the many destinations through elegant lattices of pressor deck stairways and paths, all clad in a layer of valicrete that had been cast to look like simple and elegant white stone.

Greymalkin stood on one of the atrium overlooks, arms folded into the thick black sleeves of his formal cassock, watching hundreds of the visitors newly arrived for the forty-nine days of symposia and convenings that the Abbot had decreed. The artistic intricacy of the cloisters' atrium delighted the newcomers with its three-dimensional network of stairs and pathways leading away and up to arched entrances, each of which led to one of the ecosystem mini-parks or other destinations. The pressors in the paths and stairways were tunable to six different orthogonal para-gravity axis choices, and the visitors were happily exploring the different orientations in which they could walk around the atrium. The atria paths had been one of Greymalkin's favorite places when he had first arrived as an eleven year-old novice in the Order, wide-eyed and awe-struck at the incredible cathedral-class memory ark. But now the vertical maze of laughing visitors oriented sideways from one another and the cloisters of meticulously maintained planters full of the myriad flora from a hundred different garden worlds simply made him feel even more alone.

He checked the time and saw that he still had almost an hour before he had to arrive at the transept dock to meet the delegation to which he'd been assigned. He had carefully chosen this isolated overlook to watch the visitors arriving from the docks below so that he would encounter as few Sojourners as possible. However, there was one railed stairway that led up through the overlook, and now he heard two familiar noisy voices approaching him from above. He started to pull his hood down to obscure his face, but it was too late.

Shaw and Lee came jogging down the stairs in their colorful cassocks... and locked eyes with him for a second. They both instantly stopped talking and gave him frosty scowls before continuing down the stairs silently.

Inside, Greymalkin felt hollow and echoing. He pulled his black hood down over his forehead and walked away, trying to avoid recognition by other Sojourners. He had been treated as a pariah by almost everyone during the months since the ark had been beached in normal space. Everyone knew what they had seen and heard in the ship-wide communal channel. They had heard the Abbot give him the choice of whether or not to beach the ship, and then had seen him turn back to the primary Helm console a moment before the ark's continuity manifold had collapsed.

The Abbot was the one who really beached the ship, not me! But I can't prove it, and everybody blames me! It infuriated Greymalkin that no one blamed the Abbot for the beaching, even though he had actually been the one that made the decision and shut off the manifold. Greymalkin still wondered if the Abbot had been corrupted by the Burani. He thought it over sullenly for the thousandth time.

Ever since he'd learned as a child in the orphanage that he was born Bereft, Greymalkin had always had a lurking sense of shame. Everyone thought of the Bereft as uncivilized barbarians. Now he was ostracized from what few friends that he'd had, because everyone associated him personally with the disastrous end of the millennium-long journey. Every morning when he woke up and remembered it all, it felt like a rock settled in his stomach again. He felt utterly humiliated and depressed when he was around others. On a crowded starship, that was virtually *all* of the time.

He decided that even though he was an hour early, he would go down to the transept dock to meet the delegation to which he'd been assigned as a guide during the Grand Celebration of Acceptance, as the Abbot had dubbed the weeks of symposia to come. It was the first remotely interesting duty he'd received since the horrific beaching of the ship. After the ark had been stranded in normal space there had effectively been no need for Helm personnel, so he'd been reassigned to pursue his linguistic, cultural, and other scientific studies.

That had been perfectly fine with Greymalkin, since he had fallen far behind in his academic pursuits due to the absurdly steep learning curve of ark helm control training on the bridge as an Initiate. In the intervening months he'd actually caught up on all of his assignments, and had even completed his secondary scholastic thesis on endosymbiosis, a project so difficult that the memory of it still made him groan mentally. That research assignment had turned out to be an incredibly complicated topic that entailed studying not only tiny microorganisms from Old Earth but all manner of exotic alien species nested inside one another. The research had the same effect on him as most topics, generating more questions in his mind than answers. After studying hundreds of alien species he'd become lost in the quandaries of deciding exactly when an interspecies symbiotic relationship became parasitic or commensal rather than mutualistic. He'd initially been fascinated by the topic, but then overwhelmed.

And the mental isolation had definitely weighed on him. After immersing himself in his studies for months, he'd become so lonely that he'd repeatedly tried to reconnect with former friends from the Bridge Crew and other parts of the vast memory ark, but that had been a disaster. It wasn't even the stigma of the beaching, but sometimes just the sight of his robes that made others turn away from him. Now he felt that the black robes with the silver labyrinth brocade of the Helm Crew that he had once coveted so badly had become a millstone hung around his neck, because everyone knew that there was no longer any need for helmsmen on an immobile starship. Wherever he went on the ark, even if he wasn't immediately recognized as the specific helmsman that had beached the ship, people looked at him with a mix of puzzlement and pity as a member of the now specifically superfluous helm subsection of the Bridge Crew. The days of studying quietly by himself in the Great Nave had long ago begun to wear on him because no matter where he tried to sequester himself in the gigantic space, sooner or later someone happened upon him and proceeded to glare at him accusingly. When the announcement had come concerning the symposia series, together with a call for volunteers to serve as liaisons and guides, Greymalkin had been one of the first people to sign up.

The extra time for his studies had proved particularly useful when he received his assignment for the symposia series. He would serve as liaison guide for a delegation from the incredibly distant realm of Sadoria that lay on the other side of human space, almost seventeen hundred parsecs away from where the ark was now drifting around Burdock in the Alban Realm. He knew relatively little about Sadoria, giving him a perfect excuse to completely focus on it.

The realm had certainly proven to be an interesting research topic. He'd had a vague understanding of Sadoria as a wealthy but distant realm on the edge of the Orion Arm Frontier, verging on the ancient, forbidden border of the Sagittarius Arm. It was a dangerously exposed region of human space in a very hostile region of the Milky Way Galaxy. But when he'd delved in earnest into studying Sadoria, he was gripped with the very welcome distraction of becoming immersed in its culture and history. The historical links between Sadoria and the Al Sufi culture that had originally explored and settled the region around the yellow supergiant star Gamma Cygni led Greymalkin down a dozen lines of research.

He'd studied what was known about both the past of Sadoria and its current alliances, which were extensive. Sadoria had strong defense treaties in place with the even more fantastically wealthy human realm of Deneb, as well as the enigmatic and advanced alien Thubans. But Greymalkin thought that the most interesting aspect of Sadoria was *why* they needed so many strong alliances; it was precisely because of their proximity with the Sagittarius Arm and the xenophobic aliens called the Carinans that inhabited that portion of the Galaxy. The Sadorians had previously been antagonistic toward the Carinans, and had famously encroached on and even raided Carinan space in the distant past. Greymalkin had tried to memorize as much about the Sadorians and their language as he could in the time before their arrival. Now he wished he'd had years to study them. Given how angry everyone was at him over his presumed role in beaching the ship, he was fearful of making any protocol mistakes with the Sadorian delegation. As he approached the gateway where he was supposed to meet with the delegation, he ran through the details of their culture one last time in his mind.

The designated meeting point was the arched gateway that led down to the transept dock below. He found a position where he could easily see the entire ramp down to the dock entrance.

There was a slow but steady stream of visitors coming up the ramp as they exited from the various shuttles and wherries bringing them to the ark from the huge port at Burdock where most of them were transferring from. Knowing he had time, Greymalkin began composing himself, chanting a calming meditation chant in his head. As he slowed his breathing and focused his attention, he noticed that there was a very alert man standing just to the side of the ramp, and who was closely observing him. Even apart from the way he was watching Greymalkin, there were things about the fellow that immediately made the young Sojourner uneasy. For one thing, the stranger was enormous and built like a wrestler. But after a few moments the man smiled in a friendly manner and walked up to Greymalkin with his hands upturned.

"May I presume that you might be Brother Greymalkin Thomas?" the visitor asked. Greymalkin's first surprise was that the visitor's words were spoken in very deep but nevertheless very clearly enunciated Peretian, the same scholarly language that the Sojourners routinely spoke among themselves. When Greymalkin nervously nodded, the big man continued in perfect Peretian, all the while still smiling pleasantly as he looked down at the young Sojourner, "Then we have both arrived early. Allow me to introduce myself to you. My name is Hayan, and I am a member of the Sadorian delegation visiting your magnificent library vessel."

On the surface, Hayan seemed to be a very straightforward, if rather large, individual. He wore a simple dun-colored kaftan, a garment that would never attract a second glance. The only adornment that the man wore was an unpolished band of some bronze-like metal wrapped tightly around the rugged cliffs of his head and close-cropped brown hair. The man inclined his head politely and enveloped both of Greymalkin's hands in an oddly entwined double handshake. As they touched hands, the young Sojourner felt a blast of bizarre and overwhelming images overlaid for a fraction of a second on the form of the big Sadorian. The synesthesia flooding his mind came from his shadow sense, generated by the shadow jewel in Greymalkin's forebrain.

Instead of thick cloth and human hands, Greymalkin had an indirect sense of something with truly gigantic mass and inertia, as if he were shaking hands with a vast spacecraft and not a human being. And for a scant instant it was as if Greymalkin was not looking into the big man's friendly brown eyes, but at glimpsed flashes of light from a hidden shadow jewel the size of a boulder that emitted blazing citrine rays from behind intermittently thick curtains hanging from a golden ring encircling the blinding gem.

Greymalkin was momentarily speechless at the utterly bizarre synesthesia, and then looked down dumbly at the massive knuckles that engulfed his hands and wrists. The synesthesia illusion had already passed, but in that brief moment it had felt as if Greymalkin's arms had been embedded in a solid block of valitanium. Hayan seemed to sense that something was wrong and released his gentle grip with concern. After a very genuine double take, Greymalkin saw that Hayan was only a human being after all, a simple mendicant now standing before him with palms upturned apologetically.

"I am sorry if I have given offense somehow," Hayan rumbled. After a second of regathering his wits, Greymalkin quickly shook his head.

"N-No, please accept my sincerest apologies, sir!" Greymalkin said. "I-I was... distracted, just trying to access my files on your delegation to properly welcome you. Now let me see, Mister Hayan... yes, now I have your entry among the registrations. You are...." Greymalkin abruptly felt his mouth run dry and almost choked. After trying to conceal the resulting gasp for air, the young Sojourner said incredulously, "Ah, ah, my information says that you are a *prince* of the Emirate of Sadoria? C-Can that possibly be the case, sir? I mean, my lord, ah, *your majesty*?"

Hayan's eyebrows went up and he laughed warmly. "No need for such formality, my friend! Please, simply address me as Hayan. I am only the second prince in any event; my older brother is the heir. I am a scholar and man of faith, like you."

Greymalkin nodded, feeling confused and very embarrassed at his protocol oversight. *Great Providence, this man is royalty! And I've been assigned as his liaison!* Greymalkin asked uncertainly, "So, you must be the head of the Sadorian delegation, then?"

Hayan laughed again, and said, "No, no, certainly not. I am but a humble student and follower of my superior, she who is graced with the name of Kuanian." Greymalkin searched through the registered names of visitors and found the entry. Oddly, it listed no title or other information for the name Kuanian.

"I-I see," Greymalkin said, although he understood nothing and was even more confused. "Will Kuanian or any of the other Sadorians be joining us for this orientation tour, then?"

"Oh, my apologies again for any misunderstanding," Hayan said. "You see, only Kuanian and myself were able to come. And I do not know if Kuanian will join us or not. I believe she is meeting with your Abbot at the moment."

Greymalkin clenched his jaw to keep it from dropping open. *The Abbot is meeting with her? What could they possibly be talking about? What's happening here? What is going on with the Abbot and his "symposia"?* After he absorbed the information, Greymalkin could think of nothing to say except, again, "I see."

Hayan smiled innocuously again and said, "You look concerned, Brother Thomas. If you are wondering, no, I do not know exactly what business Kuanian has with your Abbot. It probably has something to do with his interest in selling portions of your ark's remarkable archives. The offer is of course quite intriguing." This time Greymalkin's jaw did drop open, and it was Hayan's turn to look abashed. "Oh dear. Perhaps

I was supposed to keep that information in confidence. Please excuse my error and, if you would, consider this simply a misstatement on my part for the moment. I do not wish to cause an incident."

"Of course," Greymalkin said stupidly, now stunned. *The Abbot is going to sell off the ark's archives??* The thought was appalling beyond words. After a moment, he volunteered, "I will keep this between us." Hayan looked even more embarrassed.

"I won't ask that of you," Hayan said. "If this was not generally announced already, I think it will be common knowledge in a few hours. It was said to be one of the main topics that will be discussed in the opening session of the symposia today."

After staring at Hayan for a moment and almost repeating "I see" again out of a loss for words, Greymalkin simply nodded and folded his arms even more deeply into the sleeves of his cassock. He knew that he had to halt his mind and his tongue from running away with themselves. *I have an assignment,* he reminded himself, and tried to drive out the torrent of questions swirling through his head. Instead he simply smiled as pleasantly as he could manage and asked, "Shall I take you on a brief tour and then show you to your quarters, then?"

Hayan nodded, clearly grateful to be able to drop the discussion. Greymalkin showed the big Sadorian around the more interesting of the locations in the cloisters, keeping up the patter of historical facts that he had been taught as a guide for visitors. All of the arcades and parks had been given fanciful ancient names long ago to commemorate bygone civilizations and events. This seemed to entertain Hayan, and there were only a couple of moments when he thought he detected anything but genuine delight in his large Sadorian guest. One occurred when Greymalkin began to describe the main plaza at the base of the atrium, which was called the Platform of Canopus. Greymalkin noticed that Hayan frowned at the name, and paused.

"Canopus, you say? And this... arm... of your great memory library vessel that we are in, what did you call it?" Hayan asked.

"We are in what is called, for reasons of historical commemoration dating back millennia to Old Earth, the Southern Transept," Greymalkin said. "You see, we Sojourners love old memorial traditions, and the term 'Southern' was one of four cardinal –"

"I am familiar with the history of Old Earth and its traditions," Hayan said, looking around warily now. "But the star system of Canopus has... troubling connotations in Sadoria. Did you say that our temporary living quarters will be in this section of your vessel?"

Greymalkin looked at the big Sadorian blankly for a moment, lost again. Then he understood. *Canopus is a Burani system, and the Sadorians have a longstanding cultural enmity with the Burani!*

"Ah, yes," Greymalkin said, but quickly recovered. "We can relocate your living accommodations. Although the names of the locations in the Southern Transept are purely because of the historical accident that stars such as Canopus, Spica, and Achernar were visible in the Southern..." Greymalkin trailed off as Hayan's scowl became deeper and deeper as he named more of the other major Burani star systems. He cursed inwardly.

"Our dislike of the Accursed may seem extreme," Hayan said, using an old and traditional term for the Burani. "However, we have found that they are vain and drawn to places that celebrate their realms and accomplishments. And the Accursed are dangerous and violent tyrants, make no mistake. They hold power by destroying knowledge wherever they go. They rule by fostering ignorance and harmful misinformation. Above all, the Accursed stoke suspicion, fear, and hatred. Unfortunately, we have reason to believe that they may be coming here to attend your event, they seem to have taken an interest in your Order for some undoubtedly nefarious reason. So, yes, we would like to avoid places named for them while we are here. They are evil."

"Certainly," Greymalkin said, now becoming worried. "We will relocate your rooms." *The Burani, here?* And he hadn't realized that the Sadorian dislike of the notorious Burani was so extreme.

Hayan smiled then, and moved on lightly. "And is this lovely botanical park also named after one of the Accursed systems?" Greymalkin swallowed timidly, and shook his head.

"No, your majesty. I mean, no... friend Hayan," Greymalkin said, forcing himself to use the familiar form of address. "This micro-biome is named the Arboretum of Acrux." *And thankfully, the Crucians are allies of the Sadorians,* Greymalkin remembered.

Hayan smiled again. "A most august appellation. And see how wonderful a meeting we have now! There, coming toward us, is none other than my honored superior, *Kuanian.*"

Greymalkin looked to where Hayan was pointing and cringed inside. Sure enough, he could see the figure of a woman in an elegant white kaftan in the central space of the arboretum ahead. However, he could also see three male figures in the black robes of the command deck, one of which was unmistakably the Abbot. As Hayan hurried forward down the path to greet the woman in white, Greymalkin hesitated for a very long moment before following. As he and Hayan approached the group, they all turned in mild surprise.

The other two men with the Abbot were none other than the Claustral Bridge Prior Master Burke, and Greymalkin's mentor Father Johannes. The Abbot did not look particularly happy to see Greymalkin, but Johannes grinned and nodded to him as he came up. The tall and thin woman at the center of the group turned to Greymalkin after a final cool glance of suspicion at the Abbot, and then came forward smiling to greet the young monk. She had exotically beautiful facial features that were accentuated by the warmth of her expression. Like Hayan, she wore a simple kaftan, although hers was pure white. She wore an ample head scarf, but Greymalkin could see that she too wore a bronze circlet around her forehead. Also like Hayan, she took his hands in the same entwined double handshake.

Greymalkin gasped. He'd wondered if the same strange sensation would accompany this handshake, but it was radically different, and he swooned in shock. The momentary synesthetic sensations that exploded through his mind were even stronger, but nothing like the impression of enormous mass and solidity that he had felt in Hayan. This time the perception he had was of tremendous energy, as if he had touched two of the ark's primary power couplings. There was also a brief image that came to him of the smiling woman illuminated by blinding light, a huge array framing her face like a headpiece of diaphanous silver feathers and blazing sapphires, with complex blue and white silken robes billowing around her body. Her figure was covered in a mass of rapidly flowing symbols and diagrams that swirled down the elegant contours of her neck, shoulders, arms, and torso. Greymalkin staggered backwards a step, but the woman's hands were surprisingly strong and steadied him instantly.

The sensations were transitory, as before. When his vision had cleared, the first thing he saw were her concerned jade green eyes looking into his from a handsbreadth away. His head still spun, but when she spoke softly to him the effect seemed to dissipate. "Are you all right?"

Greymalkin nodded weakly, unable to speak. The woman glanced to the side at Hayan, who had come up next to them. Greymalkin had a feeling that the two of them were communing, discussing him. Then the woman communed directly with him, her thoughts pouring into his mind like a warm and comforting draught. «I am so sorry, my dear Brother Sojourner! You have a *very* unusual shadow jewel in your mind. My name is Kuanian, and I am very pleased to make your acquaintance. Are you able to stand now?»

Greymalkin felt that his knees might buckle the second she let go of him, but he nevertheless tried to convey confidence in his reply. «I'm...

fine. My sincere apologies, my lady. It was just a momentary dizziness.» The woman smiled at him again and wrapped her arm firmly around his, steadying him again with surprising strength.

«Good! Hayan informs me that you are our guide while on board. I am so pleased.» Kuanian's thoughts resonated in his mind in a way he had never felt before. Strangely, he felt stronger and sturdier by the moment. As she walked forward, arm in arm with him, rather than feeling shaken to his core by the experience, he felt oddly at peace. The intimate touch of her arm around his and the warmth of her body by his side was reassuring rather than anything else. He looked to his side at her uncertainly, but then the Abbot and the others approached them with a phalanx of frowns.

"You appear ill; perhaps you need some further rest, Brother Thomas?" Master Burke asked through gritted teeth. Greymalkin wanted to shrink away. Burke was as angry as ever, and disapproving of everything he saw, especially Greymalkin. The Claustral Prior was another one of those that blamed Greymalkin for the beaching of the ark, and had been the one that had pointedly relieved Greymalkin of all his duties following the event.

"Young Brother Greymalkin is our shipboard guide," Kuanian said sweetly. "You have assigned him to assist Hayan and myself while we are here. A most excellent choice. Thank you for your time, lord Abbot. Our discussion was illuminating."

To Greymalkin's surprise, the Abbot and the others bowed solemnly to Kuanian. The Abbot seemed to consider his words carefully before replying to her. Greymalkin was again surprised when he heard what the Abbot had to say, and how he addressed her. "We are deeply grateful for the generosity of all your proposals, most Holy Eminence. As I have indicated, while I am unable to accept some of your... more extraordinary offers, many of the other propositions you have put forward to us are acceptable, even if the specifics of the proposed exchanges have yet to be precisely determined. We look forward to continuing our dialogue during the symposia of the Grand Celebration of Acceptance. Now if you will pardon us, we must prepare for the opening ceremonies of the symposia series. We will leave you..." As the Abbot paused, he seemed to notice Greymalkin on Kuanian's arm for the first time. The slightest hint of an amused smirk touched the corner of his mouth, and he continued, "...in the capable hands of our distinguished Apprentice Helmsman. Farewell." With that, the Abbot and his officers bowed again and departed.

Greymalkin felt his face redden with a combination of shame and simmering resentment at the Abbot, but as Kuanian steered him back into the trees of the arboretum he found it impossible to stay angry. She radiated like a star with a friendly and reassuring presence.

"My, these trees are lovely," Kuanian said. "And such fragrant blossoms! One finds such interesting discoveries in such unlikely places." She gave him a sidelong glance and smile, and then leaned over to speak quietly in his ear. "Are you feeling recovered now?"

"Yes, fully. Thank you... Holy Eminence," he said hesitantly. Kuanian laughed.

"Please, please, no such titles from you, my young Sojourner! May I always simply be Kuanian to you," she said, and gave his arm a final squeeze before releasing it. "Now dear Brother Greymalkin, I would like to ask a favor of you. Will you hear it?"

"Of-of *course*," Greymalkin said. He had no idea what his strange experiences with the two Sadorians meant, but he knew with a profound conviction that he wanted to please her.

"I would like you to attend a session of the symposium this afternoon, a presentation that you will see on the schedule in which I am slated to discuss a certain endeavor of mine. And please, invite all your friends to attend as well."

Greymalkin ruefully thought about just how few friends he still had on the ark, but he still grinned and nodded. "I most certainly will do so! Now, may I show you to your new lodging accommodations? I told Hayan I would relocate you both."

Kuanian looked to Hayan for a moment, and Greymalkin could tell they were communing once more. Kuanian raised an eyebrow and said, "Very well, then. Thank you, Brother Greymalkin."

* * *

It took him some time to get the two Sadorian visitors resituated in one of the grandest visitors' accommodations in the Western Transept. As they toured the ship he tried to keep them entertained with additional details about the traditions and locations within the great memory ark. Unlike Hayan, Kuanian seemed uninterested in the ship and mostly asked Greymalkin questions about himself, which made him very uncomfortable.

Much to his embarrassment, she quickly managed to discover that he was a Bereft orphan. He had wondered how she would look at him then, but if anything it seemed to interest her even more in his background. The fact that she seemed sincerely curious in talking with him and treated him in a kindly manner quickly endeared Kuanian to Greymalkin. He was genuinely sad when he finally left the two Sadorians at the end of his watch, promising again to attend Kuanian's presentation with his friends. After he logged his notes on his activities as a tour guide and was relieved from his watch, he took time for a very quick meal. He saw that the opening ceremonies of the symposia series were now almost over, and after Hayan's ominous comments he very much wanted to hear what the Abbot had to say.

Greymalkin hurried up to the immense Amphitheater of Orion, the portion of the Great Nave where the opening ceremonies were being held. There was an enormous crowd of thousands there, and the sounds of myriad voices reacting to the ceremonies were generalized roars of laughter and cheering. As Greymalkin found a place near the back of the crowd, he found the general address communal network and connected to it. He was in luck, the previous speakers were just now finishing their comments and handing the rostrum off to the Abbot, now wearing his most ostentatious official robes with an ornate white and gold chasuble draped over his dark black command cassock that was festooned with golden brocade. He opened his address with an extended formal invocation in High Peretian that called out the authority of *Ashaloth*, the Galactic Faith of All Humanity, then the Sojourner Order, and finally Humanity's place in Providence in the pursuit of compassion and wisdom for the benefit of all.

Normally Greymalkin appreciated Sojourner addresses and technical sermons, but nothing the Abbot said would ever inspire him again. And looking around at the audience, he could see that even the simplified translations they were hearing of the archaic and complex High Peretian invocation mystified or just bored many of the visiting delegations that he stood among. But the sheer size and variety of the crowd itself awed Greymalkin.

He had never seen such a large and diverse assortment of visitors personally attending a ceremony on the ark. Certainly, there were many Albans from the nearby Burdock megahabitation that the ark now orbited in normal space, but he could also see dozens of other ethnicities and cultures around him from far flung parts of the Periphery that were distant from the Alban Realm. There were stern groups of Canisians in austere apparel from various parts of their empire, glowering at almost everyone around them whenever they deigned to notice others. He saw many colorfully garbed groups from dispersed parts of the vast Erisian Realm, chattering away in scattered languages that sounded bizarre even to Greymalkin.

And then there were delegations that must have already been visiting Burdock for other purposes, because they were clearly from the even more distant realms of the Old High Core and surely could not have made the long journey here in the few months since the ark had been beached. He saw a characteristically stoic party of scholars that were obviously from one of the Xestan cultures, an affable looking group of Dillies from Kabdhilinan in the Tauran Realm, and even an exotic group that he was sure must be Sybarians all the way from Purpuris. One of the women in the party saw him looking in their direction and gave him a very suggestive smile. Greymalkin's cheeks reddened, and he looked down quickly.

Then Greymalkin saw a party that gave him a distinct chill down his back. There was a large group of tall and richly dressed Burani not so far from where Greymalkin stood. From the look of them, he supposed they had to be Stormvalers from the Achernar Realm. There was something particularly cruel about their eyes that made him certain he was looking at members of the infamous slave-taking culture. Greymalkin felt slightly ill looking at them. What kind of people would cybernetically enslave other humans purely for amusement and as a mark of prestige? The enmity that Hayan had expressed for the Burani made complete sense to Greymalkin. In fact, it seemed shocking to him that the Abbot, even as evil as Greymalkin now thought he was, would actually allow delegations on the ark from a culture as despicable as the Burani. *Unless... he really is in league with them...?*

But what could possibly interest the Burani in a symposium on a Sojourner ark? Both the Sojourner Order and most of the varied cultures that he could see in the huge amphitheater were members of the sprawling and inclusive Ashaloth Assembly of Faiths from across all the vastly separated myriad realms that made up *human space*, the span of the Orion Arm of the Galaxy populated by humans. Assembly realms varied as much as their constituent cultures, but they all shared a set of loosely similar consensus beliefs about both the sanctity of sapient life and the original Thannic scientific discoveries concerning human psyches that dated all the way back to the First Interstellar Exodus. All the cultures of the Assembly shared some version of those principles... but not the Burani. The Burani were not members of the Assembly, they didn't believe in precepts of compassion, preserving sapient life, or... much of anything. *Themselves, maybe,* he thought. *Domination of others, perhaps?* He had never heard of Burani espousing anything but those two principles in any of their writings.

But why would they come to a Sojourner symposium, then? Maybe there's something in our archives that piqued their curiosity? Or that they want? There was certainly a vast amount of technical information in the archives of the *Dragon King*. *That must be it,* he thought, and it made sense the more he thought about it. But the conclusion that emerged from the thought was more revolting than anything that had yet occurred to him. This "symposia series" was no gathering of scholars to share discoveries, or any of the typical Sojourner purposes in such gatherings. The only reason the Burani could have been admitted was because they had great wealth and might become high bidders for the collections that made up the core of the ancient starship. The idea of the Burani buying up the archives of the Sojourners made Greymalkin feel even more ill than he had before.

The Abbot was finally finishing his opening invocation of the faith. *I wonder if he believes anything that he just said,* Greymalkin thought cynically. It seemed difficult for Greymalkin to believe anything the man said now. As the Abbot transitioned into yet another version of his sermon on Acceptance that he'd been lecturing to the crew of the ark ever since it was beached, the crowd was clearly still bored and distracted. But then the Abbot introduced a new theme, and Greymalkin together with the entire crowd of visitors actually began to listen.

«So many of you, our honored guests, have come from so many different realms to help us celebrate the triumphant conclusion of the millennium long journey of the *Dragon King* and its long accumulation of treasured archives. I once again bid you all welcome. We, the Order of Universal Sojourners, have spent long centuries of itinerant travel with the sole desire to benefit others. Now that our arduous and tormented voyages have finally come to an end, we may at last cease to hoard our troves and begin to fully share the bounty of our long travail.»

Greymalkin inhaled sharply, understanding exactly what the Abbot meant with his flowery communal thoughts. *He is going to do it, he is actually going to sell off the archives!* Evidently Greymalkin was not the only one troubled by the Abbot's message, because he was suddenly aware of the side eruption of a dozen communal channels of threaded thought among a large number of irate Sojourners listening to the address. «He can't be serious!» «I don't believe it!» «To think I've lived to see this day!» The sense of outrage grew quickly.

«As if we ever hoarded information and refused to share it!» Greymalkin hurled his own incensed thoughts into one of the channels between Sojourners he still trusted. The Abbot continued with his address, weaving in carefully selected phrases that were innocuous in isolation, like "accepting the largess of our visitors" and "to achieve the greatest utility for all". He never came out and said anything directly, but the direction of his address was clear. The throng of visitors were clearly feeling encouraged and even flattered by his words, but here and there were Sojourners who had heard enough, and began to thread their way out of the great hall shaking their heads in anger and despair. After a few more minutes, Greymalkin joined them.

Greymalkin felt shaky and unsteady as he walked away from the clamor of the amphitheater. He felt profoundly disoriented. Just a few months ago, everything in his life had been boring, but made sense. Now every day was a new disaster, and nothing made sense at all. As he paced away, unsure where he was even thinking of going, he heard someone call his name. He turned around and saw Father Johannes hurrying down the corridor.

"I'm glad I saw ye just now, Grey," Johannes said breathlessly. "I dinnae have much time just at the moment, but we need tae have a talk. I'm sure ye have many questions after the Abbot's address."

Greymalkin stared at his old friend for a moment and then nodded with exasperation. "Well, yes, I suppose you could say that," he finally agreed sarcastically. "But what is there to talk about after that... that... *betrayal*?"

Johannes ignored the derision, but his normally stern face was very drawn and sad now as he seemed momentarily at a loss for words. Abruptly, Greymalkin realized something. *This was what made Father Johannes despair all those months ago. He must have found out what the Abbot was planning. That, and the abandonment of all those skete missionaries in the Erymia.* Greymalkin felt unhappy for Johannes, but also angry at the man for not telling him any of this. *But then, he couldn't, could he? Not without proof, and not without straight-up mutiny against the Abbot.*

Johannes looked miserable as he said, "I understand why ye feel the way ye do. A great many things have changed in recent days." When Greymalkin began to sputter in indignation, Johannes simply held up his hand and continued, "Aye. *Believe me* when I say I understand, lad! I've been afraid this day was coming for months. These days have made me doubt a great many things that I've believed my whole life. But it's happened now, and we have tae deal with it. *All* 'o this blasted *mishanter*. The fact is that ye simply can't continue as a helmsman now, obviously. That's why I want tae talk with ye. I believe I can arrange a transfer for ye tae Operations. That way ye can keep yer Bridge Crew rank, and I can look after ye. The bridge has become... uncertain as of late."

The offer surprised Greymalkin, and he thought about it for a moment before frowning. "Thank you, Brother. But I'm not sure that I want to stay on the bridge. Not after the way I've been treated there."

Johannes put a hand on Greymalkin's arm with a concerned smile, and repeated himself. "I understand completely. But ye have tae do somethin' in the Order, nae? I should have advised ye against service as a helmsman; I realize that now. But ye were so eager, and I didn't know everything that would happen. It'll be different in Operations. Trust me."

Greymalkin looked down, and shuffled his feet a little. "I don't know. The Abbot...." He wondered if he would ever feel the same thrill to do anything on the bridge again. Johannes squeezed his shoulder.

"Think this oer carefully," Johannes said. "I have tae go, but I want tae discuss this with ye further. Let's talk this oer. Where will ye be at the end of the next watch? We can talk then, but nae before. I have long and... unpleasant duties tae attend."

"I was going to go to the presentation by the Sadorians this afternoon," Greymalkin said, and then frowned slightly again. "What was the Abbot discussing with Kuanian earlier in the arboretum anyway?" That matter still troubled him.

Johannes looked pained for a moment. "It would take some time tae explain *that* business," he finally said uncomfortably. "I have tae go now, but I will meet ye after the Sadorian talk, if nae before. Think about what I've said. *Please.*" With that, he hurried off.

Greymalkin stood in the corridor for a long while, wondering what he should do about Johannes' offer. He reluctantly had to admit that he didn't have many options. Helmsmen were no longer needed on a stationary beached memory ark. But the thought of going back to the bridge repelled him. The more he thought about it, the stranger and more ironic it seemed to him that a year ago he could have scarcely imagined serving on the bridge, much less piloting the ark, and now he didn't even want to set foot there again.

After brooding on the matter for so long, he now realized that none of the other Helm Crew had wanted to be the one who would be remembered for beaching the ship; they had all been trying to avoid it. *I was the only one stupid enough to fall for that trick by the Abbot,* he thought. It was obvious enough to him now why the Abbot had asked him to take the ark through the Shoals. *He thought I'd surely fail and force Sister Bora to beach the ship. But I got us through.* Greymalkin still felt proud of the piloting feat he'd accomplished, and still felt incredulous that he'd actually managed to steer the gigantic ark through a passage only fit for tiny channel cats. And it infuriated him that no one remembered him for doing *that*, only that he had been the scurrilous *gremmie* that beached the ark.

Eventually, after he had stood there indecisively wondering what to do for a long enough time, the crowd started pouring out of the amphitheater exits and he realized the opening ceremonies were over. He stomped away, angrily wondering what depressing news the rest of the day would bring.

* * *

Hours later, he made his way along through the corridors and down the grand staircases in the midst of a crowd of visitors until he found the lecture hall where Kuanian would be speaking. After simmering in a funk over the Abbot's address, Greymalkin's excitement was rising again. It was now time for Kuanian's mysterious talk.

The hall was mostly empty when he arrived, but there were two Sojourners in black Bridge Crew robes standing near the front of the room talking quietly. As he approached them he was interested to see that it was Sister Bora and Brother Soren. When they saw him, they both nodded in greeting. He nodded back to them cautiously.

He had not spoken to either of them in many weeks, and it occurred to Greymalkin belatedly that these two fellow Helm Crew were likely some of the few on board the ship that would not hold the beaching of the ark against him, especially Bora. She had been castigated and demoted in the hearings to which the Abbot had subjected her, and she was now avoided by the crew of the ark almost as much as Greymalkin. But her old colleagues of the Helm Crew were still loyal to her.

"Hello, Brother Thomas," Sister Bora said. "I'm not surprised to see yet another helmsman here to learn more about this hare-brained Sadorian scheme. Since none of us will ever take the helm again, I cannot criticize you or anyone here for considering a plan that may simply be suicidal. But I say that you are much too young to contemplate this madness."

Greymalkin stopped in confusion. "What? I'm here because I was assigned as shipboard guide to the Sadorians," he said. "What suicidal plan are you talking about?"

Bora and Soren looked at each other with doleful expressions. "Oh dear," Brother Soren muttered, and folded his arms into his sleeves. "Well, perhaps we should let this odd Sadorian mystic explain it all herself." Sister Bora said nothing, her face becoming an emotionless mask. He saw that she was watching the entrance to the room and turned. Others were starting to arrive for the talk, and the motley composition of the audience intrigued him.

While there were a few other Sojourners (and they were all indeed helmsmen, interestingly enough), most of the people arriving for the talk were rough looking men and women in battered jumpsuits that all had a stylized X symbol on the breast and sleeves. The symbol was familiar-looking to him, but he could not immediately place it. Greymalkin studied them uncertainly, and eventually asked Brother Soren in a low whisper, "Who are they?"

Soren scowled before answering. "Xenocorpsmen. Not surprising, given the nature of what the Sadorians will be discussing."

Greymalkin's head jerked back to the newcomers. The Xenocorps! Like everyone, he had heard of them and had studied many mnemotomes recounting the fantastic tales of Xenocorps exploits down through history. But he had never seen any in person. "How interesting! They're an Order of explorers, a bit like us, correct?"

Soren snorted, and Bora's expression darkened. "They are nothing like us," Brother Soren said dismissively. "Profiteering thugs and enforcers, the lot of them. Where we would reverently study an archaeological site, they'd rob and loot it."

"But all the tomes I studied described them as brave, honorable, and... *inquisitive*," Greymalkin protested. Soren shrugged, and did not take his eyes off the hardened strangers.

"They're certainly well-trained," the older helmsman said warily. "I'll grant them that. And they're quite willing to venture into dangerous unknown places if they think there's something to be gained. But I'd guess the tomes that you studied were *written* by Xenocorpsmen, to aggrandize their own achievements. They're all quite full of themselves, as well as their supposed grand history of discoveries outside human space. And their organization is absolutely as wealthy as sin itself."

"Their organization is wealthy because it is very old," Sister Bora said, evidently having decided to make some of her rare pronouncements. "Even older than our Order. Wherever they go, there will be something of value, and they will bring violence and theft. But sometimes they are themselves hired to maintain a coarse sort of law where none exists. And it also must be admitted, *they keep their word*, and they always honor their contracts to the letter."

Other Sojourners were gathering around them in a group, and many were watching the Xenocorps agents in the same guarded way as

Brother Soren. While some of the weathered corpsmen gave the Sojourners noncommittal looks, none of them seemed interested in the monks. They were watching the speakers' dais expectantly.

Greymalkin began to wonder where Kuanian was, as it was almost time for her presentation. He looked around and saw that other visitors were now entering the room. There were some stern Canisians, and two sly-looking men at the very back of the room that he could not identify. He was starting to feel alarmed. *What in all of space is Kuanian going to discuss that has attracted this bizarre mix of a crowd?*

Then Kuanian and Hayan swept into the room and quickly took the stage. Greymalkin wondered if he should join them to see if they needed anything, but Hayan immediately stepped purposefully to the front of the dais. The sight of his enormous form silenced the room. Without pausing, he summarily introduced Kuanian with a chain of rapid-fire phrases and then stepped to the side and backwards as she came forward smiling. The introduction was so abrupt that Greymalkin did not fully absorb the jumble of bizarre titles in Sadorian that Hayan gave as preface to her name. There was something like "her beatitude" and another phrase that he thought meant something akin to "the awakened rectitude", but he was still a beginner with Sadorian and Hayan spoke very quickly. Thankfully, when Kuanian spoke it was once again in familiar Peretian.

"Dear Sojourner friends and all honored guests of this magnificent memory ark, I come before you today at the beginning of our Sojourner hosts' remarkable symposia series in order to share news of an extraordinary endeavor and associated invitation. I know that many of you have already received word of this undertaking, so I will therefore be brief in my summary so that we may proceed to the questions you undoubtedly have for me. I know several of you are impatient to present your inquiries. But we must begin with a clear statement of the purpose and significance of this grand commission, and I will start by framing the profound significance of the task that I am here to represent."

Greymalkin felt relieved; for a moment he was becoming convinced that everyone *except* him knew what Kuanian was talking about. Some of the Canisians, Bora and Soren, and all of the Xenocorpsmen already looked impatient to speak as Kuanian continued.

"Those assembled here today are among the most experienced explorers in all of human space, and you are undoubtedly aware of the boundaries that have enclosed Humankind for so long. Since the dawn of humanity's interstellar age of travel three and a half millennia ago, all such travel has been effectively constrained to that which we have always termed the Orion Arm, or more properly *spur*, of the Galaxy. The combination of impassably hostile alien territories and the intractable distances to other arms of the Galaxy have long comprised the boundaries of human space... until now."

With the last statement she smiled broadly, and Greymalkin immediately felt profoundly disoriented. He'd had no idea what she would be addressing in her talk, but the presentation had taken a dizzyingly unexpected step outward in perspective. He could see that he was not the only one surprised in the audience, as there were raised eyebrows and mutters all around him. But the groups that had looked impatient to speak before were now starting to shout questions. Kuanian held up her hand for silence, and when the chatter died down she continued.

"We will have plenty of time for questions, my friends! But now that I have framed the significance for you, I must explain the specific purpose that brings us together today. As many of you know, Sadoria has long led the cause of breaching the boundaries of human space and gaining access to the vast expanse of the Sagittarius Arm that lies inward from us in the direction of the galactic core. Today I am privileged to announce the greatest expedition to the Sagittarius Arm in all of human history. The target of this venture is no less than the Eta Carina Nebula and its surrounding star clusters."

The room exploded in shouts, and Greymalkin felt as if he'd been physically rocked backward onto his heels. The Carinae! While there were a thousand fabulously unreachable destinations that he could imagine setting one's sights on, there was no other location that had the spectacular combination of danger and mystery that the Carinae embodied. There were any number of accounts describing the Carinae and its recurring history of near supernova explosions that had been passed down indirectly to humans from far older alien species like the Thubans. But those stories amounted to little more than rumors, folktales, and myths. He tried to remember if there had ever been a human expedition that had explored the inconceivably violent Eta Carina Nebulae. It seemed that he could remember *something* about such a previous expedition in history, but the memory was elusive. If Kuanian had announced that she was mounting an expedition into some supernatural location out of a legend it would probably have seemed more attainable.

After the chaotic shouting subsided and people began asking to be heard in an orderly fashion, it was actually Sister Bora who spoke first. In her typical clipped and acerbic tones she stated what Greymalkin assumed many people must be thinking. "No human interbrachial expedition to the Sagittarius Arm has ever been successful. The alien species of the Carinae behave in a psychotically paranoid fashion toward Humankind, and many are far more advanced in their technologies than any human civilization. Then there is the matter of the intercultural Xenopax Accords that have long been in place between humans and other alien species of the Galaxy. Any expedition to the Sagittarius Arm would violate the treaty that has kept the peace between us and the various alien species of the Galaxy for a thousand standard years. Finally, the task of crossing the interbrachial Rift between the Orion and

Sagittarian Arms has been rendered absurdly perilous over the centuries because of the ever-increasing dangers in the Rift over the last three centuries. Specifically, the growing presence in the Rift of antagonistic beings so simultaneously advanced and dangerous that even the Thubans avoid them. In short, no one can get there safely, it's illegal to go there in the first place, and you'd most likely be killed if you managed to get there anyway."

Bora made her statements in the same sardonic, blunt tone that one would assert that water was wet. Many of the Sojourners in the audience were nodding at her words, and from around the room came supportive interjections. Greymalkin looked at Kuanian and saw that she was grinning impishly now, clearly savoring whatever she had to say as a rejoinder.

"Successful interbrachial expeditions are rare, but not unheard of," Kuanian said. "There was the Danariad, for instance."

"The Danariad expedition was *outward*, to the *Perseus* Arm, not *inward* to the *Sagittarius* Arm," Bora said sourly. "And I would hardly call it a success; the leadership and most of the expedition perished. And the colony they founded did not survive."

Kuanian was still grinning, and Greymalkin thought she was enjoying the exchange. She said, "I seem to recall that the Xenocorps mounted a successful expedition to the Sagittarius Arm some three centuries ago." This made Bora genuinely annoyed.

"Again, hardly a success!" Bora said, glancing to her side at the crowd of Xenocorpsmen. "They can speak for themselves, but I've read the accounts. It was a gigantic expedition of tens of thousands of Xenocorps agents and hundreds of ships that set out. And only one damaged ship with just a few survivors ever returned!"

The Xenocorps troopers finally broke their silence. A tall, weathered woman, evidently the group's leader, spoke up. "That is true. All the records of the retreat were horrific. It was a running battle all the way back to the Orion Arm, with terrible losses among our forces. However..." She paused, and looked up at Kuanian pensively before continuing, "Despite the disastrous losses, the expedition returned an incredible number of tantalizing discoveries and treasures. It therefore actually turned a profit. We've never since mounted a similar effort. But now that your enterprise has been announced... it may open new possibilities."

"The point is moot," Bora said, shaking her head. "Humans are forbidden from crossing the Rift by the treaty. And, as you surely know, to attempt to cross the Rift is *lethal*."

"That is correct," Kuanian said. She had lowered her gaze to look directly at Bora, but she was still smiling, albeit a bit ominously. "However, no one here but Hayan and myself truly understand the nature of this lethality."

The room became totally silent then. Greymalkin looked around, nervously noting the way that the Xenocorpsmen had become even more grim, and many of the Canisians and Sojourners appeared fearful. Bora's expression was now troubled as she said, "None of us understands the... *Presence* in the Rift that destroys anyone that ventures there. Some suspect that it is a group of *Abyssals*, the powerful and poorly understood entities that inhabit the Carinae. But the Xenocorps were able to evade *those* beings." Bora glanced at the troopers questioningly. The tall, rugged Xenocorps leader scowled.

"You speak the truth," the tall woman said. "We learned how to evade the Abyssals of the Carinae during our last mission. But they are *not* the destructive force that haunts the Rift; we believe that even the psychopathic Carinans and Abyssals that inhabit the Carinae region fear the destructive entity in the Rift. Whatever the source of the... *annihilation* in the Rift may be, it manifested *after* we fled the Carinae. We have been trying to discover its nature throughout the centuries since."

"And what have you learned?" Kuanian asked, still smiling darkly. The scowl of the Xenocorps woman now became uncertain.

"Very little," she admitted. Then she squinted back at Bora. "But there are old stories, tales from millennia past that we have learned from our Sojourner colleagues." When everyone looked back to Bora, she shrugged.

"The annihilating force that we are speaking of lays in the direction that in the days of Old Earth was termed the constellation Vela," Bora said absently now, apparently thinking to herself. "It is true that the *Presence* there in the Rift has waxed and waned over time. There were ancient rumors from the Thannic Colonizers as long ago as the First Interstellar Exodus of beings with unimaginable power there in the Rift. Because they still thought in terms of the constellations of Old Earth, the Thannics named these entities Velans, although they sometimes also claimed that there was only one being, a single being of inconceivable power that they simply called *The Velan*." Bora glared at everyone around her then. "There were reports of distant sightings, but never recordings. *Bah!* There have been tales of monster sightings as long as humans have lived. Such stories have never been confirmed, by us or anyone else."

"We suspect..." the Xenocorps leader said slowly, now returning her attention to Kuanian, "that the destructive entity in the Rift may be one of the Old Ones, the Builders, the entities that were known to exist millions of years ago and that left so many incomprehensible ruins behind throughout the Galaxy. But the Sojourner is correct; no one knows what the thing is that lies in wait there in the Rift. The only thing that is certain is that for the past three centuries, no humans that venture there ever return. Neither do the Thubans venture there. Even the brazen Jotuns fear the region, although they are said to sometimes attempt furtive crossings. It was explicitly forbidden to humans by the intergalactic treaty with the Andromedans a millennium ago. When we ignored that prohibition three centuries past, we learned the hard way that the treaty was made with good reason, and we paid the price in lakes of blood for our transgression. But you still propose crossing the Rift?"

Kuanian slowly surveyed the room, still smiling as she looked into all the skeptical and fearful faces one by one. Finally she said, "It may interest you to know that there are *exemptions* within the Accords which allow the expedition I am describing, and that I have secured *safe passage* for anyone that accompanies me in crossing the Rift."

Sister Bora and everyone else looked shocked at that statement, and the room exploded with exclamations once again. "That's impossible!" "Safe passage? How?" After Bora glared at everyone around her long enough, the noise died down and she faced Kuanian again.

"Such an expedition," Bora hissed in outrage, "a return to the Sagittarius Arm, will surely never be launched, and I am skeptical of your claim of safe passage for anyone attempting the crossing. In fact, I find this entire discussion rather fanciful!" At this point, Kuanian's grin turned into a sprightly laugh.

"Daring and fanciful, yes!" she said, her eyes flashing with excitement. "But also a *fact* at this point! Our expedition was launched without fanfare *a year ago*. We have now established a foothold of bases throughout the Carinae. And what we have found *beggars the imagination*. Astonishing natural resources and wealth, yes, of course. That much has always been known concerning the Carinae.

"But we have also found the *unprecedented*! We have discovered not simply the traces of the former Xenocorps expedition there, *but evidence of living human colonies in the Carinae that long predate the previous expedition!* We have come here to this symposium precisely because we need the help of Sojourners to unravel this mystery. Why? Because the ruins of human societies we have discovered are *millennia* old, and the living human colonies we have encountered *are what you term Bereft.* Fallen, despairing human survivor cultures that have somehow persisted despite their proximity to the Carinans, and desperately need assistance of the kind that you are best prepared to provide. We thought of you because this opportunity is precisely the sort of challenge that your Order is dedicated to addressing, is it not?"

Once again the room exploded in clamoring voices, and Greymalkin felt light-headed. *Ancient Bereft human civilizations in the Carinae?* It sounded impossible. He looked at Sister Bora. She and all the other Sojourners stood incredulous and astonished. Here and there he saw that some of the Brothers and Sisters were brightening with grins of wondering delight, and he realized that the same grin was on his face. In the moment, he did not know what to think, other than that something amazing had just happened. *Have we been given a new purpose?*

"And there is more!" Kuanian somehow made her voice audible above the din. "The most provocative aspect of the Carinae! You speak of the Old Ones, the Builders? Through our own investigations my people have learned that an ancient trove of secret knowledge can be found in this region, a trove left behind *by the Builders themselves*, secrets that may be the most valuable of all the treasures to be gained in this expedition!"

Now the room became deafening as everyone in it began to shout out questions and exclamations. Greymalkin put his hands on his head for a moment. This was unheard of. Data troves of the Builders had always been the greatest treasures to be found in all human space. Access to the undiscovered information of a major Builder trove was the ultimate prize imaginable to any crew of Sojourners. *She's offering us the chance to access untold amounts of ancient information in the Carinae and bring it back for all of Humankind? This could reinvigorate the Order itself, not just our memory ark!* He wondered if he was dreaming for a moment.

When the bedlam finally died down again after several minutes, Kuanian asked them in an exultant tone, "Well? What have you to say? Would you be interested in joining our expedition or not?"

Bora recovered from her shock and said, "Well... *yes*, this changes a great deal. We will have to think about what you have shared with us very carefully."

Then the Xenocorps leader spoke up again, looking from Bora to Kuanian with a frown. "These... *scholars* are all well and good, however, you will also need those trained to deal with dangerous and chaotic environments such as the Carinae. We are experts in such matters."

Many of the Sojourners made derisive noises, and someone (he thought it was Soren) called out, "We can take care of ourselves!" Kuanian's smile remained, but her eyes narrowed appreciably as she faced the Xenocorps leader. Hayan looked irritated, and his deep voice rang out through the room. "We have sufficient security forces already," the big Sadorian said. The tall Xenocorps leader raised one eyebrow.

"Do you?" she asked in a neutral tone. "We heard rumors of this project before it began. Some of your... *other allies* in this enterprise have certainly found utility in the Xenocorps. They have covertly hired many of our units, and we have been keeping their bases safe for them. We think you might be well-advised to do so as well."

The dour Canisians now finally spoke up. They were all burly men and women with the dull utility clothing typical of their capitol realm Omicron Canis Majoris, marked by the impassive, flat faces and muscular, squat builds of the countless heavy-gravity warrens there called the *Jabhah*. An older, thickly bearded man that was evidently their leader said, "And consider us as well! Not for protection, but gaining new wealth! We are miners of shadow gems, aureate, and flux. Your expedition is surely very expensive. All know that the Carinae possess vast resources. We can help you realize riches untold!"

Kuanian studied the Xenocorps agents and the miners. Eventually she said, "Perhaps. But we already have many such as you at work in the Carinae now. What we lack are, indeed, *scholars* to research and attend to the mysteries we have uncovered there." She turned back to Bora with an inquisitive expression.

Bora and Soren had been staring at one another, communing privately. Now Bora spoke again, this time in a quiet voice. "We may be able to help. What research specialties do you most need?"

"Archaeologists and linguists to search the ruins for the secrets of which I spoke. And your famous civilization rescuing missionaries to assist the collapsed human societies we have found. But do the Sojourners attending this meeting have these skills? I was told—" and Kuanian briefly shot a friendly glance at Greymalkin before continuing, "I have it on good authority that the particular variety of black robes that all the members of your group are wearing represent those who are experts at *helm control*." Greymalkin winced. He *had* mentioned that detail to her as he had shown Kuanian and Hayan around. Sister Bora noticed Kuanian looking at Greymalkin, and sniffed slightly before replying in a tone that sounded faintly insulted.

"You were correctly informed, but perhaps your source of information failed to mention that all Sojourners have both operational and *research* specialties. Here for example; this is my colleague Brother Soren, who is not only a senior helmsman but also an experienced researcher in precisely the field you are seeking, archaeology. Not only this, but the fact that we are all Helm Crew is doubly fortunate for you. Surely you are aware that this memory ark has become permanently stranded here in normal space. The vessel no longer requires the services of the Helm Crew, and we now have the option to leave our duties here for other prospects."

Kuanian nodded and said, "I see! Excellent! Who among you are interested then?" The Sojourners looked at each other nervously.

Greymalkin had heard enough. His heart was pounding but he screwed up his courage and prepared to raise his hand. Before he could move, a new voice from the back of the room spoke up that had a nasal, reeding quality to it.

"Before any of you jump into her soup bowl, you may wish to know a little about what lies in wait for you in the Carinae." Everyone looked around for who had spoken, and Greymalkin saw that it was one of the two sly-looking men in the back with folded arms. The thin man that spoke gave everyone an unpleasant leer and then fixed Sister Bora with an intense stare. "*You* said it, *you* named the central problems with this lunatic scheme. The *Carinans and the Abyssals*. Murderous butchers and monstrous fiends! Anyone that attempts to go to the Carinae is simply sticking their head into an execution slot!"

"Who are you?" Brother Soren asked loudly. The wily fellow shrugged.

"Just an interested observer. My friend and I wanted to see if anyone would be stupid enough to fall for this Sadorian trick. I give them credit, they're convincing. But you may wish to find out a bit more about what you're getting into before being dropped into that nightmare."

When Greymalkin turned to see how Kuanian would react, he saw that she and Hayan had become cold and still. Then Hayan boomed at the scrawny man, "Hold your foul tongue, Accursed cybe!" Greymalkin blinked in surprise at the term that Hayan had used. *Did he mean that purely as an insult, or was he actually serious?* 'Cybe' was the common term for a cybernetically conditioned slave.

"Slander me all you like, Sadorian!" the lean-faced man sneered. "But you're the fool, because *everyone knows that what I say is true.*" Hushed discussions started in the audience. Hayan tensed for a moment, but Kuanian put a hand on his huge arm.

"What is your answer, then?" Sister Bora asked Kuanian directly. "He has a point. The Carinans have always slaughtered any intruders in their space."

Kuanian broke her icy stare at the thin man and took in the room, solemnly this time. She finally turned to Bora, and said, "I will not say there is no risk in this endeavor. Certainly, the Carinans are extremely dangerous. However, the time for beginning our project was very carefully selected. Our realm has studied the Carinans cautiously for centuries, much longer than any other human society. We selected this time for the expedition because of the Carinan cultural and biological cycles which we have observed. They periodically all withdraw deeper into the Sagittarian Arm for an extended period. We also know when they will return. As for the Abyssals, while it is true that they are even more advanced and dangerous than the Carinans, we have become quite adept at avoiding them ourselves. But it is true that there are many other dangers in and on the way to the Carinae beyond the presence of Abyssals and the Carinans, not least the *Velan* threat in the Rift which you have mentioned. *No one* should expect this journey to be anything but extremely hazardous. But I tell you this in solemn pledge, neither the Carinans, the Abyssals, nor *any other menace* will present problems for anyone who accompanies me in *our* transits to the Sagittarius Arm. And I promise you in all sincerity, this mission to the Carinae is the most significant historical event of our time."

The audience began chattering again. After first looking surprised and then scowling furiously, the scrawny fellow in the back practically shrieked, "Liar! She does not know this! She cannot know! Anyone who follows her will die horribly!" After Hayan gave the man a truly menacing stare, the incensed little man and his companion fled, stomping out of the hall angrily. Greymalkin saw that just as they were leaving in rage, Father Johannes was entering the hall. He looked after the two men in confusion, but then saw Greymalkin and began to make his way through the crowd to him.

"Please, my friends, listen to me," Kuanian said, her voice now calm and reassuring, "Those two are Burani servants, and all here know that the Burani have long been our enemies. They always spread fear and dissension; this is no different."

"But there is indeed great danger where this expedition will be going," the rugged Xenocorps leader said levelly. "You said it yourself. Any who join this endeavor will need protection. You must take precautions." The murmurs in the audience rose slightly.

Kuanian looked down for a moment, and Greymalkin thought he saw her nod ever so slightly to herself. Then she looked up and smiled wanly, her gaze resting on the Sojourners. Many of them now looked troubled, and became more so as she spoke again. "The greatest precaution one can have is to be forewarned, and I will honestly share with you the most worrisome detail that we have uncovered so far. The Burani do indeed appear to be very interested in our endeavor. We are concerned that they may have infiltrated themselves among some of the personnel our other allies brought to the Carinae. If you choose to join this expedition, be wary! As I said before, there are vast sources of information that may be acquired in the Carinae. The Burani always seek to control and hoard knowledge above all other resources. Keeping secrets for their own gain is one of their most successful strategies. Again, be wary of them, always!"

After a pregnant silence, Bora spoke up again. "If we have additional questions, may we speak with you again later?"

"I will hold several more discussions during the days of your symposia series," Kuanian said. "Despite the dangers, I hope to convince many of you to join our endeavor. What will be accomplished through this journey will be *wondrous*. We will continue this conversation later. For now, though, please consider what I have said to you today." With that, she and Hayan swept back out of the room as quickly as they had come. Kuanian followed Hayan, and everyone scattered out of the way of the huge Sadorian as he strode directly for the entrance to the hall. Then they were gone.

Father Johannes came up to Greymalkin, obviously puzzled. "What was that all about?" he asked. Greymalkin wondered how to best explain everything that had happened. In the wake of the Sadorians' departure, the other members of the audience were all leaving the room. Sister Bora passed Johannes, and the two former colleagues glared silently at one another for a moment. Greymalkin held his breath, hoping that the two might somehow reconcile. But both of them were stubborn and proud. *I know that Johannes thinks Bora endangered the ark, and surely Bora is just as bitter as I am.* The moment passed. Bora and the other Helm Crew filed out of the room without saying anything, leaving Johannes and Greymalkin alone. The older Sojourner looked at him expectantly.

"You missed a most... interesting presentation," Greymalkin finally said. Johannes looked at the backs of the last Sojourners retreating down the corridor.

"Evidently so," Johannes said. "Can ye accompany me tae the refectory and tell me about it oer a mug of something hot? I've not eaten. And I still wish tae continue our discussion regarding my proposal tae ye."

Greymalkin nodded, remembering their last conversation. He began to recount Kuanian's presentation as they walked down the corridor, but paused as he did so. It had suddenly occurred to him that he now had *options*. He'd been stuck, conceptually in limbo ever since the ark had been beached. What else was there for him but the *Dragon King*, even if the ship was now a dead monolith? But the words of Trystia from so many months ago came back to him. *"You were meant to navigate the stars. But it really is your decision, Greymalkin."*

And now he actually had an enticing second option! It was as Bora had said: *Yes, this changes a great deal.* But as he recounted every detail of Kuanian's amazing story, he saw that it was neither news nor enticing to Johannes, who simply grunted in affirmation at key points in the retelling. By the time he finally reached the end of the story they were sitting in the refectory, and Johannes was looking troubled after finishing his meal. He shook his head.

"Yes, I was aware of this mad adventure from confidential reports the senior Bridge Crew received months ago. So they've finally announced it publicly, and now they've even come tae us. But I doubt she'll get any volunteers," Johannes said in a resigned tone.

"Why not?" Greymalkin asked in genuine surprise. "Not even Sister Bora?"

"Come now, Grey," Johannes said, his voice tired. "Even Bora, despite her disgrace, is nae a reckless fool. I'm nae admirer o' scum like the Burani cybes, but *they're not wrong.*"

Greymalkin scowled. "The Burani and their cybes, that's another thing that astonishes me. How could the Abbot allow such depravity on the ark? Not only letting Burani on the ship, but to also permit them to actually bring enslaved human beings on board? Disgusting!"

"I agree with ye on that, Grey," Johannes said, lowering his voice significantly. Greymalkin gaped at what Johannes said next in a vicious whisper. "Black blast the Abbot! There's nae mistakin' his treachery now! He was always a cruel man, but to be in league with those scum? I did nae believe it myself before, but somehow they got to him! "

"What!" Greymalkin exclaimed, and then dropped his voice as well. "What do you mean? Is he actually... *working* with the Burani? In all space, *why?*"

"I dinnae know the whole of it," Johannes said, very quietly. "It's part o' somethin' much larger that I don't yet fully ken. No one knows all of it, and there many like me throughout the Order that are fightin' it quietly. But you must understand, Grey, this treachery is why he'll nae be the Abbot forever."

"He's what... *leaving*, then?" Greymalkin hissed. "Being withdrawn by the Order? Will... will it be soon?"

"Nothing so dramatic or immediate," Johannes whispered bitterly. "It may take years still, but the choices he and the other corrupted ones in the Order have made will nae go unpunished. Those among us who still have sense understand that it was his choice to have the *Dragon King* beached, and how black and foul it was to put off the blame on ye! It may take some time, but he'll be gone. That's why ye must come tae Operations for the time being! Ye'll have a future there where I can protect ye, not like poor scapegoat Bora and the other Helm Crew."

Greymalkin looked down sullenly, thinking for a long moment on what Johannes had said. It changed everything, and yet, it also changed nothing. "I'm still Helm Crew at the moment," he said. "I can't stand the way everyone looks at me. I'm glad you know what happened, but everyone else blames *me* for what happened. It's outrageous! And he'll be here for *years*, you say? I can't stay on the bridge and abide that... that *traitorous tyrant*."

"What else will ye do, then?" Johannes said impatiently. "Get ye'rself demoted to go back and start oer as an Initiate somewhere else on the ark? Be sensible."

After hesitating, Greymalkin said softly, "Well, there's the Carinae, then."

Johannes had leaned in close for the conversation. Now his eyes flared, and he jerked up in his chair before quietly snapping back comments under his breath. "Dinnae be *thick*, Grey! That's nae a path forward, it's just *death*. Be serious!" When Greymalkin sat silently, Johannes began to speak very quickly, earnestly, and in the most concerned tone he had ever heard his old friend adopt. "*Now ye listen to me, laddie.* Ye've never been on a Bereft mission, ye've never even been on a lawless and savage planet among *Sojourners*, much less among the sort o' *cutthroats and thieves* that'll be skulkin' through the lairs and holes in the Carinae!"

"The Sadorians seemed honest enough. And they said they'd planned carefully," Greymalkin said stubbornly. Now Johannes actually looked frightened, which was more alarming to Greymalkin than anything the Xenocorps leader had said. He'd never seen fear on his friend's face, and he knew Johannes was not afraid for himself.

"There's something ye need tae know about those two Sadorians," Johannes said, his voice dropping even lower. "The Abbot made me swear that I'd keep it a secret, but his own word is worthless, and I'll share it with ye if I must, if ye're seriously considerin' this madness."

Now it was Greymalkin's turn to feel uncertain again. "What is it, then?" he whispered.

"These two Sadorians, Kuanian and Hayan. Ye remember that I met with them earlier, along with the Abbot and Burke?" Johannes paused. He seemed very troubled. "I can nae tell ye about all o' that business, but understand this—those two are not like ye or me."

"Meaning what, exactly?" Greymalkin asked, confused again. Johannes seemed to wrestle with himself for a moment, but finally continued.

"Ye've read about them, I'm sure, or at least those like them," Johannes muttered. "But I'll dare say ye probably never thought tae actually encounter their like. I certainly never thought I would! They're *Risen*."

Greymalkin froze. "That... seems hard to believe."

"But ye know what I'm talking about?" Johannes pressed. "As studious as ye are, ye must have read about them...."

"Yes, I've read about them quite a bit. But, no, I never thought I'd meet any of them," Greymalkin said very quietly.

"They're the most extreme category o' the transhumans, metahumans, transcendents, whichever o' the various terms ye want tae use for truly *enhanced* humans, the ones that consort with far more advanced alien species that traverse human space. In the case o' the Sadorians, ye surely know that they've long been allies with the Thubans."

"Yes," Greymalkin said in a small voice. He was thinking of the incomprehensible synesthesia effects he'd experienced when he'd touched Hayan and Kuanian. "I felt... *very strange* when I shook hands with them." Johannes jumped on his statement.

"That blasted huge shadow jewel in yer head, laddie! It seems tae give ye a twisted piece o' good luck every now and again. Good, then ye'll believe me when I tell ye that they are *not normal*; they consider themselves higher beings than we are. We're just tools tae them, board pieces in whatever games they scheme at playing. And they will nae hesitate tae move a pawn into a death trap if it advances their goals."

Greymalkin's insides turned queasy. He thought it over, and felt unnerved. "But... they seem trustworthy to me," he said. Johannes tilted his head to the side.

"A fine sort of cunning-clever scoundrel ye'd be if ye could nae come all convincing! I'm telling ye lad, ye can nae trust them. Do *not* throw yer life away!"

Greymalkin tried to think of something to say, and eventually just closed his mouth. *What do I actually know for certain about any of this, really?* he thought to himself.

But after a long moment of looking at Johannes' pleading expression, he realized that there were at least two things that he was certain of, deep down. The Abbot had bullied him, made him feel ashamed of who he was, and hopeless about ever doing anything with his life.

But Kuanian and Hayan, whatever bizarre sort of higher beings Johannes thought they might be, had been friendly to him, made him feel proud of who he was, and had made him feel that he could achieve something *inspiring and meaningful*. Johannes seemed to panic as he saw Greymalkin's expression change, as they both realized that the young Sojourner had made the most important decision of his life.

RIFTS

Greymalkin had been sitting in the dark metallic space simply staring at the wall for an indeterminate time when a thought finally occurred to him. It took him another full minute to realize that the thought had been, *What just happened?*

He looked around himself uncertainly and gasped in pain, realizing that his head hurt horribly. He was in some kind of mechanical space, and a few meters away from him a huge object rolled by on a rail in the dark at incredible speed. A few moments later, another one zoomed past. Intuitively, it seemed to him that it was not a good idea to be sitting dazed in a dark mechanical space with large moving objects zipping along nearby. But he found that he could barely make his body move at all, and wasn't sure that trying to move was such a great idea when his head felt this bad. But as the objects continued to speed past him in the darkness, his anxiety level began to climb almost as rapidly. *Where am I? What just happened to me?*

He tried to think, but the pain in his head was pounding so badly that it drove out everything else. He tried to remember what had just happened. *I'm neuro-stunned. That guy, the Naotian. He stunned me.* An image flashed in his mind of a Naotian pointing something at him, and then incredible pain and lights erupting in his head. But what had happened then? For a moment there was nothing and then another memory flashed by in his mind. *I fell. I fell off the catwalk. But why was I up there?*

Greymalkin groaned and rolled over onto his hands, trying to get up. But his hands were wet with some dark liquid, and he slipped, almost smashing his face into the deck. He stayed like that for a moment, the tip of his nose touching the icy metal. He couldn't get up, not yet. He eased himself down, and tried to roll onto his back. But something (a pack?) was strapped onto his back, and all he could do was lay on his side. Alarms were trying to go off in his mind like blaring klaxons, but everything was clouded by the pain. *What happened? What in blazes happened to me?! I've got to remember. I've got to get up!*

Trying to remember caused a torrent of random memories to fly through his swirling mind in no kind of order, ranging from instantaneous images like the Naotian to various events that had happened to him recently.

Pieces of all the planning that had taken place after the day of Kuanian's presentation came back to him. He remembered conversations, not so much in the details but how he'd felt about them, whether frustrated or intrigued. He remembered long discussions with Sister Bora and Brother Soren about all manner of preparatory activities, and things he'd said in embarrassment or frustration, like when Soren kept hounding him about preparatory training. *Blast it, Soren, I did just complete the entire emergency preparedness training course series on travel in hazardous realms! I know it will be dangerous, I get it!* But then again, nothing in that course had taught him what it was like to actually be neuro-stunned.

He raised his head to try to orient himself. *I'm on the Naotian hoard-lair starship. I must be somewhere in the human supercargo section, maybe the hold?* He wasn't sure; their ship was so big it was very easy to get lost. He remembered the initial staggering impression of size and scale when he'd come onto the hoard-lair. The thing was even bigger than the *Dragon King*, and he recalled the confusing process of trying to learn the bizarre organization of the vast interior, especially in order to avoid the forbidden central cavity where the huge Jotun pilot dwelled like a gigantic cyborganic octopus wrapped around the central mast of the ship. *But wait, why in all space did we get on a Naotian vessel?* He couldn't remember yet, his brain was still a vicious buzzing storm spinning around in circles.

He abruptly felt sick and retched violently onto the deck. The random thought that occurred to him was, *Thank Benevolence that there's air here and I'm not wearing a helmet!* Helmet? He wasn't even wearing a void suit. *Why not?* There were so many questions that flashed and disappeared like his memories. But the question of why they would be on a Jotun galactic transporter nagged at him fiercely, like someone was yanking on his robe sleeves incessantly to get his attention. Then, as he finally levered himself up onto his hands and knees, a piece of that complicated story flew past through his consciousness.

Something had happened in the weeks after Kuanian's presentation that disrupted her plans. *That's right, she told us that the Burani had bribed the Alban authorities, and all of a sudden the Albans would not permit the Sadorians to transport us out of the Periphery and across the Rift.* He remembered how sad Kuanian had looked, and the depression that they'd all briefly fallen into. Even as powerful as she was, Kuanian was not willing to violate Alban laws and decrees. It appeared they would not be joining the expedition after all.

But then Brother Soren spoke to the Xenocorps. Soren! He seemed so against the Xenocorps, but it turned out he'd worked with them much more than he let on. They told him about another way to get to the Sagittarius Arm, a surreptitious approach that they'd planned to take if they could ever convince Kuanian to hire them. But it would be expensive, and that put an end to that idea for a while. Monks like Soren and Greymalkin didn't have the needed funds. *But then Soren asked Kuanian for the money.*

Greymalkin remembered the conversation between Kuanian and Soren. Soren hadn't wanted Greymalkin there, but Kuanian had come to trust the young Sojourner during the weeks he'd served as her guide on the ship and insisted. After she'd questioned him repeatedly, and Soren finally admitted that the idea was to bribe a Jotun to smuggle them across the rift. Greymalkin had known that Jotuns traveled throughout most of the Galaxy, but he had not known that *any* humans traveled with them, not even the Jotuns' human servitors. Kuanian had not liked the idea. She didn't trust the Jotuns, even though the Xenocorps claimed they could be trusted. It had required a long argument, but Kuanian finally reluctantly agreed and gave Soren the required funds so that they could book Jotun passage and join the expedition.

Then... then.... Greymalkin had only been semi-conscious for seconds, but even through the horrendous pain, his mind, body, and memory was starting to function again. He heard gears shifting somewhere, and realized he was laying on top of rails, the rails of an automated cargo transfer system. He was *inside* a big mechanical assembly of heavy moving cargo shuttles, and probably had seconds left before one of them came flying down the tunnel he was in. *Get up! Get out of here!* Through a supreme effort he stood up and staggered out of the cargo shuttle tunnel into a maintenance walkway, just in time to avoid getting pulped by one of the big transporter pods shooting through the space he'd been laying. He stumbled a few meters up the tilted walkway in the darkness towards a source of light, and managed to safely reach the access walkway exit pit. It was still dim, but there was a little more light than where he had been before. He looked up. He could see the catwalk above him, and realized it was the same catwalk where the Naotian had stunned him. Greymalkin looked down into the dark space that he knew led into the cargo shuttle tunnels. *I must have fallen down here, and then I rolled down that ramp onto the rails.* He *probably thought I was dead, and I almost was! But, I couldn't have been down there for more than a few minutes....*

Greymalkin swooned for a moment, almost losing consciousness again. He leaned back against the wall of the metal pit and took a moment to catch his breath. Events were flooding back into his mind, all the subsequent weeks of preparations Greymalkin had undertaken with Bora and Soren. The three of them were the only Sojourners that had agreed to go. *Kuanian was so worried about the three of us going alone.* But they had all been determined. Bora and Soren had not wanted to take Greymalkin, but he'd insisted, threatening that he would tell the Abbot about the plan if they wouldn't take him. They finally agreed.

And then there was all the equipment, supplies, and information Kuanian had given them. She'd even acquired a skiff for them that they'd picked up at the main Burdock spaceport after they left. And Greymalkin remembered some of the more mysterious equipment she'd given them. *She made such a fuss about that special gold-colored garment and the multi-tool. Said those two items alone would save us if we got in trouble.* He remembered that Bora and Soren had just looked at each other, and then at Greymalkin before insisting that *he* take the special gear. *Right, I put all that stuff from Kuanian in my pack,* he thought. *And I've got my pack here.* In the dim light he was now seeing, and not just feeling, the straps of the pack around his shoulders. But something about the pack triggered a terrible sense of dread in his mind. *Wait, the pack... something about when I put on the pack....*

Then he heard voices above him on the catwalk, and crouched down hiding immediately, even though the movement greatly aggravated the pain in his head. There were Naotians talking up above him somewhere.

Greymalkin grit his teeth in abrupt anger. More memories of what had happened were now flooding back. *Those bastards! They sold us out!* He thought back over the disturbing weeks they had been on the hoard-lair among the Naotians, trying to put the memories back together in sequence.

* * *

He still remembered the shock of meeting the Naotians. After the trio had left the ark, it had taken weeks of travel in the skiff that Kuanian had given them to reach the rendezvous. They'd stopped for resupply at two widely separated Sojourner arks, monastic communities that were much smaller than the *Dragon King*. The Sojourners of the two priories they'd stopped at had been happy to help them, and had not doubted their cover story of being on a missionary voyage. The trip out had been relatively easy; Greymalkin had been exhilarated. It was fun.

Then when they finally reached the remote location where they were to meet the Jotun starship from Naos, things became much darker. The Sojourners had learned that the Naotians were actually engaged in illegal traffic across the Rift with groups in the Sagittarius Arm. Apparently the Jotuns did illicit business with the Carinans, and for a price would smuggle the Sojourners all the way across the Rift between the two galactic arms. Sister Bora had especially disliked the idea of dealing with Jotuns, but Brother Soren had reminded her that it was the only way they could reach the Carinae. The huge aliens were afraid of the danger in the Rift, but also the only ones brash enough to risk the transit. It had sounded like a logical plan when they had discussed it along the way, and Greymalkin had been in a good mood from the two cheerful visits they'd had with the Sojourner priories on the way. But when the ominous and gigantic black egg of the Jotun hoard-lair blotted out the stars and pulled the skiff inside one of its vast holds, their trip became far darker.

After the skiff had been pulled in and clamped down, the hold had quickly become pressurized, and he'd felt a pressor deck activate under them. When he, Bora, and Soren had exited the skiff the grotesque

Naotian crew had been there to meet them. And all Greymalkin could think was that the Naotians were the most disturbing humans he'd ever encountered.

Greymalkin had always thought the history of the star Naos was interesting, and the fact that humans had long ago been enticed into willingly becoming indentured servants there to the incredibly advanced gigantic aliens. The Jotuns were an old galactic species named after creatures from ancient human mythology. They had evolved beyond their original biological forms into immense cyborgs when humans were pre-sapient hominids on Old Earth. He'd studied many mnemotomes on both the Jotuns and their Naotian human vassals, but they were deeply unsettling to actually meet. In person, the Naotians looked like walking corpses with blank white eyes, and had personalities to match their appearance. They'd taken the Sojourners from the dock hold straight to their austere living module. On the way there Greymalkin had been able to look up through big transparent panels of eoncrystal into the vast central cavity of the Jotun hoard-lair where the pilot dwelled among its unknowable treasures mounted in huge containers around the interior of the colossal space. The Jotun itself was every bit as big as he'd imagined. Its mass of cyborganic tentacles were wrapped around the starship's primary central mast, and at the end of all the tentacles was the swollen shape of what was evidently the alien's main body or perhaps head, propped up on a perch overlooking its domain. But Greymalkin had no clear understanding whether the immense black bulb at the end of the tentacles was actually the creature's head or not. The mnemotomes he'd read had no information on the innards of the huge aliens. The steely-black mass glittered with small lights in the darkness, and the only visually distinct feature was a colossal hole in the middle of the thing's gaunt "face". It might be an eye, an ear, or an anus for all Greymalkin knew.

He had wondered what to call the monstrous pilot of the hoard-lair starship. When Greymalkin timidly asked the Naotians, they had curtly informed him that the Jotun's name translated into the ominous, if aptly descriptive, human phrase "Lord of the Forbidden Ways." None of the Naotian humans seemed to have names or designations other than the one that was the apparent leader, an unnerving female (at least, Greymalkin thought the Naotian was female) that called herself the Warden of the Forbidden Ways.

The Warden was the only member of the crew that ever spoke to them in the gloomy days that followed as the Jotun hoard-lair starship hurtled through shadow space across the empty void of the interbrachial Rift toward the Sagittarius Arm and the Carinae. It turned out that there were a handful of Canisian miners on board as well as the Sojourners, but they kept to themselves, just as Bora and Soren had mostly either stayed in their quarters or done maintenance work on the skiff. Greymalkin had been the only one interested in trying to talk to the Naotians, despite their disturbing appearance and behavior. The Warden had seemed slightly interested in talking to him initially. He was intrigued with her at first, and had tried to have coherent conversations with her despite her unsettling demeanor.

Greymalkin had heard that Naotians had long ago adapted their minds to the alien thought processes of the Jotuns, and that was very evident as he tried to follow her bizarre chains of associations and statements in conversations. But he'd eventually made some progress and learned a few things. The Naotians communed mentally with one another much like other civilizations throughout human space, through signals transmitted from the shadow jewels embedded in their brains from the time they were infants. However, the Naotians were rather blunt in such practices. They only seemed to use one unencrypted network for all such communal thoughts between them, unlike the complex channels for directing communal thoughts that Greymalkin was accustomed to among Sojourners. But they also communed *constantly* with their Jotun overlord on a special channel encrypted like nothing Greymalkin had ever encountered. He came to realize that although they were technically individual organisms, their entire lives were centered on nothing but obeying and pleasing the Jotun. He became uncomfortable when he understood that they were less like a crew of the huge ship, and more like the Jotun's cybes.

The horrible realization had finally come to him that if all Naotians were like these, then they were effectively a race of impassive slaves owned by aliens. *Or completely absorbed by them.* Greymalkin had discovered that the Warden did not seem to have thoughts like an individual person, or even like a human being. Rather, she seemed more akin to an organelle of the composite being that was comprised of the Jotun and its retainers, which made a strange sort of surreal sense given their circumstances, even though he personally found it appalling. Although they were effectively enslaved by the Jotun, that characterization didn't actually seem accurate to him, simply because they no longer seemed to possess any kind of distinct sense of self *apart* from the enormous alien. Remembering his studies of endosymbiotic organisms, he tried to classify her relationship to the Jotun. While he'd first labeled the Jotuns as parasites, he began to wonder if the relationship was actually *commensal*, because the humans really did not seem to care about themselves at all. The Jotun benefitted, but the humans that had effectively become a part of the vast alien life form no longer seemed to either truly benefit or truly suffer. *Because they no longer exist. They're completely changed, transformed into something totally new and different from humans. Not even separate individuals, just instrumentality of the Jotun.* Try as he might to accept them and their culture, their utter subservience still made them seem like grotesque mockeries of human beings to him. It sometimes made his skin crawl, and he had occasionally thought it was the most obscene relationship he'd ever imagined.

Because of the mental differences separating him from the Naotians, it was difficult to discern whether they even possessed personal interests and motivations any longer. The only things they thought about were what the Jotun cared about, mainly its greed and acquisitiveness, and occasionally its fears. Greymalkin gathered that, interestingly, they were indeed all very afraid of being detected by the interbrachial entity that Bora had called the Velan. He remembered the discussions on the *Dragon King* with Kuanian about the danger of the Velan before they had left; it was the single biggest risk of crossing without her that she'd expressed. The Velan was indeed related to the Old Ones, the Builders, a broad category of truly ancient and unknowable beings. They seemed to inhabit only shadow space and came and went in the interbrachial voids through means that no one understood, not even the alien species that were far older and more advanced than human beings like Jotuns and Thubans. The Velan terrified the Jotuns, because the only thing that they evidently knew about it was that the thing was very territorial, and attacked and destroyed anything that moved between the galactic arms, even the mighty hoard-lairs of the Jotuns.

In fact, the Jotuns were apparently fearful that the Velan, whatever it was, was actually *hunting* them, seeking for them whenever they transited the Rift. Initially, that had briefly struck Greymalkin as oddly humorous, that the inconceivably powerful Jotuns were themselves terrified of a still *more* powerful being. *I guess that no matter how powerful you are, somewhere in the Galaxy there is always something more powerful for you to be afraid of. How funny.* But then Greymalkin had thought about what would happen to the Sojourners if this Velan monster succeeded in finding the Naotians, and it had not seemed very amusing to him anymore.

Wait, the Velan.... Hiding in the dark access pit, listening to the Naotians talking on the catwalk above him, Greymalkin had fought through the agony in his mind and remembered more of what had happened. *The others were on the lookout for the Velan. Now I recall, there were more than just the one Jotun on the hoard-lair.*

The sense of anxiety in his mind rose even more than the pain as he thought about the other Jotuns. He felt dizzy and leaned against the cold metal wall again, letting his head droop. Then he noticed that something was dripping off his forehead. He reached up and touched his temple, and almost yelled in even worse pain. The acute new pain jolted him into taking several deep breaths, and he felt more aware than before. The new pain came from a substantial wound on the side of his forehead, and he could feel a line of blood down the side of his face. *The dart. The Naotian shot me with a neuro-stun dart. That must be where it hit me. But... my hands....*

Greymalkin looked at his hands in the dim light, seeing now that they were totally covered in blood, far more than could have possibly come from the wound on his head. *Blood?* Then he froze in horror, his mouth gaping open. He squeezed his eyes shut, moaned low in his throat, and slumped against the wall. He was finally becoming fully conscious, and everything had come back to him.

He'd been coming back from checking on the skiff. The word from the Naotians was that the hoard-lair was finally drawing near to the Sagittarius Arm and would be there in another day. Bora and Soren had become exceedingly paranoid about anything happening to their small ship, and had asked him to run yet another diagnostic on it. As he was returning to their quarters he'd seen something incredible. The vast central bay of the hoard-lair was visible through the big eoncrystal panels above the skiff. The huge Jotun-sized doors of the central bay had opened to the void, and he could see and feel the billows of shadow space passing by them at an incredible pace.

Then through the big doors came two enormous black shapes one after the other. Two additional Jotuns had joined the first one curled around the central ship's mast. He was surprised at how fast the immense alien cyborgs could move. And dropping from the two behemoths were the tiny forms of humans in dark void suits, presumably more Naotians. The pressor deck was slowly dropping them to the interior hull, and he'd realized they would land fairly near him. Some instinct had made Greymalkin hide at that point, although he was not sure why. Perhaps it was the atypically fast movements of the Naotians. He'd never seen them hurry, but these were leaping and bounding across the deck to the airlock, which they cycled through in a rush. As they emerged on the side of the hold with air, he'd seen the Warden emerge and meet them. The Warden had spoken quickly with two of the arriving Naotians, and at first Greymalkin had simply been pleased to gain more practice in understanding the Naotian language that he had been studying for weeks. But the conversation had chilled him to the core.

"Welcome to you, fellow Wardens! How fared your masters, the Lord of Vigilant Power and the Lord of Persistent Defense? Did they find our opponent?" the female Warden had asked. Greymalkin had been pleased that he could understand her speaking rapidly; it was the most animated that he'd ever seen her. The two new Wardens were both male. They lost no time in delivering their information.

"Yes, the Velan is near, but was detected in time. Our Lords are conferring above, and adjusting course to avoid our adversary," the biggest male Warden said, and although his voice was flat and almost emotionless, Greymalkin nevertheless thought he could hear a tinge of some kind of impatient excitement. The next statement from the man revealed what the emotion was. *Bloodlust.* "But we also bring word from our Burani suppliants. The contract was completed, payment was made, and it is now time. All of the passengers must be put to the sword. No trace may remain afterwards."

Greymalkin's blood had run cold, and he'd crouched even lower in his hiding place. The panicked fear that had turned his intestines to jelly had also made his legs wobbly. He saw the female Warden nod curtly, and all the Naotians had pulled out ranged weapons, shadow blades from the look, weapons that could project a blade through shadow space at a distance. Then the Naotians had bounded off into the corridors of the ship toward the passenger compartments, leaving Greymalkin petrified.

There had been a few terrible moments of uncertainty, but then Greymalkin had unsteadily run after the Naotians, hoping desperately that he could evade them and reach Bora and Soren first. He briefly got lost in the confusing warren tunnels of the hoard-lair, and then had a fright when he almost ran headlong into another group of Naotians, a group that proved to be headed for the Canisians. He heard blood-curdling screams erupt from the Canisian quarters and ran on in anguish. Greymalkin wondered fearfully what he would do if the Naotians were already there at the Sojourner quarters. Should he try to distract them to give Bora and Soren a chance? At almost the last second, he dodged back into a side corridor as he heard a group of the Naotians pounding toward him. He caught only a few words of what one of them was saying.

"—wants the last one alive to question! Hurry up with the rest of this!" the big male Warden barked. When they'd passed, Greymalkin got up, heart pounding, and rounded the last turn. What he saw made his vision constrict into a tunnel view as he ran forward.

The wall and door to the Sojourner quarters had been hacked to pieces. He could already see that the walls of their quarters were splattered with a mass of blood, but he forced himself inside to be sure neither of his friends was still alive. When he saw the interior of the room he did not scream, because his consciousness simply locked up for a few seconds. There were no bodies; the Naotians must have taken them. But the number of arterial blood sprays on the walls was simply incomprehensible to him. In some distant part of his mind still functioning, he clung to the thought that Bora and Soren had probably been killed almost instantly as the Naotians tore them to shreds with the shadow blades from outside the quarters, straight through the wall. It certainly hadn't been painless, but it *had* been quick.

He looked around the room in quivering shock. When he realized from the fetid smell that some gobbets of flesh on the wall were viscera from one of his friends, he finally threw up. That had been when he fell onto his forearms retching, and his hands had been thrust into the pools of blood. Despite his utter panic, he made himself take a few seconds to look around the room for anything that might be usable as a weapon. That was when he had seen his pack amid the torn debris and blood. He thought of the multi-tool in the pack, grabbed the strap with a hand trembling like a leaf, pulled the pack out of the blood, and ran.

Greymalkin had dashed several meters down the corridor before he skidded to a stop, feeling like ice water had been dumped over his head. He had absolutely no idea where to go or what to do. The Naotians were looking for him and had an entire ship of incredibly advanced technology with which to find him. *What do I do? What can I do?!*

Then he thought of the skiff. It seemed impossible, but escaping in it was the only thing he could think of at the moment. He'd sprinted away down the corridor, and up into the catwalks toward the hold where the skiff was locked down.

* * *

That's when that Naotian shot me, Greymalkin thought, at last reassembling his memories. *They were trying to capture me, and not kill me for some reason. But I fell down into their cargo handling system, and they were afraid to follow me until they shut the system down. They'll be looking for me any time now. I've got to get out of here!*

Although the combination of the neuro-stun and the adrenaline pumping through his body made it seem like hours, it could only have been a few minutes since Bora and Soren were killed. Trying to ignore the pain, Greymalkin peered around the deck under the catwalk. The Naotians were only a short distance away and hadn't seen him. They were still talking, probably trying to figure out how to shut down the cargo handling system so they could go down and find his body. *They're in no rush, because they think I'm dead. I have to go now, before they come back here.*

He took several deep breaths, and then crawled out of the access pit and into the shadows under the catwalk. He tried to be as silent as possible, but every scuff or scratch against the deck sounded incredibly loud to him. He made his way toward the hold with the skiff in it, but then paused thinking.

How in blazes will I get the locks off the skiff? Or for that matter, how can I possibly launch the ship? He thought about it furiously. If he could free the locks, get inside the cockpit, and then somehow open the hatch doors underneath the skiff, it would just fall out into the void. But surely there would be codes required to operate everything in the hold. They'd probably locked the access door to the hold by now. He wondered if he could use the multi-tool to pry open the door. Greymalkin knelt down, tried to wipe some of the blood off his hands onto his jumpsuit, and opened the pack. He fumbled through the pack, first finding the elegant clothing that Kuanian had given him, and then the multi-tool. The strange tool was elegant, beautiful... and totally unfamiliar to him. And it seemed to be inert. It didn't do anything when he tried to activate it. What had she said about these items? She'd provided Bora and Soren with some sort of verbal instructions, some of which he'd overheard, but now he couldn't recall anything that she'd said. He thought he heard the Naotians talking in the distance again, and cowered down again for a moment. Then he looked at the tool once more, searching his memory. Finally some of what Kuanian had said came back to him.

She said these two things had to be "claimed" by one of us, that they would "attune" themselves to the person and the circumstances. And then he remembered that she'd indicated a small pad on each item where you were supposed to press your finger for a few seconds. Trembling, he pressed on the tool's pad, holding his thumb on it.

For a few seconds nothing happened. Then, to his relief, the tool activated. But just as he was about to test its controller, something wholly unexpected happened that made him gasp. The tool emitted an astonishingly bright pulse of energy into shadow space, so bright that it completely blinded his synesthetic senses. His normal human eyes were unaffected, but now he had no idea how or if he would be able to pilot the skiff. *What in all of space was that?!*

Apparently the pulse of energy had been so brilliant that it had blinded the Naotians as well, for he heard them screaming a hundred meters away across the deck. And as he blinked, looking around himself in disorientation, he saw that high above him even the three Jotuns holding to the hoard-lair's central mast were squirming around in agitation. Frantic to not be seen, Greymalkin scuttled away through the shadows under the catwalk, zig-zagging right and then left toward the skiff, to try to put more space between himself and the Naotians. He finally approached the vicinity of the hold, and started to climb back up onto the catwalk to reach the pressure door into the hold. But then he heard shouting voices inside and hid again. Several Naotians, including the female Warden, came pouring out of the hold door holding their heads and practically screaming in pain. He heard her shout, "What caused that cursed flare? Check the sensors! Did it draw the attention of the—" After the Naotians bolted away on the catwalks, he cautiously climbed up and lunged at the slowly closing door. He managed to catch the edge of the door just before it could swing shut again.

Hunh. It looks like that sudden flare of energy from the tool hurt them even more than me, Greymalkin mused. He didn't know if it had permanently blinded his shadow sense or not, but at least it had distracted the Naotians.

He cautiously looked inside the hold. The long and dim space held a row of huge containers even bigger than the skiff, all held tight in docking clamps. The Sojourner skiff was hanging there at the end, an ovoid of mirrorshell with the mast extending out of the stern of the ship. It was held tight vertically, the massive docking clamps clutched around it. Greymalkin listened carefully for a few seconds, wondering if there might still be Naotians somewhere inside the big hold. But there was no time for caution; he had to take his chance while he had it. He crept into the hold, and let the heavy pressure door close behind him with a thud.

And now it came down to it. He didn't know how the Naotian systems worked, how to activate them, or how to open the big clamshell pressure door that led to the void outside. Deciding that he had to do something, even if he wasn't sure what, he scampered across the catwalk to the closest docking clamp. The thing was colossal, and was firmly in place around the stern of the skiff. He looked at it closely from the edge of the catwalk, walking back and forth to try to get an idea of how it worked mechanically. *I don't have time for this, they'll be coming back!* His panic began to swell inside him as if it were rising water lapping around his neck, and starting to swamp him in blind fear. He looked around the vast room for any sort of clues.

Then, looking back down the catwalk toward the wall of the hold, he noticed a set of control panels. He ran back to them and, after taking a deep breath and trying to focus, examined them carefully. He knew enough Naotian to understand that the panels were some sort of emergency controls, but the indicators were too cryptic. Then furious communal thoughts flooded his mind, and he could not help but utter a terrified shriek.

«The emergency systems are not active, Sojourner.» The thoughts of the female Warden came to him like a flood of burning acid. He looked around wildly, and his panic exploded when he finally spotted her and two other Naotians behind the window of the hold's control blister high above him. He cursed in his mind. *She's seen me! I'm dead, I'm dead!*

«The emergency systems aren't active yet, but we are having a bit of a crisis, nevertheless. So, I don't have proper time for you. I like you though, so I'll give you a small opportunity. If you can climb to the top of your spacecraft and board it quickly, I'll release you into shadow space. You might even activate your ship's continuity manifold in time to avoid being obliterated. Go ahead. Climb quickly and you may survive!» Her thoughts were angry, and he couldn't tell if she was sincere or not. Since he had no other options, however, he sprinted toward the stern of the skiff.

As he grabbed handholds, he thought about what a long vertical climb it was to the top of the ship. As he levered himself up the side of the skiff desperately, he wished they would turn off the pressor deck function in the hold so he could float up. *Small chance of her doing that!* he thought bitterly. She undoubtedly had turned off the safety systems in the pressor deck mechanism, so that if he lost his grip she could enjoy watching him fall to his death against the hold's clamshell doors hundreds of meters below him. He tried not to think about that possibility.

And then he thought of the secondary airlock on the skiff.

The secondary was much closer to him, but it was on almost the *opposite* side of the ship from him. *But it's out of her line of sight! Will she have that side of the ship on a camera view, though?* Trying not to be obvious about his intentions, he started randomly grabbing protrusions on the hull that led toward the side of the skiff where the secondary lock was located.

When he could see the secondary airlock doors just ahead of him on the hull and felt a gasp of hope against the panic and still ringing pain in his head, the Warden communed with him again. «Canny, Sojourner. I didn't see that additional pressure lock at first. You might have actually reached it. But I just wanted to get you off the platform and onto your ship before I expelled it. If you hadn't set off that flare I'd have more time to play with you and make you climb back around until you fell. But now we've got to focus on evasion maneuvers, and I need to say goodbye.»

High above him, he saw the Warden give him a skin-crawling smile and then leave the control blister. There was a heavy sound far beneath him, like huge bolts being unlatched. Then a wind in his face quickly built up into a blast that loosened his fingers' grasp on the skiff. Greymalkin screamed and felt himself slipping.

His last grip on the skiff slid away and he felt himself falling. He started to scream again, but his breath was knocked out of him when his arm and back impacted on something. Stunned again, he found himself lying on another one of the catwalks, staring up at the empty control blister. Above him there were more heavy clunks and then the sound of metal grinding on metal. He registered that the clamps on the skiff had been released, and he saw the ship falling past him, almost within reach of the catwalk he lay on. He tried to roll toward it, wondering vaguely if he could jump onto it. But he was caught on something, and too dazed by the fall to move quickly enough.

He looked around and saw that his pack had been caught on some sharp protrusion. One of the straps and the top had been ripped open onto the catwalk. The odd gold-colored garment had partly come out of the pack. Its intricate and elegant patterns were spread out right in front of his eyes. He sadly reached out to touch it as he felt his ears popping. The air was quickly blowing out of the hold, and he knew these were his last few seconds.

I failed Bora and Soren. I failed myself. And I failed Kuanian. As the wind grew thin and quiet around him, he wished he had been able to see the Carinae just once. He'd known that Father Johannes had been right; he would probably be killed if he went to the Sagittarius Arm. But he'd wanted to accomplish that one wondrous thing, something that he could feel proud of once again, something to go together with the moment of personal triumph he'd felt in steering the Dragon King through the shoals. So he wouldn't feel ashamed. So he wouldn't disappoint Kuanian. But now, that would not be happening. He felt the tears in his eyes boiling away into the vacuum.

As he reached for the golden garment in those last seconds of clarity, he glimpsed the tab on it and wanted to claim the gift from Kuanian before he died. It was the last connection he had with her or anyone that he considered a friend. He touched the tab and held the tip of his finger down on it with a small, sad smile. He was gasping for air, but there wasn't any. He knew hypoxia would make his last moments less painful, so he opened his mouth fully.

Which made it all the more startling when the golden garment exploded towards him violently and engulfed his face with the soft punch of a fabric fist. Because his mouth had been open the satiny cloth jammed down on his tongue all the way back to his throat. He was already so stunned that he had no conscious thought other than to simply blink and flinch backward forcefully enough that he slipped out of the remaining pack strap, the backward roll sending him falling off the catwalk into empty space. In an instant the supple cloth had poured over his entire body, and through the contact around his head he distinctly heard it *snap* crisply all around him tightly. Then came an even more astonishing moment as he felt the cloth in his throat pucker and expel air into his lungs, inflating him like an empty balloon. Greymalkin gasped the air into his raw, burning lungs. His head was not only horrendously dizzy, but he realized as he opened his eyes that he was literally spinning. He could see the open clamshell doors of the Jotun hoard-lair starship spinning through his field of vision every few seconds... *and he was seeing them from outside the ship.*

Greymalkin would have screamed again if he hadn't been desperately sucking air into his lungs. His joints ached from the brief depressurization, and his head was such a mass of different flavors of agony that coherent thoughts were impossible. He found that he could move, albeit painfully, and cautiously felt his chest and limbs. It was gradually dawning on him that he was still alive somehow. *That gold-colored robe... it was some kind of cybernetically aware void suit. It deployed onto me when I activated it.* Blinking, he realized that his vision had cleared, and he found that a transparent helmet now surrounded his head. His shadow space synesthesia was slowly clearing as well, as he began to perceive the shadow space billows all around him, flying past in waves as the Jotun hoard-lair hurtled forward.

I'm drifting away from the Jotun starship, he realized, and some weak echo of his previous panic came back. *I'll hit the edge of their continuity manifold soon! I've got to get to the skiff somehow.* He looked around the spinning sky until he saw the skiff slowly tumbling through the void a few hundred meters away from him.

Several things happened simultaneously over a few seconds. His synesthesia cleared enough that he realized the golden void suit had a control display, and that it included a labeled section that grabbed his attention: *void maneuvering controls.* He had just managed to halt his spin, and was facing the slowly turning skiff when something happened that he couldn't understand or even fully process. Out of the distance in the void, a complex and shifting bone white structure emerged rapidly. It quickly filled his entire field of view and then whirled past him. The impossibly complicated form of the thing was shifting rapidly before his eyes, and he realized he was seeing some kind of four-dimensional structure crossing through his three-dimensional space.

What is it? Greymalkin had no idea if it was an artificial structure or some kind of inconceivably large cybernetic organism. As it passed him, the far flung beams and pillars of the smallest parts of the structure grew larger and larger as they approached and then swept around and past him. Seeing those portions of the structure pass around him finally gave him some sense of scale of the thing, and he gasped. It wasn't simply kilometers wide, it was the size of a small planet, and it was moving fast. As the vast object flew past him eerily in the complete silence of space it seemed totally unreal to him... until he saw one of the giant structural beams graze the comparatively tiny skiff. The impact must have been incredible, because fragments of the sturdy little vehicle actually chipped off and flew away in a spray. The skiff spun away from him then, whirling so violently he couldn't even follow the motion. He stared at the spray of tiny chips scattering away in the distance of the void. The hull of the skiff was made of mirrorshell, an incredibly tough shadow space stabilized substance that was harder and tougher than any simple alloy of metal. He watched a few more of the structural beams pass by him, knowing that if any of them hit him he'd instantly be rendered into a suit shaped bag of bloody fluids. But the thing continued by him, now slowing as rapidly as it had arrived.

He tried to scan through the half of the sky that the thing occluded in his vision. There seemed to be a centroid to the vast moving object, and he realized that it was following the Jotun hoard-lair. The immense shape quickly engulfed the asteroid-sized Jotun starship, despite the Jotun dodging back and forth like a frightened bird in a cage. Then the enormous array of shifting structures and beams contracted abruptly, like a constricting fist. He saw a blaze of incredibly bright reflected light from inside the clenched cage of structures, a blaze that briefly dazzled both his eyes and shadow sense synesthesia alike. And just like that, the imposing Jotun hoard-lair was gone.

Greymalkin blinked again, and wanted to rub his eyes. He could barely see anything, but had a sense that the stark white network of shifting structures was now constricting around him. He couldn't help experiencing a moment of dark humor. *I actually survived getting thrown out of a moving starship into shadow space... and now I'll be squashed like a bug.*

He waited while the shapes converged around him, his senses beginning to clear. He wondered why it was taking the thing so long. It had crushed the Jotun starship in short order. The complicated structures were shifting and unfurling out of other dimensions closer and closer around him. Then his mind seemed to simply slow down with a combined sense of dread and awe. Through the shadow jewel in his head, he felt a *Presence* all around him. He looked up into the mass of elegantly shifting forms that blanketed his view... and knew the Presence had a mind beyond anything he had ever imagined in his wildest dreams.

The sensation was like communing, except that the Presence didn't seem to be intentionally communicating with him. It was so all-encompassing that it felt more as if it was merely considering him, and its thoughts were so limitless that they had *subsumed* his own existence. In the twinkling of an eye he knew many things that Presence knew or *was thinking* as it studied him. This vast being was what Bora had called the Velan, and this was its territory. The three small tricksters (*the Jotuns?!*) had known that they were forbidden from entering its territory, but had done so anyway. They had crossed through the space too often, and now the Velan had dealt with them. But here was a tiny, tiny being that had managed to escape them....

Greymalkin saw himself as the Velan saw him, a kind of microscopic organism. The tiny organism *interested* the Velan as it scrutinized the infinitesimal mind and memories of the larval being. Then the Velan realized that the tiny creature was alone and in terrible pain. The Presence reacted as it considered those facts. Greymalkin had no words or concepts for what the Velan thought, its mind was much too complicated. It seemed to Greymalkin that there was almost every emotion and sentiment he could conceive of there in the Presence of the Velan. Utterly implacable resolve. Boundless benevolence. A sense of intrigue deeper than an ocean.

Despite the fact that compared to the Jotuns he was virtually an innocent bystander, apparently Greymalkin's presence in the forbidden territory of the Velan had still condemned him to death.

Greymalkin could not help thinking this was incredibly unfair, that he had done nothing at all, had not even known that he was trespassing in what the Velan considered its personal space to protect, and yet still had to die for some reason after surviving everything that had just happened. But as the huge being examined him even more closely, he quailed before it, feeling as if his mind would burst with the torrent of feelings and thoughts pouring through him from the vast alien. Then the Velan's thoughts seemed to look far away for an interminable moment. Greymalkin had no idea if it was looking across the Galaxy, or into the past or the future, or something else entirely, that he couldn't understand at all. But he had the sense that the Velan might have discovered a... *loophole* in whatever hard-hearted rule that had condemned the Sojourner to death.

It came to him that the Velan was considering asking him a question. It was a monumental question of some sort, and apparently Greymalkin could be set free if he answered correctly. But there was a problem. If Greymalkin was asked the question (*whatever it was!*), providing him with the context and background of the question would also serve to *invalidate the loophole*. The young Sojourner began to panic again. It sounded like one of the many philosophical dilemmas he had studied long ago, dilemmas that had no answer. In desperation, he tried to shut down his terror and think logically. Then he thought of another way to approach the dilemma. *But how do I communicate with this being?*

He did not know the Velan's language (or even if it had something humans would understand as language), but he could try *direct communing*. The technique was essentially what was already happening as Greymalkin sensed the Velan's general thoughts through his shadow jewel implant, albeit as a one-way communication. He didn't know if his mind could generate a sufficiently strong signal for the Velan to sense what he was thinking, but he tried anyway.

«Can you sense my thoughts?» His communing seemed like an insignificant noise in comparison to the Velan's mind. Yet, the vast being seemed to be focused on him, so Greymalkin continued. «You can read me, I think, literally like a book. I understand that.» He sent the thought in acceptance of how miniscule he was in comparison to the Velan. «Whatever the 'question' is, ask *yourself* what I would answer. I'll accept whatever the outcome of your analysis is, as long as there's a chance that you'll *spare* me.»

Greymalkin felt that the Presence of the Velan was examining him closely. Then there was a change of some kind, and the Velan seemed to be... *making something?* He had the sense that it was doing the equivalent of writing a program. Or maybe a poem, for all Greymalkin knew. Then the Velan seemed to look deep into his mind, and Greymalkin felt an utterly bizarre sensation of delicate... *shifts* in his thoughts. He felt as if he was hypnotized, staring into the shifting four-dimensional structure of the Velan for an interminable time.

A great peace settled over Greymalkin's mind then. He didn't know why. It was probably some effect of communing with the Velan. He felt a sense of acceptance and inevitability spreading out into infinity around him. Slowly, he closed his eyes. The last thought he had before losing consciousness was simply, *Let it be, then*.

Prisoners

At some point, Greymalkin regained consciousness. He knew only that he had slept in a long dreamless sleep somewhere warm, and when he finally woke up he found to his surprise that he was in the medical pod on the skiff. The cover of the pod had just retracted, along with the medical bands across his chest and head. Apparently the pod had successfully healed his most grievous injuries in the time he'd been unconscious.

For several minutes he simply laid there, completely relaxed, and remembering nothing at first. Then everything came back to him, like a crushing weight settling steadily down on his chest. He sat up in the pod, and slowly began to sob quietly. Bora and Soren were dead. Murdered. The memory of the ghastly room of fresh bloodstains was as horrific in his mind as when he'd first seen it. He sat there alone, with the finality of it sinking in on him. He would never speak to either of them again. He'd known elder Sojourners who had passed away peacefully on the ark, but none of them had been his friends. Sister Bora might have been stern, and Brother Soren was sometimes aloof. But they had been his friends, and they had embarked on this ill-fated journey together. Now they were gone, and he couldn't help thinking he had failed them.

I should have been with them. I should be dead as well, he thought. But then he sat up straight, remembering the overwhelming, stupefying awe of encountering the Velan. And yet again, he ruefully found himself wondering, *Wait! What just happened?*

He looked around the cramped interior of the ship with his eyes, and scanned outward with his shadow sense. The skiff was adrift in the immense channel that the Jotuns had been following toward the Sagittarius Arm. There was nothing around him but endless shadow space for parsec after parsec into the distance. He felt utterly alone.

Greymalkin wondered what the Velan had done to him. He searched his memories and then his thoughts... and had an immediate shock. *There was something else in his mind.* It was not a second set of thoughts, but was definitely not his mind either. It felt uncanny, like a wordless, imageless, yet structured memory. No, not a memory. It was more like a frozen echo, but of what he didn't know. He thought about it, searching through all the strange stories he'd ever learned of similar phenomena in the years he had studied on the ark. Then the symptoms of what he was feeling finally found a match in his memory. And he felt intimidated.

It's a covenant, he thought, becoming depressed. The most sophisticated cybernetic programs overlaid onto human minds were called covenants, and included the directive cybernetic programs that the Burani and others used to transform humans into cybes. *But what's it for?* he wondered. *I don't feel compelled to do anything. Or not do anything.* His mood became even more morose. *Bora and Soren are dead. And now I'm a cybe.* But something about that last thought did not ring true. He had felt the Velan's mind directly. It had no interest in human slaves. None. He was sure of that now, if nothing else.

And the structure in his mind was unbelievably complex. It had been grafted onto the shadow jewel in his mind, a vast cybernetic fractal resonance web of cryptic information. Examining the structure he began to realize that the data there was even more complicated than *his brain*. It reminded him of the Velan, except that it was intangible. Then he realized that, more accurately, it reminded him of the *Presence* of the strange being, not the physically gigantic structure of the alien. The

Velan had left him with a mandate of some kind, a complex set of instructions that he might or might not be compelled to obey without question.

And I have no idea what it's for or does. Great, just great. He knew he had no one to blame but himself. After all, he'd been the one to propose the bargain with the Velan. But at least he was alive, there was that....

After feeling miserable for a while, he decided that he'd better try to get on top of the situation. He climbed out of the medical pod and, since he was naked, went to look for a flight suit. When he went into the tiny cubby that he had claimed as a bunk on the trip out, he stopped, staring. On his bunk were the neatly folded gold garment and the multi-tool. He slowly picked up the golden robes cautiously, wondering if they were going to explode all over him again. But nothing happened. He looked at the multi-tool, wondering how it had gotten here. After thinking about it for a minute, he wondered how *he* had gotten here. He hadn't been in any shape to reach the skiff. The Velan must have returned him to his vessel. For all he knew it had made him sleepwalk into the medical pod. Then the memory came back of how the Velan had collided with the skiff and damaged it. His eyes widened, and he dropped the two artifacts and ran to the cockpit.

Once there, he quickly did a status check on the skiff. Unsurprisingly, he found that the skiff was significantly damaged from the impact. After sorting through all the damage, he saw that the biggest problem was that the ship's mast was out of alignment. He grimaced. That limited his options. The skiff was not going to function very well, and not for terribly long. If he was going to reach any kind of help, he'd have to do it soon. He groaned and looked out at the shadow space surroundings. There were relatively few gas clouds here and the skiff was not actively moving, so there was no sense of passing billows.

Instead, it seemed perfectly still. There were star systems out there, but all of them were many parsecs away. Greymalkin sat back to think carefully about his next actions. He had to admit, his situation looked grim. He started ticking off his liabilities. He was alone, and knew no help would be coming. The skiff was damaged, and while he had ample shadow flux in the tank, the ship would be very inefficient with a misaligned mast. He'd run out of flux relatively quickly. His assets? *Well, number one I'm alive.* While he was alive there was hope. Two, the skiff. Even damaged, it was still keeping him alive and provided a means of movement. What else did he have? He thought for moment. *Three, all the stuff Kuanian gave us.* He knew that Bora and Soren had stored a large archive of information that she'd given them in a special mnemotome of which they'd been very protective. Greymalkin had not studied it as intensively as they had. He'd trusted to their wisdom and judgement.

And, of course, there were the two mysterious artifacts that she had given them, the golden garment and tool. After mulling it over, he decided that while he definitely needed to examine the garment and tool, he'd do so after first checking the files in Kuanian's mnemotome. He needed to get the ship moving while he was still able, and without the guidance in her files he didn't know where to go that would be remotely safe.

It weighed on him that the Naotians had mentioned that the Burani had bribed them to kill all of the passengers on the ship. Why had the Burani done that? Kuanian had said they had also bribed the Alban authorities to prevent their departure through the original departure point that Kuanian had planned. So, he could well imagine that it would also have been consistent for them to bribe the Naotians to kill them.

He remembered the Burani cybes that had attended the first presentation Kuanian had given. They were obviously against the expedition, but what was motivating this extreme reaction? And what would happen when they realized that he was still alive? But that was unlikely to happen soon, he thought, given that the Jotun hoard-lair and everyone on it had been destroyed by the Velan. No one except Greymalkin would know what happened for the foreseeable future. But if he successfully managed to reach the Sadorian expedition, then they would likely find out, surely? And when they eventually found out that he had survived, they'd likely come after him again. The overwhelming fact of Bora and Soren's murder made him paranoid. *I need some sort of protection.* He went to find the mnemotome from Kuanian.

Everything in the ship that had been loose when the Velan collided with the ship was either broken or jumbled around the interior of the skiff. He eventually found the eoncrystal mnemotome that he remembered among Bora's scattered personal effects. It was in a box together with other items that Kuanian had assembled for them. Greymalkin said a sad remembrance chant for Bora and Soren, and then activated the tome to study it.

An hour later he was still studying the contents. Kuanian had provided them with what information she had about the Carinae, and had made many arrangements for them. He knew that the original plan had been for the Jotuns to drop off both the Sojourners and the Canisian miners at the primary basecamp of the expedition. Once there, she had arranged for the Sojourners to transfer to another vehicle she'd purchased for them that was better suited to the shadow space environs of the Carinae. It relieved Greymalkin slightly to think that there was another vehicle to replace the skiff, until he remembered that he was nowhere near the base, and also that if the Burani were trying to kill them that they'd almost certainly be waiting there for him. He began checking the shadow space topography of the region of the Sagittarius Arm that the channel led towards. He eventually realized that he could not reach the basecamp at his current rate of flux consumption. He'd have to stop at one of the secondary caches that were closer.

But one way or the other, I need protection, he thought again grimly. He scanned through the mnemotome looking at the entries that listed potential allies. There were several individuals that Kuanian had arranged for the Sojourners to meet up with... but none of them were near the arrival base.

He kept scanning until he found an entry that caught his attention. It was described as an emergency option to be used only if they felt themselves in extreme danger. *That tracks with where I am now,* he thought sourly. He kept skimming the entry, which was ominously labeled "A Prisoner to be Freed Only in Extremis" within the tome. By the end of it he felt more perplexed than anything else.

The entry was hesitant and somewhat cryptic, as if Kuanian had not really wanted them to avail themselves of the option it described. He now recalled a brief discussion about this 'Prisoner' that he had overheard between Kuanian, Hayan, Bora, and Soren. Like so many other details of the journey he had not paid much attention at the time, but now he wished he had.

The discussion had been prompted by Soren, who had been the most paranoid of the entire group. *And he was justified, as it turns out,* Greymalkin thought. *Although it didn't do him any good in the end.* Soren had been worried about being attacked by unforeseen enemies in the Carinae, and at that point Kuanian had reluctantly discussed the 'Prisoner'. Once they reached the Carinae, if they felt that they were in grave peril they should consider availing themselves of the option. *Too bad we were attacked before we ever got to the Carinae,* Greymalkin reflected.

He remembered the way that Kuanian had reluctantly discussed the matter. She had said that there was an imprisoned being that could be freed and co-opted to aid and protect the Sojourners in the Carinae.

But when she had brought up the option, Hayan had immediately objected strenuously. That was why Greymalkin remembered the exchange at all; it was the only time that he could remember Hayan ever disagreeing with *anything* that Kuanian proposed. He had been curious about the reason for it. Thinking back now, Greymalkin tried to recall what Hayan had actually said.

He remembered it had been something akin to, "Mistress, you cannot recommend freeing that wretched monster, especially given what happened the last time it was loose!" His comments had immediately convinced the Sojourners that it was a bad idea, but Greymalkin remembered that Kuanian had persisted.

"You have asked about a scenario of extremis," she had said to Soren, ignoring Hayan. "If you are in true danger, seek out this imprisoned being. It is indeed a formidable combatant, and will be able to defeat virtually any threat you may encounter. But if you do avail yourself of this option, be absolutely certain to first activate the deterrence measures in *this* device." She'd held up an odd looking device that looked alien in origin. Now Greymalkin saw that the odd apparatus was among the other items she'd included in the box. "This device will imprint anyone who activates it with a special code. This code will both prevent the imprisoned individual from harming you and will also ensure that it will obey your commands for a period of up to one standard year."

"You're saying that this device will make the prisoner into a cybe? An enslaved being?" Sister Bora had asked skeptically. Both she and Soren had shaken their heads, saying, "Sojourners do not purposefully enslave intelligent beings. We are sworn to oppose such practices." Kuanian had smiled gently, and shaken her head at them in turn.

"It will not *enslave* the imprisoned one. Admittedly, it will forcibly prevent the creature from attacking you, but that is not enslavement; it is simply protecting you from its violent tendencies. And the creature will not be forced to obey you. Rather, I am certain that it *will* obey you because of its desire for the reward that it will be offered through this exchange." When Bora and Soren had looked at her in confusion, she'd elaborated, "The creature will very willingly obey you in exchange for knowledge that it will receive in exchange for serving you for a year. You have my assurances on this point."

"Still, this seems like a decidedly... capricious and wayward course of action," Sister Bora had pronounced, frowning. Kuanian had nodded.

"Agreed. This is why I instruct you solemnly to abjure this option except in the greatest extremis," she had said. At the time, Greymalkin had thought the matter closed, and that they would never need to consider it again.

Now he was just as sure that he *absolutely* needed to avail himself of this 'Prisoner' that would supposedly 'be able to defeat virtually any threat you may encounter'. He was alone, and knew that someone had intentionally tried to kill him. That felt like extremis to him. After a bit of searching through the charts that Kuanian had given them, he realized that he would probably have enough flux to reach the relevant star system that was marked as the location of the imprisoned being.

He sat back in his seat, thinking. This was only the first of many decisions he knew that he'd be faced with in the Carinae, but it felt like a choice that would have enormous consequences either way. The image of the blood-soaked room came back to him again, and he shuddered. He charted a course for the star system of the Prisoner. It would take a few days to reach it. He was barely on the edge of the Sagittarius Arm.

In the days that followed he continued reading through Kuanian's notes, repairing parts of the skiff wherever possible, and meditating to calm and center himself. He reluctantly looked through the equipment on the ship to identify anything he could use as a weapon. Eventually he came upon some shadow space mining tools in a locker. There were two runcibles, tools that could be extended into and out of shadow space for mining or sample collection. The tools were peaceful applications of the same technology as the shadow blades that the Naotians had used to kill Bora and Soren. But even thinking about the idea of using tools like these to slice up a human being made him ill. He put the runcibles back in the locker.

He followed the channel and then the subsequent branches he had mapped out. Over the next few days he steadily got closer to the star system, and steadily became more nervous. Not only did he have little idea what he would find there, but the continuity mast of the skiff was continuing to warp further out of alignment. He was also watching the meter on the skiff's flux tank slowly dwindle. He looked out at the endless shadow space billows and stars before him, and felt decidedly vulnerable.

The day finally came when he reached the system and slowed to a crawl at its outskirts. It was a typical system with many small rocky planets and a few huge gaseous ones. His target was a moon of the biggest gas giant. He had barely pulled into orbit around the gas giant when it happened. Greymalkin was skimming the skiff around the rim of the planetary system when the bubble of his continuity manifold weakened and failed. He had been carefully keeping his distance from the enormous and vivid blue shadow space echo cast by the gas giant, together with the sharp traces of the widespread rings that circled the huge planet. The gas giant had dozens of moons, some of which were so big that they were essentially planets in their own right. He had to make sure to avoid them all on his approach, and it had distracted his attention from the mast and the continuity manifold. He caught the flicker of the manifold only at the last moment, when it was too late.

The emergency shunt failsafe kicked in at the last microsecond and dumped the skiff into normal space abruptly, with a wrenching sensation that made him gasp. *Every ship I pilot lately seems to end up beached,* he thought morosely. He looked up through the main view port. In normal space the gas giant was a vast angry orb of brown, orange, and red stripes. The rings were a fantastic array of amber and saffron hues shot through with ochre tinges. He took a moment to appreciate the view. He had not visited that many planetary systems before, and always found them breathtaking. While he had never set foot on a habitable planet, he had also rarely set foot on even airless rocks. This would have been a treat for him if he had not felt so exposed and vulnerable.

Greymalkin got out a small amplifier and began using the shadow jewel in his head to scan the gas giant system for energy sources and signs of living organisms, whether organic, cyborganic, or purely cybernetic. He immediately detected many telltale patterns in orbit around the gas giant, some of which looked to be at least small communities or clusters of some kind of cyborganic organisms. He also noticed something that gave him an uneasy sense of anticipation; there were three beings vectoring towards him rapidly from different directions, two cybernetic and one cyborganic. Judging by their acceleration rates, they would rendezvous with his orbital position within minutes. That would likely not give him enough time to try to reset the mast and depart. He put down the amplifier, very worried. If they were not friendly....

He quickly donned a void suit and, after a moment of hesitation, retrieved one of the runcibles from the locker. Greymalkin wondered what he should do. Contact the entities approaching him? Go outside the skiff to meet them? He decided that he wanted the protection of the ship and stayed inside. He busied himself trying to hastily reset the mast so that he could make a quick getaway.

As expected, he didn't have enough time. The first two cybernetic entities approached him very rapidly, in fact, they flew past him and collided with one another. As they flew past the skiff he gasped, and his fear boiled up instantly into near panic.

Although the exact taxonomic variations were unknown to him, he recognized the two cybernetic beings as fragmentivores, yet another example of the many feral descendants of cyborgs created in the dim past by the ancient Builders millions of years ago. Most cybernetic paleontologists thought that fragmentivores, or just fragvors, had originally been created by the Builders as recycling cyborgs designed to tear down and process wreckage. The feral descendants of those creatures survived by scavenging in environments that had old ruins or wrecks. They were extremely dangerous creatures to encounter alone in the wild. And Greymalkin was about as helpless as was possible.

"*Sard me!*" Greymalkin cursed in angry frustration. It looked like he was going to be killed no matter what he did. The two fragvors were evidently fighting each other over the right to scavenge his ship, and of course they would not hesitate to carve him up with the skiff. He desperately kept trying to finish resetting the continuity mast so that he could escape before they settled their differences. But the bigger fragvor had evidently already intimidated the smaller one, which was retreating. The monster was much bigger than the skiff, and came towards him with an array of cutting and drilling limbs already deployed. He tried to think of something to do to drive it off, but he was too terrified to think clearly. However, at the last moment, the creature spun around toward the third oncoming being that he had detected, which was now close.

The newcomer was not a fragvor. It was evidently a spacecraft of some kind, albeit very primitive looking to Greymalkin's eyes. But it was heavily armed. Missiles erupted from it and all of them streaked toward the charging fragvor. The explosions dazzled his vision, and he saw the big cybernetic scavenger thrown backward by the blasts. The explosions actually blew a large hole through the creature, and it abruptly went inert, spinning away into the distance. Greymalkin watched it go, and then looked at the oncoming spacecraft apprehensively.

The vehicle was simply a big framework of weapons rigged around a massively sized archaic fusion engine and fuel tank assembly. The only other thing of note that he could see as the primitive vehicle jetted to a stop outside of his view port was the perch for the pilot, who was sitting naked in the open vacuum of space looking at him curiously. Greymalkin gawked. It was a human being, or if not wholly human, at least a somewhat close *variation* on a human being.

By the look of him, the pilot was clearly one of the Scorpian variants of humanity, inhabitants of the human-descended civilizations of Girtab, Sargas, Graffias and other allied star systems in that region of the Orion Arm. Scorpians had long ago chosen to genetically modify themselves in drastic ways for survival in deep space, with adaptations like spiky exoskeletons and modified internal organs that enabled them to live in a vacuum without breathable air. The pilot was a particularly rugged looking individual, and some of the many spikes and knobs of his hard, dark grey exoskeleton were weathered and broken off.

As Greymalkin took in the pilot's appearance, he noticed that the primitive fellow did not have a shadow jewel implant and was actually emitting modulated electromagnetic waves. *He's communicating with radio waves?* Greymalkin was briefly surprised, but then realized that given the relatively crude nature of his technology, radio communication made sense. After analyzing the signals, Greymalkin was able to identify the modulation code; it was a common ancient standard that had been used for centuries historically. And the language the pilot was speaking was recognizably classic Scorpian, which had been one of the main linguistic trees Greymalkin had focused on in his studies. The pilot was asking simple questions that were easy to understand.

"Are you alright? Can you understand me? My apologies if I scared you, but that scavenger was threatening you," the pilot said. The fellow was in vacuum, so his vocalizations from inside his torso must have been transmitted through some sort of embedded microphone. Greymalkin caught his breath, and then carefully composed a response in his mind before speaking. The abrasive clicks and glottal stops of the Scorpian language were harsh, but he had practiced the language a great deal in the past.

"Many thanks! That was a very timely assist, indeed! I would have surely been killed by those fragvors," Greymalkin said over an emulated radio modulation that he activated in the communications array of the skiff. The pilot sent back an odd barking sound, which Greymalkin realized after a moment was laughter.

"No thanks necessary, my friend!" the pilot said boisterously. "I hunt these scavengers, and you handily drew them out of their hiding places for me. I can salvage a great many components and substances from the carcass of the one I just killed. One moment, I need to retrieve it before it spins too far away. I'll return shortly." The clunky looking vehicle pivoted and roared away with surprising speed and grace toward the steadily spinning fragvor body. Greymalkin used the time before the pilot returned to think about what to do.

Do I trust him? I don't have much choice except to do so, and after all, he just saved my life. But the thing that gave Greymalkin pause was the memory that historically the Scorpian cultures had often been allies with the Burani. Could this barbarian be yet another threat? As the Scorpian pilot jetted back out of the distance, the big carcass of the fragvor clamped securely on the front of his vehicle, Greymalkin decided to watch him carefully. *But I desperately need help.* The mast would require a lengthy realignment process with heavier tools than he had on board. He started to form a polite inquiry, but the pilot beat him to it.

"Do you need repairs? Your ship appears to be immobile, but I see that it is one of the interstellar vehicles of the Ancients, yes? I do not know how they function and can't fix it, but I can at least offer you a haven to work on repairing it, if that would help," the pilot said. Greymalkin grinned. Even through the thick Scorpian accent, he could hear that the fellow had a hearty, good-natured tone.

"Thank you! Thank you very much!" Greymalkin said. "I would greatly appreciate that. I don't have much, but maybe I can give you something in return...."

The Scorpian leaped out of his seat, and began fastening the skiff onto the front of his vehicle next to the fragvor. "No need for that!" the pilot laughed. "Keep your stuff, you'll need it out here in the wilderness. What in the name of the Ancients are you doing out here, anyway? From what I can see of you through that porthole, you look like a soft-skin. I haven't seen one of you in many years. And how do you know my language?"

"I'm a Sojourner," Greymalkin explained, nervously watching the big Scorpian nudging the entire skiff around with his bare hands. Granted, they were in a weightless environment, but it was still impressive how quickly the Scorpian could move around the thousands of tons that the skiff massed with nothing more than the muscles in his body. "I'm a scholar; I study languages of different cultures." The spiky head of the pilot looked around at him with eyes widened in a very human expression, even though his pupils were glowing with blue light inside grey sclera.

"A monk!" the pilot exclaimed. "We've heard of your kind, but only in legends and old folktales! The old stories say you were people of learning and wisdom that voyaged across the Galaxy to help people."

"Yes, that is our goal," Greymalkin said, pleased that in the middle of nowhere he'd found someone that actually seemed to have a favorable idea of Sojourners. After a moment he volunteered, "That's why I'm here. I've come all the way from the Orion Arm of the Galaxy, but I didn't expect to find any humans or near-humans like you here." The Scorpian finished securing the skiff to an extension of his vehicle's frame, and then gave himself a shove that sent him drifting up to the view port. He looked inside from only an arm's length away at Greymalkin, who apprehensively realized that the big man was more than two and a half meters tall, and muscled like a construction vehicle. The gnarled pilot looked at him with an expression that, to Greymalkin's surprise, also seemed anxious.

"Then it is fortunate that I have met you this day," the Scorpian said solemnly. "Good monk, my name is Bokin. I am just a scavenger myself out here in the ice rings and rocks, but I try to care for my family all the same. You are a man of learning. My father is very ill. Could you perhaps help him?"

Greymalkin was taken aback, but quickly said, "Pleased to meet you, Bokin; I am Brother Greymalkin Thomas! I have only very basic medical training, and I am no expert on your physiognomy, but I will of course do anything I can for your father in thanks for your help. I cannot promise that I can do anything for him, though."

The Scorpian nodded, and backflipped nimbly away from the skiff, landing squarely in the centrally mounted seat in his vehicle. "That is all I can ask. We go now." The fusion engine on the crude spacecraft fired again with a gigantic blast, and Greymalkin fell face first into the viewport with the resulting thrust before the pressor deck in the skiff could compensate. Although Bokin's vehicle was primitive, it certainly had plenty of thrust. Greymalkin could see that they were retracing the entire path that Bokin had taken when he first approached.

* * *

Because the skiff was mounted prow down, Bokin and his rig filled the viewport. As time wore on in the rig's steady burn and Greymalkin examined the Scorpian technology, he realized that much of it looked handmade. The rig was nothing but metal beams welded together. Speculating, he asked, "Bokin, how did you come to be here? I've only known your people to live in the Orion Arm."

The Scorpian looked up from his console with a solemn expression, and said, "The old stories must be true, then. It is said that our families first came here, to the wilderness, long ago as part of a venture of the mighty Xee explorers. The stories say that we were left behind when the Xee fled from the Great Hunters."

Greymalkin's mind raced. "You call them Xee?" he asked. "Could the explorers you speak of be the Xenocorps? They came here in the last great expedition to this region three hundred years ago."

Bokin lifted his arms in a gesture very close to a shrug, but his shoulders evidently did not move up and down. "The word sounds ancient, maybe that was their name? I don't know lore. But here we are."

"How many of you are there? You said you don't know about interstellar ship systems. Are you just here in the orbit of that big gas giant?" Greymalkin asked. Bokin glanced at the huge gas giant.

"You mean Big Orange?" Bokin asked. "Yes, our families live on the moons and rocks of Big Orange, although it is said that others live around other lights in the sky. I don't know how many we are. There are many of us on the moons. But fewer lately, because of disease and hunger. And the Great Hunters."

The scenario emerged in a straightforward way to Greymalkin, even though he still had many questions. There must have been humans from the Scorpia systems in the Xenocorps expedition three centuries ago. When the Carinans attacked and drove off the other Xenocorps forces, the remaining Scorpian explorers had survived by hiding wherever they could, and that evidently included the moons and rings of this gas giant. Without resupply, much of their technology would have failed over time. Now the descendants of the survivors were doomed to scrounge parts from feral cyborgs and whatever else they could find. *But what is their overall ecosystem? Have they developed mutualistic relationships with pre-existing cybernetic life forms like the fragvors? How?* Then Greymalkin gave a slight gasp.

Just like that, he realized he had discovered his first Bereft civilization. He felt a tightness in his chest and an electric thrill ran down his spine. *They... they need my help! I thought I just needed them, but they are Bereft.* Exactly the kind of fallen civilization that Sojourners were dedicated to helping. But reflecting, he realized that this was truly an exposed and dangerous region for anyone to survive, much less a Bereft society.

"Bokin, you mentioned the Great Hunters. Who are they?" Greymalkin asked. The big Scorpian paused before answering in a quieter tone.

"They live among the stars here. They come when we build structures that are too large. They do not want us to grow powerful or wise. Especially not wise. Always when they come they first make sure to destroy all our records of the old knowledge. They want us to be stupid so that we cannot fight back. We have learned to hide from them, but we also know the *Words of Peace*. The Great Hunters do not always abide by the Words, but the Words have saved us many times," Bokin said slowly.

Great Hunters. That must be the Carinans, then. But what in space are these Words he's describing? Greymalkin's mind continued to sort information and follow little trails of data as he thought about where this system was located in relation to the main Carinan areas in Kuanian's star charts. Greymalkin asked hesitantly, "Bokin, can you share the Words of Peace with me? I may meet the Great Hunters, and I do not know the Words."

Bokin brightened. "Yes! I can teach them to you," he said cheerfully. "They are not a secret, even though we learned them from the secret guardians, those who helped our first tribes. The Words of Peace are part of their scripture."

Confused, Greymalkin asked, "Who are the secret guardians? Are they humans or aliens?" Belatedly, he realized that he needed to adopt a mindset that prepared him to know nothing about the strange new realm of the Sagittarian Arm. And he realized that he needed to begin taking serious notes. Any minor information might be stray data that saved his life here.

"The secret guardians are humans," Bokin said, laughing again. "I forget, you have come from far away. The secret guardians are soft-skins, like you. They have always been here, or came here so long ago that even they have probably forgotten when. They spread the scripture of their goddess Holy Mother May. She discovered the Words of Peace and much more, but that was all long, long ago according to the Guardians. Hold tight, Brother Greymalkin Thomas, I must flip us over for deceleration."

As Bokin spun his vehicle and its cargo around to decelerate the rest of the way to his destination, Greymalkin marveled over these new pieces of what he already sensed would be a vast puzzle, the puzzle of the Carinae. *If I survive here long enough, maybe I'll figure it out.* But the bits he already had were fascinating. Apparently there were humans here that *predated* the Xenocorps expedition. If he could find them, he suspected they'd have many answers for him.

"Here are the Words of Peace," Bokin said. "Now listen carefully because you must say them very precisely. If you don't say them precisely to the Great Hunters when you meet them, they will kill you." Then the Scorpian emitted a truly bizarre sequence of modulated radio waves that just seemed like grating and screeching noise to Greymalkin. He had been prepared though, and had recorded the sequence.

"Can you say that a few more times?" Greymalkin asked. If he could identify the median sequences and analyze them, it might be a start on understanding these bizarre 'Words'. Bokin happily complied, and Greymalkin realized that the big Scorpian was enjoying this. Maybe it made him feel smart? After recording the sequence several times, Greymalkin put it through his linguistic analysis routines. The signals did not resemble any human language in his entire database, and even if translated into sounds, they didn't actually seem like phonemes that a human glottis and mouth would normally make. He identified the core sequence and adapted his vocalizer system to emit it as radio waves. The signals emulated regular sonic patterns, but were meaningless by themselves. After he was ready, he tried it out on Bokin.

"That's good!" the Scorpian proclaimed. "You are definitely a wise boy to learn it so fast. Now, say those words if the Great Hunters ever find you." After a moment he added, "If they give you a chance to say anything."

Greymalkin nodded. From the surviving accounts of the Carinans, he doubted he'd get a chance. They seemed more like killing machines than debaters. But this was something to start with. The signals were not human, so they might actually be a statement in whatever language the Carinans possessed. He wondered how the 'goddess' of the secret guardians had elicited the code phrase from them. *How could anyone have possibly gained access to that information?* After thinking about it for a time, he asked, "Bokin, do you know what that statement means?"

The big Scorpian man shrugged again. "No one knows, except maybe the guardians. You could ask them. If you can find them. They are very good at hiding from the Great Hunters. Whatever it means, it works. I've used it myself, and I'm still here! And now we are arriving at my home. Welcome, Brother Greymalkin Thomas." The thrust from Bokin's vehicle was dwindling, and Greymalkin briefly glimpsed an icy surface in the background behind the frame of Bokin's vehicle. Then he saw a big pair of slowly opening metal doors which were painted to look just like the icy surface. The vehicle passed into a big hangar concealed by the doors, and they bumped to a stop.

The big Scorpian clambered out of his seat and climbed up to the ship's main viewport. Bokin peered in at him, and asked, "Can you come out of your ship? We use oxygen, but not in an atmosphere environment like soft-skins." Greymalkin nodded.

Greymalkin was still wearing the void suit, and said, "Yes, I can come out. I have a suit that protects me from vacuum." Bokin grimaced, and Greymalkin realized that it was a smile.

"Good!" Bokin exclaimed. "Come meet my family!" Greymalkin saw that there were other Scorpians entering and adroitly bouncing around in the microgravity of the hangar shed. On the way in he had scanned Bokin's home, and had seen that it was nothing but a primitive habitat built into the mountain of ice and rock orbiting the gas giant. Greymalkin cautiously exited the skiff, and was immediately the focus of attention by the mob of Scorpians. They were all much larger than Greymalkin and apparently were also all Bokin's children. The Scorpian children were all males and had frightful spiked faces, but they were also very curious about Greymalkin. After their father had barked commands to them, the group tended to the vehicle and its cargo, dismounting the fragvor body and the skiff.

Greymalkin noted that Bokin had heavy equipment in the shed which the young Sojourner might be able to use for a makeshift realignment of the skiff's mast. After the hubbub of stowing and securing everything was finished, Bokin took him inside the habitat. Although it was as airless as space, the tunnels were well-lit and even felt somewhat homey. He was introduced to Bokin's extended family which included a wife, Bokin's parents, his wife's parents, and several other extended family members. He recorded everything, so that even though he quickly lost track of who was cousin to who, he could play back the introductions later if need be.

Although he was ready to examine Bokin's father immediately, the Scorpians insisted on having a meal to welcome him, as he seemed to be the most interesting new event in their lives in quite some time. Bokin corralled his boisterous family eventually and they came together in a room that he decided must be a dining room.

He found the Scorpians endlessly fascinating. They communicated amongst themselves with a mixture of sign language and radio communication. While he was observing the children gesticulating at each other and repeatedly banging one another on the head so hard that it would have readily crushed Greymalkin's skull, he also studied the interior of the habitat. To his surprise, he saw that much of it was mirrorshell, and must have originated from the *nemora*, the old growth feral cybernetic forests of the Builders. If this system had fragvors, it would make sense that it would have other feral cyborg creations of the Builders. Nemora meta-trees were massive cybernetic composite sessile growths of mirrorshell found in the cometary belts of solar systems throughout the Galaxy. It would make sense that the massive mirrorshell trees of the Builders were also to be found in the Sagittarius Arm.

Eventually the familial commotion settled down, and Bokin's wife brought out large clusters of containers radiating heat. A container was placed on a rack in front of each member of the family and the children began to tear into them, but Bokin whacked their knobby arms soundly, saying that they must wait for their guest to eat first.

Greymalkin opened the container, and found a series of what looked like steaming sausages inside. He pulled one off the spike it was stuck on and eyed it. To start with, he couldn't eat through his void suit helmet, but the 'sausage' looked decidedly unappetizing. He took out a sample probe from his utility belt and tested the sausage while he asked Bokin and the family to eat. After they understood that he could not eat in a vacuum like them, Bokin allowed members of his family to dig in and they did so ravenously.

Bokin insisted that Greymalkin take the food back with him to eat later, and Greymalkin agreed. If nothing else, he would be intrigued to analyze exactly what the Scorpians ate. Their exoskeletons and other biological differences undoubtedly meant that their nutritional needs were radically different from standard humans. The sample probe indicated that the sausage object had toxic levels of many compounds that would be indigestible to Greymalkin.

After the family had devoured the food in practically no time, they cleaned up the remnants of the meal just as quickly. Bokin finally took Greymalkin to his father who was isolated in a different room. Greymalkin had brought a medkit, and approached the Scorpian cautiously. The man was even bigger and knobbier than Bokin, and Greymalkin immediately saw that his exoskeleton was discolored with a bright red tinge. After Bokin explained that Greymalkin was here to examine him, the old Scorpian nodded and simply floated there passively trembling in pain. Greymalkin got out the sensors in the medkit and got to work.

After examining the Scorpian for the better part of an hour and comparing the observations with the tomes that he had brought from the skiff, Greymalkin was reasonably sure of what was wrong with the old fellow. The symptoms matched a Scorpian disease that was labeled bronchial ataxia in the data about Scorpians. Basically, the closed respiration system inside the Scorpian's body was losing its ability to process oxygen internally. After figuring out how to hammer the probe through a weak spot in the Scorpians exoskeleton (a process that did not seem to bother the old man in the slightest), Greymalkin took some test samples back to the medical pod on the skiff. By the time he returned, he had synthesized the relevant vaccine from the medical pod's database.

After asking Bokin and the old man for their approval to proceed, he again hammered the probe through the Scorpian's exoskeleton and injected him with the vaccine. When nothing happened immediately,

Greymalkin explained to the confused Bokin that the treatment would require hours to take effect. After his father fell asleep Bokin shrugged resignedly and went off to sleep himself, but Greymalkin stayed with the old man, taking measurements every hour to monitor his condition. Although there was no sound in the airless tunnels, Greymalkin had been able to feel vibrations through the walls as the Scorpians bounced around the compartments. The habitat grew still as the other members of Bokin's family retired, evidently to sleep as well.

Greymalkin watched over the old Scorpian as he slept. The big man trembled violently every once in a while, a sign of what Greymalkin had recognized as the equivalent of coughing. The young Sojourner thought about the long life this old man had led here in a wilderness that Greymalkin had never imagined. He gradually felt a protective impulse toward the old man. Greymalkin knew he was not much of a doctor, but he had more information and medical supplies than these poor people did. He hoped that he could help the old man, and dreaded what might happen if he could not.

After a few hours he could tell that the treatment was taking effect. Greymalkin kept observing him with gradually increasing hope for the Scorpian. The old man stopped coughing and the bright red tint to parts of the exoskeleton began fading away. When Bokin finally returned after what must have been his normal sleep cycle, Greymalkin was smiling. The old man was sleeping peacefully now, and all signs of the disease had vanished. Bokin was astonished and thanked him repeatedly. Greymalkin went back to his skiff to sleep feeling a sense of accomplishment. He'd done something worthwhile. He'd saved a stranger's life.

Over the next few days Greymalkin had a growing feeling of accomplishment that began to give him hope again. Bokin's father was soon up and moving, albeit still weak. The Scorpian family fussed over Greymalkin, thanking him endlessly. Bokin helped him perform makeshift repairs to the skiff, and they managed to gradually, marginally, work through the process of realigning the mast.

Bokin turned out to be relatively chatty, and they had many conversations as they worked. Greymalkin asked the big Scorpian questions about his people, and Bokin asked reverent questions about the endless technical topics that were far beyond the experience of the simple but unpretentious man. Greymalkin found his childlike curiosity refreshing. It turned out that Bokin was intensely curious about interstellar travel. The fact that his society had collapsed to the point that they no longer had starships was tantalizing to the scavenger. He was confused by many of Greymalkin's statements and asked questions for hours on end as they worked.

"You say that you must exchange this starship for another when you reach the big base. But why? If we fix this ship, can't you use it then?" Bokin asked, handing Greymalkin a tool, who shook his head and tried to think of a way to explain the matter simply.

"The conditions and potential pathways through shadow space are enormously varied. Because of this, there are many different types of starships," Greymalkin said slowly. "Each type is optimally configured for a specific kind of shadow space traversal."

Bokin nodded, but his fierce looking face was screwed up into a grimace of concentration, and he asked, "Okay. But how many kinds? Are there many-many?"

Greymalkin laughed. "No, not so many, I suppose. There are three main types of paths that can be traversed through shadow space." He tried to think of simple analogies that Sojourners were taught to use in explaining shadow space travel. The usual way of explaining the three shadow space continua to Bereft that lived on planets were to compare them to rivers, plains, and the sky. In that analogy, shadow channels were like rivers that a boat could float down, shadow planes were like the surface of a planet that a cart could be pulled across, and shadow volumes were like the sky that a bird could fly through. But Bokin lived in *space*, not on a typical terrestrial planet surface. After a moment of further thought, Greymalkin shrugged and tried a simple geometric explanation.

"When you shift a ship into a shadow space continuity you separate it from many limitations of normal space. You're in a separate continuity, effectively a separate tiny universe that can move around and then rejoin the normal universe. Separating and joining universe continuities is not subject to the hard limit of the speed of light *inside of* a continuity.

"But there are other limits that affect the potential pathways for a ship in its separate little universe to move and then rejoin the normal universe. And these potential pathways are similar to how you can move in three dimensions. If you only move in one dimension, back and forth along a line, that's similar to what happens in a shadow *channel*. Channels usually lead from one star or big mass to another; they form lines of potential traversal for a ship shifted into shadow space. But you might also move in two dimensions, like people on a planet following the surface of the world. That's akin to what happens on a shadow *plane*. Again, it's just potential ways to traverse a particular kind of shadow space potential, but the constraints are two-dimensional rather than one dimensional. You need different types of starship for each type of travel."

Bokin grunted in understanding, and said, "And the third category must be potential for movement in three-dimensions?" Greymalkin grinned and nodded.

"Correct, that's called shadow *volume* traversal, and it requires yet another kind of mast configuration. There are many tradeoffs in the optimization of different configurations, but those are the three basic starship rig categories: shadow channel, shadow plane, and shadow volume."

"And what type do you need, then?" Bokin asked, clearly intrigued. Greymalkin pursed his lips, thinking.

"There are greater or lesser pathways of all three kinds anywhere in the Galaxy," Greymalkin said. "But around here? I can sense these potential pathways clearly with the jewel in my head. That's one of the reasons we have them in our minds in civilizations with starships. And most of the pathway potentials here are shadow *planes*, so I need to exchange this skiff for what's called a rover. That is, assuming we can get this skiff moving again so I can reach the expedition bases at the end of the channel we're in."

Over the next few days they made progress repairing the ship. It would take a fully equipped starship drydock to fully realign the mast, but it gradually worked well enough that a day came that Greymalkin felt that he could depart. But he wondered if he should.

He had thought about the Bereft Scorpian society he'd discovered long and hard while he worked among them. Although they looked frightful, they were affable enough when one got to know them, albeit a bit violent. He couldn't fault them, as they lived in a very violent environment. While part of him would have been happy to simply stay with them and go on to tutor this family and others and slowly help them improve their technology and living conditions, he began to see the wisdom in what Mother Advisor Trystia had said about helping the Bereft. Yes, a single Sojourner could do many things to help them. But a group of Sojourners with more resources could do far more. And the problem that loomed over these Scorpians and any other Bereft human societies here were the Carinans. Whatever the case was with Bokin's vaunted Words of Peace, the Scorpians clearly lived in terror of the aliens. If he was really going to help them, he had to try to discover more about what was actually happening in the Carinae. He had to actually join Kuanian's expedition, as had been the original plan. And the thought of the Burani had not left his mind. What if they found out he was here? Would they be a threat to Bokin and his family as well as Greymalkin? *I have to go. For the best interests of Bokin and his people, I need to go.*

And that meant that he still needed the protection of Kuanian's mysterious Prisoner. So it was that after he had given Bokin a basic archive of information to use and share with other Scorpian families, one day he asked if his scavenger host would escort him to the moon that he was seeking.

Bokin became uncharacteristically silent, and Greymalkin wondered if he had offended the man in some way. Finally, Bokin asked, "Are you sure you want to go to that moon?"

"Why?" Greymalkin asked. "Is there something wrong with it?"

The Scorpian seemed to be pondering something for a long moment, then said, "Yes, very wrong. There are old stories about that moon. It is cursed. It is called the Ghost Moon." Greymalkin fought the urge to smile superciliously at the superstitions of his primitive friend.

"I'm sure it will be fine, Bokin," he said. "I can go by myself; I don't need to bother you with this task. You've done so much for me already."

"You think I am a simple and stupid man," Bokin said, sounding slightly hurt. "But we were told these stories by the secret guardians. They are our wisest allies, and are never wrong. I tell you this in truth, there is something evil and dangerous on that moon. If you must go there, then I will go with you. But although I owe you a great deal for healing my father, I must also think about my family. I will take you to the Ghost Moon. But I will leave you then."

Greymalkin felt humbled by Bokin's simple integrity. He had come to respect the Scorpian a great deal, he realized. "That will be fine, Bokin. Thank you again for all your help."

Bokin insisted on ferrying Greymalkin's skiff to the moon, where he would leave him. So, after Greymalkin said goodbye to Bokin's jostling, rowdy family, and his void suit had almost been punctured many times by being bear-hugged by the big spiky Scorpians, he watched Bokin and his sons once again mount his skiff back on the front of the primitive Scorpian vehicle and they took off. The two of them flew most of the trip in silence sitting next to each other, but when the pale moon that was his destination finally hove into view the Scorpian spoke again, saying, "I do not know why you want to go to this cursed place, but please be careful, Brother Greymalkin."

Greymalkin was busy scanning the moon, but looked up and said seriously, "You have been a very good friend, Bokin. I am extremely lucky to have encountered you by chance. You saved my life, and I will never forget that." The big Scorpian laughed then, busying himself with the process of landing the ship.

"I am the lucky one," Bokin said, as the framework vehicle descended to the surface of the icy moon. "Good luck on your big expedition, my friend. This is where we must leave each other." Both of them jumped onto the silent snowy surface. Bokin dismounted the skiff from his vehicle, and through his feet Greymalkin felt it thump heavily into the snow of the moon. The landscape was very dark. Greymalkin watched his friend depart with a blinding blast of fusion thrust. The young Sojourner watched his friend leave until the vehicle was a distant light among the stars.

* * *

Greymalkin looked around. Without Bokin present, the moon seemed eerily dead and unfriendly. He bounced across the snow in the low gravity and climbed into the skiff, trying to shake off the sense of foreboding. Once inside, he took off his void suit and warmed up before going to the cockpit of the little starship. Checking the coordinates from Kuanian's notes he saw that he was roughly forty kilometers from the location she had indicated. He activated the ship's pressor lifts, rose to a height of several hundred meters, and began moving forward toward his goal. All the while he was reviewing Kuanian's information in his mind and thinking through what he would do if he actually found the being she called the Prisoner. After a short time he saw a small mountain coming over the moon's horizon that matched the images in Kuanian's files. He circled the mountain until he saw what appeared to be a cave opening. Greymalkin set the ship down in the snow just a few meters from the opening. It looked pitch black inside the cave. He looked at it, drumming his fingers on the console. *Well, I came all this way....*

The first thing Greymalkin did was cautiously pick up the alien device that Kuanian had provided. The thing was a simple bronze colored oval band of metal. Now that he thought about it, it resembled the head bands that both Hayan and Kuanian had worn. After reviewing her notes one last time, he set the device on his head and turned it on. The thing lit up immediately and presented him with a single prompt communed into his mind. «*Activate?*»

Greymalkin thought a long time before responding. But no matter how he looked at the situation, no matter how frightened he might be of the endless list of things he didn't know, this still seemed like a necessary next step. So, he activated the device.

The sensation was strange. At first it reminded him of nothing so much as a feeling of ephemeral threads falling on his head and then vanishing. But the impression built and built until it felt nearly intolerable, as if quickly disappearing threads were being crammed into his brain with a hydraulic press. He gasped and reached up to yank the band off his head, but before he could reach it the sensations stopped. A single message communed into his mind, and then the device became inert. «*Process complete.*»

He tore the band off his head, feeling flustered. After shivering with sheer nervous energy, he thought to himself, *Okay, I don't know what I expected, but not that.* He cautiously searched through the sensations he was feeling and was shocked to find yet *another* covenant in place within his mind. He stomped around the cramped skiff interior cursing and yelling at no one in particular. He couldn't feel angry at Kuanian because he had chosen to activate the device. *I just wish she'd told me what to expect,* he thought. His shadow jewel and brain felt so stuffed full of covenant programming that he was claustrophobic for a moment.

Then a different thought came to him. He'd been thinking of the covenant that the Velan had placed on his mind as some kind of binding, a set of chains. But if what Kuanian had indicated in her notes was true, the new covenant that had just been installed on his shadow jewel (and consequently his brain) was an asset, not a liability. *Maybe the Velan was trying to help me as well?*

He shook his head, trying to shake off the sense of dizzy congestion in his mind. The feeling faded away gradually and became almost imperceptible, but if he sought for them he could immediately feel both covenants in his mind. Irritated, he put the device away and went back to his preparations, which involved yet another of Kuanian's supposed 'gifts'.

He picked up the golden robes. He had experimented with them in the days he had lived among the Scorpians, and had figured out a few things concerning the garment. It could reconfigure itself into several different kinds of garb, ranging from the void suit form that had saved his life to several different kinds of simpler clothing. He was still not sure of all its capabilities, but for all its uncertainties the thing had become a kind of good luck charm in his mind. He reconfigured it into a void suit and put it on in the normal way. Then he took up the multi-tool, also with some slight suspicion.

Like the robes, he'd discovered that the golden tool could reconfigure itself into many forms. If anything, it seemed to have far more possible forms to assume than the robes. It annoyed him no end that, while they had clearly identified *settings*, neither item appeared to have any discernible kind of overall manual or instructions, forcing him into trial and error experiments to figure them out. He'd thought about leaving them both behind, but still placed a dogged trust in Kuanian. If she had given them these items, Greymalkin felt that they must be useful.

He crammed a few more standard items into a pack and then exited the skiff. The yawning black orifice of the cave was an imposing sight in front of the ship. Greymalkin activated a light source and approached it slowly. The cave spiraled downwards at a gradual angle, the dark walls becoming more regular in form as he walked forward warily. Very soon the passage became pitch black except for his light source. Becoming steadily more anxious, Greymalkin followed the passage until he saw a wall of some kind ahead of him. Kuanian's notes had only said that the tunnel would end at the 'Lock'. Now that he had found what he was looking for, Greymalkin felt scared almost out of his mind.

A huge round object was mounted in the wall of black rock at the end of the tunnel. He could see a myriad of inscriptions carved concentrically around the surface of the round disc. Unsurprisingly, he could not read the inscriptions, since he assumed it was an alien artifact. Then, to his shock, he realized that some of the glyphs were actually in a recognizable human writing system. It was a very *old* writing system, but he had studied antiquities inscribed with these characters, which dated all the way back to the first interstellar exodus of mankind. He approached the giant metal disc, trembling and trying to shine his light on the letters to make them out.

Although the inscribed message looked eroded and chipped with age, it was still very clear. It said simply: DANGER. HIGH RISK. DO NOT TOUCH. He looked around the entirety of the disc, but there were no other characters that he recognized as human. The only other distinguishing feature of the ancient disc was a shining metal cube embedded in the center. Greymalkin leaned back away from the disc and nodded to himself. *That's it. The release mechanism that Kuanian describes in her notes.* He was gathering up his courage to reach out and touch the elaborately carved cube when something happened that petrified him. Out of nowhere, a communed voice spoke to him in perfectly understandable Peretian.

«Hello.»

Greymalkin almost wet the golden void suit. He staggered backward and shined the light around in the darkness wildly. But there was nothing and no one there except him. Stuttering in fear, he communed a response.

«W-who are you? A-and *where* are you?» Greymalkin extended his shadow sense, but there was nothing around him but ice and rock. Except, there was a heavy metal column that ran straight down from the rear of the big metal disc. The column extended into the depths farther than he could trace purely by means of his shadow sense.

«I am far beneath you. Please do not be alarmed. I am very glad that you are here.» The communed thoughts felt ominously deep, massive, and hard as stone to Greymalkin. In his panic he fought the urge to run. *This must be the Prisoner I came for,* he thought. *But I didn't think he'd talk to me!* The strange, communed thoughts continued to echo in his mind. «Are you here to release me? Did Kuanian send you?»

Hearing the familiar name gave him something to hold onto psychologically, and he tried to think. «Yes. Kuanian sent me. How do you know her?»

There was a sense of amusement in the response, but also a disquieting amount of anger. «She was the last person that came here to speak with me. She said that she might send someone to come back here and free me if I behaved myself.» Then the steely thoughts closed around Greymalkin with intensity. «Are you going to free me?»

«I'm... thinking about it, yes.» Greymalkin looked down, trying to sense where the imprisoned being was held. But there was nothing beneath him but kilometers of ice and rock. Realizing that his answer had probably not been what the Prisoner wanted to hear, he asked a question to interrupt any angry retort. «You say you're beneath me? I don't sense anything beneath me, though.» When the response came, it was indeed fuming with anger.

«I am directly below you at the center of this ball of frost and dirt!» There was an almost animalistic snarl in the thoughts, and Greymalkin felt that coming here had been a very bad idea. As he cast his shadow sense farther and farther down into the substrata of the moon, he could finally, dimly perceive an object thousands of kilometers beneath him from which the communed thoughts were emanating all the way up through the column. He blanched and looked down in horror. *It wasn't exaggerating! It's actually imprisoned in the core of this moon!*

Far, far beneath him, Greymalkin could indistinctly make out a peculiar shape, a rhombic dodecahedron, with diamond shaped facets. The structure must have been gigantic for him to be able to make it out at this distance. It was glowing with heat, and it was the center-point of some kind of network of power cables that stretched away into the volume of the moon in various directions. He thought about the implications of that for a moment, and the walls of the airless cave felt like they were closing in on him. He started to run back the way he had come. But the communed thoughts of the imprisoned being returned to him, and they felt calm and reasonable.

«Please do not be alarmed. I am eager to help Kuanian in achieving her goals. I am eager to help *you*. Please, please, free me!» The thoughts of the being became more emotional and frantic. Greymalkin paused and stepped back to the huge disc. There was something poignant about the thoughts of the being, and Greymalkin felt a twinge of pity at the despair he sensed in it. He thought the situation over again. He thought about retracing his steps back up through the tunnel to the surface and his ship. Greymalkin knew he could flee back to the Scorpians, but the same issues that he had faced before remained. He needed to join the expedition, and he needed protection to survive to do it.

But what am I releasing if I free this creature? That uncertainty still brought him up short. He finally sent the being a response. «Why are you imprisoned here?»

«Kuanian did not tell you?» The thoughts became amused again, and Greymalkin sensed that the mind he was communing with was erratic and impulsive to the extreme. It felt enraged one second, then despairing, and then falling down with laughter the next moment. «I committed crimes and was eventually caught and imprisoned here.»

«What crimes?» Greymalkin wondered if he could trust whatever answer the being gave him, but was surprised by the honesty of the response.

«All of them, I believe. But I have learned my lesson. I will behave myself and I will help you. Free me!» The thoughts of the imprisoned being sounded truly sad, and he hated the thought of abandoning this wretched thing here to its prison. Greymalkin made up his mind. Kuanian had given him this option and he trusted her.

«I will free you. Kuanian left me instructions on how to release you. Do you need to make any preparations?» He wondered how long it would actually take the creature to burrow up through thousands of kilometers of the moon.

«No, but you do. Once you release the seal, go back to your little ship and fly away from where you are now. I will meet you soon afterwards.»

It knows I came in a ship? «How far away should I fly?» Greymalkin still wondered if he would be regretting this decision shortly.

«At least as far as you flew when you came across the surface the first time. You know, from where you left the scavenger man when he flew away.»

«You saw that??» Greymalkin felt taken aback. «Can you see me from down where you are imprisoned?»

«Of course! How else would I know to contact you? Now, please, free me!»

Feeling that he was making a huge mistake, Greymalkin reached out to the shining cube at the center of the disc. There were no instructions on the disc, but Kuanian had provided them. The cube turned stiffly, but it did turn at the touch of his hand. He rotated it through three turns counterclockwise, and then pressed on it, hard. The cube slowly depressed until it was flush with the surface of the disc. It then began to glow with an angry red light.

Greymalkin hurried away back up the tunnel, stumbling and falling several times in his nervousness to get away. He couldn't help thinking repeatedly, *What have I done? What really just happened?*

He got into the skiff and lifted off the ground, flying quickly back above the ice fields in the direction he had come. It only took a few minutes for him to fly back to roughly the spot where he had said goodbye to Bokin. He exited the skiff again and waited on the snowy plain.

He didn't have long to wait. The snow around him suddenly shook violently into a powder that flew up around him, knocking him off his feet. Huge blocks of ice crumpled upward through the snow in vast rows across the surface of the moon to the horizon. Greymalkin cursed and tried to get back onto his feet, but the ground was a slurry of snow flying in all directions. He glimpsed the sky for a moment and saw an enormous fountain of rock and ice slowly rising up over the horizon and out into space. *Why did I get out of the ship?* he wondered ruefully, but too late. The ground kept heaving for at least a minute, before it settled into a kind of ongoing rumbling spasm that gradually began to subside.

When he could stand up again, he got back up and looked around. Then he froze stock still. Something that radiated enormous heat was floating a few meters away from him above a patch of snow that was visibly melting. He stared at the pulsating black thing that hung there above a rapidly widening puddle of melting snow.

It was pitch black, with reflective highlights. Parts of it slowly bubbled in and out of view in a disturbing way that reminded him of the four-dimensional structure of the Velan. At first he'd thought the thing had a vaguely humanoid form, but now he saw that wasn't true. While it had a melted-looking blob of blackness where a head would be, and had extensions and stumps that could loosely be interpreted as limbs, there were too many of them to resemble a humanoid form. And they kept shifting in and out of view, like a shadow in a nightmare. Although the figure was actually shorter than Greymalkin, it was wider than it was tall, with grotesque extensions like strangling arms hanging out to the side. And it did not stand on its stumps, but rather just floated there before him with distortions in the vapor fumes radiating off it and the liquified surface underneath it. Greymalkin had never seen anything remotely like it, and simply stared goggle-eyed at the monstrosity in horror.

The amorphous black creature abruptly extended a spike from one of its arms directly at his head, far too quickly to avoid. The tip slowed just before touching him lightly on the forehead of his void suit, just above his faceplate. And Greymalkin's mind exploded in synesthetic images.

Greymalkin had come to recognize the momentary plunging immersion of synesthesia when he was touched physically by a higher order being like Hayan or Kuanian, even though it seemed to be a radically different experience with each such being. This was the most disorienting experience yet, however, and virtually nothing made any coherent sense. He had the impression of falling through vast and intricately organized vertical halls of dark stone with countless branches extending to the sides as he fell, each of which appeared to store innumerable carved artifacts. Then the stone halls fragmented with cracks, shattering into pieces that fell alongside him. The fragments dissolved, becoming huge viscous blobs of black fluid that recombined and solidified instantly into a new endless pattern of a different style of corridors, again with myriad chambers full of strange artifacts opening off to the sides. He could glimpse creatures in some of the chambers, and even some humans standing here and there in conversational groups. *Are these recordings? Live images? Or what?* The bizarre matrix of tunnels and rooms flew apart and reassembled in an accelerating cycle of changes until he found it unbearable, and Greymalkin screamed inside his mind.

He gasped and fell backwards away from the black spike that had touched his forehead. The inky-dark thing floating before him pulled the spike back into itself in a liquid motion.

«So it is true!» the communed voice of the thing exclaimed in his mind. «Kuanian warned me that I would not be able to harm anyone she sent to free me! You will be pleased to know, human, that I am unable to intentionally kill you.» The tone of amusement had returned in the thing's thoughts. Greymalkin kept gasping in irked shock.

«Y-you... *just tried to kill me??*» Greymalkin's thoughts were as livid as he felt. There was a trickling and bubbling sensation in the thought-stream of the thing that Greymalkin realized after a few moments was its equivalent to laughter. Then it seemed to incline its entire ruinously flowing black metallic-stony body towards him for a moment.

«Forgive me, but I was very curious. I do not know how Kuanian obtained my master control code restrictions, but somehow she did. However, you should feel pleased and happy that I cannot harm you!

And I am very glad that you are here. Thank you for unleashing me upon the universe again!» Now that the being was close by and not buried under thousands of kilometers of moon, the communed signal was overwhelmingly strong. Greymalkin had the impression that the entire body of the creature was transmitting its thoughts, rather than a single shadow jewel source such as he had in his head. Greymalkin stared at the thing, wondering what it was. He'd never heard of anything that resembled this abomination.

«How long were you locked up down there?» Greymalkin inquired finally, but then wondered if he actually wanted to know.

«Far too long a time!» the thing practically roared back at him, enraged again. «But now I have been released finally, by a human cybe no less. How ignominious.»

Greymalkin felt his ire rise at the creature, and despite how horrifying it appeared, snapped back at it. «I am not a cybe! How do you even know that word? And what in blazes are you, anyway? How do you know my language?»

The trickling sensation from the monster broadened into a communed bubbling gurgle. «Absurd! You have so many swatches of programming layered on your mind I'm surprised that you can even move. You're certainly a cybe.»

«I got these from Kuanian, and, and a thing called a... Velan.» As soon as he had let slip the sentence, Greymalkin wanted to choke himself. *I shouldn't give this creature any information!*

The black floating thing seemed to appreciate the statement though. When Greymalkin had thought of the Velan, the thoughts of the black horror had perked up in recognition. «Oh, so *that* one did this to you! I retract my insult, I consider that one a friend. And Kuanian, for all her mischief, must be thanked for releasing me from that prison. Very good then, human. What should I call you? Your kind have names and designations, correct?»

True, we haven't been introduced, Greymalkin thought. *Since it evidently isn't going to kill me, at least for the moment, I guess I should try to get to know it.* He cleared his throat, more as a matter of habit than necessity. None of this conversation had been spoken. He doubted the thing even had a mouth from the look of it.

«I am a monk of the Sojourner Order. You may address me as Brother Greymalkin Thomas.» After a moment's hesitation, unsure what else to do, he inclined his head slightly to the horror. This elicited a torrent of burbling thoughts from the monster.

«Well, well, how *do you do*? How polite you are! I like you already, you're extremely odd.» The thoughts of the thing were distinctly amused. Greymalkin grit his teeth.

«And how should I address you, then?» Greymalkin was straining to keep his thoughts polite, but couldn't help adding a sarcastic comment on to his inquiry. «I mean, since you are apparently so familiar with my language, I'm so pleased to converse with you, and don't want to address you as 'horrible black rock blob'.»

The nightmare actually spun around in a circle while issuing gargling thoughts that grated on Greymalkin's nerves. «I think I like that name better than anything else your kind have given me in the past! But I suppose we will have to have more decorum, now, won't we? Yes, I've known many humans in the past, and there was a name that they gave me which was used most often. They called me *Bruno*.»

«Bruno?» Greymalkin thought that was a ridiculous name for this ghoulish nightmare, but so be it. «And where are all of these human comrades of yours?» *Maybe I can find someone with some answers,* he thought.

«All dead, unfortunately.» The answer chilled Greymalkin to the core, and he wondered again what he had done by freeing this monster. The floating black horror seemed to discern some of his thoughts, and responded. «I did not kill them, if that's what you are wondering, even though they lacked Kuanian's miraculous codes to keep me at bay. It's simply that I knew them a very long time ago, as time is judged by your kind. But time and circumstances are not easygoing on humans. They are all now long expired.»

Isn't that the truth, Greymalkin thought nervously, and staggered on his feet as a huge block of ice in the disrupted plains around them collapsed with a shattering vibration felt through his boots. He looked out at the landscape of chaos this creature had created simply by rejoining the universe, rubble and fragments still falling everywhere. *Well, it's a start, I suppose.*

Meetings

Greymalkin sat tensely in the cockpit of the skiff, watching all of his instruments and especially the camera he had trained on the amorphous black abomination that had asked to be called Bruno. As far as he could tell, the thing had been innocently floating outside the skiff tranquilly throughout the hours since he had departed the prison moon. It seemed content to simply accompany him, riding along inside the continuity manifold of his ship but outside the hull, which was fine with Greymalkin. He did not want the thing inside the cabin of the skiff. He kept imagining it committing fiendish acts. But it just remained there, floating along.

He looked out at the passing billows of the shadow channel and the star systems that he was slowly passing. It was a beautiful region of the Galaxy, although he was much too anxious to enjoy the surroundings. He nervously checked the flux tank for the hundredth time, confirming that the inefficiency rate in the flux consumption had not increased. By his calculations he would have just enough flux to reach the outermost resupply base of the expedition. It was one of the smallest bases in the entire operation, but he should be able to refill his tank there. And that would allow him enough range to reach his goal, the primary expedition base.

Mostly to distract himself, he tried talking to his nightmarish guest again. Soon after he had freed it the thing had become bored with his questions and refused to answer any more. But he had to try to find out a bit more about the creature. He tried reverse psychology this time, communing, «It's probably better that you don't tell me anything about yourself. Kuanian must have instructed you to not divulge what you are to me. I think that's for the best.» Happily, this provoked exactly the response he was hoping for.

«Kuanian? Feh. To obtain what I want, I'll comply with her bargain and act as your bodyguard for the specified time. But I owe her nothing, and certainly wouldn't obey her orders blindly. Or yours. And she knows almost nothing about me or my kind anyway. Still, I suppose that to fulfill the agreement with her, I will have to obey your commands. Just remember that there is a limit to my patience. I'm not your slave.» The creature oscillated in its emotional sentiments wildly, even while it was rambling through a sentence. This was one of the things that made him the most worried about the creature. How would it respond in an actual crisis? Yet, he had to learn how to interact with it.

«Kuanian is the best informed person I know.» Greymalkin had no trouble feeling confident of that in his thoughts.

«Hardly! She simply referred to me as a *protean*. How nonspecifically speculative!» The thing became more amorphous when it was agitated, and now it began to look like boiling tar. But Greymalkin's eyebrows rose slightly with interest.

A protean? He's right, that's a nonspecific term, but.... While the term simply meant something that could change form, Greymalkin had seen it in another context referring to some of the reported cybernetic organisms that had been encountered historically in the Sagittarius Arm. The Xenocorps expedition of three centuries ago had described encountering creatures that they termed 'Abyssal Proteans'. But that was merely a phrase that combined a term for something that shapeshifted with the 'Abyssal' label for bizarrely powerful creatures almost like the Velan that were routinely encountered in the space between the Orion and Sagittarius Arms. The working hypothesis of the Xenocorps had been that the Abyssal Proteans were yet another of the myriad feral cybernetic species that had been created by the prolific Builders millions of years ago. But that had never been confirmed or even been built out as a theory.

Greymalkin examined the creature once again. It was so dark that it would have been impossible to see in the blackness of space. But the thing was different in shadow space. In Greymalkin's shadow synesthesia the thing glowed with an eldritch blue nimbus of light. His synesthesia also seemed to perceive weird sounds and smells from the creature occasionally, ranging from almost subsonic growls to strangely juxtaposed scents like acidic onions and sweet peaches. Everything about it was unnerving. The phrase Abyssal Protean was as good as anything else for it. But he suspected that Bruno was right, and that even Kuanian did not fully understand this creature.

Then he saw that his target, the resupply base, was finally coming into view. It had a transponder to locate it at short distances, and he could detect the blinking beacon in his amplifier. He breathed a sigh of relief, but thought to communicate with Bruno again.

«Okay, we agreed that you will stay out of sight, correct?» Greymalkin felt as if he was nagging the creature, and it apparently did as well.

«I have confirmed that request three times, human. While I am with you, you're the boss! I grow unsure of why you even wanted me to accompany you.» The thoughts of the thing called Bruno felt very annoyed.

«I will likely need you in the future, when my life may be threatened.» Greymalkin had not yet decided how or if he would explain the presence of Bruno to the people at the base, but he did not want to add the bizarre presence of the creature to what would already be an awkward moment of introductions. «I just need to quickly pick up some shadow flux for this skiff.» The skiff was now on close approach with the base. Greymalkin shut down the continuity manifold when he was close enough to reach the resupply station in normal space. The skiff dropped back into the universe and through the viewport he again saw the expected field of stars and nebulae spread out before him.

But *what* stars, and *what* nebulae! Many of the stars in the Carinae were flaring variables that glowed brilliantly to his shadow sense, even through the skiff's hull, along with the blazing shapes of the vast emission nebula around them in the sky. Synesthesia made the various energy sources in the breathtaking sky not simply glow, but also generated distinct sounds and aromas in his mind. The brightest stars recalled crisp scents that his brain interpreted as spice and incense, and his auditory system interpreted their signals as haunting rumbles far away. In the middle of it all was the foreboding hourglass shape of the enigmatic Homunculus Nebula and the searing light from the stars at its center. With an effort, he shook off the dazzling sights of the tableaux and focused on docking with the base ahead of them.

The resupply base was nothing much to look at. Once again, it was simply some hulls buried inside an asteroid-sized mass of rock. However, the messaging it was emitting was far more sophisticated than the primitive habitat within which Bokin dwelled. When Greymalkin communed a tentative hail, the base flight controller responded immediately. He saw a huge door recessed into the surface open, and he carefully steered the skiff into the hangar.

The door closed far above the skiff just as large mechanical grapples extended and grasped the skiff to pull it into a standard dock. He felt the reassuring thump of a pier tunnel settle onto the airlock of the skiff, and knew that he would not have to don a void suit for egress. He briefly scanned around the exterior of the ship. Bruno was nowhere to be seen. Greymalkin relaxed. He didn't know where the creature was hiding, and did not really care to know either as long as it stayed out of sight.

Before he went to the airlock he paused, thinking, and then took along his pack with the golden garment and tool.

When he exited the ship he found a sleepy looking Canisian dock manager waiting for him. The man eyed him in confusion, yawning.

"Who are you?" the man asked in a befuddled tone. The particularly gruff Canisian dialect told Greymalkin that the fellow was from one of the lowest class levels of the vast warrens that made up so many of the megahabitats in the Canis Major realm. But the man seemed friendly enough. "We weren't expecting anyone from the main base. Did you log your flight plan?"

Greymalkin shook his head and launched into his long explanation. As he recounted the various details of the harrowing destruction of the Jotun hoard-lair the man's eyes got wider and wider, although Greymalkin omitted the story of freeing Bruno on the way here. By the time he'd finished, the dock manager was both fully awake and speechless. He finally said, "Good grief! I can't believe you survived all that! Well, we can certainly resupply you; what's your expedition ID number? We have to charge it back to the appropriate account."

Bureaucrats and procedures, Greymalkin mused. *I suppose it's encouraging that they are the same everywhere, at least.* He gave the man the number that he'd been assigned as part of the expedition and the fellow took him to a kind of canteen to wait while the skiff's flux tank was refilled. Greymalkin sat down in the quiet, empty room and closed his eyes for a moment. It had been a long day. He drifted off into a brief nap that was ended by an abrupt, horrific nightmare. In the nightmare, he was instantly plunged into a mass of cold metal tentacles that were wrapping around him tighter and tighter, like an ocean of grasping limbs holding him in a grip of steel. Behind the thick coils of tentacles was a shadowy human figure that seemed to absorb light like a hole into the void. He could not tell if the nightmare was only a second or two or if it was hours, but he was just drawing in breath to scream when he woke up trembling.

A hand had gently shaken his shoulder. Greymalkin startled awake instantly, looking around for the iron-like tentacles, but only saw the hand withdrawn from his shoulder as the person silhouetted against the ceiling lights above him stood up. It was a handsome older man with greying hair, smiling down at Greymalkin with an avuncular expression. His face was wizened, but had a strong jawline and broad forehead. His squinting eyes had irises that were so very light an amber brown that they looked almost yellow. They were expressive, intense eyes and they watched Greymalkin very closely. The older man wore a dark, old-fashioned jumpsuit with a name stenciled over the breast pocket, 'R. Flavopallio'. When he spoke, Greymalkin found that the man had a resonant voice that sounded accustomed to commanding attention.

"Hello, Brother Thomas. We weren't expecting you here, but we're very glad to see you. I'm an expedition representative. If you can come with me, I have just a few questions, and then we'll send you on your way." Greymalkin nodded. *More bureaucracy. It's to be expected.* He followed the man out of the canteen.

"Has the Sojourner priory at the main base been informed of your arrival?" the grey-haired man asked. "If not, would you like us to send them a message for you?"

"I would appreciate that," Greymalkin said, feeling slightly dizzy, heart pounding. He was still throwing off the panic of the nightmare.

"Certainly," the grey-haired man said, looking back at him with that reassuring smile. Greymalkin soon felt calmed and encouraged as he followed the man down some halls to what appeared to be simply a storeroom. Everything would be alright. Just as the man waved him in, Greymalkin became annoyed at the realization that he had left his pack behind in the canteen. He resolved to go back for it as he stepped through the door.

Two things hit Greymalkin instantaneously, one a gruesome sight and the other a physical punch to his stomach. The dock manager was lying in a corner of the room, unmoving and bloodied. The punch came from a hidden man that had been standing to the side of the door just inside the room. He'd savagely slugged Greymalkin in the solar plexus as he stepped through the door. The blow made Greymalkin's universe explode into exquisite gasping pain, followed in short order by a terrific blow to the face. His vision blackened and all he saw for a moment were brilliantly flashing points of light. His sight gradually began to clear, just in time for his shoulders to be seized by people behind him, and his head to be hauled up violently by the hair. Standing in front of Greymalkin once again was the man in the dark jumpsuit, still smiling pleasantly, but now with folded arms.

"I wish you were a little less like me, child," the smiling man said cryptically, and then he nodded to someone behind Greymalkin. Before Greymalkin could form a coherent thought, he experienced yet again the now familiar agony of a neuro-stunner. Someone had shot him in the back near his spine, and it was having a spectacular effect on his nervous system. Between the punch to his stomach and the dart, he could not even draw enough breath to scream. He lost his awareness for an indeterminate period.

He did not immediately regain full consciousness, but became cognizant that the continuing pain of the neuro-stun had lessened somewhat. Despite the agony and other effects of the stun, he could vaguely discern that several more voices had joined them in the storeroom. His mind began running around in erratic circles, looking for a coherent thought. He caught bits of what they were discussing in low voices, "...can't believe this idiot survived the Jotun ship being destroyed... how did Rodo know the kid would arrive here of all places?... we'll get a bonus for wrapping this up so quickly!... tweak the records and no one will know what happened to the dock manager, or that this guy was ever here... what the blazes was that stuff in his pack?... forget it, Rodo already took it with him to the main base... I don't know *why*, maybe he wanted to report it... why did it take you so long to bring down those cutter blades?... let's get on with this, Rodo said to take care of this guy quick... I think he's waking up...."

Then Greymalkin was abruptly hauled up off the deck roughly, bringing him almost fully awake for a moment. Opening his eyes, he dizzily saw that there were several figures around him now. He barely had enough presence of mind to send out a blaring communed signal with what strength his scattered concentration could muster. «Bruno! Help me! Get them...»

He was dropped to the deck just as suddenly as he'd been picked up when a tremendous sound of metal being torn apart echoed through the room deafeningly. He tried to get his hands underneath him, but his muscles were still in spasm. He again heard only fragments of what his assailants were now shouting. "What in all space is *this* thing, then?... hit it with the shadow blades!"

Bruno's communed thoughts came into his head, still full of the same amused and bubbling tones. «Do not worry, boss! These persons are simply here to provide us with some amusement, information... and perhaps pocket change!» What Greymalkin heard next was an utterly horrific chorus of screams set against the backdrop of what sounded like tubs of gelatin being splattered against the walls. In a few seconds the noise resolved itself into the sound of one man's shrieking and pleading voice. He murkily sensed Bruno communing with the man, asking questions. The man's screams became steadily higher pitched and then were abruptly punctuated with a sound like snapping sticks. Greymalkin tried one last time to push himself off the deck and failed, falling unconscious again this time.

When he awoke, he wished he hadn't. He was propped up sitting against a cold metal wall that felt very wet. The slowly morphing form of Bruno filled his view, apparently examining him for a moment. The head-bulb of the protean moved out of his view then, revealing the room behind him. Greymalkin's gorge surged up and he vomited onto the deck. All the trauma of seeing what had happened to Bora and Soren flooded him again, but worse.

What coated the walls of the storage room was apparently all that was left of the men that had knocked him out and captured him. It was the most inconceivably disgusting sight he had ever imagined, and he knew he had to get out of the room as fast as he could or his mind would snap. «G-get me out of here, Bruno!» Greymalkin's communed thoughts were every bit as broken as he felt.

«Certainly!» Bruno's thoughts were disconcertingly coherent and perfectly cheerful. Greymalkin closed his eyes against the pain that surged up again in his head as he was lifted up, promptly losing consciousness once more.

When he opened his eyes again, he found himself in the pier tunnel just outside the skiff. Bruno communed with him again. «How do you feel now? Can you pilot your ship?»

«I... I don't know, but I'll damned-well try!» Greymalkin staggered to his feet, leaning against the curved tunnel walls. He took a moment to try to gather his completely fragmented thoughts, mostly because he could barely stand up. «But... the base recorded us docking. They'll know....» He swallowed, trying to wrap his mind around the full horror of what had just happened.

Those men. They had been criminals, obviously. And they had been preparing to *kill him*. But what Bruno had done to them.... Greymalkin looked with shock at the serenely bubbling protean floating in front of him. Bruno had not just killed those men. He had *casually slaughtered* them like stomping bugs flat. *And it's my fault! I told him to....*

Greymalkin paused. What exactly *had* he told Bruno to do? In the heat of the moment he had no recollection; it had happened too fast. Then his mind began racing in random panicked directions. *What will the expedition do to me? What will Kuanian think of me?*

«The recording systems of this base have registered nothing at all.» Bruno's thoughts were still very amused. «This is certainly not the first time I have had to make a 'getaway'. I am extremely well-versed in the process of erasing evidence. Your vehicle has been restocked with shadow flux. Shall we go?»

As he tried to look at the monster, Greymalkin found that his vision was swerving up, down, and sideways. His eyes were still jittery, pitching and rolling with the effects of the neuro-stun. He felt so utterly panicked at this point that he would have considered normal panic to constitute a clear and calm mind.

Rather than try to think the situation through further, he simply nodded while wiping vomit off his chin. Looking down at his blood-drenched hand, he realized that all he had accomplished was replacing the bile with viscera. When his stomach threatened to heave again, he instead forced himself to open the airlock, get in the cockpit, and somehow manage to take off. He did not question why the dock clamps retracted or how the hangar door opened, but he did notice Bruno outside the viewport ahead of him the entire way out.

By carefully focusing on each key step in the process slowly, he was able to set the ship on course down the center of the shadow channel toward the main expedition base. He then programmed the autopilot to drop them out of shadow space if it detected any obstacles. Finally, feeling like he would pass out at any moment, he staggered into the medical pod, laid down, and promptly lost consciousness again.

The last thing he was aware of was Bruno cackling away with his bubbling laugh as he sent a communed thought. «Gracious, I was so wrong! This arrangement with Kuanian is going to be enormous fun after all!»

*　*　*

There was a very long period of unconsciousness and then sleep that was punctuated by nightmares. A few times he jolted awake briefly, only to find that he was inside the medical pod again when he banged his forehead on the cover above his face while trying to sit up. Greymalkin did not know if he fell asleep again naturally in those moments, or if the pod sedated him. He woke up twice, screaming against the oxygen tube down his throat and trying to free himself, but the pod had restrained him by then.

He finally woke up fully just as the pod cover was retracting and the restraints slid off his limbs. This time the pod communed a concerned-sounding recording into his head. «Attention! This unit has noted that you have suffered repeated serious neurological trauma. Emergency medical care has been administered and has repaired the most immediate physical damage, but you should seek the care of a qualified medical practitioner immediately. Please review the full diagnostic log at your earliest convenience. Repeat...Attention!....»

Greymalkin shut it off, moaned, and sat up rubbing his head and neck. He felt thick-headed, dazed, and numb. *Where am I?* All he did was stare around the cabin of the skiff at first. His hands were trembling, he noticed abstractly.

He climbed out of the pod, trembling even worse with each step. He had a suspicion that the pod had administered some kind of drug to blunt his emotions and calm him down because of the way he felt. Some of his muscle groups felt sore as he hobbled toward the cockpit. There was a generalized sense of anxiety and confusion that he thought seemed to be associated with someone else, but the one thing he was certain of was that he needed to get to the controls of the skiff. When he got there, the first thing he did was check where he was. The ship was still moving down the shadow channel toward the main expedition base. *Right, that's the course I set. I think. But, why am I worried about that?* He shook his head and tried to remember what had happened. *Why does that sound like such a familiar thought to me?*

«You're up! How are you feeling?» A deep, accented, and chipper stream of communed thoughts flowed into his mind, and he cringed without knowing why. *The creature, it... protected me, right? But, it....*

Then it all came back to him in an instant, together with a hot layer of panic pouring down over him. He accessed the hull cameras quickly, and saw that once again the creature Bruno was floating along in the void just outside the ship. He tried to think through everything that had happened, and soon felt the urgent need to ask the protean some questions, even though he was afraid of what it would say. Although it hurt his head at first, he focused on communing with the alien cyborg.

«Bruno, you... *killed* all those men.»

«Yes, I did. Sorry I waited so long! I wasn't sure what you wanted me to do, so I just watched from a distance until you gave me instructions. They really seemed to be hurting you! I was glad when you finally contacted me.»

«You... saw what they did to me?»

«Oh, yes; all of it. I hope you aren't upset at how long I waited. I'm just not sure of how you want me to handle these sorts of situations yet.»

Inside his mind, Greymalkin went through a twisting sequence of thoughts. At first, despite the calming drugs in his system, he felt an exploding sense of anger that the alien had not helped him when he was attacked. Then, as he tried to think it through from the creature's point of view, his anger drained away, leaving him simply feeling empty.

That's true. I didn't tell him what I wanted him to do ahead of time. I didn't think ahead. I've just been reacting ever since Bora and Soren were killed. Then Greymalkin held his face and sobbed for a few moments before wiping his face and gritting his teeth hard. *Okay, I've got to get on top of this situation and think it through!* He checked the flight log. He still had several days before he reached the main expedition base. In that time he could try to think some things through, and get better prepared.

He performed a traditional Sojourner calming chant while breathing deeply for a few minutes. Then he slowly started making a mental list of what he needed to work through while he got some water and a food bar. While he still felt emotionally broken inside, he felt at least a bit more centered. Greymalkin wasn't eager to talk to the horrific alien cyborg any further, but knew he had to debrief with it. After thinking through his questions, he started conversing with the creature. Bruno seemed to be in good spirits and happy to answer questions for once. He wondered if butchering people cheered it up? After talking to the creature for more than an hour, Greymalkin felt that a coherent picture emerged of what had happened.

It grated on him that Bruno had apparently just watched him being beaten and captured, but the alien obviously did not regard such topics in the same way he did. It also had no hint of remorse at killing the men (there had been *six* of them, apparently), and did not understand any suggestions on his part as to why that might have been an extreme reaction. The creature found the idea of simply subduing the men bizarre, with the only possible motivation being to get more information from them. But as it also pointed out, Bruno had paused long enough to interrogate the last man thoroughly before proceeding to kill him without a second thought. The alien understood the need to get information from the group but evidently did not possess the slightest trace of mercy or common human decency in its thinking about what it had done. As it turned out, however, Bruno had actually discovered a great deal during the interrogation before summarily snapping the man's neck.

Bruno confirmed that the six men had been Burani operatives. Their leader was named Rodolfo, although the others simply called him 'Rodo'. He was apparently the same man that had woken Greymalkin up in the canteen. After leaving Greymalkin with his men, Rodo had quickly departed the resupply base well before Bruno had attacked. Greymalkin's stomach sank even lower when Bruno also verified that Rodo had indeed taken the pack with him that contained the golden garment and tool.

Greymalkin briefly felt like shouting, *Then why didn't you stop him??* However, everything came back to the simple fact that the creature had been operating without any guidance. In fact, given its obvious propensity for violence, he was somewhat surprised at the initial restraint it had shown. It gradually dawned on Greymalkin that if there was anyone he should be angry at, it was himself. The situation could actually have been totally in his control if he had just taken the time and caution to have been prepared.

Thinking about it, at first Greymalkin found it hard to feel much sympathy for the men that had been about to kill him just as casually, but then the memory of the room flooded with their entrails came back to him and he trembled uncontrollably for ten minutes straight before he could continue with the conversation. Bruno seemed briefly puzzled by his silence, and Greymalkin started to understand that the creature was simply too alien to understand most human reactions. As he reflected on this, Greymalkin gradually realized that he had been confused because of the alien's ability to commune with him in a familiar language. *I suppose that just because it can communicate with me doesn't mean it thinks like me.* That was a sobering lesson that he would need to internalize. *If I live through this, that is.*

Whatever was happening here in the Carinae, there were interests at work that had no hesitation at committing murder. He thought about how correct Father Johannes had been every time that he had admonished Greymalkin and pleaded with him not to go. This was indeed a lawless region where violence prevailed. *I was wrong and he was right. It's as simple as that. Bora, Soren, and I were all wrong to come here. They paid with their lives, and now I've become an accessory to murder myself.* But then a counter-thought occurred to him.

We weren't wrong to come here, we just weren't prepared. If we had known what they would do to us.... But then he shook his head. It wasn't his fault that they'd attacked him, and it certainly wasn't the fault of Bora and Soren that they'd been killed! He gripped the pilot couch harder and harder until his hands became drained of blood as he grew angrier and angrier at a central realization that was dawning on him. *From this moment on, if I'm not prepared, it will be my fault.*

In that moment Greymalkin felt a profound shift in his worldview. Even though he had been a Sojourner for as long as he could remember, there had always been some parts of his training in the Order that he had not truly understood, and many of those were the parts that addressed the dangers of mission work. He thought back now to the countless drills that had emphasized a desperate importance in physical awareness of surroundings and rapid analysis of environmental threats. He realized now why he'd never done well in those drills. He'd always felt *safe*. He remembered preceptors like Johannes that had seemed so harsh to him in the moments when he'd been absent-minded or day-dreaming.

Once, when Greymalkin had walked obliviously through a training simulation while blithely ignoring signs of hostile life-forms, Johannes had deactivated the mental safety settings in the synesthesia and allowed the young boy to actually feel the terrifying sensations of being thrown to the ground and mauled by a predator. At the time, Greymalkin had felt shocked and outraged, sulking for a week over Johannes' admonishment that, "The Galaxy is nae a safe place outside the calm walls of this monastery! In the field, *never* simply wonder if danger is out there! Expect that it's *always* there, and *always* comin' for ye! What ye're tae do is just this, *make sure that you discover it before it discovers you!"*

After all the intervening years, Greymalkin finally felt that shift in worldview taking hold of him firmly now that he had gone into the field. Johannes had always said that pain and fear were the best teachers of new safety instincts. As grim as the transformation in perspective was, as bitter as he felt about having to internalize it, he knew he would never again wander into an unknown setting blindly. And he sadly reflected that this was likely not the last such transformation he would experience in the Carinae. In fact, he now wondered if he could change *enough* to actually survive the place. But this newly acute sense of caution in his mind immediately brought him back to the moment when his companions had been killed in the Rift. Now more than ever, he felt like he owed it to Bora and Soren to set things right, be more cautious, and succeed at what they had all set out to do.

And Greymalkin couldn't help wondering *why* this was happening to them. *Why are these Burani lunatics so blasted determined to make sure we don't arrive? What did we ever do to them?* Then a suspicion crawled into his mind, curled up, and made a nest there.

It's not anything we've done yet. It's something they're afraid we'll do. Or find out.

He pounded on the couch arm so hard that it made his head hurt again. But now he realized had a purpose, a purpose that had been carved into his mind with a bloody knife. *I have to honor Bora and Soren and do what they would have done if they had lived. I have to do what Sojourners are supposed to do, help people and record knowledge.*

«Are you feeling okay, boss?» The cyborg's thoughts seemed curious, rather than concerned. Greymalkin unclenched his hands and jaws, and responded with subdued anger.

«I wish you hadn't let the Burani leader get away. We don't know where he's going. And I hate to lose that pack.» Greymalkin felt empty again. The two gifts from Kuanian had felt like good luck charms, and now they were gone.

«Oh, I haven't lost track of that fellow! I know exactly where he is.» Bruno bubbled away with his cackling alien laugh as Greymalkin blinked.

«What!? I thought you said he left the resupply base?»

«He did, but I wouldn't let somebody just beat up my boss and get away for good! His ship is much faster than yours, but he's in this same channel way up ahead of us.»

«How do you know that?» Greymalkin found it hard to believe that even this creature could observe objects in isolated continuity bubbles parsecs away.

«Simple! I can divide myself into many parts, and still keep track of all of me. I hid a small bit of me on his ship. I can track him wherever he goes.»

Greymalkin's eyes widened. That changed a lot. He began thinking, sorting the situation into compartments and analyzing each one in turn. His normally smooth internal mental analysis process felt like a jangling havoc of sifting through falling rocks because of everything that had happened to him in the last few days, but he was determined to become better prepared.

And the monstrous alien cyborg, for all of its horrifically violent capabilities, was proving to be just as important an asset as he had anticipated. He gave thanks that he had stuck to his instincts and freed it from its prison. He went back to questioning the alien, and it turned into a conversation that lasted on and off through the next few days. By the time they finally reached the main expedition base, while he still didn't feel prepared for every possibility, he felt a hundred times more organized than when he had set foot in the resupply base.

When the main expedition base came into view floating in deep space, it proved to be a substantial center of operations. He could identify dozens of large facilities and hundreds of starships, some of them quite large indeed. The base transponder marked the main docks as located in the hollow trunk of a gigantic dead nemora meta-tree husk that the expedition had probably used as a convenient starting point for the base. The crown of the tree was a delicate looking spherical spray dozens of kilometers wide in the vacuum of the void, with more than a hundred silvery gossamer branches that all ended in a bulb that was likely being used as a habitat. Although the kilometers-long branches looked frail, he knew that the mirrorshell material of the branches and other parts of the tree was far, far stronger than any normal metal since the bonds that held it together extended into shadow space in a dense interdimensional structure. The toughness of mirrorshell was why arks and so many other starships were constructed from the stuff. He wondered what could have killed this huge tree, supposing it must have been some sort of internal rot or disease. Cyborganic species like this were found throughout the Galaxy, and could live for many millennia.

He eyed the huge bulbs on the ends of the dead branches, which typically only matured after thousands of years of slow growth. If they weren't harvested by humans or other star-faring species, in living trees the bulbs would eventually detach and become the larval form of the species, with the base of each bulb functioning as an independent shadow space mast to propel and disperse the larva across interstellar distances. The 'trunk' of the main meta-tree was comprised of thickly clustered pillars of mirrorshell that gradually accreted around the original shadow space mast of the tree, and extended straight down from the center of the spherical crown of branches for many kilometers.

Greymalkin thought back to when he had first encountered nemora meta-trees as a child. The cyborganic life-forms were found all through the Orion Arm of the Galaxy, and he'd played inside the cavernous hollow branches and bulbs of the forests around the orphanage as a young boy with the other oblates. He had always wondered what the *Builders* had used the trees for, but that mystery had occupied scientists for centuries. As he approached the main docks he saw that the entrance was a nearly kilometer-wide gap carved through the thickest cluster of silvery pillars low on the trunk. Greymalkin carefully steered the skiff into the entryway and then toward the particular dock the transponder indicated. Clamps slowly grasped the skiff. A standard pier tunnel extended out from the dock and thumped against the skiff's airlock.

Greymalkin took a deep breath, trying to calm his nerves. After his last experience, he felt frightened at the thought of boarding the base. But he also felt an angry sense of alert vigilance. He'd rehearsed what to do in many possible scenarios with Bruno over the last days, and this time he maintained a close communal link with the hidden alien cyborg as he went to the airlock to exit the ship. He paused to go over everything with the alien cyborg one last time.

«Okay, to reiterate, this 'Rodo' guy, the Burani operative, is not here, correct?» Greymalkin knew he was obsessing about the Burani, but he couldn't help it. *They almost killed me twice!* The protean responded quickly; it seemed to be in one of its cheerful, manic phases.

«Yes, boss! He reached this location a day before us, and left again after only a few hours in a different ship, rover-configuration. I wasn't able to record everything he did while he was here, but he visited a particular module of the main base which is apparently the Sojourner habitation here. Well, at least, it is according to *you*.» Bruno had replayed recordings of the man Rodo visiting various locations in the expedition base, and one locale immediately stood out as a missionary priory to Greymalkin for the simple reason that it had been full of Sojourners. Greymalkin knew the man's face all too well, now. He had studied it long and hard to be able to spot the man even if disguised. When he wasn't smiling pleasantly, Rodo was a cold-looking older man with a narrow, somber face. The elegant dark jumpsuit he wore seemed old but otherwise unremarkable. That is, other than the fact that it had several pouches on the belt that were obviously big enough to hold a small shadow blade. And he was wearing Greymalkin's pack. Greymalkin did not look forward to encountering the man again, and it especially troubled him that he had specifically visited the Sojourners on the base. Kuanian had said she had recruited other Sojourners from different parts of the Orion Arm. The idea had been for Greymalkin, Bora, and Soren to join them. Now Greymalkin felt guarded about even *that* idea.

«How did you get all these recordings again? I thought your... *fragment* stayed with Rodo's skiff.» Greymalkin was still trying to understand the nature and extent of the protean's abilities. He didn't trust it, but it was certainly a powerful ally.

«They aren't very sophisticated with their security systems. I just tapped into their internal camera system on the base. This wasn't fancy work, boss, *you* could probably do it.» Bruno's trickling chuckle-thoughts were less and less annoying to Greymalkin, as was its sarcastic use of the term 'boss' whenever he communed with it. *If it puts the thing in a good mood to make fun of me, all the better. I need to stay on its good side.* Bruno had been noticeably more cooperative than at first. «He stayed a while with the Sojourners and then left, still with your pack. He picked up that rover from this pen and then took off right away.» Bruno communed an image of a dozen or so rover starships, but something looked odd to Greymalkin about them.

«Did you say pen? That's not a dock? I can see humans in void suits on the periphery.» Greymalkin was confused.

«Yes, but notice how they are outside of the barriers? The humans are avoiding the individual rovers that have not been dock-clamped. Those starships are not simple artifacts, they are intelligent feral cyborgs.» Bruno's thoughts felt amused at Greymalkin's confusion.

«What! But... enslaving intelligent beings is....» Greymalkin began to feel ill again.

Bruno finished his thought for him. «...is not uncommon here in the Carinae. You are clearly not from this region, boss. Things are much more brutal here than where you come from. I suggest you become accustomed to it.»

He could sense Bruno's bubbling laughter in the back of his mind, and realized that the monster was actually hoping for some kind of violence to break out again. That made Greymalkin's stomach flutter in fear, and he again had a desire to run away. But there was nowhere to run, except forward. Scowling, he decided he'd talked to Bruno enough, opened the airlock door, and cautiously stepped into the pier tunnel.

What he encountered there made his eyebrows shoot up, and he crouched warily.

An alien was standing (crouching?) in the tunnel on the walkway, studying a silvery tablet. It was like no species he had ever seen before, and his observational habits kicked in trying to classify it. *Bilateral symmetry (uncommon, as in humans), vestigial predatory features....* Greymalkin started recording details. The creature had speckled brown and white fur (or feathers?) visible where its branching limbs emerged from the utility jumpsuit it wore. The large head had big, alert-looking ears that directionally focused on sounds. There were four eyes arranged in widely separated pairs that were each surrounded by a white ruff of fur, giving it an odd goggle-eyed appearance. The eyes all had yellow pupils that looked up at him above a prominent beak-like structure, and the entire 'face' was framed by something like big horns that emerged from the top of the head and curved down below the ears. It walked up to Greymalkin with a surprisingly agile gait (he noticed nervously how heavily muscled its limbs were), and actually bowed to him.

And then, astonishingly, it *spoke*, in a deep and resonate voice.

"Greetings to you, human Brother Thomas," the alien said. It had only a slightly odd Peretian accent that actually made it sound strangely erudite to Greymalkin. "I am called Huhonen, and will be your dock manager. At your service!"

Greymalkin eyed the alien cautiously and before he said anything, communed with Bruno. «Have you ever seen a species like this before?»

«Oh, certainly, boss.» Bruno sounded only moderately bored already, now that the creature had not attacked Greymalkin. «It's just a Crotani. You can find them in many of the systems around here.»

«Why haven't I heard of them before?»

«Probably because you're dumb.» Bruno said with sincerity, annoying Greymalkin. «That, and they're boring little savants that no one cares about. Or maybe you humans have simply never encountered them before. It appears they've put them to work here, though.»

Greymalkin stifled an urge to snap a retort back at Bruno, and instead took a breath. He nodded to the alien and said, "Thank you, Huhonen. How do you know who I am?"

"Your skiff was registered with the expedition in advance by the Lady Kuanian, along with the names and images of yourself and your companions," the Crotani said. Its four eyes glanced at the tablet for a second, and as they did so a fifth sensing organ blinked open in the center of its forehead. *Is it or isn't it an eye?* Greymalkin wondered for a moment, as the organ didn't look like the other eyes. Perhaps an infrared sensing surface? "Are a 'Sister Bora' and a 'Brother Soren' waiting to exit your ship?" it asked.

Greymalkin groaned inwardly, but again went through the painful story of what had happened to them on the way to the Carinae, omitting the parts about Bruno and his visit to the resupply base. At first the Crotani did not seem to react, but then began bobbing up and down and blinking quickly.

"That is terrible!" Huhonen bellowed in a louder voice, although its voice did not seem capable of conveying much of anything approaching an emotional tone other than by volume. The beak chomped open and shut a few times, and he could see several fleshy lips and tongues inside its mouth. "Do you require medical attention? Shall I summon human medical technicians?"

"No, thank you," Greymalkin said warily. If he wanted it later, he would seek out the base infirmary. "I would like to visit the Sojourner mission priory here, though. Can you direct me?"

Huhonen blinked at him a few more times with various eyes, and then said, "Yes, I will take you myself. Follow me, please." It turned around and began bounding away, forcing Greymalkin to almost run after it. The odd alien ran to the end of the pier tunnel, which turned out to be the stepping-off entrance to a big transit column. Huhonen waited for Greymalkin to catch up with him and then they both stepped off the pressor deck into the huge empty space of the transit column. They began accelerating upward, the wind making his flight suit flap a bit.

From the size of the nemora meta-tree, Greymalkin knew that it would take them a few minutes to reach the center of the tree's crown, which was presumably where they would then ride another transit column out to one of the habitat bulbs. He took the opportunity to question the alien further. "You are a Crotani, is that correct? I have never encountered your species before."

Huhonen whipped his big head 90 degrees around to look at Greymalkin, and said, "Yes, human Brother Thomas. We are native only to the Sagittarius Arm of the Galaxy. We are very grateful for the help of Sojourners, the Xenocorps, and especially Lady Kuanian for your assistance and the gift of knowledge about shadow space technology."

Greymalkin suddenly realized that the Crotani had no shadow jewel in its cranium. It had not attempted to commune with him, and now that he actively sought for it he could feel the absence of any communing signal within the creature. *That* led directly to interesting inferences. "Wait, are your people system-bound? I was told that your species was to be found in many star systems of this region."

"Yes, that is true. And we hope to one day rejoin the civilizations that travel among the stars. We did so long ago, but lost that knowledge. When your mission first visited my people, it changed everything for us. I volunteered immediately to assist your expedition."

Greymalkin stared in disbelief at the alien. *Yet another Bereft civilization? And this one is alien?* But then he felt even more incredulous. "You learned to speak Peretian this well in only a year's time?"

The Crotani bowed again, an interesting gymnastic feat given that they were hurtling upward together through an open air column. "My people have some skill with languages. And we are eager to learn about humans. Thank you so much!" It again bellowed the last words for emphasis rather than expressing enthusiasm in its tone, but now that dissonance seemed more understandable given how short a time the creature had studied his language. It was incredible to Greymalkin that Huhonen had learned a wholly alien language so quickly. *But then, I can pick up a new language in a year. Why am I skeptical that this alien could do it?* He started to feel a new linguistic kinship with Huhonen.

They reached the end of the transit column and stepped out into a gigantic transitway junction that was evidently the center of the huge tree's crown of branches. Looking up, Greymalkin saw that the roughly spherical junction was almost a kilometer across, with hundreds of transit openings around the interior. Huhonen led Greymalkin to the entrance of a glideway path marked on the floor of the huge chamber. They both stepped up onto the invisible path and it whisked them away sideways around the interior of the junction, presumably toward the transit entrance that led to the Sojourner mission.

"How many Sojourners are there in the mission?" he asked the alien. Huhonen's large head again whipped around in that disconcerting manner, this time almost directly backwards from the way the alien was facing.

"I do not know, but their habitat is the largest bulb on the entire tree," the alien said. "I would assume hundreds, perhaps thousands, but I do not know. We will be there soon; you can ask them. This way, please." The Crotani stepped off the glideway and quickly strode to another transit entrance, waiting again for Greymalkin to catch up. As he ran up to the alien, he wondered if he should ask it to slow down for him, but the alien stepped into the transit column immediately and Greymalkin followed it.

As they descended through the column rapidly, Greymalkin asked, "Since you are a dock manager, may I ask you if the Sojourners take many trips out into the Carinae?" The alien shook its head back and forth in an exaggerated way that made him dizzy just looking at it.

"I have rarely seen them venture off of the base," Huhonen said. That surprised Greymalkin more than almost anything else the alien had said. He had assumed they would be exploring the region, and had intended to ask where they went most frequently. A missionary priory of Sojourners that *did not sojourn*? It made little sense, especially in an incredible region like this. As he mulled this over they descended into a reception space at the end of the transit column. Huhonen bounded away the second their feet touched the floor, and Greymalkin hurried after him into the next room. The entire jaunt across the tree had only taken a few minutes. *Those transit columns were rigged for efficiency, not comfort. Interesting.*

The door they approached was surprisingly massive. As Huhonen touched a contact that was apparently a summons, Greymalkin examined the big door frowning. What was the purpose of a barrier like this? It certainly wasn't a simple pressure door. Something this big implied a need for physical security against weapons. It took a long time for anyone to respond, even after his alien guide had touched the summons twice more. When Greymalkin had started to wonder what was wrong, a smaller section of the big door unlatched heavily from the inside and opened.

The Sojourner that emerged wore hooded robes, but the colors and markings were unfamiliar to Greymalkin. This fellow might have been from the other side of human space for all he knew. And he seemed extraordinarily angry.

"Why do you summon repeatedly, fool Crotani?" the man yelled at Huhonen, who cowered down and stepped back from the entrance. "You must have seen the notice that we are in mourning!" Then the man saw Greymalkin, and his eyes widened.

Greymalkin looked around the big door, but there was no notice that he could see. "I see no such notice, Brother," Greymalkin said. The man bowed and walked up to Greymalkin through the small door, looking up and backwards at the door. He snorted and activated a control, and then a very large sign lit up with a litany repeated in several languages that basically amounted to variations on *Go Away, In Mourning!*

"Apologies, young Brother. We were not expecting any new arrivals. Who are you and what...." The man trailed off, peering at Greymalkin with a strange expression that first seemed startled and then repulsed. Greymalkin cursed inside his mind.

It's the covenants. He had worried about this, whether or not the layered communal patterns piled on his shadow jewel would be immediately obvious to others with shadow jewels. Apparently they were. The man looked Greymalkin up and down distastefully.

"You surely cannot be a Brother Sojourner," the man finally said. "The Order does not allow cybes to be ordained with active...."

"I am an Apprentice in good standing with the Order," Greymalkin said curtly, his cheeks and ears beginning to burn with the realization that everyone in the Order was likely going to treat him this way now. "These... *cybernetic systems* were placed on my shadow jewel without my assent while en route here. My name is Brother Greymalkin Thomas. I have endured a very trying journey to reach this mission, and would appreciate the courtesy of being admitted!"

The other monk squinted at him skeptically. "There was a Brother Thomas scheduled to arrive some days ago along with others. But we were told not to expect you; that your conveyance had been destroyed on the way here. And now you claim to be Brother Thomas, but with these...." He gestured vaguely to Greymalkin's head in disgust. It incensed the young monk.

"I demand to be admitted!" Greymalkin shouted in fury, and was surprised at his own anger. *But then, I've been through some moments lately,* he thought. Both Huhonen and the monk seemed intimidated by his rage. The monk made a placating gesture.

"Now, now, young Brother," the monk said. "I didn't say I would not admit you. It's just that you've arrived at an inopportune time; we are in mourning over the death of our most senior Brother. Please come in." The monk stepped back to allow Greymalkin entrance.

Greymalkin turned to the Crotani and tried to recover from his angry outburst. The cringing alien looked agitated, and was glancing back toward the transit column. "Thank you most sincerely, Huhonen," Greymalkin said to the alien, bowing. "I am grateful for your kindness and prompt attention to my requests. You have been a model of hospitality, unlike some others here." He could not resist the irritated comment directed toward the other Sojourner.

The Crotani bowed several times again. "You are most welcome! I will take my leave then!" the creature bellowed, and then ran back to leap into the transit column and vanish upward. Greymalkin felt ashamed of his anger, and turned back to stomp through the door after the other monk, who led him into the compound.

"Now, please be mindful of the service we're holding and keep silent when we reach the other Brothers and Sisters," the monk said as they walked. "You can speak to the Prior after the service is concluded."

"Who died?" Greymalkin asked, still slightly sullen, but sensitive to the idea of the death of a friend. The other monk winced.

"It was aged Brother Vairoc," he said. "He was found dead yesterday."

Greymalkin frowned and nodded. "I see. He was old, you say?"

"Indeed, he was the oldest monk anyone among us in the Order have ever encountered. He had reached his three hundred and seventieth year," the monk said. Greymalkin felt disoriented by the statement.

"What sort of years are you talking about?" Greymalkin asked. "Surely not standard years, unless he was a cyborg or revenant recreated after death?" The monk shook his head.

"Standard years. And he was a living man, not an unnatural revenant. Brother Vairoc was unusual and renowned for his knowledge of life-preserving technologies."

Greymalkin looked askance. "Excuse me, but that seems hard to believe. I've heard of extreme life-preserving techniques that can carry a person to perhaps two hundred years, but not longer. And if he was actually so extremely aged, what in all space was he doing here on this expedition in the midst of... such danger?"

The other monk shrugged. "He was still in reasonable health despite his age, and greatly wanted to come. He was one of the few survivors of the last expedition to the Sagittarius Arm three centuries ago. And he had apparently made new discoveries about the Carinae that he was going to reveal to us. Something profound about the central Eta Carinae star system."

Everything about this seems odd, Greymalkin thought with immediate suspicion, and noted with bitterness how quick he had become to distrust situations now. *This place is twisting me up.* "What did he die of, then?"

The other monk paused for a long moment, eyed Greymalkin sidelong, and then said, "Sadly, we believe he killed himself."

"What! How?" Greymalkin's alarm bells were already jangling.

"Violently. He smashed himself into a wall, running. The impact crushed his skull."

Greymalkin stared dumbfounded at the other monk. *Can he really believe that?* Greymalkin tried not to sound condescending as he asked, "Uh, have you considered foul play?"

"Obviously we considered it," the monk said, irritated. "But many of us saw him retire to his quarters, which are in common view. We all saw that no one else entered for hours, and the base system logs confirm that no one else was admitted to his quarters to see him. Now please be silent; we are approaching the chapel where the service is being held." Indeed, an entrance ahead of them was surrounded with Sojourners in meditation pose, and he could hear chanting inside. Apparently there was not enough room in their chapel for everyone, and the overflow were listening from out here. The monk left Greymalkin alone and shoved his way inside.

Greymalkin listened to the service for a few minutes, long enough to confirm that it was the long form of the *Journey's End* mourning ceremony. He had made up his mind already about what had happened, but nevertheless communed with Bruno. «You said that the man Rodo came here to the Sojourner priory? Did you see what he did here?»

«No. All the recordings became scrambled when he entered where you are now. It seems likely he was involved, though.» The alien cyborg sounded only mildly interested. *Not enough immediate violence to entertain that ghoul, I guess. But I'm certain that this poor old Brother must have been killed by the Burani.* He felt simultaneously nervous and seething through the entire *Journey's End* service as people shared memories of the dead man, and then afterwards when a seemingly interminable flood of Sojourners exited the chapel. He waited unobtrusively in an alcove until he could identify the monk that he thought must be the Prior from the small crowd of monks that followed him dutifully out of the chapel. Summoning up his courage, he went up to the man and bowed, presenting himself with a brief introduction.

All of the older monks in the group scowled at Greymalkin, pointedly studying his head. Greymalkin tried to stay neutral and not to react. The man that he thought must be the Prior looked at him coldly and said, "Yes, greetings, Brother Thomas. We were informed of your arrival during the service. Please accompany me." The procession of monks wound through the warren of tunnels in the priory, finally reaching a suite of drab offices.

The Prior sat down behind an imposing desk and set of consoles, and two belligerent looking Subpriors stood behind him with their arms folded. Greymalkin stood before the desk uncertainly as they all glowered at him, until the Prior said, "A few bits of your incredible account were relayed to me during the service, but I wish to hear the entire tale from your lips. Please proceed."

Greymalkin wailed inside, but set about retelling his journey with the Jotuns and its disastrous ending. He again omitted the stories of Bruno and the refueling base. *In for a bit, in for the whole thing....* he thought irritably.

When he was finally done, the Subpriors looked somewhat more sympathetic, but the Prior appeared unconvinced. He drummed his fingers on his desk, and asked, "And you somehow escaped the destruction of a vessel as mighty as one of the Jotuns' transporters? And you also claim that the layers of covenants engraved on your mind's shadow jewel were forced upon you by the monstrous 'Velan' that wreaked such destruction upon the huge Jotun vessel?"

"Yes, well, one of the covenants," Greymalkin said. "Although in a real sense I accepted it as the price of being spared by the creature. And I do not believe that the covenant has enslaved me, as I have not felt compelled to do anything against my will. And I cannot, in good conscience, claim the other was forced on me either. I willingly accepted it from Lady Kuanian."

"The Lady Kuanian?" the Prior seemed even more skeptical. "I find it difficult to believe that one of the prime sponsors of our entire expedition would enslave you."

Greymalkin shook his head. "I say again, she did not enslave me. I believe that her cybernetic mental encoding holds vital information."

"For what possible purpose?" the Prior said, scowling. Greymalkin hesitated.

Now it comes to it, he thought. He'd been dreading being questioned about this matter, but he had made up his mind to not reveal the presence of Bruno just yet. "That is between the Lady and me," Greymalkin said sullenly. The Prior leaned back in his chair.

"Which is precisely the kind of absurd story that a covenant would lay on you to claim," the Prior said, his brows knitted. As Greymalkin began an exclamation, the Prior's expression softened, and the man held up his hand. "Pardon me, young Brother. It is not your fault that you were accosted and enslaved, most likely by one of the many nefarious human barbarian tribes that inhabit this dreadful region. Or worse, one of the alien species that have sprung from its depths."

"You cannot believe that," Greymalkin said incredulously. "If I were truly enslaved, I could neither have disobeyed or taken leave of my captor."

"No," the Prior said. "But you may not have done so. You have, after all, been transformed. You may have been sent here under orders by your captors to infiltrate our missionaries and betray us."

"What!" Greymalkin cried. He started to make a counter-argument, but struggled to find a flaw in the Prior's argument. The Prior shook his head sadly.

"You need not posture or seek to argue with me any further, my boy," the Prior said. "We know how torturous the rigors of cybernetic enslavement can be. We can send you home on the next Sadorian galleon that arrives here with those returning to the Orion Arm."

Greymalkin felt panicky again. *I cannot be summarily sent home after all I have done to reach this place!* He tried another tack. "I understand your concerns. But let me prove that I am under no coercion!"

"How could you possibly do that?" the Prior said, raising an eyebrow.

"Give me some task to accomplish," Greymalkin pleaded. "I am an expert helmsman, and there is the ship I arrived in. There surely must be some nonessential cargo I can transport for you."

"There are myriad useful courier duties, but you have forgotten something," the Prior said, "That skiff belongs to the expedition, not you. You were tasked by the lady Kuanian with bringing it here, and then transferring to another small starship, a cyneget rover."

"Then let me use the new vessel and serve as courier through a shadow plane route," Greymalkin begged.

"There is a problem; when you did not arrive, the option on that vehicle expired, albeit just a day ago," the Prior said. "The vendor is one of the more scurrilous types that have gravitated to this base in search of the fabled profits of the Carinae. I do not think he will give you the cyneget now, and we have no power to compel him."

Greymalkin stared at the Prior for a moment, and finally held his head, stomped his foot, and exclaimed angrily, "Blast it all!" When the other Sojourners looked at him with even more pity, Greymalkin could not stand it. He could hardly believe that these individuals were even Sojourners. *Where is the mutual support of the Order? They should be trying to help me, not show me contempt!* Finally the young monk spat out, "Well then, if I go and convince this... *vendor* to abide by the original intent of the contract with lady Kuanian, forgive the one tardy day, and give me the rover, will you then allow me to try to prove myself?!"

"You can try, young Brother," the Prior said, quietly now. "But when you fail, I cannot allow you to live within the walls of the Priory while you wait for the next ship home to the Orion Arm. You are a risk to us, you see. You will have to stay in the base warrens with the unsolicited miners and other fortune-seekers that have become camp followers here."

Greymalkin felt himself about to explode, but clenched his jaws together and counted to ten slowly. Then he said, "Very well. I cannot ask you to put your monastic community at risk, after all." Greymalkin barely succeeded in keeping the sarcasm out of his voice. "Where may I find this vendor? And how do I identify the rover?" The other monks looked at each other for a moment skeptically, and then one spoke up.

"His name is Trauerstrom," the Subprior said. "Adler Trauerstrom. You can find him down by the main docks. Anyone down there or in one of the taverns can direct you. And here is the identification code for the rover." The man gave him a number that Greymalkin remembered to record.

Trembling in frustration and fear, Greymalkin could barely keep from losing his temper further, but managed to hold it inside. He took a breath, bowed, and said, "Thank you, Brothers. May Providence be with you."

"And with you," the Prior said, looking away in boredom, obviously impatient to go on to other matters. With a final scowl, Greymalkin spun on his heel and left.

* * *

As he strode rapidly back to the entrance of the priory, Bruno communed with him flippantly. «You have a lot of restraint. I'd have just killed them.» Greymalkin grit his teeth.

«I have to find this guy, Trauerstrom, but keep monitoring me. If anyone attacks me, stick to the plan.» Greymalkin at least felt that he would not be ambushed this time.

«Do I have to keep hiding until then? I could protect you better if I was closer to you.» Bruno sounded more bored than protective.

Greymalkin rolled his eyes. «No. This time we have a plan. Just make sure that you stay close enough outside the station that you can get to me quickly if I need you.» The protean didn't respond other than to commune the bizarre grinding thought that Greymalkin had learned was the cyborg's equivalent of an exasperated sigh.

Greymalkin jumped into the transit column and retraced his path down toward the docks. When he reached the main transit junction for the docks, he wondered briefly if he should seek out the Crotani dock manager, but decided that he had bothered the alien enough for his first day at the base. Greymalkin still felt so angry over his interaction with the Prior that he wanted to explore the base by himself for the moment. He looked around at the various transit entrances leading away to different dock clusters. When he saw no obvious directional clues, he remembered what the Subprior had said. *Ask at a tavern.*

He looked around and quickly saw a prominent entrance to what appeared to be a large social space. He walked up to it and heard many voices inside. The entrance opened out into branching side sections, each of which had dozens of humans eating, drinking, and conversing. He nodded to himself and walked in.

The place was packed, mostly with rough-looking Canisian miners drinking from tubes of liquid. Some of them looked like they had just arrived because they still wore their void suits. A few even had runcibles with them, big shadow space tools for extracting flux and aureate across dimensional boundaries. Hesitating, he looked around shyly, but there was no one that looked particularly approachable in the tavern. He finally marched up to one of the miners and tapped him on the shoulder. The fellow squinted at Greymalkin, but his expression became more reserved when he saw the Sojourner Galaxy-shaped S symbol on his flight suit and the strangely large shadow jewel in his head.

"Excuse me," Greymalkin said in Canisian. "Can you tell me where I can find a man named Trauerstrom?" The man seemed to think for a moment, and then shook his head.

"I don't know him, but then I only arrived recently," the miner said candidly.

"Is there anybody here that you think would know a lot of people at the base?" Greymalkin asked. The miner nodded quickly.

"Oh sure, just ask Tatter," he said.

"Who is that?" Greymalkin asked, frowning. The man seemed to chuckle, but Greymalkin noticed that it was a slightly nervous laugh.

"Tatterdemalion. She runs this place; she knows everybody," the man said. Then he lowered his voice, "But, uh, stay out of her way."

"Why?" Greymalkin asked.

"She causes a lot of trouble," the miner said, evasively. "She works with Old Gower, the base operations manager, and his son's gang. I'm not sure exactly what their arrangement is. But..." There was something the man was obviously hesitating to say, Greymalkin thought.

"But what? Come on, tell me."

"She... never mind. It's just, she causes lots of trouble around here," the miner finally said. "Watch out when you're around her. She's over there, bringing drinks out to that bunch." He pointed to a mob of men nearby.

"Thanks for the advice," Greymalkin said. He paused, wondering if he should go somewhere else for information, but then decided he didn't have any better options. He worked his way through the tavern crowd toward the big group. He could see someone female in the middle of the miners, but there were so many people, and they were talking so loudly that he couldn't make himself heard. When the group showed no signs of moving apart, he tried to worm his way through a little. That proved to be a mistake. A big miner turned unexpectedly, and his huge shin swept Greymalkin's feet out from under him. The pressor field in the tavern was apparently not tuned for safety, because it simply threw Greymalkin down through the crowd to the floor, rather than steadying him. The noise of the crowd died down appreciably as people realized he'd fallen.

Greymalkin cursed under his breath, but before he could get his hands underneath him, someone with a powerful grip grabbed his arm and violently yanked him up onto his feet. Greymalkin was ready to yell at the person who had almost pulled his arm off so rudely, but he hadn't gotten his footing yet and stumbled against them. The strong arm that had hauled him up went around his back and pulled him tight to steady him. And then the room vanished around him for a split second that seemed to linger on indefinitely.

Greymalkin seemed to be looking down into a huge meadow of strange alien plant life at the back of a child sitting alone, faced away from him, wearing a red hooded garment. The child was singing sadly in an eerie language he had never heard before, and seemed to be playing by itself quietly. There was something so lonely about the small, hooded figure that he had unconsciously reached down to touch the child's shoulder in concern. The little figure turned to face him, still singing forlornly. He tried to scream, but was frozen in horror and rooted to the spot. The face within the hood was that of a blue-grey fiend with dagger-like fangs and only glittering, smooth surfaces where eyes would have been on a human child. The small form seemed to expand dramatically before him, with massive limbs of corded muscles and dark armor languidly stretching out to pull him close. The hard greyish lips retracted farther, revealing more of the array of wet, dagger-fangs which parted as Greymalkin's face was pulled closer to the grisly maw. Paralyzed, he tried again to draw in his breath to scream, but instead nightmarishly found himself leaning in to kiss the ghoul's mouth. Just as he felt his lips and tongue meet the harsh fangs, the awful hallucination vanished.

That was when he became aware of a very human, and extremely *female* form pressed against him. He found himself nose to nose with an exhausted young woman's face. He was stunned for a moment by how beautiful she was, but he also noted how careworn her expressive features were. As the woman eased Greymalkin down away from her, he saw that she was somehow also juggling a half dozen big drink tubes in her other arm, all while she had simultaneously snatched him up off the deck with one hand. Her attention was sideways, on the armful of drinks, as she set Greymalkin down on his feet.

"Are you okay, bud?" the young woman asked in a distracted, tired voice, and then glanced at him. Her gaze drilled into him, the exhausted expression vanished, and her eyes flashed as she took him in quickly. Then she smiled broadly and brightened immeasurably, her face becoming what seemed to Greymalkin to be nothing but a gigantic grin of white teeth and big dark brown eyes that blotted out the rest of the room, paralyzing him for a moment. She'd noticed how petrified he was while she held him up against her. After abruptly erupting in a loud guffaw that was then echoed by the entire crowd, the woman's huge grin turned into a widely dimpled mouth that bawled at him with a deeply amused and bawdy contralto voice, "Hunh! I think you may have had enough already, pal! You feel a little... *stiff*. But what can I do you for, then?"

Greymalkin tried to find his voice, which wasn't easy given that he was still shoved up against the buxom woman by the packed crowd. He was just becoming aware of how deeply her jumpsuit front was unzipped when he quickly averted his eyes. She noticed that too, and simply grinned at him even more brightly if it was possible.

"Uh, are you Tatterdemalion?" he finally asked. She paused, obviously enjoying herself as she stared at him, leaning in to look up at him from under thick eyebrows and eyelashes, her face framed by a bushy chestnut mane. He tried to avoid staring into her hypnotic eyes, and instead wound up lost in her flashing smile.

"Now, who else would I be?" she practically roared at him in the noise of the room. The big smile danced in her voice, and then sparked another round of guffaws by the crowd around them. It came to him that despite her obvious fatigue she seemed to be managing the situation adeptly. *And, is she... flirting with me or something?* Embarrassed, Greymalkin finally asked his question as she proceeded to hand out the drink-tubes to the men around him. He noticed uncomfortably that she was very intentionally brushing against him while she did so.

"Do you know where I can find a man named Adler Trauerstrom?" he asked. The woman raised one thick eyebrow at the question, but after a moment, grinned again.

"That anus?" she said, more as a statement than a question. "He runs a cyneget pen that takes up all of Dock Fifteen. Why're you looking for him?"

"He owes me a rover," Greymalkin said with a scowl. The woman handed out the last of the drink tubes, and then shrugged while making a face.

"Well, good luck with that, pal," she said. She grinned again as she turned, shoving the big miners out of her way effortlessly with surprising physical strength. "But take it from me, you only get one thing out of an anus!" The crowd resounded with laughter again, and Greymalkin felt his cheeks redden even more.

He pushed his way out of the tavern as quickly as he could, muttering in a low voice to himself, "Yeah, I *bet* that woman causes a lot of trouble." He had forgotten that Bruno was monitoring him, and jumped when the cyborg's communed thoughts came into his head.

«That was not a woman.» The thoughts bubbled and hissed with amusement. «I actually like her, but she's not a human female. Well, not *only* a human female.»

One of Greymalkin's eyebrows went up in baffled curiosity at the statement. He looked through the signage to the transit entrances for the one marked 'Dock Fifteen'. Greymalkin found the correct entrance and jumped into it. As he did so, he communed with the alien cyborg. «What do you mean, not 'only' a human female.»

«I believe that in your language they are called *Sylphids*, a species that primarily inhabits shadow space. They are also protean shape-shifters, although quite dissimilar to me. These creatures are powerfully biogenic life forms. But that one groping you had a significant amount of human DNA in her organs.»

Greymalkin clucked his tongue, searching through his mnemotechnic arrays to confirm what he thought he recalled. «She's likely a *Morganan*, then. I've heard that Sylphids can intentionally interbreed with humans if they want to, and the Morganan Realm is known for hybrids like that.» He frowned. The presence of a Morganan here seemed very odd to him. «The Morganan Realm is near the Garnet Star; it's a red hypergiant star far, far away in the Inner Frontier. Very wealthy, for all kinds of reasons. It's supposed to be a major source of the best bloodstone shadow jewels in the Orion Arm. I wonder why she would come all the way out here?» He noted the pace at which he was moving down the transit column. He'd reach Dock Fifteen quickly.

«I have no idea.» Bruno was starting to sound bored again, but it communed an afterthought. «I think she likes you. Her human body has a cardiovascular pulse, and I noticed that it accelerated when she fondled you.»

«She didn't 'fondle' me, and I seriously doubt that an alien would be attracted to me.» Greymalkin stepped off the transit column into the dock entrance, trying unsuccessfully to shrug off the memory of Tatter, her body, and her curves pressed up against him.

«I also observed the same reaction in *you*.» Bruno's thoughts briefly bubbled with humor, and Greymalkin felt his cheeks redden. Then the protean's thoughts became serious. «But I would not recommend... *fraternizing* with the Sylphid.»

That raised Greymalkin's curiosity. «Why not?»

«Several of my former human companions became attracted to Sylphids long ago... to their detriment.» Bruno's thoughts were pensive now. «Sylphids intentionally adopt human forms that are hypersexualized in order to attract and manipulate your kind. They can be quite adept at such tactics.»

«Thank you for the warning.» Greymalkin filed the information away absently for future reference just as he walked through the entrance into a large space that he saw doubled as a repair workshop and viewing bay.

The main dock area was a giant enclosed space hundreds of meters across, and was visible through a huge viewport. Tatter had called this a cyneget pen, and he thought through the implications of that phrase with distaste. The word 'cyneget' was an old term for feral Builder cyborgs possessing minds that were *sentient* but not fully *sapient*, and therefore considered acceptable as chattel, much as domesticated animals like dogs had been on Old Earth long ago. But such assessments all too often involved very subjective judgements, and the practice was frowned upon throughout human space. *Well, outside of Burani realms, that is.* He made his way through the bay until he saw a dockman in a dirty jumpsuit at a control panel looking into the dock. As he approached the man Greymalkin scanned the dock area beyond the viewport.

Most of the dock space was occupied by a large cargo module, but there were a number of huge cyborgs, each a hundred meters long or more. The cyborgs looked familiar; he'd seen images of creatures like them, or at least the same cyborganic clade category before. Similar to the habitat pods of the huge nemora meta-tree and so many of the other feral cybernetic species the enigmatic Builders had left behind, the bodies of these cyborgs resembled ovoid bulbs arranged in a sequence on a central stalk, but with long grasping limbs emerging from the stalks.

Fascinating. Cynegets. Living starships. Like the larval form of the nemora meta-tree seeds, Greymalkin knew that these cyborgs must have the ability to travel through shadow space, but with far, far more agility and speed than nemora larvae. The creatures' natural cyborganic mirrorshell exoskeletons had central axial stalks that served the same function as shadow space manifold masts in constructed starships, although the cynegets were sleekly elegant in a way distinct from any starship he'd ever seen. He saw that where the central stalks grew out from the rear of the cyborgs there were telltale cross-stalks, so he knew that the creatures must effectively have rover-configuration shadow space transit capabilities. That made sense, since the primary shadow space transitways here were planar. The Builders had bred them as beasts of burden, with cyborganic minds and largely hollow ovoid mirrorshell carapaces that could carry cargo.

But they're held so tightly, in ship docking clamps! He scowled at the cruelty of what he was seeing. The creatures were struggling pitifully in the docking clamps, much as any living things would struggle with harsh rings clamped around their necks and limbs. He could sense keening communed signals from them, like moans and whines from animals in pain. He stomped up to the dockman, trying to restrain his anger but not succeeding.

"Adler Trauerstrom?" he demanded. The dockman was wiry, with knotted muscles bunched up in the filthy jumpsuit, topped by a lumpy face with a sneering expression covered in stubble. He did not look away from the console as he answered Greymalkin in a distracted tone.

"Yeah. Whotcher want?" he asked in a gravelly voice. Greymalkin frowned. The man had answered in a Burani dialect of Peretian. *Not another Burani, surely!*

"I'm looking for a particular rover," Greymalkin said tensely. "It was said to be in your possession. Here's the tracking number." He read off the string of digits the Subprior had given him. The man uttered an evil little laugh.

"You mean little Royce, here," Trauerstrom chuckled, nudging his chin out toward the viewport. "You're a bit late. I don't think little Royce will last much longer." Just then, an omnidirectional communed shriek of agony erupted from the dock area, making Greymalkin jump again. Bewildered, he looked through the viewport to try to understand what was happening there.

He immediately saw that one of the rover cyborgs was clamped to the base of the huge cargo module, which was itself clamped to the dock. The communed shriek had come from the cyborg, which was frantically pushing against the giant clamped cargo pod. Greymalkin stared at the cyneget rover in horror. The cyborg was one of the most elegantly formed organisms he'd ever seen, but it had been *maimed*. The body was comprised of three beautifully formed mirrorshell ovoid bulbs linked by stalks but, grotesquely, the external grapple-limbs of the cyneget had been brutally hacked off, mutilating the creature and denying it the ability to resist or try to free itself. The limb stumps were frantically flexing. There was also a muzzle-lock around its mast-stalk array, preventing it from either escaping into shadow space or defending itself with a manifold vertex attack. Wide-eyed, Greymalkin looked down at the virtual controls the man was operating on the console, and realized that Trauerstrom was administering steadily increasing amounts of pain to the creature.

"*What are you doing to it?!*" Greymalkin yelled. The man chuckled again.

"Destructive motivational testing," Trauerstrom said absently. "My wholesaler delivered this cyneget to me pre-owned, and I don't do pre-owned 'jets. But I've been wanting a sample subject to destructively test. Royce here is the lucky one that I picked." He advanced the pain setting, and the cyborg's mind howled again. Greymalkin looked askance at the cargo pod to which the creature was clamped.

"That cargo pod must mass a million tons! And you've got it clamped down, anyway!" Greymalkin shouted. "The cyneget can't possibly move it!"

"It *might* move it. At least, if it pushes hard enough to break the clamp grip," Trauerstrom grunted. "Why do you care?"

"That rover's mine!" Greymalkin yelled. "I'm contracted to pick it up from you for the Sojourners." Trauerstrom snorted.

"Wrong," the man said derisively. "Maybe you *were* contracted, but that expired yesterday. So, now I got my sample for testing." He grinned and adjusted the pain setting higher. Greymalkin looked at the console and could see the cognitive metrics on the cyborg going berserk as the creature howled again, this time in desperation.

"You're just going to agonize it until you fry its mind??" Greymalkin felt appalled. He'd never seen anything so inhuman, and didn't know what to do.

Trauerstrom snarled, and left the console for a moment. The cyborg went inert, its systems almost burnt out. The man turned while starting to shout something, but then stared at Greymalkin's head. Then Trauerstrom burst out laughing at Greymalkin.

"Cor, look what dragged in here!" the wiry fellow laughed. "A cybe! When I got here from Doradus nobody told me that they allowed human cybes on this base! Good to know for future reference. Run along, cybe. Tell your master they got owned fair and square. This is my 'jet now." He turned the pain signal on again even harder, and the cyborg shrieked in despair. Greymalkin stared, horrified.

"Let it go!" Greymalkin yelled. "You're going to scramble its mind!"

"That's the whole idea, wanker," Trauerstrom snapped. "I want to know how much pain this type of 'jet can take. I've tested other types, but not this variety. Now get out of here or I'll beat you bloody. Or maybe I'll get out my shadow blade and just dice you up, you little shit."

«Can I kill this scum, boss?» Bruno's thoughts actually seemed as angry as Greymalkin felt.

«No, don't kill him, but....» Greymalkin had a panic-reaction then, thinking of the two rooms he'd seen splashed with blood, weeks ago now but still fresh in his mind. As he heard the communing cyborg in the dock wail piteously again, he felt some mental chord snap, and his mind boiled over. «Bruno, can you come in here without blowing a hole in the wall?»

«Already here, boss.» The alien cyborg's thoughts felt close, and when Greymalkin turned he flinched at the sight of the morphing black shape just behind him.

«Good. Can you grab that guy tightly without killing him?» Greymalkin's face had gone from red to white. He had never felt so furious.

In answer, the protean instantly reached out with one of its huge strangler limbs and seized the slaver. Trauerstrom shouted in surprise, looked at the big graspers wrapped around him, and then at Bruno in shock. Greymalkin stepped forward. He first turned off the pain console and then made sure the cyneget in the dock was alright. Trembling like a leaf, he turned to Trauerstrom. The Burani's mouth was gaping open, and he was gasping for air against Bruno's monstrous grip. To the surprise of both Trauerstrom and Greymalkin alike, Bruno actually *spoke*, then. The voice was horrific, more like a deep, inhuman snarl than actual speech.

"May I paint the walls with him now?" the alien cyborg growled. Trauerstrom tried to speak, but Bruno squeezed him so hard that his pale, balding head became a dark red plum.

"No," Greymalkin said, his voice cracking. "Don't kill him. Not unless he gives me any more arguments." Greymalkin leaned over, still trembling, and glared into the face of the Burani. As he did so, for a second Greymalkin saw his own reflection in Bruno's glossy black limb. The reflection of his own eyes looked so insane that the sight actually frightened him.

Greymalkin swallowed, trying to get his anger under control, and said, "Trauerstrom, this is what you're going to do. Reassign the ownership and control codes of that cyborg to me. And you aren't going to tell anyone this happened, either. You get one chance to agree. Otherwise, my friend gets his wish. Let him talk, Bruno." The big black stony-metallic fist wrapped around Trauerstrom relaxed slightly, and a stream of incomprehensibly terrified gibberish came out of the Burani's mouth. After a moment it resolved into something understandable.

"Yes, yes, yes! *Don't kill me!* I'll transfer little Royce over to you! So sorry, so sorry! Don't kill me...." After the man had subsided into babbling sobs, Greymalkin nodded to the alien monster that held him.

"Let him go," Greymalkin said. "But watch him. If he does anything suspicious...."

"Yessss...." Bruno's snarl was both convincing and utterly terrifying as it dropped the man. The Burani crawled across the deck shakily

sobbing, and began entering codes into the console while still sniveling wetly.

Greymalkin saw the clamps release the cyneget in the dock space, and the creature became comatose. Then he glanced at his own reflection again in Bruno's morphing black surface, and was startled once more, almost not recognizing his own transformed features. It was the face of a stranger, and it wore an expression that was nothing less than *psychotic*. He found himself wondering once more, *What just happened?*

Assaults

He woke up screaming. Again.

This time Greymalkin bit off his own scream before it could ramp up into a full-throated wail. After so many nightmares about Bora and Soren being killed, the recurring sense of panic and fear had begun making him feel more frustrated than terror-stricken. He was sick and tired of not being able to sleep soundly because of the panic attacks that tended to hit him when he dozed off. And worse, he realized the nightmares made Royce panic as well whenever they were connected through the helm systems. Greymalkin had taken the dangerous measure of snatching naps while connected through the helm interface to the cyneget and underway in shadow space. He knew it was risky, but he was desperate to make up lost time on the courier trips he had been undertaking for weeks. And something else had changed profoundly. He no longer felt *alone*. Between the two cyborg companions he now had in Bruno and Royce, he now felt like he had some support to rely on while navigating the treacherous shadow planes of the Carinae.

He sat up in the cockpit almost instantly alert, even after waking up abruptly from the nightmare, and already calming the jumpy mind of the cyneget. Greymalkin was still getting to know the creature, but he had immediately perceived that Royce was almost constantly nervous and filled with anxiety. It was a bond the two of them shared. The effects of the abuse at the hands of Trauerstrom had profoundly affected the small living starship, a being which Greymalkin had come to realize was much more intelligent than an animal, but simply lacking in the verbal abilities of a human being. He soothed the cyneget mentally, and Royce settled back down to its steady focus on the task of impelling its manifold through shadow space. He was aware of Bruno briefly studying them both for a moment, but then the protean went back to scanning the path ahead of them silently. In the weeks they'd been traveling together, the trio were already becoming accustomed to non-verbal communication during their exhausting treks.

Greymalkin looked out at the spectacular shadow space landscape that stretched out for parsecs around them. The Carinae was a dramatically dangerous region, and looked it. Around them was the vast panoply of hot stars frozen in the act of roiling the thick nebulae of the Carinae. Navigating the pathways through these tangled virtual planes of deadly obstacles was nerve-wracking enough without panic nightmares brought on by traumatic memories. He soothed the cyneget again mentally, and Royce settled down to its task of skimming across the shadow space plane.

Greymalkin climbed out of the cockpit while maintaining the Helm Link. He began silently caring for the little cyneget, checking on its slowly regrowing limbs and tending to its other cyborganic needs. He had cared for living things before, both organic and cyborganic creatures, but never something as complex as a sentient starship. Yet, he found that the routine of caring for the creature reassured both Royce *and him*. It was a tangible way of demonstrating that he appreciated Royce's well-being, and it gave him something routine and positive to focus on. He obviously depended on Royce for his survival in shadow space, but until he had taken up providing for the cyborg he had not realized how urgently both he and the cyneget simply needed someone to show them *compassion*. The irony was not lost on Greymalkin that caring for a being that needed him had been helpful in dealing with his own trauma.

They passed the white dwarf star that served as his mental cue to begin preparing for arrival at the base, which was now only a short distance ahead of them. Greymalkin returned to the cockpit. «Bruno, when we arrive, help me dock Royce, okay?» The monster gave a growl of assent, and he wondered about it again. Bruno had become increasingly helpful to him over the intervening weeks, making fewer and fewer overt insults and threats. It seemed to actually be appreciating its role as his protector, and the brute definitely enjoyed intimidating the miners and other personnel at the expedition base. As he had feared, word about his harassment and outright robbery of Trauerstrom had spread like wildfire. But no one had come after them, and Greymalkin had come to realize that there was very little law or order on the base other than what one brought to it.

To his great annoyance, Greymalkin had come to be known throughout the base as the 'lunatic cybe-Sojourner with the dangerous alien bodyguard monster'. And even more irritating (although convenient for his purposes), he had quickly become in demand for courier duties, not because he was a good pilot, but because the various skulking gangs of thugs in and around the base that threatened other potential couriers did not dare bother Bruno. Even though the priory had denied him any funds for maintaining Royce, the Sojourners had grudgingly sought him out on a regular basis as a courier, and these assignments had provided him with a slow but steady source of income. And he had also begun to occasionally gain funds through his own initiatives with other expedition groups, even though the Sojourners were still his main source of income.

And I still need the Order for information, he thought again in grim frustration, resolving to confront the Prior once again as he approached the main dock. He carefully docked the ship and went through the other extended tasks required with Royce to provide for the cyneget's basic needs of sustenance and cyborganic maintenance. From the purring signals that the cyborg communed to him, he knew that Royce deeply appreciated the simple consideration he showed. Greymalkin wondered if anyone had ever simply been *kind* to the creature before. He could feel how Royce became calmer all around him as he tended to it, settling down for its resting cycle as he finished diagnostics and clearing out waste products from the cyneget's internal organs more efficiently than it could.

Greymalkin was gradually becoming accustomed to the novelty of flying through shadow space within a living being. Now the standard skiffs and flitters that he had flown before seemed grotesque to him in at least one way—the mirrorshell hulls. He had never before questioned why the hull shapes of skiffs were so standardized, but it was now obvious to him. *They get the hulls from the bodies of dead cyborgs.* The ovoid mirrorshell shapes of the vast majority of the smaller ships humans used had been created through the simple expedient of hollowing out once living shells harvested from nemora meta-tree bulbs or other similar dead cyborganic creatures. He knew he'd heard this before, but the reality of how small starship hulls were created had never sunk in before. He hoped that none of the ships he'd ever flown in had come from living cyborganic creatures killed simply for their carapaces. The thought sickened him now that it occurred to him, yet another perspective transformed by the Carinae.

But Royce's interior was still alive, not like the hollowed-out and installed starship interiors he had always used before. Certainly, he had scavenged many artificial components from the skiff he had arrived in, carrying them over to Royce's interior without admitting it to the other Sojourners here, who he no longer trusted. These included items like the medical pod, cockpit seats, some of the cabin fixtures, and most of the equipment that Bora and Soren had brought.

While the Builders had bred the cynegets to have hollow interiors to accommodate such cargo, the remainder of the creature's body cavity was filled with living organs contained within the interior integument of the creature. Visually and to the touch, cyneget interior hide was a tough white material resembling fine-scaled leather, albeit tougher than woven steel. Before now, Greymalkin had known only the rudiments of Builder cyborgs and their physiology, mainly from helping tend the nemora meta-tree groves near the orphanage where he'd grown up. Now he was literally immersed in maintaining a living starship from the inside, and quickly learning how to do so out of necessity. It was wholly different from flying inside dead artifacts. He found it fascinating.

After he finished tending to Royce, the cyborg was quite calm, and it obediently went into its hibernation mode for healing and regeneration. He was gathering up some of the smaller stray items that he had brought back on this trip when he noticed movement in the dock outside the viewport. The berth next to the one he had been assigned for Royce was used by the tavern where he had asked directions weeks ago. In fact, the back of the tavern structure extended all the way out to the dock, and he'd routinely seen cargo moved directly from the dock into the rear storage areas of the tavern.

Greymalkin found it suspicious that although there never seemed to be a ship docked, there were always many cargo pallets and modules. And the pallets were usually being moved inside by the same immense individual, a huge alien being that he had eventually learned was the tavern owner herself, albeit *not* in the human form she had taken when he'd met her. She was there now, moving in and out of the shadows and the harsh dock spotlights, unpacking several large cargo pallets. After thinking about it for a moment, Greymalkin decided to try to talk to her. He put on his void suit and exited through Royce's airlock.

Because of the non-human form she took while working in vacuum, Greymalkin sometimes found it a bit unnerving being dock neighbors with the alien Sylphid who went by the name Tatterdemalion. When he'd asked if this was her actual name, she had laughed and explained that someone had insulted her with the term when she had first arrived. But she decided she liked it, and took it on as her nickname, or just Tatter. It had occurred to him that this might also simply be a convenient cover story to avoid using her real name, whatever it was.

As he exited Royce he saw that she was working there amid a small group of armed thugs who were hanging back in the shadows. The son of the old base operations manager Gower was also there. The younger Gower was a big and sullen brute, continually surrounded by his gang of thugs and taking inventory. All the while, Tatter did the actual heavy work of moving the massive cargo pallets by hand. She worked without a void suit in the harsh vacuum, and therefore could not use her deceptively attractive human figure. Instead, she manifested in her natural alien physique. And that transformation was rather unbelievably frightening.

The Morganan's monstrous native form was only vaguely humanoid. He was never completely sure if she was simply nude and the gnarled bluish-grey integument and slabs of darker plates were her natural exoskeleton or if it was some kind of armored array of garments. Either way, the Morganan stood more than five meters tall, with elegantly twisted parodies of human arms and legs. Her powerful elongated limbs were layered with massively thick knots of rope-like muscles that came together at the joints. The Sylphid's limbs were not only long, but had *more* joints than those of a human. Her head was all fearsome bony ridge structures, festooned with multiple whipcord-like antennae that constantly moved around her head. The 'face' of the creature was all the more uncanny for the grotesquely distorted features which lacked clearly defined eyes and was only disturbingly reminiscent of a human countenance.

The pseudo-smile of the alien was the most chilling thing of all, a frightful parade of jaws and spiked tusks. He thought back to the strange hallucination he'd had when she first touched him in the tavern. The memory of that touch and even the electric *taste* of the Sylphid's fangs had not faded. He felt a shiver go down his back, and wondered again what that eerie vision had meant. *Why did I lean down? Surely not to... kiss her?*

Despite how alien her form was, as he watched Tatter's smoothly streamlined muscles glinting in and out the harsh dock lights and shadows, he found himself admiring the sheer strength, poise, and vitality she exuded. There was an uncanny grace and deadliness to the shape of the Morganan as she moved, something both terrifying but also enthralling in the lethality visible there. As he watched her lift and lunge with the huge crates in her arms, he wondered if he actually found her somewhat... *intriguing to view?* While Greymalkin had been frightened before, he'd rarely been *repulsed* by alien beings, no matter how strange. Another shiver went down his back.

Greymalkin kept his distance, watching the half-Sylphid and her human guards for a few minutes as he sat perched on Royce's hull in the zero gee. The group eventually noticed him and took an interest. The humans fingered their weapons, which were mostly shadow blades. Greymalkin knew that they could easily pick him off or slice him into pieces from where they were, but Bruno had silently appeared from nowhere, looming behind him without needing to be asked. The gang simply watched the slowly morphing form of the alien cyborg, silently alert. Greymalkin grinned tensely. He knew that Bruno was the only reason they left him alone. But it was somewhat amusing to watch them squirm.

He eventually decided to commune a greeting. Something quixotic stirred in him then, and on the spur of the moment, he decided to push things outside of everyone's comfort zone with a grin while doing it. «Ho, Tatter! Do you need any help? I'll come over!» Before being invited, he proceeded to take a slow, lazy zero gee flip across the distance separating the two dock berths. The pressor deck caught him, but he touched down closer than he had planned, right beside the looming form of the Morganan, who proceeded to look down at him with the horrifically spikey smile right above his helmet. The thugs in the shadows appeared agitated, as if they wanted to rush him, but then looked back to where the silent sentinel protean floated by Royce. Younger Gower simply looked thoughtful. But a gruesome rictus spread across Tatter's giant head. Greymalkin felt the same terrified shiver run down his back, but he stood his ground while grinning up at her jaws.

«Hi there, love!» Jarringly, her thoughts still felt human and had the same flirtatious tone, despite how threatening her current ghoulish form appeared. But now he could tease out the alien tinges in her thoughts, like strangely subtle tastes in exotic food. «Thanks for the offer, but no, I've got this.»

Greymalkin looked at the pallet of containers she was casually moving around with whip-corded muscles. The containers held suspension bottles of a psychogenic substance that he knew was colloquially called *gnari*. He was not sure what it actually was, only that it was forbidden on Sojourner arks. He'd heard tales of the liquid and its mind-warping effects from older monks. He also knew that it was a controlled substance often smuggled illegally back in the Alban Realm. The containers Tatter was slinging around probably massed a thousand kilos, but she just grinned and set them down easily while she communed with him. «Drop by the tavern later, hmm? We've got some real *treats* in this shipment. I'm serious, this is the *good* stuff. You should absolutely come by and try it.»

Greymalkin nodded with an innocent smile, although he was starting to involuntarily tremble at just how close her fangs were, and her sheer scale as she towered over him. He turned to go, but then interjected his question as if it had just occurred to him. «You know, you always bring in so many shipments, but I never see a ship. What's your secret?»

«Aren't you nosy!» Tatter had laughter in her thoughts, but the big jaws full of spiked tusks opened and snapped shut, making him flinch. «Mind your own business! A girl deserves some secrets.»

Greymalkin nodded, trying not to tremble in fear too uncontrollably as he squatted. He deactivated Tatter's pressor deck's grip on him, and then jumped all the way back to his own berth, where his own pressor deck caught him again. The thugs visibly relaxed, but kept watching both him and also Bruno alertly. Greymalkin went about his business, unhurriedly removing his own cargo off of Royce's exterior mount points and transferring it onto a big autocart. He steered the autocart ponderously into the base interior through the berth airlock and then stood waiting for Bruno before closing the hatch.

Without being prompted, Bruno pulled a couple of the cyborg's incomprehensible protean tricks. First, it simply vanished from the berth and appeared again next to him inside the big airlock. Then the alien cyborg morphed itself into a smaller and smaller form as the airlock cycled, until it was finally no bigger than a large spider the size of his hand. Somewhat dreading what was coming, Greymalkin simply closed his eyes and waited for the protean to leap onto his shoulder and cling there tightly.

When the protean clung to his shoulder, the contact still resulted in a vastly reduced version of the brief moment of shocking sensations that Greymalkin had come to expect. The young Sojourner did not understand why contact with some beings like Hayan, Kuanian, and even Tatter had evoked such intense sensations in him, but Bruno was the most extreme of all. The first time the alien monster had perched on his shoulder he had almost lost consciousness from the blast of thoughts and impulses. In addition to the imagery it had been like being swept away in a vortex of pure aggression and fury that made the universe itself spin. The storm of combat instincts and reactions that was evidently Bruno's essence had been totally overwhelming at first, but Greymalkin now simply grit his teeth until the momentary sensation passed.

Greymalkin looked sideways down at the black tarantulan shape on his shoulder. It was a mystery how or *where* Bruno parked its enormous mass while in this tiny form, but it felt light as a feather. He had the impression that the monster's true mass was untold orders of magnitude more than what it typically exhibited. The protean had taken to manifesting in this much smaller form for practical reasons when they moved about inside the base, but had also demonstrated at times that it could change into almost any form or size in the twinkling of an eye.

After the moment of disorientation at Bruno's touch had passed, Greymalkin began making the now familiar trek up through the nemora meta-tree trunk, and then out through the long hollow branch to the priory. After he had loudly demanded entrance for several minutes, the gate monk finally admitted him, nervously eyeing the tiny but menacing form of Bruno splayed out on Greymalkin's shoulder. It required a seemingly interminable delay of queries, but finally the monk took him into the Prior's audience chamber.

Being admitted into the presence of the Prior for the entire Sojourner mission was still slightly intimidating, but Greymalkin's anger and resentment had now reduced this intimidation to the point that he found himself unceremoniously dumping the contents of the big autocart onto the floor. The Subpriors scowled at his cavalier behavior, but the Prior knelt and eagerly examined the artifacts Greymalkin had brought back.

"This is everything Sister Constance gave me to bring back from the dig site this time," Greymalkin said impatiently. He had already looked through the entire cargo of ancient human and alien artifacts, and knew just how precious it was.

"Very good, Brother Thomas," the Prior said happily as he held up the individual items appraisingly. "You will receive the usual courier fee."

Greymalkin folded his arms and scowled. "Great; that's all well and good. But I have been wondering about something." He studied the Prior before asking the question that he knew would set them off. "Why have you not dispatched more of the monks here at the priory out to that dig site and all the others I've now visited?"

"Be silent!" snapped one of the Subpriors, a red-faced man. "That is none of your concern, Brother Thomas." In irritation, Greymalkin tapped his foot and rudely ignored the Subprior, something he would never have thought to do before he had found himself in the upside-down Carinae.

"They have only a handful of Sojourners out at the archaeological dig sites," Greymalkin said. "You have hundreds and hundreds of monks here at the main base."

"Our monks here are occupied studying and cataloging the artifacts that Sister Constance and her teams have recovered," said the other Subprior, a scrawny Sojourner with a crinkled and cracked voice that grated on his ears. Greymalkin found it telling that none of the three had ever bothered to introduce themselves to him or even give him their names.

"Nonsense," Greymalkin said bluntly. All three of the other monks glared at him as he continued. "I've spoken to Constance repeatedly now, and I've discovered several things. She and the others at the dig sites are the only other Sojourners in addition to me that were directly recruited by Lady Kuanian. And it shows." He looked the others in their eyes, feeling nervous about making his next statement to their faces. But his jittery nerves had shattered his patience. "I think that the monks hiding here inside this priory are both cowards and corrupt."

The Subpriors stiffened in anger, but the Prior did not react and continued fingering the artifacts before finally saying, "The Brothers and Sisters here are well-occupied."

"Hardly," Greymalkin said curtly. The Subpriors looked as if they were going to explode in anger, but Greymalkin gestured to the artifacts and said, "There is clear evidence here that humans have existed in the Carinae for thousands of years, sometimes living side by side with native intelligent species. That is an astonishing fact. It means that, somehow, humans from the time of the First Interstellar Exodus reached the Carinae. But that implies an even greater mystery than the mere fact of ancient human encampments and habitations here."

The Prior slowly rose and motioned for the Subpriors to take away the artifacts. He smiled at Greymalkin and said neutrally, "Really? Why is that?"

Greymalkin blinked in surprise at the man's blatant insincerity, then scowled. "Obviously, because the First Exodus had only sub-light spacecraft! They could not possibly have *reached* the Carinae thousands of years ago with such vehicles, they would still be in transit *today*! That indicates something no one has ever suspected, that the Thannic explorers must have *discovered shadow space travel* at some point after they departed Old Earth. That's an incredible finding; it changes all of our fundamental concepts of history and how humans spread across the Orion Arm in those early times! And also this: humans have evidently been here in the Sagittarius Arm for millennia, but *where are they now*? I myself encountered a Bereft human culture on my way here, but they appear to date from the Xenocorps expedition three centuries ago. That makes sense. Humans from the Scorpian Realm did not yet exist at the time of the First Exodus. Who, then, left behind all these artifacts that Constance has discovered? *What happened here?* You must be at least a little curious!"

"You are not a trained archaeologist, Apprentice. Your fantasies are uninformed," the Prior said, looking at him levelly. It infuriated Greymalkin. As the Subpriors piled the artifacts back onto the autocart, the Prior said, "Now then, I have another courier assignment for you...."

"Why me?" Greymalkin snapped. "I mean, you think I'm merely an uninformed, deluded, and untrustworthy cybe after all, correct?"

The Prior's smile became brittle. "Yes, however, you have a most useful guardian that obeys you," the Prior said, nodding toward the splayed form of Bruno on his shoulder.

"I've been thinking about that as well," said Greymalkin slowly. "My 'guardian', as you call him, indeed gives me a rather unique asset. But why did Lady Kuanian entrust this protean solely to the ill-fated party that I joined? For example, why not provide the protean to *you* as the official Prior of the mission, for the benefit and protection of the entire expedition?"

The Prior's smile vanished, and he said in a tone that was suddenly frosty, "And what is your conclusion as to that matter, then?"

"Simple," Greymalkin said, lowering his voice. "She did not provide you with the protean because she must no longer trust you as leader of this mission. It seems obvious that she did not recruit you as leader for this mission. And at some point she rightly began suspecting that treachery and corruption were sabotaging the expedition as a whole. She is a good judge of character. She knew that our group would hold to the purposes to which she set us. And she wanted to protect us." Before the Prior could spit a rejoinder at him, Greymalkin continued, "By the way, when is the Lady Kuanian due to rejoin the expedition?"

"She is unlikely to return here for several more months," the Prior said with a vague gesture of his hand. "Perhaps she is off recruiting additional sterling persons such as yourself. Now, as to your next courier assignment..."

"I have another task to take care of first," Greymalkin said tersely. "I will let you know when I am again available for your errands." Before the Prior could protest, Greymalkin turned and strode out of the room. He'd heard and seen enough to confirm everything he had suspected.

* * *

As Greymalkin returned to the docks, he could feel Bruno squirming around on his shoulder. For a time he ignored this, but finally grew tired of it. «Yes? What is it now?»

«Nothing.» Bruno's thoughts squirmed even more than the tiny twisting form on his shoulder. Greymalkin waited. Obviously, the creature had some thought that it wanted to share. And the alien cyborg finally did so, long before they reached the docks. «I thought that you still needed additional funds. As irritating as that individual is, should you not accept the opportunity for additional payment?»

Greymalkin did not respond until they exited the transit column and entered the docks. He set his jaw. «We have sufficient funds. And I want to finally retrieve my stolen pack and the gifts from Kuanian. You told me that you had devised a plan for recovering them?»

«Yes. However....» Bruno seemed surprisingly hesitant. Greymalkin waited him out. The protean finally continued. «While I have carefully observed our targets for weeks now, I think they are concealing something.»

Greymalkin waited, but then became impatient. «What is it, then, Bruno? I'm surprised at your hesitation. You usually just want to charge in.»

«This human, Rodolfo. He is definitely concealing... something.» The thoughts of the alien cyborg seemed oddly cautious and tentative. Greymalkin snorted and kept walking.

«What a surprise. Obviously, he's concealing many things.» Greymalkin felt impatient. And hungry. He realized he had not eaten in almost a day, but he was sick of the cheap emergency rations and foodbars on which he'd been subsisting. Tatterdemalion's tavern was ahead of them, and he made a snap decision.

He walked through the entrance and looked around for an empty table, but as usual every spot he saw was occupied. He finally saw a relatively small table in a corner occupied by only a single man. Greymalkin did not like sitting with strangers, but he still felt angry and impatient. *I'm hungry,* he thought again. He walked up to the seated man, who quickly glanced up.

"Excuse me, do you mind if I sit... here...." Greymalkin trailed off, looking at the man's head in growing dismay. The fellow was intense-looking, weathered, and had blond hair that was extremely close cut. He wore a very old-fashioned jumpsuit that seemed vaguely familiar, but that was not why Greymalkin stared. His shadow sense had immediately focused on the man's head. Specifically, his brain. Or lack thereof.

More precisely, Greymalkin realized that while his shadow sense could feel that the man had a normal biological body, what occupied his cranium was an *artificial* mind. Normally, his own shadow jewel resonated with the bright emanations of the shadow jewels in the forebrains of other humans, subliminally swirling with the traces of thoughts. It was something that he knew everyone felt while among other people, the basic precursor perception that enabled communed thought between humans. The absence in this man's skull was grotesquely obvious, a gaping, empty hole where a living mind should have been. After Greymalkin had stared at the fellow in consternation for several seconds, the blond man rolled his eyes in mild disgust, stood up, and said in a gruff voice, "Here, you can have the table, I'm done. And kid, with what you've got layered on your mind and draped over your shoulder, I wouldn't stare."

Greymalkin instantly felt ashamed, because that comment was nothing but the truth. The young Sojourner had become extremely tired of people's revolted reactions to the covenants laid on his shadow jewel, as well as the presence of Bruno beside him over the last few weeks. *And yet, I had the very same reaction to this... person.* As the blond man started to walk away, Greymalkin motioned him to stop.

"Please! My sincere apologies," Greymalkin said firmly. "I was wrong to stare at you. My name is Greymalkin Thomas." He had no idea if the man would glare at him, shun him, or simply spit on him. Greymalkin decided that he wouldn't blame him for any response. Instead the fellow met his eyes, and then mustered a very slight, sad smile.

"I'm Lex," the man said, and very much did *not* stare at Greymalkin's head, but only met his gaze for a moment. Greymalkin felt a slight shiver; in that moment it struck him that those eyes were like two still, ancient blue pools at the bottom of shadowed wells. The faint, wry smile faded away then, and the man walked away without volunteering anything else, leaving Greymalkin very confused as he sat down. *Is he a cyborg then? An organic telepresence unit? Or... what is he? What could possibly have transformed him that drastically without simply killing him?*

As the young Sojourner sat down and watched the unusual old blond fellow disappear through the crowd, two other familiar figures shoved past him and seated themselves across from Greymalkin. They were the two men named Gower, the older father that was the influential but corrupt base operations manager, and the younger son that Greymalkin had seen at the tavern dock earlier. He knew the younger man led many of the gang members on the base. Greymalkin eyed the younger Gower suspiciously and tensed for a second. *Did he follow me all the way from the docks to the priory and back here? Why?* Greymalkin looked at them uncertainly, but neither one seemed threatening or unfriendly. In fact, the older man actually seemed to be awkwardly struggling to put on a friendly expression.

"Hello, my dear Brother Thomas," old Gower said. Greymalkin had noticed that the man spoke Canisian with a low-caste accent, but in an unctuous and oily manner that was clearly intended to sound urbane. Gower continued, his seedy voice dripping like a broken sewer line, "I'm so glad you came into our tavern tonight. We wanted to talk to you."

Greymalkin frowned, and then said, "I thought Tatter was the owner? Never mind; it doesn't matter. What do you want?" The two men glanced at each other uncomfortably.

"Yes, well, you see...." Old Gower said, clearing his throat noisily. Young Gower folded his thickly muscled arms and dropped his eyes to the table silently, letting his father do the talking. "Tatterdemalion is actually the topic we wanted to discuss with you."

Greymalkin's eyebrows went up. He was baffled. "Okay, I'm listening."

"It cannot have escaped your attention, that our local tavern girl is... not entirely typical," old Gower said. At first Greymalkin wondered if this was some kind of prank or joke, but the older man looked not only earnest but also upset.

"Uh, she's a Sylphid," Greymalkin said. "Well, half-Sylphid, anyway. A Morganan. That was my understanding, anyway." He looked from one man to the other questioningly. Then the younger man spoke for the first time, in a voice full of loathing.

"She's a shag husk," Young Gower snarled, using an incredibly vulgar Canisian slur. The coarse language made it even more obvious to Greymalkin that the man was an unsophisticated thug. The young Sojourner blinked in surprise, and wondered what had happened between the man and Tatter to evoke such anger.

"Okay, uh, sorry to hear that?" Greymalkin said, hesitantly. "I gather you won't be working with her anymore, then?" The younger man dropped his gaze again and the older man seemed to wince.

"Ah, yes, well...." Old Gower began. "You see, our business arrangement with Tatterdemalion has not progressed as we hoped it would. I assumed she would provide more... *direct* assistance in our work activities. She has not cooperated as I wished, despite my generous backing of this tavern. I've allowed the situation to drag on unresolved until now because my son..." The old man glanced at his son with obvious contempt, and the younger man scowled, still looking down. "My son was somewhat... *smitten* with her initially."

I'll bet he was, Greymalkin thought, remembering the encounter he'd had with Tatter in her oh-so-voluptuous human form. "So, what do you want me to do about it?"

"Ah, yes, to the matter itself," Old Gower said, clearing his throat again. The older man nodded at the splayed form of Bruno draped over Greymalkin's shoulder and said, "We've all heard the stories about how you put that odious scum Trauerstrom in his place. We were wondering if you might agree to something of the sort with Tatterdemalion as well."

Greymalkin raised his eyebrows and said, "Really? Why do you need my help?"

"Yes, well, you may be familiar with the physical capabilities of Sylphids?" Old Gower asked with a pained smile. "You see, well, that is... we're concerned that...."

"Tatter will rip my guys' heads off. And mine too," Young Gower said bluntly. "She's strong enough to punch through a bulkhead. And her alien hide is harder than steel."

"Of course, I'll make sure that you're well compensated," Old Gower said quickly, and named a figure that made Greymalkin's jaw drop. The young Sojourner recoiled.

"No," he said flatly. "What do you think I am, an assassin?"

"Oh, you don't have to kill her," Old Gower said. "Just have your... *companion* do the same that it did with Trauerstrom. She'll leave the base just as he did." Greymalkin shook his head. He still regretted losing his temper with the cyneget pen master, even though it had indeed resulted in the evil man selling off the cyborgs he'd been abusing and then quietly fleeing.

Old Gower gave him another greasy smile and said, "Ah, so you're hard to motivate, eh? I suppose that I can go slightly higher with your fee." Then he named an even greater amount. Now it just made Greymalkin scowl and prepare an insulting retort. Then, all three of them were surprised when they heard a low, almost subsonic growl from Greymalkin's shoulder.

"How much did you say?" Bruno rumbled. The sound produced by the innocuously tiny form of the protean was far larger and more ominous than seemed possible. People at the tables around them stopped talking and looked nervously at Bruno. The old and young Gowers looked speculatively at the cyborg. Greymalkin glared sidelong at the alien cyborg, and stood up.

"Thank you both, but I can't agree to that," he said curtly, and walked away. *I guess it's foodbars for dinner again after all*, he thought glumly as he stalked out of the tavern.

Bruno was silent at first, but it had raised itself up off his shoulder slightly, like an alert spider. Greymalkin waited. He was getting to know the creature quite well, and indeed it eventually piped up. «There might be some utility in reconsidering the offer of that individual. You need significantly more funding to continue your pursuits.»

"Why do you care?» Greymalkin was actually puzzled. «You're my bodyguard, not my advisor.» When the protean finally answered, its thoughts seemed puzzled as well.

«That is correct.» The protean flopped back down onto his shoulder morosely. «I suppose I am starting to internalize your absurd avocational perspectives. It comes from being so bored. But I do have to keep you alive long enough to collect my reward from Kuanian.»

«What I'm doing is not an avocation or a hobby.» Greymalkin folded his arms as he walked slowly toward Royce's berth. As he often did lately, he was thinking sadly about Bora and Soren. «Maybe, at first, I thought this would be some kind of big adventure. Perhaps I'd make some big discovery and feel better about some things in my life. But that's changed. My friends and I made a promise to Kuanian. And my friends were murdered because of that promise. I'm the only one left of the three of us. Me, the one that was most poorly prepared for any of this. But I will not leave this cursed area till I do my best to honor that promise, help some of the abandoned people here, and find out what damnable secrets are hidden here.»

«Why do you think that something's hidden here?» The protean was bored again.

«What *isn't* being hidden here?!» Greymalkin communed angrily. «And you're no help, either! You've obviously existed here for a very long time, but you won't give me any details about the history of the Carinae, or anything else I ask you!»

«I already told you, I never frequented this region, I was simply imprisoned here.»

«So tell me about the regions you *did* frequent, then.» Greymalkin knew this line of questioning would lead nowhere; he had tried to engage the protean countless times in the weeks the creature had served as his bodyguard, to no avail. He found it maddening to be in the presence of a being that seemed so enigmatically powerful but also so profoundly stubborn and immature. Bruno obviously must have incredible historical knowledge, but simply refused to share it.

«I find the past tedious to discuss. I prefer to act in the present.» The protean's attention had already drifted away again, Greymalkin could tell. It seemed to have an incredibly short attention span.

«Good, then, let us act. I want to retrieve my possessions.» Greymalkin clenched his fist in conflicted uncertainty. Part of his mind advised him to let the pack go, that it wasn't critical to his mission. Another fearful part of him worried that he would need it for the unknown capabilities of the garment and tool. And another, stubborn, hurt, and angry emotional part of him just *wanted* the pack. Mulling it over, he realized why.

The pack and its contents were his only links with that happy moment at the beginning, the moment when this endeavor that now seemed so nightmarish had instead seemed joyful and hopeful. He had been floundering steadily down into despair further and further, day by slow depressing day. He found that he desperately wanted the pack as reassurance that he might feel good about things once more, at least, *some day*. «You told me that you have reconnoitered the location where Rodolfo met with the others you've described? You seemed concerned about one of the other... *beings* in this location, this... *lair*?»

Bruno's thoughts were guarded. «Yes. I have closely watched this particular individual. It is clearly the ruler of the lair. Rodolfo appears to be on good terms with it. It is what you would call an *Abyssal*, a being somewhat like me. But a different kind. You understand?»

Greymalkin frowned as he reached Royce's berth, and walked to the end of the pier tunnel before replying to Bruno. «I do *not* understand. 'Abyssal' is just another nonspecific human term, more evocative than substantive. We use that word to refer to something we don't understand, something that 'arises from the abyss of time'. I have no idea what *you* are, Bruno; what would I know about another Abyssal that was different?»

«But, you do know about us. We are constructs of the Old Ones.»

Greymalkin finished cycling the airlock and shrugged. «What you call the 'Old Ones', we call the Builders. But that civilization has been gone for millions of years. Their abandoned structures and the feral descendants of the cybernetic creatures they created are found everywhere. Humans scavenge the things they left behind, like using the hollowed out shells of the nemora larval seeds for starship hulls. But we don't understand their technology.»

«Nobody knew or understood the Old Ones, or most of their spawn for that matter.» Bruno's thoughts were slow and uncharacteristically pensive. «And that seems to be what this one that I have observed is. What you call Abyssals are just the spawn of the Old Ones that are more advanced than you humans. And there are many of us. Many such spawn. But this one is also different somehow.»

Greymalkin flopped down onto one of the horizontal surfaces inside Royce. He felt exhausted, but wanted to try to tease more information out of Bruno before falling asleep. Trying to keep his eyes open, he once again asked a key question that never seemed to elicit any intelligible response from Bruno. "Hey, whatever happened to the Builders, the Old Ones?»

«Nobody knows.» Bruno had given similar responses before, and Greymalkin laid back to go to sleep. But then the protean communed something that jolted him awake. «They probably just changed over time into the Central Ones.»

Greymalkin tried not to react overtly, and pretended to yawn. «The Central Ones? Who are they?»

When Bruno answered, its thoughts seemed confused. «They are the Ones in the Center, obviously. Why do you ask about them?»

Greymalkin started to ask a dozen questions, but then thought better of it. The protean always became evasive and then irritated when he peppered it with questions. *I'll come back to it later, when I'm ready,* he thought to himself. *But now I have a very big thread to pull on.* He turned over on his side, pondering what the protean's cryptic comment might have meant. At some point he fell into a restless sleep.

For the first time in several days, he did not fall into troubled nightmares of murder and death. Instead, he found himself in an absurd dream in which Bruno first was scheming with the two Gowers over insidious plots. Then Bruno and Royce were arguing back and forth, although he could not understand the disagreement. He woke with a start, for a moment thinking he had actually sensed Bruno communing with the cyneget. He sat up muzzy and self-conscious, aware that both cyborgs were alert and observing him. When he communed, he directed his thoughts at both of them. «Anything amiss?»

«No.» Bruno's thoughts seemed oddly subdued, though. Nervous, even? «I double-checked the operational steps that I discussed with you, and I have provided your transport with the relevant flight plan information. We are ready to go whenever you give your consent.»

The last statement made Greymalkin pause. It was the first time he could recall the protean explicitly waiting for his approval on anything. Greymalkin usually had to engage in an extended harangue to even get the creature to acknowledge his statements. «You still seem hesitant. Are you having second thoughts?»

«No.» Bruno seemed to be thinking *something* over, however. Greymalkin busied himself in a pre-flight check sequence, and waited. The protean finally communicated with him. «If I am cautious, it is only because this is your first combat mission. I am unsure if you are sufficiently prepared mentally.»

Greymalkin frowned. «What do you mean by 'combat'? I thought you had figured out how to retrieve the pack without violence? I told you, don't kill anyone else!»

«Yes, I understand that.» The protean seemed impatient again. «However, *you* must understand that there is always some risk of violence in this kind of situation. We cannot predict what will happen. It's a remote possibility, do not obsess over it again! Just be prepared.»

«That is not particularly reassuring.» Greymalkin momentarily thought it through one last time, but found himself as impatient as Bruno. He'd already made up his mind. «Alright, then; let's go.» He connected his thoughts with Royce's mind through the helm control system, and the rover cyborg gracefully swept out of the dock into space and then effortlessly shifted into shadow space.

* * *

As Greymalkin steered it forward, the cyneget began accelerating out across the ghostly blue shadow plane that stretched out endlessly before them. The ethereal surface extended into the distance, a virtual sheet of potential transition paths that he could sense more than see through his shadow jewel. He could feel the surface of the shadow plane almost like a faint extension of his own skin, stretched out tight and tingling in the places where it draped over the most energetic stars in the distance. The passage of Royce's continuity manifold felt almost like a tickling insect skittering across that sheet of skin, scrabbling occasionally for purchase on the slippery surface.

Greymalkin focused his attention on the path ahead of them. The location they were traveling toward would require most of a day's travel. Both he and Bruno had thought it quite interesting that the lair of the other Abyssal was so close to the main expedition base. It seemed likely that there could easily have been other humans beyond Rodo that might have had dealings with the lair.

He thought about pursuing the question of the "Central Ones" with Bruno, but somehow felt that it wasn't yet the right moment. Instead, Greymalkin divided his attention while en route between directing Royce across the shadow plane and sorting through his mnemotome journal entries. It was high time that he started organizing the copious observations and notes he'd been recording in his journal since arriving in the Carinae. He'd steadily been working on a variety of basic tasks that he'd been shocked to discover the Sojourners at the main base had neglected, everything from basic stellar topography to charting the locations of the various archaeological research sites that Sister Constance and her teams had investigated.

Constance was an older Sojourner, but Greymalkin had immediately recognized in her a kindred spirit that reminded him of Mother Advisor Trystia. She and the Sojourners working with her were genuinely devoted to the exciting but daunting task of investigating the Carinae. The lack of anything remotely resembling adequate time or personnel for exploring so large a region made the task that much more overwhelming. The Carinae was so vast a space that generations of Sojourners could have researched it and barely scratched the surface. What little research they could accomplish in their random investigations must have felt frustrating and tantalizing to them.

Constance had been profoundly grateful for the addition of a skilled courier like Greymalkin, and had gladly dispatched him on half a dozen urgent retrieval trips to sites where her scattered team had performed rapid evaluative surveys and sampling efforts. Even though she and her skeleton crew of Sojourners were operating at an overtaxed pace, they were achieving incredible results. Despite his inexperience, that was obvious to Greymalkin as he cross-referenced the many sites to which Constance had sent him. And a general picture was starting to emerge.

There was clear and obvious evidence of many ancient human habitations throughout the Carinae, even though that idea flew in the face of every long-established historical account of human exploration that he'd ever heard. Apparently, despite all historical perceptions, at least some of the Thannic Colonizers of the First Interstellar Exodus had achieved superluminal travel and crossed the thousands of light-years to the Sagittarius Arm long ago. The remnants of habitations and fragments of spacecraft hulls discovered by Constance's researchers showed all the signs of the First Exodus fleets. There were extensive ruins, as if the Colonizers had begun their traditional activities of preparing to terraform planets and seed new colonies throughout the region in earnest. But everything seemed to have abruptly halted three millennia ago. In a few places there were damaged ruins as if the Colonizers had been attacked, but mostly the bases seemed to have simply been abandoned.

However, the strangest thing Constance had discovered was that in a few scattered locations there were traces of very *recent* habitations. These vestiges had been concealed but then dug up, violently destroyed, and then scattered about the sites. The pattern of the destruction suggested what was known of the Carinans. That led Greymalkin to the same conclusion that Constance and her team had reached. Humans of ancient origin had been here, and might *still* be here, but they were hiding from and being hunted by the Carinans.

The hours of the passage went by quickly while Greymalkin was focused on his research. Before he knew it, Royce had swiftly carried them to the edge of the target star system. They dropped out of shadow space, and he scanned the planets of the system with his amplifier.

The target planet was a massive ball of rock with a metal core. The gravity on its surface would be so strong that Greymalkin would barely be able to stand up, much less walk. Not that he had any intention of getting anywhere near it. «Do you think they will have seen us?» He was careful to tightly focus his communed thoughts toward Bruno, who was inside Royce with him. The hulking protean seemed even larger and more menacing in close proximity.

«It depends on how alert they are.» The alien cyborg's thoughts seemed distracted for a moment as it continued to scan their surroundings, but then he felt the full intensity of Bruno's attention. «I need to go *now*, before they have further opportunity to see me coming. Well? Have you reached a decision?»

Greymalkin nodded. After he had harangued the protean repeatedly about not killing anyone, as part of its plan Bruno had offered to link their minds during the infiltration. The protean had described the process as similar to the Helm Link that Greymalkin could activate with Royce, but even more direct. Greymalkin could not understand how such a link could be maintained across so great a distance, but he had no alternative ideas. «Yes. Proceed with your link, then.»

The protean did not hesitate, and reached out to touch him lightly on the forehead. Greymalkin felt the usual shock of the creature's violent thoughts, but this time the sensation seemed to suffuse his entire body, and he flinched back away from Bruno. The sensation was akin to a very strong telepresence link, and Greymalkin felt almost as if he was in two places at once. He felt his human body in the cockpit seat, but he also felt... what Bruno felt.

What Bruno felt was raw, pulsing, thrumming exhilaration. Greymalkin realized that the protean was primed and ready for battle, the instinctive preparation of a predator for carnage. He started to remind it again that the explicit goal was *not* to fight, but immediately knew that message would simply antagonize Bruno further. He waved the cyborg away. «Go. Get my pack and possessions as quickly as you can.»

The protean communed nothing, but simply vanished out of the spacecraft interior into shadow space with only a faint pop of displaced air. That was frightening in itself to Greymalkin. A continuity manifold that refined was incredible. The protean never ceased to terrify.

Greymalkin settled into the cockpit, observing as the protean flew like a hidden ripple through shadow space toward the planet, billions of kilometers away. He'd brought Royce out of shadow space on the very edge of the system at Bruno's urging. It seemed impossible to imagine that anything could detect them out here, but he had a healthy respect for the protean's advice in such matters. He felt reassured as Bruno made the incredibly rapid transit to the planet. Even closely linked to the protean as he was, he could barely detect its presence.

It would have taken many hours for a beam of light to reach the planet, but Bruno was there in what seemed like seconds. In fact, because the protean reacted at electronic speeds, it was hard for Greymalkin to clearly follow the sequence of what happened next. He could only tell that, in what seemed like the blink of an eye, the alien cyborg had slipped in through a very small aperture into a large internal space beneath the planet's surface. Bruno was furtively springing from one hiding place to another when the surroundings of the protean seemed to explode in a blinding explosion that made Greymalkin scream from the indirect pain.

After that things happened so quickly that it was even harder to tell what was happening under the surface of the distant planet. He had a flashed perception that Bruno had engaged in a quite long (for the cyborg) and very angry communication exchange with another being, an exchange that had taken place so fast that Greymalkin barely had time to register that anything had happened. The details were lost on him, all he'd had time to discern was that the other creature was utterly enraged at the protean's intrusion into its domain. Then the explosions began again in earnest, and the surface of the planet erupted across a hundred kilometers with blasts of light from below, tearing the surface apart.

Greymalkin was startled, but then even more so when he felt rather than heard Royce commune a signal unlike anything the cyneget had ever transmitted before, something that resembled an alarming and inchoate snarl of rage. Greymalkin flinched, but immediately realized that the cyneget had not snarled at him, but something else entirely. He started to scan his instruments but then felt a chill down his back *at the presence of someone else in the cockpit with him.*

"You are remarkably resourceful, Brother Thomas," a resonant voice said from roughly a meter away. Instead of further startling him, Greymalkin felt petrified. He looked around slowly, straight into an intense pair of eyes with yellow irises around black pupils. Rodo, the now all too familiar-looking older man, was sitting across from Greymalkin. He looked very relaxed. There was a slight smile on his handsome, slender face.

Bruno's agitated thoughts crashed into Greymalkin's mind. «I have good news and bad news.» Another series of explosions enveloped Bruno, atomizing the rock around him into plasma. «I have successfully managed to secure your bag. However, the Abyssal that possessed it is proving to be a bit of a problem. And I have strong reason to believe that your ship has been boarded by the individual you encountered previously, Rodolfo Flavopallio.»

«Thank you, Bruno.» Greymalkin felt an immense sadness and sense of regret settle over him as he looked at Rodo's eerie eyes and smile. *I am so, so stupid. I could have easily avoided this. Now I'm dead.*

Rodo seemed puzzled for a second, and then his eyebrows lifted. "Oh dear, please excuse how dense I am! I've given you the impression that you've attracted my anger." He smiled broadly then, and shook his head. "Far from it! You've attracted my interest, my boy."

Greymalkin was aware of several threads of events going on at the same time. The battle between Bruno and the Abyssal was reaching truly epic proportions, with vast city-sized pieces of the planet's surface erupting upwards amid the explosions, sending enormous clouds of debris in slow arcs out into sub-orbital paths radiating away from the location of the duel. Much closer, Royce was emitting a low continuing snarl, and trying to figure out some way of attacking Rodo without injuring Greymalkin. And closest of all, Greymalkin realized he had suddenly become very calm as he desperately sorted through options in his mind, seeking some way out of the predicament.

"Really. Please, tell me about it," Greymalkin said woodenly. *Maybe if I have Royce depressurize the cabin....*

"My young friend, please don't do anything rash," Rodo said, appearing genuinely friendly and concerned. "Your apprehension is understandable, certainly, given our first meeting! I *am* sorry about that. I had no idea you were this *interesting*. I'm only here to talk."

Greymalkin hesitated uncertainly, feeling frozen by the man's unblinking stare, and then said, "Your friend on the planet doesn't seem to be interested in talking, only attacking."

Rodo nodded sympathetically, and said, "Yes, your associate definitely stirred up a hornet's nest there, no doubt about it."

Greymalkin frowned, and asked, "What is a 'hornet'? Some kind of animal?"

Rodo looked surprised, and then delighted. "So innovative and brave, but so inexperienced! My young friend, I have so much that I can teach you. Please say that you'll come with me? I've wanted someone to mentor for a very long time. Can we perhaps reach an understanding?"

Greymalkin was shocked at the statement, but jumped on it in desperation. He could feel that Bruno was expending energy at an unbelievable rate, and although the protean appeared to be giving as well as he received, the battle was not going well. And Royce seemed ready to try to turn inside out to get at Rodo. Greymalkin communed conciliatory thoughts. "I will be happy to let you have my pack. I was a fool to come after it; it isn't worth all this violence."

"Pack?" Rodo said, muddled for a second. "Oh, your little artifacts! They are of no consequence. Interesting toys from the Sadorian. I gave them to my friend as an amusement. That is not what's caused all the commotion down on the planet. Your associate invaded a sacrosanct stronghold. I'm afraid my friend will fight to the death over that incursion."

Greymalkin felt his heart jump, and said, "Surely there is something we can do or trade to settle this?" Through the link he felt Bruno's increasing pain at the damage it was incurring.

Rodo smiled broadly again. "Oh, please! Surely you aren't worried about your associate!? I have no idea if it will defeat my friend or the other way around; they seem rather evenly matched. But that should hardly matter to us! I say again, come with me. The two of us have much more in common than you and that boiling black catastrophe! We're both Sojourners, after all."

Greymalkin stared, speechless. He finally whispered, "What did you say?"

"Oh, you hadn't discerned that yet?" Rodo said. "Yes, indeed, our origins and aims are aligned. I've just been here *much* longer than you. Since the last such expedition three centuries ago, in fact."

Greymalkin's mind raced as he wondered if anything Rodo said could possibly be true. A Sojourner? Now that he thought about it, there was something about the man that reminded him of senior Sojourners. In fact, *both the Prior and the Abbot*. That thought made him shudder. As his thoughts chased themselves in a circle, Bruno roared at him through the link.

«Do not go with that individual! I'll be there momentarily, you've given me an idea!» The protean then had another incredibly fast discussion with the Abyssal for all of a second. Greymalkin only caught that Bruno was making some kind of offer to the other creature, but the constant stream of explosions stopped. In the sudden pause, clouds of millions of tons of debris began to fall slowly down around Bruno and the Abyssal throughout the huge cavity in the surface of the planet carved out by their battle.

Rodo sighed deeply and then stood up. "Oh well, we can continue this conversation subsequently, Brother Thomas. We have plenty of time. I only ask you to consider my offer."

"What is your offer?" Greymalkin asked, his thoughts a jumble of distractions. Desperate, Royce was about to flood the cabin with supercooled gas. And he had no idea what the frozen tableaux of Bruno and the Abyssal facing one another signified.

"Join me," Rodo said, smiling. "You are seeking information. Information is the key to power, here and everywhere. I can help you gain information *and* power. We can help each other."

"Help each other do what?" Greymalkin pressed. "Explore this territory?" Bruno had vanished into shadow space, and Greymalkin could feel that the protean was racing back toward him. But the Abyssal was not pursuing. It had vanished as well.

"No," Rodo said with a small, wry shake of his head. "*Rule* this territory. Goodbye for now, Brother Thomas." Unbelievably, he simply vanished before Greymalkin's eyes. The young Sojourner had a vague perception of something rocketing away through shadow space at incredible speed, even for a starship. He couldn't track it because he was too occupied restraining the panicked Royce from flooding the cabin with liquid nitrogen. By the time he had calmed down the cyneget, Bruno had appeared outside the hull.

«Did the Rodo sham-thing depart, then?» Bruno was a boiling black lava physically, and its thoughts were even hotter as it scanned around them in different directions.

«Sham-thing?»

«*You cannot possibly believe that creature is a human!*» Bruno's mind was a white-hot fury of frustration blasting at him so powerfully that Greymalkin winced and broke the link with the protean. The feedback from the alien cyborg's combat frenzy had started bubbling up through Greymalkin. Even Royce felt it. The living starship squalled a frightened signal and frantically spun around away from the protean, throwing Greymalkin into the side of the cockpit. He had to calm down the agitated cyneget all over again.

After he'd soothed the little starship, Greymalkin slumped down into the cockpit seat. «You may be right. How did you make peace with the Abyssal?»

Even though he'd broken the link with the protean, Greymalkin could tangibly feel Bruno's rage subsiding, but oh so slowly, like boiling water cooling. «I did not make peace with it. I made a bargain with it in order to delay our conflict. You gave me the idea with your comment to the Rodo-thing.»

That got Greymalkin's attention. «A bargain? For what?»

«I offered to share Kuanian's reward with it.» The protean now seemed subdued, but Greymalkin felt even more shocked.

«Truly? I... suppose I am surprised. The reward seems rather important to you.»

Bruno's communed thoughts were irritated. «The reward is *very* important to me, yes. But Kuanian's reward is information, and the nature of the information is...What is the human term? *Non-rivalrous*. I lose nothing by sharing it. And offering to share it stopped the battle. For the time being.»

How interesting, Greymalkin thought. Then he communed another thought, very cautiously. «So, you were unable to defeat the Abyssal?»

Bruno sulked for a moment before responding. «No, surprisingly. Dark Nebula is rather powerful.»

«Dark what?»

«The Abyssal told me its name at one point. The name essentially translates as 'Dark Nebula' or 'Black Stellar Wind' in your language. By the way, here is your precious garment bag.» Bruno dropped out of shadow space inside Royce's cabin for a fraction of a second, dropping the pack near Greymalkin's feet. Even for that split second, Greymalkin felt a blast of heat radiating from the protean. The battle had raised the cyborg's temperature incredibly.

The pack was singed, and very hot to the touch when Greymalkin opened it. The golden garment and tool were both there, but he only looked at the two gifts and did not touch them. *What a fool I was to cause all this havoc for these... possessions.* He finally sealed the pack and stowed it away. He sat back in the cockpit and began the process of linking to Royce's helm control, communing with Bruno as he did so. «I admit it, I was unprepared. I was wrong. You warned me. I apologize for causing this conflict, Bruno.»

«Why?» The protean's thoughts were confused. «We retrieved your items. And that was a *magnificent* battle. I greatly enjoyed it, and you and I both survived.»

«Those outcomes might have been very different.» Greymalkin closed his eyes, directing Royce into shadow space. The protean followed silently, floating along just outside the hull. Finally Greymalkin asked the question that he had been dreading to broach. «Were there any other living beings on that planet?»

«Oh, yes. Dark Nebula had a great many Crotani servants in the lair.» Bruno's thoughts were very matter of fact. Greymalkin felt his heart sink. He did not ask anything more during the trip back, instead simply meditating on how terribly he had failed in this venture, and resolving repeatedly to himself to never again act without thinking carefully about the potential consequences. He did not want to know how many Crotani had died because of his stupidity.

By the time they reached the expedition base, he felt exhausted. It had been a horrendous day, and he felt another of his recently recurring migraines coming on now. He mechanically went through the process of docking Royce and tending to the cyneget. It took a long time for the agitated starship to settle into dormancy. Greymalkin eventually found himself in a near trance of fatigue, simply sitting in the cockpit and staring out the forward viewport at the darkened loading dock of the tavern. Neither Tatter nor the gang members were there. Everything seemed quiet as he tried to ignore the migraine, and finally drifted off to sleep.

Greymalkin woke abruptly when a loud and very weighty thump against the hull knocked his head against the cockpit wall. He came awake instantly, just as Royce blared a klaxon warning signal and twisted violently in the dock berth. Communed screams were coming from two minds just outside the rover starship who were apparently in actual direct contact with Royce, because Greymalkin could also *hear* muffled echoes of the same screams vibrating *directly through the hull*. He looked around, frantically trying to figure out what was happening just as several more thumps jarred the hull heavily.

Then two unmistakable individuals slammed into the viewport right in front of him. One was Bruno. The protean was morphing even as it collided with the viewport, evidently trying to envelop the other individual... who was Tatterdemalion. The Morganan was in alien form and was not holding back, actually throwing *off* the protean even as Greymalkin watched. He registered that the entire back wall of the tavern was blown out, with fragments scattered and spinning through the dock space. In the brief moment while the two were in front of him, before they both lurched away to the side, Greymalkin had no time to do anything except simultaneously yell and commune incoherently at the two of them.

«Hey! *Hey!*» Neither of them paid him any attention. Greymalkin finally managed to form a lucid thought and statement. «Bruno, stop it! Stop attacking her!"

The protean obediently backed away, and so did Tatter. Then Greymalkin was again shocked when Royce thrust forward one of its manipulator limb stumps that had been slowly regrowing. For a fraction of a second Greymalkin thought it was also trying to punch Tatter, but then a shadow blade appeared from nowhere, lodged in the manipulator and having just missed the side of Tatter's head.

Greymalkin flinched, but then followed the direction of the blade's passage with his eyes back to the origin point. Young Gower was in the shadows with several members of his gang, holding the control handle of the blade. Everyone froze, and Greymalkin instantly understood what had happened. Gower had tried to kill Tatter with the shadow blade, and Royce had instinctively moved to protect her.

Tatter's strange alien non-eye bulges swelled, and Greymalkin picked up her communed thoughts directed at Gower in disbelief. «*Jamie? You're trying to kill me?*»

Greymalkin could not see Young Gower's face through the helmet of the void suit, but the thug's thoughts were both angry and terrified. «Get away from us, you bitch! Leave now or we'll find some way to kill you, *I swear it*!»

Even though Tatter was in her alien form, Greymalkin somehow understood the expressions that crossed her extraordinary face, perhaps through her communed thoughts. In the space of a few seconds she was first anguished, then furious, and then frightened and vulnerable. She looked around the dock, obviously seeking somewhere to retreat to cover, but there was nowhere to hide. She finally looked at the big manipulator arm in front of her where Royce had taken the attack meant for her, and moved behind it to shield herself. That brought her close to the viewport, and she suddenly saw Greymalkin from only a meter away and glowered at him.

«Was this *your* idea? To use your freak horror-fiend to kill me?» Her thoughts felt bitter and isolated. Greymalkin stared at her and shook his head hastily.

«No! I didn't know anything about this! Bruno! What in blazes is this about?» Greymalkin looked at the protean in confusion. The creature simply coalesced smaller.

«You need *funds*. They offered funds, and I thought it would be easy to defeat her.» What passed for the head of the protean was always hard to discern, but Greymalkin thought Bruno was looking at Tatter. «Unfortunately, this one is more capable than I anticipated.»

Then Gower communed angrily again. «Get lost, Tatter! Nobody wants you here! We'll kill you if you don't leave, and leave now! I mean it!»

The Morganan did not respond immediately, but simply looked around the docks again. At last her communed thoughts came sadly and slowly. «There's nowhere to go out there, Jamie. You know that.»

Greymalkin had struggled to catch up with what he was seeing. The Gowers had evidently hired Bruno to ambush Tatter in the dock area of the tavern, and the protean must have agreed without telling him. Greymalkin inwardly cursed the protean for a violent, impulsive moron. He looked at the Morganan on the other side of the viewport. As imposing as the alien was, he thought he had never sensed emotions communed from another being that felt more abandoned and betrayed.

«Tatter, I didn't have anything to do with this. I called Bruno off; you're okay now!» Greymalkin felt stricken by what the alien-human hybrid said next in a cynical tone.

«Sure. Thanks, buddy. But even a Sylphid is dead out here in the Carinae if they're by themself. *Nobody* survives this place alone.» The Morganan looked at the entrance to the dock and the harshly bright stars shining there. Greymalkin looked from her eerie alien face to the stars and back, desperately seeking a solution. *No! I can't have killed yet another person with my stupidity....* Then he found himself speaking before he knew what he was saying.

«Come with us then! Bruno's just an idiot, and you're safe from him now. Come with us!» Greymalkin could only think of how foolish and naïve his thoughts seemed while effervescing out of him. But the Morganan looked at him quickly with what seemed to be an anxious and alert expression.

«Are you serious? Crap, if you are, then we've probably got to get out of here. *Now.*» The huge alien seemed to look at him uncertainly through the viewport. Gower and his thugs were fingering their shadow blades again.

«Yeah, I'm sure! Let's go.» Greymalkin opened the outer hatch on Royce's main forward airlock. Tatter glared back at Gower and his thugs.

«I want all the money I earned for you and your dad, Jamie! I'll be back for it, do you hear me!?» Then Tatter neatly flipped herself away from Royce's manipulator and into the airlock. Greymalkin did not hesitate. He quickly steered Royce out of the berth and toward the dock entrance.

«Come on, Bruno, we're leaving!» Greymalkin saw the protean vanish from the docks and reappear next to Royce just as he launched the cyneget into shadow space. He set the helm on a course away from the expedition base and then went down to the inner airlock hesitantly, wondering if the Morganan would simply kill him when he opened the door. But he could sense that Bruno was just outside the hull, watching intently. He cycled the airlock.

When the door opened, Tatter was there inside the airlock glaring at him as she morphed rapidly from her huge, armored alien body back into her human form. And, as the antennae morphed into disheveled human hair and the hard exoskeleton became soft skin, Greymalkin uncomfortably realized with a sharply inhaled breath that a very *human* Tatter was taking form standing stark naked in front of him. When she was finally nothing but curves and a wildly tousled mop of auburn hair, she stepped forward aggressively and pushed him out of her way so hard that he slammed against the wall.

"Show's over, pal!" she snapped at him. "And you'd better have some clothes for me to wear, right now! Your black blob-monster came at me when I was trying to go to sleep." Greymalkin stopped gaping at her and nodded contritely, tearing his gaze away. After a moment's thought, he sadly went to a disused locker and pulled out one of Bora's old flight suits. He handed it behind him, and Tatter snatched it out of his hand.

After the rustling of fabric stopped, he turned around. The jumpsuit was definitely quite a bit *tighter* on the Morganan across the chest and hips than it had ever been on Bora, but Tatter had nevertheless managed to pour herself into it. She crossed her arms, and scowled at him irately. "Well? Where do we go from here, then? Any bright ideas, hmm?"

Greymalkin groaned inside. Belatedly, it was sinking in just how awkward and dodgy this was actually going to be from this point on.

Assays

Greymalkin found having a coherent conversation with Sister Constance to be a challenge, because she was always in motion. He admired her commitment to getting absolutely as much research accomplished in the time she was given, but he found being around her to be exhausting. And he could feel yet *another* migraine looming. His recurring headaches were wearying.

«Constance, where are we going? Please slow down!» As Greymalkin chased her across the enormous trunk of the nemora meta-tree, he had to struggle to keep up with her but also not accidently spin away from the smooth silvery surface into the void. The huge limbs of the living tree that they were assaying were all around them in a confusing visual tangle of reflective surfaces against the stars. He picked out Constance again, a moving human-shaped reflection among the myriad curved mirror surfaces. Perhaps because of her relentless level of activity, Constance had a thin, athletic build, and a remarkable level of coordination to go with it. As they emerged from the darkness of shadow behind one branch into the relatively bright glare of the two blue stars that the nemora meta-tree orbited, he fumbled several sample containers and had to pause to collect them before they drifted away. Constance was a hundred meters away by the time he resumed following her. She did not look back as she dove headlong into a cluster of globular seed-pods, each one bigger than a house.

«Take your time, Grey. I just have to finish collecting all my recorders before I pack up and leave this tree. Now what were you saying? Please continue.» Constance could focus on several tasks and discussion threads at the same time, he'd learned. He sighed, secured the pack of containers against his chest, and tried to remember what he'd been asking her.

«Right, *Bruno*. I haven't been able to get any more details out of him about these mysterious 'Central Ones' he mentioned. But do you really think they could be the Builders?»

«Why not? That tracks with a lot of reports we've heard over the years from different alien species.» Constance was busily gathering up a series of small sensors inside the seed-pod cluster when Greymalkin found her. After stowing away the last sensor into yet another container, she peremptorily shoved it into his arms and leaped away through the pods. Slightly annoyed, he added the container to the collection already strapped to his chest.

«What reports? I've never heard anything like that.» Greymalkin bounced out of the seed-pods into the void and saw that she was now half-way back to her own cyneget. Constance had named her cyneget Lacey, and the cyborg was huddled next to Royce. He hurried to pressor after her.

«Grey, my friend!» Constance had an amused laugh in her thoughts. «You came all the way out here, to the Carinae, and didn't read up on this part of the Galaxy? There have been comments from both the Thubans and the Jotuns for centuries about the powerful beings they've encountered in the galactic core. What else would an Abyssal like this 'Bruno' of yours call them except 'the Ones in the Center'? Okay, before we each take off, I need to give you a full copy of all my notes on the Carinae. And I want you to study the main dataset I've collected on all the sites my team and I have surveyed. Give me your thoughts on the extended hypercardioid distribution around the primary Eta Carinae nebula... Grey? Are you paying attention?»

Greymalkin sullenly caught up with her next to the two rovers. Both of the cynegets were closely observing them. «I'm paying attention. I just don't think we're *getting* anywhere. You and your team are working yourselves to death out here, but the Prior and his cronies at the main expedition base are just sitting there hoarding most of the items you've collected.»

«Oh, it's much worse than that.» Constance, for once, was not in motion. There was a momentary sense of fatigue in her thoughts, as if she found this topic tiresome. «They sell many of the artifacts we've collected to the highest bidder back home.»

«What!» Greymalkin was aghast. «Then what is all this effort for, if they're just selling everything?»

Constance shook her head quickly. «I didn't say they sold *everything*, just a lot of it, the shiny junk that I send his way to keep him off my back. I make sure that the important items get back to the Orion Arm to reputable memory arks. I'm quite familiar with such corruption in the Order; I learned how to work around it long ago.»

Greymalkin felt appalled. «That's... awful. I... didn't know there was this much corruption....» He suddenly felt very stupid. Constance again shook her head.

«I don't think it used to be this bad.» Her thoughts were now uncharacteristically slow, and reflective. "But you've surely been aware of the trend of declining support for the Order over the last century? Sojourners are respected everywhere, but arks like yours have been beached, and then just *disappearing* in recent years. The Priors and Abbots willing to oversee those collapses are usually corrupt. The senior brothers and sisters with integrity refuse, and go pursue other endeavors.»

Greymalkin thought of Trystia, and nodded sadly, before looking at Constance quizzically. «But, if that's the case, why are you here, then?»

She laughed at his comment. «Because, silly, this is a wondrous opportunity! I'm not going to let some crooked dimwits ruin that for me and everyone else. This is the first opportunity to explore the Carinae in centuries! I'm surprised at you. You're the one who's usually talking my ear off about the mysteries of this place. That reminds me, let me get the mnemotome copy of my notes that I made for you.» She launched back into frenetic activity, stowing away the containers he had carried for her while rummaging in one of the big cargo pods strapped to side of her cyneget, Lacey. The cyborg helped her with its manipulators.

While Constance rummaged in her cargo pods, Greymalkin looked up at the breathtaking tangle of nemora branches around them, and the vast forest of wild trees floating in the sky beyond. It was an awe-inspiring sight. He'd never seen such big nemora meta-forests as the ones they'd encountered here in the Carinae. Many of the *really* big forests in the Orion Arm had long ago been harvested. He had to agree with her; the Carinae was wondrous. But the thought of the corrupt Sojourners and violent gangs he'd encountered here was like the taste of bile, threatening to spoil the wonder of it all for him.

The violent sky of the Carinae behind the forest attracted his attention then, and Greymalkin looked up at the blazing Wolf-Rayet stars around them, along with the incredible sight of the central Eta Carina Homunculus Nebula that hung above them. That enormous, vicious-looking, yet seemingly motionless tableau was the still expanding remnants of a supernova explosion that had occurred millennia ago. It was one of many incredible sights adorning the Carinae that were always visible wherever he went in the region, like trophies of annihilation on the wall of the universe. In his shadow synesthesia these cosmic disasters rumbled like thunder in the distance.

And then Greymalkin caught sight of the other object that inevitably attracted his attention lately whenever he took a moment to study the Carinae, the strange Keyhole Nebula. To his synesthesia the bizarre figure-eight lemniscate of seething, fluorescing gas filaments sounded like the combination of a distant waterfall spray of ice and the steady roar of an incomprehensibly vast creature. He resolved again that he wanted to study the nebula up close at some point. His attention came back to Constance; she had finally dug out a compact mnemotome databloc, and was offering it outstretched to him.

«Here is a copy of all my observations to date, including my tentative conclusions. Remember, I want your thoughts on the distribution of sites. I think it means something, but I don't want to prejudice your thoughts about it.» Constance had an earnest intensity to her.

Greymalkin scowled. «I will. The mysteries here are what keep me going. But all these Abyssals we're encountering hereabouts must know *everything* worthwhile there is to know about the region! If they would just tell us.»

Constance laughed heartily again. «Says the only Sojourner to ever have an Abyssal at his personal beck and call. Ask your Bruno monster.»

«Agreed, I think he probably knows everything I'd want to ask. But he, or is that thing an *it*? He or it—just won't tell me. Or maybe I just can't figure out how its mind works, not well enough to get answers.»

«Then go ask one of the *other* Abyssals!» Constance's thoughts were flashing with laughter and impatience now. He could tell that she wanted to get going. «I'm afraid to approach them, because we don't have a bodyguard like you do! But I've collected information on dozens of them that have been encountered in the Carinae, and they aren't all unfriendly psychopaths. Just *most* of them. Did you ever go try to communicate with the one in the Keyhole Nebula over there? Or the one closest to us near that star formation region?»

«Not yet.» Greymalkin was delaying now. He didn't want to say goodbye to Constance just yet. She was the only Sojourner who had not reacted with disgust to the covenant systems layered on his mind. And she was the only other person here that he could actually talk to about exploring the Carinae. Conversing with her was the only time he felt like the universe was sane. «I want to, but I can't figure out how to navigate through all the turbulence around them. There are so many stars jammed so closely together here it's insane.»

«You'll figure it out. Providence is with you, brother. Farewell, for now.» She leaped into the airlock of her cyneget, and the cyborg immediately reared up off the nemora meta-tree trunk. Her rover vanished into shadow space, and Greymalkin clung to Royce, feeling alone.

But he wasn't alone, Greymalkin realized. Royce was there, and of course Bruno was there, hiding as usual. The protean had appeared at his side surreptitiously, without him noticing. As alien as Bruno was, Greymalkin could detect the irritation in his communed thoughts. «That woman seems to think I'm your pet, when it's actually more the other way around. Don't we need to be going? The Sylphid will be expecting us.»

Greymalkin grimaced and sighed. «Don't remind me. But yes, let's go.» Quickly enough, he clambered into Royce and connected with the rover's helm control. In moments they were skimming along the shadow plane toward Tatter's location.

Royce sped rapidly and smoothly across the plane, as always. Usually the sheer vitality of the rover cyborg cheered up Greymalkin, but somehow today he felt depressed. Royce in turn could feel that depression through the helm link, and it aggravated the cyneget's nervous mood. Greymalkin knew exactly what was making the cyneget agitated; it had him on edge as well. To the right of them loomed the frozen contours of the huge black nebula that had been known for millennia as *the Finger of God*. The nebula was a sheer wall of harsh turbulence generated by the ravening torrent of energy that several blazing blue giant stars poured into the dark clouds of dust and gas. Their path inevitably took them close by the black wall in order to reach Tatter's position. Even Bruno seemed to be eyeing the long black wall stretching out to the side of their path. It did seem very much like God's Finger pointing toward the roiling clouds of ionized gas ahead of them. Deep in that nightmarish thicket was the shadow mine where they had left Tatter.

«You are late.» Bruno's communed thoughts seemed amused. «The Sylphid will be displeased. Even if she is fond of you, she still does not trust you completely.»

«She's not 'fond' of me. And why should she trust *either* of us?» Greymalkin found that he was in a truly foul mood. «You tried to kill her, and I'm sure she thinks I'll abandon her just like the expedition scum did. I'm amazed she was gutsy enough to stay working in that mine all by herself.»

«She needs the wealth the mine offers. As do we.» The protean's thoughts were full of suspicion directed at Tatter. «I hope she will honor our agreement and share the profits generated. You are truly near the end of your supplies.»

Greymalkin communed nothing in response. He was now occupied with the process of steering Royce deftly up the jagged winding shadow plane path that was the only safe way to reach the location of the mine. Once they reached the entrance, he gently but firmly urged Royce down into the opening, going deeper and deeper into shadow space away from the normal universe. He and Royce both knew they would be plunging far down into shadow space, displacing their continuity bubble increasingly farther from normal space and moving directly 'below' the blazing ultraviolet giant star where the mine was situated.

He disliked diving in shadow space, for a host of reasons. Granted, it was risky, but most of all he hated the oppressive sensation. Shadow space seemed to thicken around them rapidly. His peripheral perception of the stars, almost always there in his shadow synesthesia, faded until it felt like they were flying through a thick, inky black murk. His anxiety level steadily rose, because he knew he had to stay exactly on course despite the lack of orienting stars or other features in the darkness. The path was treacherous. If either he or Royce made a serious misstep the spatial continuity manifold around them would collapse and they'd be annihilated.

He felt the helm link with Royce intensifying, as it sometimes did in these moments of close coordination. It was a very odd sensation. His mind seemed to be growing closer and closer to that of the cyneget, until it felt like they became conjoined. Where there had been a human and a rover cyborg, it now felt like there was a single hybrid being focused on navigating through shadow space. Greymalkin had read about the mental condition of communal confluence in linked minds, but had never experienced it before he had become close to Royce. But they had become totally dependent on one another throughout the weeks that had followed their meeting, and they had come to trust one another implicitly.

Before he knew it, the dock beacon loomed up out of the obscuring darkness. They had arrived at the mine, deep in shadow space. Both he and Royce felt the abrupt merging of their continuity manifold with that of the mine, and they traversed the final distance through the void increasingly slower and more carefully while decelerating. Finally, there was a heavy *thump* as he nudged Royce's forward airlock into one of the docking cradles of the mine. He realized he'd been holding his breath again out of anxiety, and began to inhale uneasily.

Greymalkin stiffly extricated himself from the cockpit and tried to relax his tense shoulders. While his shadow synesthesia was muffled, there was nevertheless a horrifically strong sensation of oppressive mass and energy pressure around him that left no doubt that he was *inside* the surface boundaries of a star. Because displacement in shadow space was actually only a matter of tiny interdimensional distances, the uncomfortable reality was that he was intimately close to the blazing thermonuclear interior of a very large, hot, and somewhat unstable star. He tried not to think about it as he donned a void suit and exited the rover, floating into the darkened zero gee tunnels of the mine. Bruno silently took on his tiny form and draped himself on the shoulder of Greymalkin's void suit.

Everything about the place was unsettling. Beyond the synesthetic sensations of being underneath a star, the mine was long abandoned and indeterminately ancient. He wondered what alien species had built it. The Carinans? The interior structures of the mine were bizarrely shaped and worn smooth with use. Tatter was secretive about what she did and did not know about the facility. *Who told her about this place?* Greymalkin wondered. *Someone* had installed human starship docking cradles in the mine, though, and he doubted that it had been Tatter. The cradles looked like they'd been there a very long time. There were markings on the walls, but they were like no language he had ever seen. He tried to hurry, jumping down the long tunnels in long zero gee leaps. He finally found the entrance to the big shadow space extraction chamber where they had last left Tatter. There were no sounds in the void, but ahead of him in the chamber he could see the telltale blindingly bright flickering flashes of a runcible in operation. Greymalkin peeped into the room.

Tatter was there in her alien Sylphid form, holding a huge alien runcible in place with her bare hands as it sparked brilliantly. Greymalkin had taken the precaution of adding a flare shield to his helmet, and it blocked most of the light that leaked through the interdimensional manifold of the runcible. Although what leaked through the manifold were only vanishingly small traces, the source was the thermonuclear exploding hell inside the giant star. The traces of plasma that came flaring through the manifold of the runcible were blindingly hot, violent, and very dangerous. Despite all of that, Tatter operated the runcible *by hand*. Greymalkin shook his head.

He definitely didn't want to startle her while she was working the runcible, so he waited until she had finished the extraction she was working on before communing to her. When the light-show stopped and she put down the device, he piped up. «Tatter, we're back.»

The Sylphid looked around at him and grinned that hideous alien smile that was packed impossibly full of needle-like teeth. «I sensed you guys coming. I wondered if you were going to come back for me or not.»

Her thoughts did not seem very *concerned*, however, Greymalkin noted. *She wasn't the least bit worried about being stranded here.* He wondered again if she had some alternate means of traveling through shadow space. «So, any luck with the mining?»

Tatter's monstrous rictus of teeth grew even broader, if that was possible. «Check it out! See what I pulled out of this big beautiful star while you guys were gone.» She gestured to the extraction bay, and his eyes went wide. There were dozens of blazing shadow jewels suspended in the collection grid, row after row of brilliantly glowing nuggets. Greymalkin went over to stare at what she had collected.

«These shadow jewels... they're enormous.» Greymalkin felt taken aback. As Tatter drifted over to loom over him uncomfortably closely, he glanced nervously at her grinning jaws and fangs, each of which were longer than one of his arms. He laughed anxiously and looked away from her to the shadow jewels. «These are adamans, right? I've never seen any this size.»

Tatter's communed laughter was disconcertingly bright and amused. «Of course you have, dummy! You see one just like them every day! Where do you think that rock in your head came from?»

Greymalkin blinked in surprise, conceding the truth of what she was saying. Now that she had pointed it out, he realized that his enormous and brilliant violet-white shadow jewel was indeed very like these gems. His communed thoughts came out in a mumbling tangle. «Well, hmm, I guess mine must have come from a big star like this one, but back in the Orion Arm....»

Tatter cocked her huge head at him. «You clearly aren't a jeweler! Me, on the other hand, I appreciate quality. Sure, I can dig and mine as well as any Canisian, but I'm also an aficionada of adamans. Oh, shadow jewels from other kinds of stars are okay, jacinths from red giants, citrines from big yellow supergiants like Polaris, and so on. But I *adore* adamans. They only come from O-class ultraviolet giants like the one we're inside. Grey, don't you understand? Giant ultraviolet stars are the rarest ones in the Galaxy; they all have unique shadow signatures and regional patterns. We Sylphids can sense that kind of thing directly. And your jewel, my friend, came from right here in the Carinae. I think it might have even come from this star, or one close by in this region. Hell, it might have been extracted in this mine!»

Greymalkin stared at her for a second. He was just now realizing that Tatter herself had a rather large adaman in her alien head. *Wait, is she serious?* Then he laughed, shaking his head. «Very funny. You know I wasn't born anywhere near here.» He snickered nervously, moving back slightly from the thicket of long teeth in Tatter's ever-widening inhuman smile that was now only centimeters from his face.

«You might not have been born here, you cute little dope, but your shadow jewel was. Why don't you ask whoever stuck it in you where they got it?» Tatter reached around him abruptly and snapped the collector shut, making him flinch and bump against her huge shoulder.

He floated away spinning slightly, and grabbed a stanchion to stop the spin. He frowned at her as she packed up the jewels.

«I *can't*, I'm an orphan. I don't know who my parents were.» Greymalkin felt disoriented. Could his shadow jewel really have come from the Carinae? It didn't seem possible. He scowled at Tatter, who now seemed wistful, or at least as wistful as an alien ghoul could appear.

«That must be nice. I wish I *didn't* know who my parents were.» Tatter finished packing up the shadow jewels while Greymalkin gawked at her in confusion. Not knowing who his parents were had haunted him for as long as he could remember. She picked up the big alien runcible and stuffed the sealed jewel case under her arm, looking at him impatiently. «Let's get going. We need to sell these off.»

«Where are you going to sell all those adamans anyway? Won't Gower and his gang be on the lookout for you back at the expedition base?» Greymalkin jumped back down the tunnel toward the dock, and Tatter followed him. «I mean, there aren't that many places out here to sell anything!»

«Says the monk!» Tatter's thoughts were brimming with giggles. «Do you think there *aren't* all kinds of under-the-table buying and selling back channels happening out here, what with all the shadow space mining going on in this expedition? Since we're sort of partners now, I suppose, and you'll find out anyway when I sell them, I'll tell you who my buyer is. He's the same guy that tipped me off about the existence of this hidden mine.»

Greymalkin's ears perked up. She was evidently in a good mood; this was the first time she'd shared any significant information with him. «Well, yes, monks aren't usually in the habit of fencing jewels. Tell me how it works.»

Tatter chuckled again in her communed thoughts. «You are so adorable! I don't need a *fence*, these aren't stolen. I just finished mining them myself! And I can sell them for a small fortune, even with the markup around here. We need to go to that outer resupply station I told you about, remember? I set up the purchase handoff with a Crotani I know named Huhonen.»

«What!» Greymalkin accidentally banged his head on the tunnel wall while trying to look around and gauge if she was joking. «He was my dock manager back at the base! But he seemed like an honest, aboveboard kind of fellow.»

To his annoyance, Tatterdemalion's communed thoughts burst out with mental gales of laughter. «You've got to be kidding me! That guy is up to his eyeballs in every end-run scheme on the base! C'mon now! Your ship's berth was right next to my tavern! You never noticed he was helping me smuggle stuff in and out all the time?»

Greymalkin grit his teeth, feeling stupid again. He also felt the migraine headache coming on now. Admittedly, the mental feeling of pressure from the star around them was getting to him, but he'd been having more and more migraines lately, when he'd never had them in the past. That worried him. They floated out of the tunnel into the dock, and Royce signaled him immediately. Greymalkin steadied himself against the cradle for a moment, and tried to steady his throbbing head as well. As she came up next to him, he frowned at the awkwardly big alien runcible Tatter was carrying in her oversized hand. «Are you really bringing that thing along with us? Did you find it here at the mine or what? I can't believe it still works, or that you actually trusted that ancient thing enough to extract shadow jewels from a star with it."

Tatter hefted the massive runcible triumphantly. «Are you kidding? This is the best damned runcible I've ever had! I can't believe what this rig can do. I think you could yank out souls with this thing! But best of all, I found it abandoned, for *free*, in this dead place!»

He shook his head again, trying to ignore the headache, and jumped over to the front of Royce's mirrorshell hull. They had to board one at a time through the airlock, because of Tatter's sheer size in her Sylphid form. He immediately went to the cockpit and made ready to depart while Tatter was cycling through the airlock. When she stepped out she was once more human, suddenly now once again dressed in one of Bora's old flight suits, albeit still stretched tightly around her every curve. He also noted that the runcible and the jewel case were nowhere to be seen, even though she'd entered the airlock with them. He'd grown frustrated with her unexplained vanishing tricks, and decided to try to broach the topic again while he released the docking cradle clamps around Royce. Tatter seemed to be in a good mood because of the jewels.

"Hey, Tatter, where'd the runcible go?" He tried to keep his thoughts casual and distracted. He'd noticed that Tatter, much like Bruno, seemed to respond more frequently to chance questions. She bounced down into the co-pilot seat while still grinning, although as he gazed at her he thought the smile was much less terrifying and far more appealing in her human form. He dropped his eyes quickly realizing that, whatever Bruno had said, Greymalkin was in fact becoming rather fond of her smile. *And her.* She raised an eyebrow at him.

"Can you not see my shadow pouch?" she asked in surprise. When he simply stared at her, she inclined her head. "I thought you could sense it with that big gem in your head, but you can't, hmm? Where did you think most of my mass goes when I shift out of Sylphid form into this teeny tiny body?"

Greymalkin nodded slowly, and scanned her more closely with his shadow jewel, shifting his perception through not only the flesh of her body, but also through the immediate quantum layers of shadow space in her body's vicinity. Straightaway, he sensed what she was referring to, and gasped. There was a huge pocket submanifold like an alien stomach or bladder surrounding her in shadow space that he had never noticed. It was jammed with both biological and technical items, many of them directly connected through huge neuronal paths that filled her human cranium and from there leading down into her human nervous system. Although he could sense her hulking alien form folded up neatly into a compact space there, the vast majority of the items were an array of strange equipment. In fact, as he scanned it he realized that there had to have been hundreds, perhaps thousands of tons of devices packed into the pocket space, virtually all of it unfamiliar. He found himself lingering as he examined both her alien form and human body in fascination.

"Hunh. No, I *didn't* see all that before. Uh, *wow*. Do all Sylphid's have something like that?" he asked in genuine fascination. She gave him a lazy smile and leaned over, putting her arms around his shoulders, making him anxious again but also sending a familiar shiver down his back. Her arms were warm and soft, but he could also feel how improbably *strong* they were.

"That's right. *All* of us, the purebred and the half-breeds like me, too. We're kind of like those human-space creatures called *turtles*; we carry our homes around with us. And...," she said, narrowing her big eyelashes ever so slightly at him, "you can stop snooping into my private parts now, love." He hastily directed his shadow sense away from her hidden innards.

"What's a 't-turtle'?" Greymalkin stuttered. She snorted, took her arms off him and sat back in the co-pilot seat.

"Good job trying to change the subject," she said, chuckling. "But you're wondering how it works, aren't you?"

Greymalkin shrugged, focusing on steering them up, away, and out of the mine. "I suppose I am. I mean, how can humans interbreed with a completely different alien species like the Sylphids, anyway? That makes no sense at all."

Tatter looked surprised, and then said with a leer, "You kinky little thing! I was still talking about the shadow pouch. But you were thinking about...."

"It-it's all part of the same topic really, isn't it?" Greymalkin snapped in embarrassed irritation. "I mean, how your physiology works, your biological origin, all of it is interrelated, right?"

Tatter rolled her eyes, and said with exaggerated sarcasm, "You monks. Are weird. Weirder than me, for sure." Then she impatiently launched into an abrupt scientific exposition that flabbergasted him as she shifted into uncharacteristically scientific language that he'd never heard her use before, but that she was clearly familiar with.

"Okay, to answer your question, *no*. Sylphids and humans don't interbreed in a direct biological sense; that's impossible. *Obviously*. But Sylphids are both biogenic and biomimetic. Our shadow space pouches can store huge quantities of additional tissue; it was an evolutionary adaptation that enabled adapting our physiology to imitate and take on the form of other creatures from our own biosphere.

"What happens with interspecies hybrids is that the Sylphid partner absorbs the human partner's DNA and creates a Sylphid offspring with... well, a little something extra. Sylphid-human hybrids generate a kind of homunculus inside of our shadow pouches, a xenobiological organism that's not actually Sylphid, and is distinct from our primary trunk. The growth is a genetic *teratoma* directly grown from the human partner's DNA, a human body that we can use as a kind of avatar to go among humans *as* a human. We can invert and evert ourselves back and forth quickly from our native Sylphid form to the teratomatic human form through shadow space. Like I said, it was an evolutionary adaptation that lets us perfectly mimic other species. Sylphid hybrids just take this adaptation to the next level with a species chosen by their Sylphid parent as a partner. Humans are one species we partner with this way; there are others, too. But understand, I really am *as much human as Sylphid*."

Greymalkin sat silently in the cockpit seat, stunned, but also utterly fascinated with this different side of Tatter. She clearly had advanced expertise as a xenobiologist. He was struggling to absorb both the unexpectedly dense explanation and the even more unexpected fact that Tatter was obviously far more studied than she'd let on. He also felt deeply chagrinned, realizing that he'd started to dismiss her mentally as a fetish, a gorgeous alien tavern-keeper wench. It infuriated him that he'd done exactly what he hated most, when people dismissed *him* as a stupid Bereft-born human. He kicked himself mentally for not remembering that Sylphids were far more intelligent and technologically advanced than human beings. *I won't make that mistake again.* Tatter picked up on his train of thought and sighed in exasperation.

"Yeah, mister oh-so supercilious science-monk, I know a lot about xenobiology in general, and interspecies reproductive biology specifically. It interests me, especially since I'm a *product* of it! Sorry if I surprised you. The rest of us don't feel the need to brag about how smart they are all the time," Tatter said with a scowl, folding her arms. Just as he was trying to think of a response, they were both startled when Bruno spoke up in the shockingly deep voice that occasionally projected from the tiny shape still splayed across Greymalkin's shoulder. The protean had been very quiet lately, to the point that they both sometimes forgot it was even there.

"He underestimated you, just as I did," the black splatter-shape rumbled from the shoulder of his void suit just under his left ear, making him jump in his seat. Greymalkin had taken off his helmet, but had left the void suit on. He'd completely overlooked the tiny form of the alien cyborg. The voice that filled the room with its monstrous snarl was as jarring as always whenever it deigned to speak. "So that's how you had sufficient strength and mass to resist my attack at the expedition base. You are most interesting, Sylphid."

"Yeah, you're just a barrel of laughs too, Bruno," Tatter said in evident disgust. She'd seemed to be getting accustomed to the protean, but clearly still didn't care much for Bruno after he'd attacked her. It seemed to put Tatter off her good mood, and she frowned at both Bruno and then Greymalkin. She leaned back in the seat and closed her eyes, saying, "Wake me up when we get to the resupply base. I've been mining nonstop ever since you left, and I'm beat." After a while Tatter began to snore. Greymalkin continued sitting in silence for the next few hours while she slept, enduring the migraine and worrying alone by himself while focusing his attention on the helm link with Royce and navigating across the hazards of the Carinae shadow plane.

In fact, he *caught up* on his worrying, fretting about virtually everything happening to him. He worried that he had obliviously misjudged the Crotani named Huhonen, and wondered how Tatter could trust such a duplicitous alien.

And he wondered about trusting Tatter, trying to reassure himself that she wasn't secretly planning to kill him without Bruno noticing. It still surprised him that she had agreed to come with them at all, given what Bruno had done to her. Even though she seemed to be friendly and jocular most of the time around him, he could occasionally sense a brittleness to the persona she projected. He had begun to realize that despite the flamboyant show Tatter put on constantly, he could occasionally glimpse subdued hints of nervous insecurity in her responses. At first he had dismissed those impressions, given how terrifying she was in her Sylphid form. It was hard for him to imagine that such an imposing being could possibly be insecure about anything, much less in her stunningly beautiful human form. But as he had spent time with her, he'd noticed more and more moments that implied a pervasive fear underneath her alternatively frightening and stunning façade.

But then, fear is the only sane response out here, he thought as he morosely looked out at the spectacle of the incredibly dangerous environment all around them in the Carinae. *Why shouldn't she feel afraid out here? And why shouldn't she be afraid of me as well as Bruno? I'm the one that everybody at the base thinks is unhinged. Why should she trust me?*

But then Greymalkin looked sidelong at her peaceful sleeping face, and found that whatever else he thought about Tatter, *he trusted her.* He wondered if he should worry about that as he furtively studied her relaxed features with sidelong glimpses. *I can't help it, I've started to like her,* he admitted to himself, feeling smitten. *I really like her.*

The migraine wracked his mind again and he worried about how agonizing it was becoming. He worried about becoming too pained and fatigued to steer alone. Most of all he worried about the turbulence and dropout gaps he encountered every few minutes in this region of the Carinae shadow plane. It was the most dangerous region he'd ever traversed.

But then he noticed something. Royce was anticipating his navigational responses and cues more and more intuitively. The cyneget was observing him and *learning* how to anticipate his helm commands. Royce had also started signaling him subtly at the times when his attention began to drift or when he started to nod off. By the time they arrived at the resupply station Greymalkin had realized that the little rover cyborg might be able to both help him spot at least *some* navigational hazards and stay alert at the same time.

When they finally reached the rendezvous point, he happily found that the shadow jewel purchase was an uneventful transaction between Tatter and Huhonen, and he was able to rest while the migraine went away. He studied the Crotani as it spoke to Tatter, and now picked up on cues that he had not found obvious before. Huhonen had a way of hiding in plain sight, he realized. The creature acted in so servile a manner that he now understood why he had overlooked its behavior before. Especially in contrast to Tatter's oversized personality, the

Crotani was virtually invisible, until he began noticing its subtly furtive habits when the alien thought no one was watching.

Greymalkin was glad when the transaction was over, and shocked at how much money Tatter had garnered from the deal. As they began restocking their supplies, he realized hopefully that if she indeed shared some of the funds they would now have enough provisions for weeks to come, if not months. While he was refueling Royce, he took advantage of the time to quickly skim through the dataset and notes that Constance had given him. By the time that Tatter and Bruno had hauled over and mounted a variety of new cargo pods full of provisions on the exterior of Royce's hull, he had selected his next destination. He watched the two aliens working together, and noted how Tatter always kept Bruno carefully in her sight. *She still doesn't trust him*, he thought. *Blazes, do I trust him? He seems much less erratic lately, but...*

Then Greymalkin paused, taking time to think back over the past few weeks. Now that he took a moment to reflect, the demeanor of the protean had changed quite significantly over the time it had been accompanying him. The changes had been gradual, but when he thought back to what the alien cyborg had been like when it had first erupted from beneath the surface of the moon where it had been imprisoned, the difference was almost startling.

When he had first encountered it, the protean had been prone to abrupt, unpredictable, and frightening mood shifts. Bruno could still become enraged, but it happened far less frequently now. And the protean seemed increasingly skilled at gauging and anticipating Greymalkin's responses. *It's almost like Bruno is studying me. Adapting to me. But why is he following me, really? And as for that, why is Tatter following me, really?*

It seemed strange that both the protean and the Sylphid now accepted requests and instructions from Greymalkin without responding with contemptuous comments or threats. What had changed? And more importantly, would they both continue to be agreeable? He studied the two aliens as they continued transferring crates, and he couldn't help wondering if *all three of them* might be watching one another with guarded optimism.

* * *

There finally came a moment when he was done refueling Royce, Bruno had returned to his shoulder, and Tatter had finished transferring all of the provisions. She came bounding up and loomed over him where he clung to Royce's hull. Greymalkin was still unsure of her huge Sylphid form's body language, but he found her sleek alien presence intriguing. Her huge form radiated a kind of raw power, graceful agility, and animal magnetism. As she quickly clasped a stanchion next to him, he looked at her scythe-like claws that were as long as his forearm... and felt an involuntary shiver down his spine.

He wondered what she was thinking about, and if she was planning to excuse herself and leave for parts unknown now that she had all the funds she needed. He suddenly realized with a pang that he would miss her if she left. Instead, she surprised him yet again by communing cheerfully, «So, what's next, love? Where are we headed now?»

Greymalkin blinked, and his forehead furrowed as he communed uncertainly. «I thought you just wanted to get hold of enough money to leave. Do you still want to come with me?»

Even despite her alien Sylphid expressions, he could feel in her communed response that Tatter felt hurt. «We're partners now! And besides, there's a *lot* more shadow jewels to be mined here in the Carinae before I go back to the Orion Arm.»

«I'm not here to make money, Tatter.» He found that his thoughts were both serious and firm. «I'm a *Sojourner*. I'm here to investigate this place and try to help the Bereft here.»

«Oh, so you don't want your portion of that adaman deal, then?» she asked, her thoughts laughing and amused.

Greymalkin paused, squirming. «Well, I need *some* of it if you're still willing to share, but not for me! I need it to keep Royce fed and cared for.»

Tatter grinned at him again with fangs like a fence, and communed back to him sweetly with warm thoughts that felt very human. «Sure! Good! So, then where are we headed?»

«Yes, do not keep us in suspense.» Bruno's thoughts rumbled in a low register. The protean still clung innocuously to his shoulder, but was obviously still attentive. It leaped off of him and began slowly growing in size. «We've wasted enough time with these logistics as it is.»

«Alright then.» Greymalkin cleared his throat and suddenly felt very self-conscious. It was dawning on him that, as ridiculous as it seemed, and at least for this moment, the two most intimidating alien beings he'd ever encountered in his life were actually looking to him as their *leader*. That was rather disorienting, and humbling. He wasn't used to anyone even being interested in his opinions, much less his directions. *I hope I made the right choice.* He communed a stellar topography chart from Constance's dataset to Bruno and Tatter.

«Constance recommended that I approach one of the other Abyssals in this region, even though they're all unfriendly, and mutual enemies of one another to boot. There are two nearby, one in the Keyhole Nebula and another one that's apparently in orbit around this star *here*.» He indicated a brilliant yellow supergiant star in the midst of a cluster of large stars near the resupply base where they were docked. Constance's stellar topographic data showed that the regional shadow plane around the cluster was horribly twisted, crunched, and folded around and through the cluster. The region around the Keyhole Nebula looked even worse. Tatter had skeptical thoughts.

«Uh, sort of rough going to get to either of those two spots, don't you think? I don't think I could find my way in or out of there even if my life depended on it.» Her thoughts were clear, even if her massive head was impassive. Greymalkin shrugged while nodding.

«You're right about it being incredibly rugged topography.» he agreed. «But look, I'm tired of wasting time fetching stuff for those corrupt characters at the main base. They don't know anything because they're *terrified* of actually exploring the Carinae. Constance has gathered lots of observations, but she and her team are far too scattered and *cautious*. The Crotani are too *primitive*. All the signs point to them being relative newcomers that lost whatever civilization they had after they arrived here. And they're completely subjugated by the Abyssals, anyway. The *only* way we're going to get any real answers is to communicate with some of the more advanced locals. The dominant species here are the Carinans, but they aren't around at the moment, and if they were they'd just try to kill us anyway. In my estimation, the *Abyssals* here have to be the best informed sapients about the Carinae. They are even more powerful than the Carinans, and there's evidence that the Carinans are allied with and serve some of them. Admittedly, there's very little information accessible about the Abyssals, but the records from the previous Xenocorps expedition indicate that they've been here a very long time. They might be convinced to communicate with us.»

«Why do you think the Abyssals will not simply try to *kill* us?» Bruno growled. After the protean had left his shoulder it had leisurely morphed into a larger and larger mass of boiling glossy black stone. Now it was more than two meters wide. Tatter was a still larger form looming closely over him to his right. He could not read her toothy alien expression, and found himself wishing she were in her human form.

«I don't know what they'll do. And, yes, the old accounts indicate that they're not disposed to being friendly.» Greymalkin admitted the point honestly. Then he scowled as he looked at Bruno. «Constance is afraid to approach any of them, she just took notes about the various ones that she heard about. But if *somebody* doesn't try to approach them, we'll never find out *anything*. And I'm the only one here that Kuanian entrusted with a *bodyguard*.» He looked pointedly at Bruno.

«So, which one of the two Abyssals, then?» Tatter now seemed entertained, and genuinely curious. «And do you want Bruno and I to scout ahead of you and Royce when we get there?»

Greymalkin looked at her with confusion. «What do you mean? Do you want Bruno to take you with him?» He was surprised that she trusted the protean enough to suggest *that*.

Tatter's huge alien face twisted into a grotesque smirk. «No need. I can travel in shadow space by myself. I've got a small personal shadow space drive in my pouch.»

Greymalkin gaped at her, and then sighed. «Of *course* you do. Just out of curiosity, if you can do all that, why did you need to come with us, then?»

«I told you before, nobody survives this place alone.» Tatter became somber, with the same tinge of fear that he'd felt before. «I never saw anybody that went solo prospecting out here in the Carinae come back, not in the entire time I've been here.»

«But you stayed behind by yourself in that shadow jewel mine. You didn't seem scared when we left.» Greymalkin still felt confused.

After she hesitated briefly, he noticed that her long antennae all moved forward, orienting on him alertly. He wondered what that meant. Tatter slowly communed a response, and he was surprised at how her thoughts now felt oddly vulnerable but also genuine. «I felt safe there mining on my own because... well, I knew you'd come back for me, Grey.»

Greymalkin swallowed. He'd felt the sincerity in her thoughts, but he'd also caught another nuance. *Feeling vulnerable is really hard for her. She didn't want to feel that way; she didn't want to think about the fact that it <u>mattered</u> to her that she could trust me.* Greymalkin instinctively sent a quiet, sincere thought back to her. «You can always count on me to come back for you, Tat. Don't worry.»

That seemed to fluster her even more, and he could feel her thoughts retreating behind a tense façade again. She leaned in close to him with smiling alien jaws wider than his shoulders as she communed a deflecting message. «And besides, you have Kuanian's personal backing, because you've got your bubbling black nightmare Bruno here, right? I've got a hunch about you, and I've learned to trust my instincts. Something tells me the smart money is going along with you two. And, you know something, you're kind of an... *interesting* little weirdo! So, count me in on this trip!»

Look who's calling me a weirdo, he thought, nervously looking at her ferocious dagger teeth again, so close that he could climb into her mouth if he'd been brave enough. Then Bruno's intense communed thoughts rattled through them both.

«Your assistance is not required, Sylphid.» The protean had continued steadily growing, Greymalkin realized. Now it was a gigantic mass of morphing rocks that dwarfed even Tatter. The protean's thoughts seemed very skeptical. «You should stay behind.»

«Hey, it's my call! And I thought I showed you back at the base that I can handle myself!» Tatter's thoughts were irritated now. She was clearly still angry at the protean.

«You merely surprised me. And I was vastly restraining my attacks. In fact, I was carefully trying to *avoid* killing you.» Bruno's thoughts were starting to heat up as well, and Greymalkin quickly interjected himself between the two.

«She'll be helpful, Bruno; let's bring her along. And uh, *thanks,* Tatter! Thank you so much for sharing the proceeds of that adaman sale, and thanks for coming with us! You're the best!» Greymalkin continued before either Bruno or Tatter could come back with another snipe at each other. «And to answer your question, Tatter, let's investigate the closer Abyssal, the one in orbit around the big yellow supergiant in the cluster near us. It'll still be hard to reach, but slightly easier than the other one.» When the two seemed like they might start up their argument again, Greymalkin quickly jumped in once more. «So, shall we be going, then?»

Tatter ultimately decided to ride with Greymalkin in Royce until they reached the vicinity of the cluster. It did not take Royce long to reach the region, even with Greymalkin dodging around all the typical sinks and traps of the Carinae along the way. They stopped at the edge of the cluster and dropped out of shadow space. Greymalkin whistled in a low tone to himself, looking out at the spectacle spread out ahead of them across the sky.

The cluster was a madhouse of bright stars and energized gas clouds. There must have been almost a thousand stars jammed into just the cubic parsec ahead of them. The view was so blindingly bright that he had dialed up the viewscreen shade enormously to block most of the light, and yet it was still dazzling. To his shadow synesthesia the stars were a howling gale of frigid wind coming at him. Worse, the wind was full of strange synesthetically rendered fetid scents he'd never encountered before. He wondered why his subconscious mind was interpreting his shadow jewel signals from the cluster in that alarming way. It smelled faintly like a breeze coming off rotten meat. Since Greymalkin was a vegetarian, that was doubly disgusting.

Greymalkin scanned the twists of the shadow plane ahead of them as it bucked and dove around the blazing star masses. Really, there was no completely stable plane of shadow space transit to navigate. For that matter, there were no stable shadow channels or even shadow *volumes* that he could detect. This region would be a nightmare to journey through, no matter what sort of starship one had.

Thinking it through further, Greymalkin wasn't even sure if Royce had enough shadow space thrust to make it up some of the gradients he was seeing. After considering the matter for a few minutes, he communed to Bruno. The alien cyborg was floating a few hundred meters away from Royce. Bruno had continued pulling more and more mass out of shadow space, and was now a huge cluster of black rocks orbiting around one another. Each black stone was dozens of meters in diameter, and glowed with a nimbus of blue light against the radiation of the cluster.

«Bruno, can you chain your shadow space impeller to Royce? We may need both of you pushing to get us to where we need to go.»

«Of course.» Bruno's thoughts were scoffing. «My manifold cannot *shunt* your cyborg into shadow space, but I won't have any difficulty towing or pushing it once shifted.»

Tatter had been lounging in the copilot's seat in her human form, but now got up and stretched before heading to the airlock. "I can help as well," she said. "Looks like it's time for me to get outside and help push. I'm tired of sitting in here anyway."

Greymalkin looked nervously from the viewport back to her as she entered the airlock. "Ah, are you sure you'll be okay out there?"

Tatter had turned, facing away from him. She unzipped Bora's jumpsuit and peeled it off down to her shapely hips while looking over her shoulder with a grin. She began to morph into her huge alien form, and as her human skin transformed into knotted bluish-grey chitin she dropped the flight suit to the deck before it ripped apart. Crouching down so as to not bang her giant head on the ceiling, she turned to him with her now monstrous smile of razor teeth, and said in a voice deepened by the transformation, "Don't worry about me; worry for anybody that crosses us." She held up the big alien runcible in one limb and, with a grin, activated it before closing the airlock.

Greymalkin shook his head at her, and then focused on Royce through the helm link. The cyneget could sense the energy boiling in the stars ahead of them as well, and was more exhilarated than ever.

Greymalkin could directly feel all of the organs and systems of the living starship through the helm link. He again marveled at how different it felt to pilot a living creature than a dead vehicle. The closest experience he could compare it to was when he had piloted the *Dragon King*, with its immense, aloof cybernetic mind. He thought sadly about the moment the huge starship's mind had died.

But Royce, even though the little starship's presence was far smaller that that of the *Dragon King*, felt more alive in a completely different way than the ark had felt, even before the immense vessel's mind had perished when it had been beached. The little rover cyneget had *vitality*, emotions and feelings of its own that surged through the link and affected Greymalkin's mood every bit as much as his affected the rover. Greymalkin could sense himself as Royce perceived him, a tiny being of intense intelligence and agency perched at the very forward-most crown of the cyneget's body, directing and controlling the creature almost like a separately animate forebrain. The cyneget was a totally loyal being; it had complete faith in him and wanted to please him by taking the young Sojourner wherever he directed. And more than anything else Royce wanted to... *run*. There was no other way to express the mood of the cyneget, it was like an animal that longed to race across a planet's surface. Greymalkin had sampled recordings in mnemotomes of the minds of big quadrupeds, and he recognized the sheer vigor of the cyborg's mind. It lived for nothing so much as racing through the stars.

The big, gnarled form of Tatter loomed up in front of the viewport outside, toothily looking in on him. «Are we ready to go?» Her thoughts were sweet, with a barely concealed fringe of nervous energy all her own. *We're all on edge. Nobody knows what we'll encounter in the cluster.*

Greymalkin communed with both Tatter and Bruno, trying to fill his thoughts with optimism. «Let's go!» At the merest hint of a command from him, Royce charged into shadow space and almost left the other two behind. But the protean and the Sylphid caught up and were quickly pacing the cyneget on either side, their continuity bubbles merging and then diverging with the rover cyborg's manifold as the two flitted around in shadow space.

He took a moment to study Tatter again, as this was the first time he'd seen her *in flight*. He was fascinated to see that she actually *did* have an implanted starflight system, and that it was *multimodal*. She was easily keeping up with Royce as the cyneget churned along the shadow plane, but she could also follow Bruno when the protean occasionally popped up off the plane into the volume above them in shadow space. He wondered if she could also follow a shadow space channel or not. Bruno seemed to be limited to only plane and volume travel.

For a moment, he felt a wistful jealousy of the three other beings he was traveling with. In stark contrast to them, physically he was a hopelessly primitive creature, limited by a body of blood and bones rather than sheer energy and impervious materials. *I'm the only one here that can't travel the stars by myself,* he thought morosely. But then they came to the first twists in the shadow plane, and he became too busy to think about anything else.

Although the distance they had to traverse was not enormous in an absolute sense, in practice it was incredibly challenging shadow space topography. They were immediately laboring up and down shadow plane impedance gradients. He could intuitively sense the resistance of most of the transitions, but sometimes he felt the forces around them abruptly shift in a way he had not anticipated. He and Royce would then almost hurtle off the invisible plane of shadow space travel that the cyneget clung to, and they would have to desperately try to hang onto the elusive trace of forces in the plane.

Neither Tatter nor Bruno even attempted to hold onto the planar path that Greymalkin was following. Instead, he could sense them flitting nimbly through the shadow volume around them. But even they were having difficulty with the turbulence of shadow space in the cluster, and they frequently had to circle around repeatedly in order to finally transit problematic regions near energetic stars. At one point Tatter became completely disoriented and briefly became lost in a snarl of twisted paths and volume currents until he dashed back after her. When he signaled her to guide her back to the correct path, he could sense the growing fear in her thoughts of becoming hopelessly lost in the cluster.

After an exhausting period of harrowing twists and turns, he found that he had successfully navigated them to the area near the yellow supergiant star. They all dropped out of shadow space, and he caught his breath. The location was incredible to behold.

The yellow supergiant was by far the brightest object in the cluster, and while they had dropped out of shadow space billions of kilometers away from it, the blazing star was still incredibly bright in the sky, to the point that he simply closed the viewport against the blinding light. The star nevertheless blasted at his shadow jewel with a radiant energy that was unbelievable. The strange synesthetic sense of a fetid wind in his face was stronger than ever, and it almost made him gag. He wondered again what was producing that bizarre sensory hallucination, and ran through a set of sensor checks to try to pin it down. But there were so many wild readings in the sensors that he had never seen before that he came away baffled, with no idea what it meant. Through the helm link he could feel Royce bristling antagonistically. *So, it isn't just me,* Greymalkin thought. He decided to commune with Tatter and Bruno.

«Are either of you having a strange shadow sense response to that star?» Even as he was sending the message he felt foolish, but Tatter came back immediately.

«Aha, so I'm not the only one!» Her thoughts were unsettled, and even more nervous. «It's throwing off an incredible combination of energies, it makes me feel sort of *ill*. Are there any planets? If we could get behind one of them, it might occlude all those ghastly signals.»

«What you sense is not the star.» There was an angry snarl building in Bruno's thoughts that Greymalkin had not felt since the battle with the Abyssal that had called itself Dark Nebula. «There is an installation of some kind ahead of us. It is in orbit around another body in this system. The unusual radiance being emitted from that location is what is causing the illusory sensations and other phenomena that we are all experiencing.»

Greymalkin absorbed that information uneasily. «Is it harmful? I mean, other than the star being bright enough to blind me, that is.» The protean did not respond immediately, but seemed to be intently observing whatever it was focused on.

«I am unsure.» The protean now sounded increasingly agitated. «Whatever the nature of this Abyssal you've sought out, it interests me keenly. Let us investigate.»

Greymalkin hesitated. He took a moment to mentally review everything that he had studied in Constance's dataset and the old records from the previous Xenocorps mission three centuries ago, especially the threats. In addition to the Abyssals, the Xenocorps had cataloged several other incredibly dangerous life forms in the Carinae, many of them additional unfamiliar varieties of feral cyborgs that had undoubtedly been created by the Builders. There were too *many* possible threats. Any of them could be deadly. But then again, they had Bruno with them, and the protean seemed to be at least as dangerous as anything in the old stories.

Greymalkin scanned the system using the amplifier he'd brought to enhance his shadow jewel's perceptions. He immediately understood what Bruno had been referring to. Although it was obscured by the blazing energy of the yellow supergiant, there was another mass in the system almost as large as a small star. He scrutinized it carefully, and realized it was a brown dwarf, a substellar-sized gas giant that must have been captured from interstellar space by the gravity of the huge star. He tried to scrutinize the brown dwarf, and could only discern that it was radiating strongly in the infrared. The energies thrown off by the yellow supergiant were too overpowering to observe any other details from this range. «I can make out the big gas giant, but nothing else because of all the glare and noise from the big star. You said there was an installation? Is it in the clouds of the gas giant planet?»

«No. There are very sizeable moons in orbit around it. The installation is on one of them.» Bruno's thoughts convulsed in anger. «I can sense *him* there. Our *opponent*. He appears to have a large contingent of lesser beings there as well, slaves no doubt.»

Greymalkin noted the rising battle-lust in the thoughts of the protean with alarm. «We aren't here for a fight, Bruno! We want to communicate with the Abyssal and ask it questions.»

«I do not think that the powerful being you seek will be cooperative, but we can give it the benefit of the doubt.» Then Bruno's thoughts bubbled in the grim way that Greymalkin had learned was the protean's equivalent of a rueful laugh. «At least, until it tries to slaughter us.»

The protean's comment triggered Greymalkin's memories of horror, the sound of panicked screams and the sight of human blood splattered against walls. He shuddered, and fought down the paralyzing sense of dread. A thought came to him then. «Give me just a minute, I want to get something.»

Greymalkin went back to his cubby, brought out his old burned and beaten pack, and then slowly took out the golden garment and multitool. He looked at the two artifacts for a moment. He wondered again what Kuanian had anticipated when she recruited Bora, Soren, and him. After a momentary pause, he configured the golden garment as a void suit and put it on. Then he clipped the tool and Constance's databloc to his belt harness and returned to the cockpit. He didn't feel any safer, but he felt like he'd done what he could to prepare himself as Kuanian would have wanted.

«Okay, let's go.» Greymalkin nudged Royce through the helm link, and the cyneget practically leaped forward. It took very little time to reach the brown dwarf, and when they dropped out of shadow space they were in orbit around the planetoid that Bruno had indicated. The vista that greeted them was incredible.

The brown dwarf was a gigantic black shadow in the sky above them, harshly backlit by the blazing yellow supergiant. Beneath them, the pock-marked surface of the planetoid was a brightly lit, sickly shade of lemon. Scanning the surface, Greymalkin quickly realized that the pallid color came from sulfur dioxide that was being ejected from volcanoes caused by tidal heating with the brown dwarf. Bruno quickly signaled him.

«I see many reflective objects on the surface. Stay here in orbit. I will descend and inspect the objects.» The thoughts of the protean were focused and alert. A small inky black blob suddenly appeared next to Greymalkin and plopped onto his shoulder, making him twitch. «I have deposited a small fragment of myself on your person to monitor your safety and stay in close communication.»

I wish he would tell me before he does that, Greymalkin thought in irritation. «Yes, I noticed. Please remember, do not act aggressively toward the Abyssal, and please do not kill any of its servants.»

«Noted.» Bruno dwindled rapidly toward the surface, followed by another familiar shape, which prompted an angry message from Bruno. «Sylphid, I told you, your presence is not required!»

Tatter's thoughts were full of laughter. «And I already told *you*, I can handle myself. Besides, I'm curious what's down there as well.»

Greymalkin rolled his eyes, wondering what the result of Bruno and Tatter trying to work together would be. He squinted up through the viewport shade at the black arc of the brown dwarf and realized that the planetoid beneath them would soon be passing through its shadow. Bruno and Tatter were already out of his sight far below, but through the communal link that Bruno had established with him, he could see Tatter flying along gracefully above the yellow planetoid. She was descending just as rapidly as the protean. He wondered if they were racing one another to the surface.

«I thought you did not wish to explore this region of space because it was too *dangerous*, Sylphid!» Bruno's thoughts were still irritated and angry. When Tatter replied, Greymalkin had the distinct sense she was trying to goad him.

"I'm not alone out here now; I have you as backup! If anything bad happens, I can run, and *you* can deal with it!» Tatter was clearly taunting the protean. «Now stay alert, there's got to be shadow jewels and other loot around here with a star that bright.»

«I do not take orders from you, Sylphid.» Bruno's thoughts suddenly became very wary. «Be cautious now! Here are the objects I scanned remotely.»

Greymalkin was first puzzled and then chilled by the sight that greeted the two as they slowed to hover above the planetoid's surface. There were indeed huge cyborganic carapaces scattered across the sludgy yellow surface of the planetoid. The objects appeared to be huge, hollow, and empty mirrorshell husks scattered across the brightly lit surface of the sulfurous yellow planetoid. Some of the silvery husks were almost completely buried in the yellow muck that covered everything on the surface. At first Greymalkin had been unable to make out anything in the harsh shadows of the bright star. Then he'd briefly thought the objects were giant carcasses with many silvery, bony limbs. After Bruno had swept close above and then even *through* some of the big empty shells it triggered a memory. He thought he knew what he was looking at, finally.

«Wait, Bruno go back to that really big one to your right.» Greymalkin paused as Bruno flew back to the big skeletal shell. «I think I recognize this from the old Xenocorps logs I read before we came here. There was a cybernetic organism they observed that shed its exoskeleton periodically. The shells it left behind looked like this, although a lot smaller. The shed exoskeletons they observed were only sixty meters long, at most. That shell in front of you must be, what, a hundred meters long?»

«In your units of measure, that husk is one hundred and forty-eight meters in length, not counting the longest of the ten limbs, the ones that trail off behind and to the sides.» Bruno rotated through a full turn, looking around alertly. A sulfur volcano on the horizon was spewing a bright yellow spray into the sky in slow motion, but other than that nothing moved. «If these are shed exoskeletons, what left them behind?»

Greymalkin was searching quickly through the old Xenocorps logs of three hundred years ago, and finally located the entry he'd been looking for. «Wait, it took me a minute, but I found the log entry. It was just a fragmentary record from one of their wide range survey scouts. The exobiologist on the scout ship took observations of these same sort of husks, and even assigned the creature a tentative reference designation. The guy obviously wanted to leave his mark on history, I guess.»

«So, what did he call it?» Tatter's thoughts were now very nervous. Greymalkin wondered if she was having second thoughts about coming along. Looking out at the sweep of the planetoid passing underneath him slowly as Royce orbited the planetoid, Greymalkin could see the dark shadow of the brown dwarf sweeping across the bright surface. He thought to check when it would darken the area of the surface where Bruno and Tatter were, and in the process he realized that he would soon be out of their sight when Royce orbited around to the other side of the planetoid.

«He said in the log that he was going to call it a 'Striated Manticore' if they ever found what left the husks, because of those long dark ridges down the sides of the exoskeletons.» Greymalkin started communing more quickly, because he was concerned about being cut off from the others. «But he never got to register the name; that was the last log entry transmitted from the scout ship. It never rejoined the main exploration fleet. Hey, you two, be aware that the brown dwarf is going to put you two in shadow soon. Also, Royce and I will be orbiting around the planetoid for a while, out of your direct line of observation.»

«All the parts of my body are in quantum-entangled communication.» Bruno's thoughts were still alert, but there was definitely a sense of smugness there. «We will stay in close communication with you no matter what happens.» As the protean completed its message, several things quickly happened at the same time. The landscape suddenly darkened as the bulk of the brown dwarf cut off the brilliant light from the yellow star, Tatter's thoughts became a scream in the communal link, and something massive slammed into Bruno violently.

Greymalkin's eyes widened, and he tried signaling the protean, but all he could sense through the link with Bruno was a confused and rapid series of furious impacts. Tatter was communing to Bruno in a panic, and then she abruptly sent a strange message that baffled Greymalkin.

«*Wait, it's empty!*» Tatter's thoughts felt astonished. «It's empty! there's nothing in there, it's just one of the husks from the surface! Somehow, it's animate!»

Bruno's thoughts were still focused and alert, and now the image Greymalkin was receiving through the link became clear. Portions of the protean had separated and formed themselves into big graspers that were firmly holding up one of the giant silvery mirrorshell husks in the darkness above the surface of the planetoid, illuminated in a spotlight that the protean was emitting. The husk was still squirming, but it was clearly empty.

«TAKE EVASIVE ACTION!» Bruno's mental roar at Greymalkin startled the young monk so much that he almost did not sense the giant shape that had abruptly materialized behind Royce, enveloping the little rover cyborg just as Royce howled out a collision tocsin. Greymalkin yelped and tried to steer away from the huge striped silvery limbs closing around them in the gloomy darkness as they orbited behind the planetoid, but it was too late. Claws longer than his body emerged directly from shadow space into the cockpit *around* him, not even bothering to tear through Royce's mirrorshell hull. Greymalkin grunted as mirrorshell digits yanked him out of the cockpit and clapped tight around him, crushing the air from his chest. He was aware of Royce bucking futilely at the monstrous limbs and the distant perception of Bruno unsuccessfully trying to leap *through the planetoid* in shadow space toward him, but then his perceptions faded away.

He seemed to be standing in a pitch black space, but Greymalkin realized that he was experiencing another of the strange dreamlike hallucinations he always seemed to have whenever he first came into contact with one of the Risen. The creature must evidently be enormously intelligent. He tried to orient himself in the darkness of the dream-vision, but the only thing he could sense initially were terrifying snarls and roars all around him. Startled, he tried to run but kept stumbling over objects in the darkness. Then he felt some kind of overwhelmingly strong squirming tentacle wrap itself around his legs and drag him backwards across the ground. In the hallucination, the darkness began to lift, revealing a dim room like a huge cage. But the thing that seized his attention was the sight of nested sets of enormous gnashing predatory teeth glowing silvery white in the darkness, becoming closer and closer as the tentacle dragged him backwards toward them. He screamed, wondering briefly if it was real or if he was still hallucinating. He was dragged down into the horrific mouth, which was like a bottomless pit full of the endlessly nested jaws, all now closing around him. Then he lost consciousness.

* * *

After some indeterminate time, Greymalkin felt a persistent vibration from a violent buzzing on his shoulder, an insistent pulsation that dragged him back to wakefulness. Blearily he looked around, and quickly realized that he was still in total pitch blackness. But now he felt that his body was being grasped by enormous claws that were carrying him along in the dark.

Bruno's thoughts poured into his mind like ice water. «Apologies for waking you from your *nap*, but I thought I should let you know that I must now eject my fragment off your person, as they are about to scan you closely. You have been taken inside the underground fortifications that I detected earlier. Be assured that I will return for you when I have an opportunity.»

Greymalkin managed to sadly commune a last message as he felt the tiny fragment-blob of Bruno leap off his shoulder and vanish into the darkness. «We should have approached the *other* Abyssal, I guess. I was dead wrong to pick this one.» Bruno's presence vanished from his mind. *And now I'm just going to be dead, I suppose,* Greymalkin thought.

While his eyes could see nothing in the darkness, his shadow sense revealed that he was being carried rapidly down a gigantic corridor more than three hundred meters wide. The corridor had many enormous structures along the walls that seemed like decorations rather than devices. Equally huge hallways led off to the side from the main corridor. The revolting synesthetic stench of something like rancid meat that he'd been sensing distantly was overpowering here and getting stronger by the second, making him fearful of vomiting inside his golden helmet. Within seconds he began to see lights in the distance, and sensed that the corridor was opening into a much larger chamber.

The vast new chamber was in the same near-vacuum with faint traces of sulfur dioxide from the surface. He was very glad he'd taken the precaution of donning the golden void suit. The big cyborg carrying him approached a gigantic assembly hundreds of meters tall that stood at the end of the chamber. The huge creature carrying him landed, and proceeded to hold him down on a vast metallic surface. Greymalkin's fear increased even more as human-sized aliens in void suits approached him from the shadowy recesses of the chamber and quickly enveloped him in some kind of sticky bindings. He tried to quickly scan all of the creatures, and also took a moment to scan the big cyborg above that had captured him and carried him here.

As he looked around at the smaller aliens manhandling him, he was momentarily surprised to realize that they were simply Crotani wearing void suits. *But that makes sense.* Other than the psychotic Carinans themselves, the Crotani seemed to be the most common sapient beings in the Carinae. What arrested his attention was the fact that, unlike the Crotani he'd met at the main expedition base, *these* Crotani actually had shadow jewels in their brains, and he could sense them communing with one another. He tentatively tried to commune with them, but immediately realized that they all had truly oppressive mental covenant systems layered onto their minds through their shadow jewels. All that he could sense of their individual minds were gaunt shells, alternatively overwhelmed with either frightened obedience or resentful rage. When it became obvious that the Crotani would not commune with him, he instead twisted his head around to look at the giant cyborg that had captured him, and saw that it was quite different.

The main trunk of the cyborg did indeed resemble the complex exoskeleton husks that it had apparently left on the surface after moulting, and he began analyzing what he was seeing, thinking all the while, *This must be the "striated manticore" that the Xenocorpsman had found evidence of three centuries ago.* The creature was immense, far bigger than Royce or many other spacecraft he had ever seen. It loomed above him in the dim chamber, its ridged cybernetic metal body darting about far quicker than he would have suspected possible. The front of the cyborg, what he assumed was the thing's "head", was festooned with antennae. He could sense that it too had a shadow jewel within its skull. The cyborg's head was pointed toward the even larger assembly on the platform in front of him, a bizarre series of shapes that loomed hundreds of meters up into the darkness. The manticore was evidently communing with some intelligence within the vast assembly on the platform, even though Greymalkin could not make out anything coherent in the thoughts of either being.

Greymalkin peered into the darkness at the gigantic assembly that occupied the platform, wondering what it could possibly be, what sort of mind was inside it, and why the manticore was so intently communing with the huge structure. Whatever the huge thing was, he had immediately recognized that it was the source of the nauseating synesthesia odor. Even though Greymalkin knew intellectually that he was in a near vacuum and was not actually smelling anything, his shadow jewel synesthesia was filling his mind with an unbearable stench, almost as if he had been jammed inside of a rotting corpse. Greymalkin struggled, trying to get away from the ghastly smell. He wondered what about the huge assembly could possibly be generating the stink in his shadow sense. He stared up at it in the blackness, but could make out nothing but a giant glowing array of golden reflections in the dim chamber. *There must be an individual there, a living being somewhere inside that giant building, a being with some sort of mind equipped with a shadow jewel.* Greymalkin decided to scan it with his shadow sense... and gasped.

His shadow sense revealed that the entire gigantic assembly was *yet another cyborg*, albeit much, much larger than even the hulking manticore. And he could also tell from his shadow sense that it was examining him intently. The huge creature moved then, proceeding to lean down over him. Greymalkin flinched. It was as if a reeking corpse the size of a building was collapsing on top of him in the darkness. But it stopped roughly twenty meters above him, simply studying him. He could feel various powerful scans going through his body, and realized that the golden void suit he wore was blocking many of the signals.

Then, as Greymalkin examined what he could of the giant being, now that it had leaned down closely above him, he was shocked to see that the enormous creature actually seemed to be constructed entirely out of a golden material very similar to that of the void suit that Greymalkin wore, the garment that Kuanian had given him. He briefly wondered what that meant, but then the enormous cyborg emitted a massive generalized communal signal that blasted resonating thoughts throughout his skull. Greymalkin realized it was trying to communicate with him. The signal was an extended interrogative, he understood that much through the communal channel, even though it was so strong that it made his head feel like exploding.

«Yes, okay, okay! I can sense your communal signal!» Greymalkin's thoughts were full of wailing fright. «Don't hurt me! I'm not armed.»

The huge golden cyborg seemed to process that, and then slowly leaned back up to a vertical orientation almost a kilometer above in the darkness. Then it surprised him with a communed message in thickly distorted *Peretian*. «You are a human, a member of the latest invasion wave that I have been observing from a distance.»

Greymalkin's eyes opened even wider. «We are not invaders, we're explorers! And I'm very pleased that we can communicate, but how do you know my language?»

«My sentinel took many captives like you during your last invasion.» The golden alien cyborganic giant mentally indicated the manticore monster that had carried Greymalkin into the chamber. «We recorded this language, among others, in the process of vivisecting the captured intruders.»

Greymalkin was now trembling so badly with fear that he felt the void suit rattling around him. «Please, please, I simply came seeking information, to have a *dialogue* with you. I'm certainly no threat to you whatsoever!»

«That is an obvious lie.» The golden giant's thoughts seemed irritated. «You just admitted that you came here seeking information.»

Greymalkin stared up in confusion. «Yes, that's right. Only information. I came with no intention of threatening you in any way.»

«Your thoughts are contradictory.» The towering cyborg slowly leaned down over him again, now orienting a battery of quavering sensory organs like eyes at Greymalkin. «Information is power. If you came with the intent of stealing my information, you came to steal my power. *That* is a threat.»

Inside his helmet, Greymalkin's eyes widened. *Wow. There's paranoia and then there is paranoia.* «I did not come to *steal* anything. Neither information nor power. I only seek dialogue with you.»

«Yes, this word 'dialogue' is recorded in the communication sequences we extracted from the other humans.» The golden giant lowered the array of sensors closer to Greymalkin, and the various lenses and other devices began to move as they scanned him. «A 'dialogue' is a kind of mutual interrogation duel, then? You are very stupid to propose such an activity; I think I will win the duel.»

Greymalkin groaned, wondering if he would be able to communicate in any useful way with the monster. «No. A dialogue is not antagonistic. The goal is to share information for mutual benefit.»

«I have no interest in benefiting you.» The sensor array of the golden giant began to swivel around Greymalkin's head, the different parts of the array disturbingly suggestive of clusters of quivering eyes staring down at him. He felt a faint buzzing sensation centered around his shadow jewel. The huge being lowered itself further, once more making him flinch again as the titan filled his entire field of view.

«But now I have discovered that the information I gain from you will benefit me greatly!» The thoughts of the golden monster now radiated greedy excitement. «It is difficult to discern through your armored covering, but I have now detected several data troves concealed in your cephalic organ.»

«My *what* organ?» Greymalkin said in confusion. Then he thought about it for a moment. «Oh. You mean... my head. My brain.» He swallowed. «Uh, the thing is, I sort of *need* my brain.»

«You sought to share information with me, did you not?» Now the immense golden being lowered itself even closer to Greymalkin, becoming a vast wall of dimly glimpsed golden shapes above him, shining darkly in the gloom of the vast chamber. As it descended, the terrified Crotani around him scattered away, back into the shadows of the vast darkened chamber. The thoughts of the golden giant had become irritated again. «I will obtain what I seek sooner or later. Why not come out of your armored shell and give it to me now?»

«I can't come out.» Greymalkin trembled again. «I won't be able to breathe. I'll die.»

«No matter.» The giant being now simply seemed distracted. «It will take me a short while to prepare the vivisection box for you. The extraction must be done delicately or I will damage the data troves.» The creature stopped communing then, evidently tired of the dialogue 'duel' with him.

I have a tiny window of time, then. I have to focus on getting it to continue talking to me, somehow. Greymalkin took deep breaths then, trying to subdue his fear. His face became solemn as he thought to himself for a few moments. *I knew I was likely to die if I made this attempt to contact it. But the only thing that matters now is getting some answers.* He looked at the huge golden surface of strangely twisted alien shapes above him. It now seemed like the nightmarish golden ceiling of a cruel palace, the ceiling of the palace where his journey would end in death. *Okay, then. Let's see what I can find out in my last moments.*

«I was serious about sharing information with you." He set aside the idea of death as inevitable, and that lessened the fear. It made it easier to be analytical. *What does it want?* He squinted at the vast golden surface and then the sensor orbs that surrounded him like pulsating eyes. «What are these 'data troves' you're referencing? If I can give them to you without dying, I will.»

For a moment the vast golden thing above him did not respond. When it did, he could detect emotions in its thoughts, strange equivalents of disbelief and amusement. «You do not even know what you carry? This makes no sense... but I can discern that you are telling the truth. Explicate! You must know that there are two large data troves in the shadow space crystal embedded in your cephalic organ?»

The covenants. It's talking about the covenants. That reoriented the situation in his mind. *I actually do have something it wants. I just need to figure out how to reason with it!* «The 'data troves' were recorded on my shadow jewel without explanation to me. I do not know their purpose.»

«Curious.» The mental stench radiating from the vast golden being was overpowering. Greymalkin winced, trying to keep his focus as the monster continued communing. «But you surely must have encountered the two entities that recorded these troves. They must have sent you.»

«I did... *encounter* them both, but in quite different ways. The larger trove was given to me by a being called the Velan. The smaller trove is from one called Kuanian. She was the one that sent me to this region, but not to you specifically. I made that choice myself.»

«I do not know these designations, but I recognize the encoding signatures of the troves.» The thoughts of the monstrous gold being had become suspicious and... fearful? «You have encountered the Magistrate and the Mediator. They are both among my enemies, so they surely sent you for some purpose harmful to me.»

Greymalkin blinked. «Magistrate? Mediator? Are you sure we're talking about the same beings? I have never heard them referred to by those... designations.»

The monster's thoughts became a low growl. It almost seemed to be thinking to itself rather than addressing him. «It was them. I recognize the encoding. And I understand the *primary* encoding on top of the larger trove. It is what I need, the guarantee of free passage that I have been seeking for so long. If I can extract it successfully, I may finally gain access to both the Forge and the Nexus....»

Greymalkin inhaled. *Now we're getting somewhere. I'm not sure where yet, but... somewhere.* «You wish to gain access to the... *Forge and Nexus*? I do not know what those names refer to, but perhaps I can assist you in your goal.»

Once again there was a long pause before the golden giant responded, and when it finally did there were once again the sequence of bizarre emotional responses, first of disbelief, then amusement, and then angry suspicion in its thoughts. «You cannot possibly be unaware of the Forge and the Nexus. They are the center and purpose of everything in this region. The Forge and the Nexus are the only reason I and all the rest are here, the only reason we subjugate ourselves to the cursed Tenax. You must be trying to misdirect me!»

Tenax? What can the 'Tenax' be, then? Greymalkin wondered. But then, for just a moment amid the torrent of raging emotions and thoughts the monster was blasting at him, there was a confused sequence of images that nevertheless seemed strangely familiar to Greymalkin. The jumbled memories were full of cold steel tentacles that seemed to wrap tighter and tighter around both the golden giant and the young Sojourner, like an ocean of grasping limbs holding both of them equally helpless. And behind the thick coils of tentacles was a shadowy human figure with glowing yellow eyes in the darkness. *Rodo?? Does this monster know him? But, even as devious as Rodo is, why would a being this powerful fear him? And where have I seen that image of clinging metal tentacles?* Greymalkin cast aside the questions for the moment as he struggled to reason with the golden monster.

«No! I promise that I'll help you if I can!" Greymalkin desperately tried to think of a response that might interest the horrendous creature. «To... *gain access*, was that it? To the... Forge, to make... whatever it is that the Forge makes. And the Nexus, for... whatever *it's* for... and the *Tenax*?» His communed thoughts trailed off awkwardly. *Blast it. I'm shooting in the dark! But I'm finally learning some things, if I can just keep it talking to me....*

«The Forge does not make particular *things*.» The golden monster's thoughts were now growing even more angry. «The Forge makes *anything requested*. And the Nexus provides the secrets to *everything*! But the Tenax controls them both! You certainly know this! You were sent to spy on me and steal *my* secrets, if not by the Magistrate and the Mediator, then by one of my other enemies.»

«I was not!» Greymalkin tried to remain conciliatory and keep his thoughts calm, but the interrogation was terrifying. «I was not sent by anyone.»

«Ah, you must have been sent by the Prosecutor. He is the closest and most dangerous of my foes, more unpredictable than even the cursed Tenax.» The thoughts of the golden giant momentarily quivered with fear, and a brief image flew by that was unmistakably the nearby Keyhole nebula. Then the monster's thoughts filled with rage. «Admit it!»

Greymalkin remembered the notes that Constance had given him about the other powerful being, the one in the Keyhole nebula. *I've got to keep that memory out of my thoughts.* «I have seen that nebula near here, obviously. We call it the Keyhole. But I have no knowledge of any enemies of yours!»

«Your communication signals betray you!» The thoughts of the golden giant pounced, even as fear of the enemy it was considering flooded its mind. «I detect your lie! You know of the Prosecutor!»

"I tell you, I don't mean you any harm!»

Abruptly, there was a vast reverberating vibration through the floor. The fearful Crotani around him all reacted, looking back down the corridor that the manticore had brought him through. Then another, even more violent rumbling tremor came through the floor. The huge golden cyborg angrily sent an even stronger communed signal through Greymalkin's head.

«That is again a lie! Even now your bodyguards are trying to blast open the entrance to our sanctuary. They will not succeed. My sentinel will now destroy them.» The giant golden cyborg sent a complex communed message to the still waiting manticore, and it whirled about, disappearing down the corridor much faster than Greymalkin would have imagined possible for something so massive. The Crotani now came swarming around him again, hauling him off the floor roughly. The giant golden cyborg continued communing with him. «Your outer shell is shadow aureate armor like my body, but we will nevertheless find a way to extract your soft interior form from it for vivisection. And I will then extract the data troves in your cephalic organ.»

«Wait, wait!» Greymalkin's communed thoughts were begging in confusion. «Surely we can reach a peaceful resolution!»

«Your armor and the data implanted in your cephalic shadow jewel were given to you by my enemies, that much is certain.» The thoughts of the giant golden alien were both furious and contemptuous. «Extracting your cephalic jewel will extinguish you. We know this from experience with your species. But I also know what these data troves contain, and their value. I will vivisect you and take the troves, after we dispose of your bodyguards.» Then the Crotani dragged him away across the vast floor of the chamber while Greymalkin spluttered and tried to commune further with the golden alien cyborg. The Crotani alternatively dragged and portered him along through dark and airless corridors until they finally reached a cell where they trussed him up with security restraints suspended from the ceiling. Frustrated, Greymalkin struggled with the bonds, but they were far too strong for him. Then he paused, thinking he had felt some sort of tremor through the bonds.

Although the restraints dampened the vibrations, he could feel occasional jolts through the ground and ceiling of the cell. Greymalkin wondered how violent the explosions had to have been to be sensed here, so far beneath the surface of the planetoid. *Bruno must be going all out to try to get in here and rescue me. But will he make it in time?*

Greymalkin almost jumped out of his skin when he abruptly felt Bruno's thoughts in his mind. «Apologies for the lack of contact until now, but I did not wish you to betray my presence to our lumbering opponent.»

«*Bruno!* You're back? Are you in here with me?» Greymalkin looked around the dim cell, and quickly realized that Bruno's tiny fragment had somehow gotten inside with him when it landed on his shoulder like a forceful tap of a finger.

«Obviously!» The protean's thoughts seemed distracted by something. «I never let you out of my observation. You had a most illuminating conversation with your captor! But we are now engaged in combat with the creature that abducted you, and I wanted you to be aware and prepared if the Sylphid and I are able to successfully penetrate the fortified compound where you are being held.»

Greymalkin groaned. He was still bound tightly and dangled suspended in the middle of the dim cell. «Can't we find some way to negotiate with it, or do *something* less violent?»

«I do not believe that will be an option.» Bruno's thoughts were agitated and full of the familiar battle rage that Greymalkin had become accustomed to from the protean. «Here, I can reconnect our full sensory link so that you can follow the progress of the battle.»

The sights and sensations of the protean flooded into his mind again, disorienting Greymalkin to the point that he almost screamed. The blazing yellow supergiant was once again in the sky above the planetoid, with the arc of the brown dwarf across the sky to the side. But everything was spinning wildly; Bruno was apparently in some kind of spiraling aerial dogfight with the manticore. Adding to the chaos, explosions were going off everywhere around the two battling cyborgs. It was no wonder the protean's thoughts were so choppy as it continued communing with him. «This creature is surprisingly elusive, and I have not been able to land a decisive attack on it during this combat encounter.»

«Where's Tatter!?» Greymalkin asked fearfully. The yellow surface of the planetoid spun wildly as Bruno maneuvered after the manticore, which always seemed to be just out of reach of the protean. It was making Greymalkin ill trying to follow the fight.

«She is also quite elusive. I lost track of her moments ago in the heat of battle.» Bruno's thoughts became jarringly staccato as the manticore landed a series of explosive attacks on the protean. Greymalkin blanched, but then gaped when he saw the manticore abruptly crash into the sulfurous surface of the planetoid in a tremendous wallop that splattered yellow sulfur dioxide snow everywhere. It remained motionless in the crater it had made where it impacted the yellow surface. Bruno descended quickly to the huge wreck of the manticore's carcass. Then Greymalkin made out a familiar figure leaning in fatigue on the huge head of the creature amidst the monster's antennae.

Tatter was crouched there, nervously extracting the long runcible from the cyborg's wreckage. She looked up as Bruno came down to hover near her. The protean communed a triumphant message to her. «Well done indeed, Sylphid! I retract my previous comments; your assistance was well timed!»

Even in her alien form, Greymalkin could tell that Tatter was exhausted and injured as she yanked the runcible out of the monstrous ridged cyborg. «This damned thing was practically impossible to kill! I had to jam the runcible drill all the way through its brain in shadow space. I wasn't sure if even *that* would work. Hey, is our monk still okay?» A rumbling in the ground curtailed any response from Bruno. Greymalkin could feel the same vibration faintly through his bonds where he dangled in his cell, and saw that both Bruno and Tatter had both spun around to face a vast stony mountain range behind them. A huge set of metallic doors were retracting there, the sight clearly visible even across the kilometers of the planetoid's steaming sulfurous yellow sludge. The doors were set deep into buried metal barriers in a devastated landscape of rock and cratered snow lying before the stony mountain range.

«I believe that we have succeeded in sufficiently angering the ruler of this fortress. Now we will have a true battle!» Bruno's communed thoughts were exultant, but Greymalkin felt petrified. He watched the terrifyingly immense and now brightly lit golden form of the alien cyborg leader that had questioned him before rising majestically through the opening. It was like watching an enormous starship lifting off. Tatter evidently shared his sentiment.

«Uh, *you* can take this one, rockhead!» With a last anxious look, Tatter vanished into shadow space as the brilliantly shining golden mass of the enraged cyborg came flying across the surface of the planetoid toward Bruno. The thing was so big that it dwarfed even the cliffs and crags of the mountain range as it flew past them, gathering speed.

«Good! Perhaps we can finally achieve a resolution, then!» Bruno's intense thoughts were full of a swirling, reckless anger that made Greymalkin feel dizzy and shocked at the utter lack of caution in the protean. Bruno was charging straight toward the golden cyborg, and Greymalkin could see a mammoth aperture opening in the huge golden head. Ominously, it was pointed straight at Bruno.

«Bruno, it's going to blast you! *Get out of there! Dodge!*» Greymalkin was frantically trying to get the protean's attention through the link when a blinding light like a supernova went off in the golden aperture.

Through the link Greymalkin felt exactly what Bruno suffered then. The agony in the mind of the protean was like nothing he had yet experienced in Bruno's thoughts. The echo of the cyborg's pain was so intense that the young monk couldn't help screaming. That agony continued on and on until Greymalkin felt himself starting to black out.

The link with the protean finally went dead. With a supreme effort Greymalkin held on to consciousness and kept himself from blacking out with the pain. But then, in horror, he glimpsed the tiny fragment of Bruno drop from his shoulder and become an inert black puddle on the floor of the cell. *No, no, no, no!*

«Bruno! Bruno, are you still there? Tatter? Royce?» Greymalkin frantically continued sending communed thoughts to no avail. The communications link the protean had provided them with was gone, and he was too far underground to commune with anyone on the surface. The young monk felt panic rising up in him, but then he closed his eyes and grit his teeth.

No. I will not panic again. It won't help anything. I've got to think clearly, now more than ever. He took deep breaths, and even though his heart was still pounding and he was trembling almost uncontrollably, his mind cleared. He quickly raced mentally through the facts of his situation and everything that had happened.

Despite what that golden atrocity bragged to me, I think that I won the 'dialogue duel' after all. I got a lot more information than it did. Greymalkin realized that he now knew about many of the fundamental dynamics of the entire Carinae region, and what the Abyssals were fighting over so fiercely. *This 'Forge' and 'Nexus', they sound like powerful Builder artifacts. The Forge can make anything? The Nexus... the golden creep said that it held the secrets to everything. That sounds like exactly what Kuanian was describing in the presentation she made to us back on the ark.* The gears of Greymalkin's mind turned through more revolutions. *That's why these Abyssals are fighting one another so viciously; it's a winner take all situation. Whoever gets control of the two artifacts wins it all. But what is the 'Tenax' it mentioned? Blast it! I'm going to have to get out of here if any of this is going to do me any good.*

Greymalkin realized that although he'd gotten at least some answers to the questions that had brought him here, it was all useless if he and his companions were dead. But as he reflected on what had happened, it occurred to him that everyone might still be *alive.*

Bruno was hurt badly and his link dropped, but he may not be dead. Surely he can't be; he's the single most invulnerable entity I've ever heard of. Although he kept repeating that statement to himself, Greymalkin was still not at all sure. He had directly felt the incinerating blast as it hit the protean, and the unbelievable pain it had caused. Then the young monk shook his head violently. *No! He's alive! I will hold onto that until I know otherwise!*

Greymalkin also anxiously wondered if Tatter was safe. *She had the sense to get out of the way of that blast, but can she get away from that* *golden lunatic? She <u>will</u>; I have faith in her! She's the smartest, most resourceful person that I know! She'll survive and escape, I'm certain of it!* But then he remembered where they were. The system was buried in the vast and impossibly tangled shadow space topography of the cluster. He remembered how she'd become disoriented and lost several times on the way in.

I have to help her! She'll be stuck here, otherwise! And Royce! Even if Royce follows her and survives, he can't navigate by himself! He looked around the dim cell and strained against the bonds desperately. *I've got to get free and get out of here! I've got to help them!*

Shaking, he stopped thrashing and thought about the biggest and most insurmountable problem he faced: the huge golden monster that had captured him and apparently defeated even Bruno. *I'm an insect compared to that thing! Even if I get out of these bonds, even if I escape, I can't defeat it! This is utterly hopeless!*

Then Greymalkin paused as a thought occurred to him in the darkness.

Wait a minute. It was <u>afraid</u>, there at the end. Afraid of the <u>other powerful being, the one</u> in the Keyhole Nebula. What did it call the other one? The Prosecutor? If I can get a message to that being... well, the enemy of my enemy is my potential ally, right? If the golden jerk is <u>that</u> afraid of the other one.... Greymalkin thought for a time, and his panic went away, becoming replaced by a jittery sense of resolve and planning. He made up his mind.

It's my fault that Tatter, Bruno, and Royce are all in this mess! But even though I'm the blasted <u>weakest</u> of all four of us, and I'm tied up <u>helpless</u> down here, I'm still alive and unharmed. I don't <u>care</u> how hopeless this situation is, I owe it to them to not give up. Blazes, I am <u>not</u> going to give up trying, <u>no matter what!</u> And anyway, I've still got my best weapon. My <u>wits</u>. Deep within the now silent alien fortress, the young Sojourner looked up at the metal and endless layers of rock that he knew lay between him, the surface, and his companions. A very long moment passed for him as his heart continued sinking. But then he grit his jaws and scowled. His face became drawn and determined inside the golden helmet.

Hang on, everybody! I don't know how yet, but <u>I'm damned well going to help you!</u>

To Be Concluded in *Pilgrim: Book Two of the Sojourner Saga*

About the Author

Dr. Martin Halbert is a librarian and digital library innovator whose career has featured decades of experimental work in developing research data repositories and collaborative institutional change projects. Halbert served as co-principal investigator for the *Transatlantic Slave Trade Database*, one of the most prominent international sources of scholarly information for researching the history of trafficking in enslaved Africans, and was the founder of Educopia, a non-profit organization that promotes knowledge sharing and capacity building among research organizations, communities, and individuals. He served as dean of libraries at two universities, and is now a tenured professor. Most recently, he completed four years as a program director and science advisor for the U.S. National Science Foundation, where he worked on open science policy for the agency. This is his first novel.

For more information on Dr. Halbert, see:
   https://martinhalbert.eposian.com/

The Sojourner Novels

Helmsman: Book One of the Sojourner Saga

Pilgrim: Book Two of the Sojourner Saga

Sylphid: Book Three of the Sojourner Saga

Oracle: Book Four of the Sojourner Saga

Xenocorpsman: Book Five of the Sojourner Saga

Wayfinder: Book Six of the Sojourner Saga

For more information on the Sojourner Saga universe, see:
https://sojourner.eposian.com/

www.ingramcontent.com/pod-product-compliance
Lightning Source LLC
LaVergne TN
LVHW011927070526
838202LV00054B/4525